Ten American Girls from History

Kate Dickinson Sweetser

Copyright © 2017 Okitoks Press

ISBN: 1977973000

ISBN-13: 978-1977973009

Table of Contents

FOREWORD

The loyalty of Pocahontas, the patriotism of Molly Pitcher and Dorothy Quincy, the devoted service of Clara Barton, the heroism of Ida Lewis, the enthusiasm of Anna Dickinson, the fine work of Louisa Alcott—all challenge the emulation of American girls of to-day. Citizen-soldiers on a field of service as wide as the world, young America has at this hour of national crisis its chance to win recognition for fidelity, for bravery, and for loyal service, with victory for American ideals as its golden reward, in a world "made safe for democracy."

My first aim in bringing the lives of these ten American girls from history to the attention of the girls of to-day has been to inspire them to like deeds of patriotism and courage. Second only to that purpose is a desire to make young Americans realize as they read these true stories of achievement along such widely varying lines of work, that history is more thrilling than fiction, and that if they will turn from these short sketches to the longer biographies from which the facts of these stories have been taken, they will find interesting and absorbing reading.

May the book accomplish its twofold object, and so justify its publication at this time of the testing of all true Americans.

Kate Dickinson Sweetser.

August 1, 1917.

TEN AMERICAN GIRLS FROM HISTORY

POCAHONTAS: THE INDIAN GIRL OF THE VIRGINIA FOREST

Sunlight glinting between huge forest trees, and blue skies over-arching the Indian village of Werewocomoco on the York River in Virginia, where Powhatan, the mighty "Werowance," or ruler over thirty tribes, was living.

Through Orapakes and Pamunkey and other forest settlements a long line of fierce warriors were marching Indian file, on their way to Werewocomoco, leading a captive white man to Powhatan for inspection and for sentence. As the warriors passed into the Indian village, they encountered crowds of dusky braves and tattooed squaws hurrying along the wood trails, and when they halted at the central clearing of the village, the crowd closed in around them to get a better view of the captive. At the same time there rose a wild clamor from the rear of the throng as a merry group of shrieking, shouting girls and boys darted forward, jostling their way through the crowd.

Their leader was a slender, straight young girl with laughing eyes such as are seldom seen among Indians, and hair as black as a crow's wing blown about her cheeks in wild disorder, while her manner was that of a happy hearty forest maiden. This was Matoaka, daughter of the Werowance Powhatan, and although he had many subjects as well as twenty sons and eleven daughters, not one was ruled so despotically as was he himself, by this slender girl with laughing eyes, for whom his pet name was Pocahontas, or in free translation, "little romp."

Having established themselves in the front row of the crowd the girls and boys stood eagerly staring at the prisoner, for many of them had never seen a white man before, and as Pocahontas watched, she looked like a forest flower in her robe of soft deer-skin, with beaded moccasins on her shapely feet, coral bracelets and anklets vying with the color in her dark cheeks, while a white plume drooping over her disordered hair proclaimed her to be the daughter of a great chief. In her health and happiness she radiated a charm which made her easily the ruling spirit among her mates, and compelled the gaze of the captive, whose eyes, looking about for some friendly face among the savage throng, fastened on the eager little maiden with a feeling of relief, for her bright glance showed such interest in the prisoner and such sympathy with him as was to endear her to his race in later years.

The long line of braves with their heads and shoulders gaily painted had wound their slow way through forest, field, and meadow to bring into the presence of the great "Werowance" a no less important captive than Captain John Smith, leader in the English Colony at Jamestown by reason of his quick wit and stout heart. The settlers having been threatened with a famine, the brave Captain had volunteered to go on an expedition among neighboring Indian villages in search of a supply of corn. The trip had been full of thrilling adventures for him,

3

and had ended disastrously in his being taken prisoner by Opechancanough, the brother of Powhatan. The news of Smith's capture having been carried to the great Werowance, he commanded that the pale-faced *Caucarouse*, or Captain, be brought to him for sentence. And that was why the warriors marched into Werewocomoco, Opechancanough in the center, with the firearms taken from Captain Smith and his companions carried before him as trophies. The prisoner followed, gripped by three stalwart Indians, while six others acted as flank guards to prevent his escape, and as they passed into Werewocomoco they were greeted by yelling savages brandishing weapons and surging forward to get a better glimpse of the white captive. The procession halted for a few minutes at the village clearing, then moved slowly on to Powhatan's "Chief Place of Council," a long arbor-like structure where the great Werowance was waiting to receive Captain Smith.

The crowd of boys and girls followed in the wake of the warriors until the Council Hall was reached, when they all dropped back except their leader. Pushing her hair from her low brow, that she might see more clearly, and walking with the erectness of a Werowance's daughter, Pocahontas entered the hall and stood near her father where she could not only watch the white captive, who appealed strongly to her fancy, but could also note Powhatan's expression as he passed judgment on the prisoner.

With inscrutable reserve and majestic dignity the great ruler bowed as the captive was led before his rustic throne, where he reclined in a gorgeous robe of raccoon-skins. On either side of the Council Hall sat rows of dusky men and women, with their heads and shoulders painted red, some of the women wearing garments trimmed with the white down from birds' breasts, while others wore long chains of white beads about their necks.

It was a picturesque sight for English eyes, and fearful though he was of foul play, the Captain could not but appreciate the brilliant mingling of gay colors and dark faces. As he stood before the Chief, there was a clapping of hands to call an Indian woman, the Queen of the Appamattock, who brought water to wash the captive's hands, while another brought a bunch of feathers to dry them on. "What next?" Captain Smith wondered as he watched further preparations being made, evidently for a feast, of which he was soon asked to partake.

Under the circumstances his appetite was not keen, but he felt obliged to pretend to a relish that he did not feel, and while he was eating his eyes lighted up with pleasure as he saw by her father's side—though he did not know then of the relationship—the little Indian girl whose interest in him had been so apparent when he saw her in the village. He dared not smile in response to her vivid glance, but his gaze lingered long on the vision of youth and loveliness, and he turned back to his meal with a better appetite.

The feast at an end, Powhatan called his councilors to his side, and while they were in earnest debate Captain Smith knew only too well that his fate was hanging in the balance. At last a stalwart brave arose and spoke to the assemblage. The captive, so he said, was known to be the leading spirit among the white settlers whose colony was too near the Indians' homes to please them, also in his expedition in search of corn he had killed four Indian warriors with "mysterious weapons which spoke with the voice of thunder and breathed the lightning," and he had been spying on their land, trying to find some secret means by which to betray them. With him out of the way their country would be freed from a dangerous menace, therefore he was condemned to death.

Doomed to die! Although he did not understand their words, there was no misunderstanding their intention. Immediately two great stones were rolled into the hall, to the feet of Powhatan, and the Captain was seized roughly, dragged forward and forced to lie down in such a position that his head lay across the stones. Life looked sweet to him as he reviewed it in a moment of quick survey while waiting for the warriors' clubs to dash out his brains. He closed his eyes. Powhatan gave the fatal signal—the clubs quivered in the hands of the executioners. A piercing shriek rang out, as Pocahontas darted from her father's side, sprang between the uplifted clubs of the savages and the prostrate Captain, twining her arms around his neck and laying her own bright head in such a position that to kill the captive would be to kill the Werowance's dearest daughter.

With horror at this staying of his royal purpose, and at the sight of his child with her arms around the white man's neck, Powhatan stared as if at a hideous vision, and closed his ears to the sound of her voice as her defiant Indian words rang out:

"No! He shall not die!"

The savages stood with upraised weapons; Powhatan sat rigid in the intensity of his emotion. Watching him closely for some sign of relenting, Pocahontas, without moving from her position, began to plead with the stern old Chief,—begged, entreated, prayed—until she had her desire.

"Let the prisoner go free!"

Through the long Council-room echoed Powhatan's order, and a perfunctory shout rose from the savage throng, who were always quick to echo their Chief's commands. Captain Smith, bewildered by the sudden turn of affairs, was helped to rise, led to the beaming girl, and told that the condition of his release from death was that he might "make hatchets and trinkets" for Pocahontas, the Werowance's dearest daughter. So his deliverer was the daughter of the great Chief! With the courtly manner which he had brought from his life in other lands he bent over the warm little hand of the Indian maiden with such sincere appreciation of her brave deed that she flushed with happiness, and she ran away with her playmates, singing as merrily as a forest bird, leaving the pale-faced *Caucarouse* with her royal father, that they might become better acquainted. Although she ran off so gaily with her comrades after having rescued Captain Smith, yet she was far from heedless of his presence in the village, and soon deserted her young friends to steal shyly back to the side of the wonderful white man whose life had been saved that he might serve her.

During the first days of his captivity—for it was that—the Captain and Powhatan became very friendly, and had many long talks by the camp-fire, by means of a sign language and such words of the Algonquin dialect as Captain Smith had learned since coming to Virginia. And often Pocahontas squatted by her father's side, her eager eyes intent on the Captain's face as he matched the old ruler's marvelous tales of hoarded gold possessed by tribes living to the west of Werewocomoco, with stories of the cities of Europe he had visited, and the strange peoples he had met in his wanderings. Sometimes as he told his thrilling tales he would hear the little Indian maid catch her breath from interest in his narrative, and he would smile responsively into her upturned face, feeling a real affection for the young girl who had saved his life.

From his talks with Powhatan the Englishman found out that the great desire of the savage ruler was to own some of the cannon and grindstones used by the colonists, and with quick diplomacy he promised to satisfy this wish if Powhatan would but let him go back to Jamestown and send with him warriors to carry the coveted articles. This the wily Indian ruler promised to do, and in return offered him a tract of land which he did not own, and from which he intended to push the settlers if they should take possession of it. And Captain Smith had no intention of giving either cannon or grindstones to Powhatan, so the shrewd old savage and the quick-witted Captain were well matched in diplomacy.

Meanwhile, Powhatan's interest in his white captive became so great that he gave him the freedom he would have accorded one of his own subjects, even allowing Pocahontas to hunt with him, and when evening came she would sit by the great fire and listen to her Captain's stories of his life told with many a graphic gesture which made them clear to her even though most of his words were unintelligible.

Then came a day when the captive was led to a cabin in the heart of the forest and seated on a mat before a smoldering fire to await he knew not what. Suddenly Powhatan appeared before him, fantastically dressed, followed by two hundred warriors as weirdly decorated as he was. Rushing in, they surrounded the frightened Captain, but quickly dispelled his fears by telling him that they were all his friends and this was only a ceremony to celebrate his speedy return to Jamestown, for the purpose of sending back cannon and grindstones to their Chief.

This was good news. The Captain showed hearty appreciation of the favor, and at once said his farewells. Powhatan, the inscrutable, who bade him a dignified good-by, repeated his promise to give him the country of the Capahowsick, which he did not own, and said he should forever honor him as his own son. Then, with an escort of twelve Indians, Captain Smith set out for Jamestown, and beside him trudged Pocahontas, looking as resolute as if she were in truth a forest Princess escorting her chosen cavalier through the wilderness.

As they picked their way along the rough trail, the Captain told her such tales of the settlement as he could make clear to her and repeated some simple English words he had been trying to teach her. As he talked and as she said over and over the words she had learned, Pocahontas gripped his arm with rapt interest and longed to follow where he led. But night was coming on, it was unwise for her to go beyond the last fork of the trail, and so, reluctantly, she parted from her new and wonderful friend. But before she left him she darted to the side of a trusty warrior and gave a passionate command, then started swiftly back on the long wood path leading to Werewocomoco. The next night no one could make her laugh or join in the dances around the big fire, nor did she show any likeness to the light-hearted, romping, singing little tomboy, ringleader among her playmates. Pocahontas had lost a comrade, and her childish heart was sore at the loss. But when the warriors returned from Jamestown she became merry and happy again, for had the *Caucarouse* not sent her back strings of beads more beautiful than any she had ever seen before, such as proved surely that he had not forgotten her?

The truth of the matter was, that on reaching the colony, Captain Smith showed the Indians a grindstone and told them to carry it back to Powhatan, but when they tried to lift it and found its great weight they were utterly disconcerted. Then the wily Captain showed them a cannon purposely loaded with stones, and had it discharged among the icicle-laden trees, which so terrified the savages that they ran away and refused to take another look at it. Then Captain Smith cleverly suggested that they carry back trinkets in place of the articles which were so heavy, and the Indians went happily away without the promised gifts, but bearing many smaller things, some of which the Captain was thoughtful enough to suggest be given to Pocahontas as a slight token of his appreciation of her great service to him.

Little he dreamed, man of the world though he was, that the small courtesy would mean as much to the Indian maiden as it did, nor could he know that from that hour the dreams of Pocahontas were all to be built around the daily life of the pale-faced men in the Jamestown settlement. Even when she joined her playmates in her favorite games of Gus-ga-e-sa-ta (deer buttons), or Gus-ka-eh (peach-pit), or even,—tomboy that she was,— when she turned somersaults with her favorite brother Nantaquaus and his comrades, she was so far from being her usual lively self that the boys and girls questioned her about the reason. In reply she only flung back her head with an indifferent gesture, and walked away from them. Later when the great fires blazed in Council Hall and Long House, she sought the trusty warrior who had accompanied Captain Smith to Jamestown, and he gave her such news of the settlers as he had heard from the Indians who loafed about Jamestown. They were on friendly terms with the white men, who let them come and go at will as long as they were peaceful and did not try to pilfer corn or firearms.

Winter came with its snow and zero weather, and Pocahontas heard of great hunger and many privations among the colonists. She held a long secret conversation with the Indian warrior who knew of her interest in the pale-faced *Caucarouse*, then, at twilight of a bitter cold day, she stole out from her wigwam, met the warrior at the beginning of the Jamestown trail, and after carefully examining the store of provisions which she had commanded him to bring, she plunged into the gloomy wood trail with her escort, hurrying along the rough path in the darkness, until she reached the rough stockade guarding the entrance to the settlement.

The man on watch, who had heard many glowing descriptions of the maiden who had saved his Captain's life, recognized her at once and admired her exceedingly as she stood there in her dusky imperiousness, demanding to see the Captain. Astonished, but pleased at her coming, Smith quickly came to greet her and was enthusiastic in his thanks for the provisions she had brought. Then by the flare of a torch he showed his eager guest as much of their little village as could be seen in the fast-falling darkness, enjoying her questions and her keen interest in such buildings and articles as she had never seen before. She responded to the Englishmen's cordiality with shy, appreciative glances and would have liked to linger, but it was too late for her to remain longer, and the colonists crowded around her with expressions of regret that she must leave and renewed thanks for her gifts. Then Pocahontas and her Indian escort started back toward Werewocomoco, taking the trail with flying feet that her absence might not be discovered.

From that day she often found her way to Jamestown, carrying stores of provisions from her father's well-filled larder, sometimes going in broad daylight, with rosy cheeks and flying hair, after her morning swim in the river, at other times starting out on her errand of mercy at twilight, always protected by a faithful warrior who was on terms of intimacy with the settlers and felt a deep pride in their admiration for Pocahontas, whom they called "The Little Angel," and well they might, for they would have gone without food many a time during that bitter winter but for her visits.

As for Powhatan, he was too well accustomed to the forest excursions of his "dearest daughter," and to having her roam the neighboring country at will, to watch her carefully. He knew that his daughter was safe on Indian territory, never dreaming that she would go beyond it, and as her guide was loyal, there was no one to prevent her from following out her heart's desires in taking food to her Captain and his people.

But as time went on and Powhatan heard more of the wonderful firearms and useful articles possessed by the white men, he became not only bitterly jealous of them, but determined to secure their arms and articles for his own use. "So when the valiant Captain made another visit to Werewocomoco and tried to barter beads and other trinkets for corn, the old chief refused to trade except for the coveted firearms, which the Captain declined to give. But he did give him a boy named Thomas Salvage, whom Powhatan adopted as his son, and in exchange gave Smith an Indian boy, Namontack. Then there were three days of feasting and dancing, but of trading there was none, and Captain Smith was determined to get corn." He showed Powhatan some blue beads which took the Indian ruler's fancy and he offered a small amount of corn in exchange for them, but the Captain laughed scornfully. Those beads were the favorite possession of Kings and Queens in other countries, why should they be sold to Powhatan? he asked. Powhatan became eager—offered more corn. The Captain hesitated, shook his head, and played his part in the transaction so well that when at last he gave in, he had secured three hundred bushels of corn for the really worthless beads!

In the following months the Indians threw off their mask of friendliness for the colonists and began to steal the firearms so coveted by Powhatan. For some time the white men were patient under the annoyance, but when knives and swords began to go, a watch was set for the thieves, and nine of them were caught and detained at the Jamestown fort, for Captain Smith suspected treachery on Powhatan's part and determined to hold them until all the stolen articles were sent back. In return the Indians captured two straggling Englishmen and came in a shouting throng to the fort clamoring for the release of the imprisoned Indians. Out came the bold Captain and demanded the instant freeing of the settlers. His force and tactics were so superior to those of the savages that they were obliged to give up their captives. Then the Captain examined his Indian prisoners and forced them into a confession of Powhatan's plot to procure all the weapons possible from the colonists, which were then to be used to kill their rightful owners. That was all the Captain wanted of the Indians, but he still kept them imprisoned, to give them a wholesome fright. Powhatan, enraged at hearing of the failure of his plot against the white men, determined that his warriors should be freed at once. He would try another way to gain his end. From his rustic throne in the Council Hall he sent for Pocahontas. She was playing a game of Gawàsa (snow-snake) with two of her comrades, but left them instantly and ran to the Council Hall. Long and earnestly Powhatan talked to her, and she listened intently. When he had finished a pleased expression flashed into her black eyes.

"I will do what you wish," she said, then ran back to join in the game she had left so suddenly.

The next morning she went swiftly along the forest trail now so familiar to her, and at length approached the settlers' stockade and demanded audience with the Captain. He was busy chopping trees at the other end of the settlement, but dropped his ax at the summons and hurried to bid the little maiden welcome with the courtly deference he always showed her, whether he really felt it or not. With folded arms and intent silence he listened to her plea:

For her sake would he not give up the Indians detained in the fort as prisoners? Powhatan was very anxious that the pleasant relations between himself and the Englishmen should not be disturbed by such an unfriendly act as holding his men captive. Would the noble *Caucarouse* not free them for the sake of that maiden who had saved his life?

Captain Smith listened with a set expression and soldierly bearing and tried to evade glancing into the girl's eager eyes, but found it impossible. One look broke down his iron determination, and bending over her hand with his Old World chivalry, he said:

"Your request shall be granted. They shall be freed, but not in justice, simply as an act of friendship for you, who saved my life."

His intention was clear, though his words were not understood. Joyfully Pocahontas beamed and blushed her rapturous thanks. Smith, none too happy over the result of Powhatan's shrewd move, called forth the sullen warriors from the fort, and sent them on their way back to Werewocomoco, led by victorious Pocahontas.

But the Indian girl did not spend all of her time in such heroic deeds as this, nor in dreaming of the pale-faced *Caucarouse*. She was usually the merry, care-free child of the forest and daily led her mates in sport and dance. Once when the Captain went to Werewocomoco to confer with Powhatan on matters concerning neighboring tribes, and found the great Chief away from home, Pocahontas did the honors of the village in her father's place. After sending an Indian runner to request the old ruler to return, she invited Smith and his companions to be seated in an open space before the huge fire which had been built for their benefit.

There, with the clear starlit sky over their heads, and the forest on all sides, they awaited the pleasure of their dusky hostess. But she remained away from them for so long that they grew uneasy, fearing some plot against them. While the Captain was wondering what to do in case of treachery, the woods suddenly resounded with wild shrieks and hideous yells. All jumped to their feet, but stepped back at sight of Pocahontas, who darted from the woods to the Captain's side and said that there was nothing to fear, that she would not allow a hair of the white men's heads to be injured, but had merely arranged a masquerade to amuse her guests while they awaited Powhatan's coming. Then she flitted back into the forest, and presently she danced out, leading a band of thirty young Indian girls, whose bodies were all stained with puccoon and painted with gay colors, while such garments as they wore were made of brilliant green leaves. "Pocahontas, as leader, wore a head-dress of buck's horns and girdle of otter-skin; across her shoulder was slung a quiver filled with arrows, and she carried a bow. Her companions all carried rattles made of dried gourds, or clubs, or wooden swords as they rushed out of the forest yelling and swaying to weird music while they formed a ring around the fire. There they joined hands and kept on dancing and singing in a weird, fantastic way for an hour, when at a whoop from their leader they all ran into the forest, but soon came back in their ordinary Indian dress, to spread a feast before the white men and spend the remainder of the evening in dancing and revels, after which, by the light of flaming torches, they escorted their guests to their tents for the night."

The next morning Powhatan came back, and was told Captain Smith's errand. He had come to invite the old Werowance to visit Jamestown, to receive gifts which Captain Newport, a colonist who had just come back from England, had brought from King James. The King had been much interested in what Newport told him about the Indian ruler, and thought it would be a fine idea to send him back some presents, also a crown, which he suggested might be placed on the savage's head with the ceremonies of a coronation, and the robe thrown over his shoulders, while he was proclaimed Emperor of his own domains. This ceremony, King James thought, might bring about a warmer friendship between the red men and the colonists,—a result much to be desired. And so Captain Smith gave the invitation while Pocahontas, never far away when her *Caucarouse* was at Werewocomoco, listened eagerly for her father's reply.

Powhatan received the invitation in silence and smoked a long time before answering. Then he said:

"If your King has sent me presents, I also am a King, and this is my land. Eight days will I stay to receive them. Your father (Newport) is to come to me, not I to him, nor yet to your fort."

Wily Powhatan! He had no intention of visiting the white men's stronghold, when by so doing he might walk into some trap they had laid for him!

And so Pocahontas was disappointed in her eager hope of going with her father to the settlement where her white friends lived, and where she could see her wonderful Captain daily. But there was no help for it. Powhatan resisted both her pleading and the arguments of the Captain, who was obliged to carry back the old Werowance's refusal to Captain Newport.

"Then we will take the gifts to him!" said Newport, stoutly. "The King would never forgive me if I did not carry out his wish."

And so to Werewocomoco went the two Captains together, bearing their offerings to Powhatan, who received them with dignity, and showed a mild interest when presented with a bedstead and a basin and pitcher such as the English used. But when Captain Smith tried to throw the coronation robe over his shoulders he drew away haughtily, wrapped his own mantle around him, and refused to listen to argument or entreaty. Namontack hastily assured him that the garments were like those worn by the English and would do him no harm, and Pocahontas, seeing the Captain's eagerness to accomplish his end, and also keenly interested in this new game, begged her father to accept the beautiful gifts. Her words influenced the old ruler, and, standing as stiff and straight as a wooden image, he let himself be dressed up in the garb of English royalty. Then he was told to kneel while the crown was placed on his head, but this was too much for even Pocahontas to expect of him. He folded his arms and stood like a pine-tree. In vain Pocahontas urged, in vain the two white men bent and bowed and knelt before him to show him what he ought to do.

At last Captain Smith grew impatient and laid a powerful hand on the Werowance's broad shoulders; unconsciously he stooped. The crown was hurriedly placed on his head, and a volley of shots was fired to show that the ceremony was over. At the shots Powhatan sprang free like a wild creature, sure that he had been trapped, and Captain Smith appealed to Pocahontas to explain to her terrified father that the firing was only part of the program. Meanwhile both Captains bowed ceremoniously before the savage ruler, calling him by his new title—Emperor—and finally soothed and reassured, he stood as erect and dignified as of old, and beckoning majestically to Namontack, bade him bring his old moccasins and mantle to send to King James in return for the crown and robe!

Much amused, Captain Newport thanked him and received the gift, but told him that more than moccasins or mantles, the Englishmen desired his aid in attacking a neighboring and hostile tribe. In this desire, however, Powhatan showed no interest, and the two Captains were obliged to leave Werewocomoco without his co-operation, which would have been of much benefit in subduing the unfriendly tribe. But the coronation ceremony had been accomplished; that was one thing for which to be thankful and Captain Newport had for the first time seen the charming Indian girl who had become such an ally of the settlers, so he felt well repaid for the visit, although to him Pocahontas showed none of the spontaneous sympathy which she gave so joyously to Captain Smith.

And now again came winter and with it privation and hunger for the colonists. Corn must be procured. There was only one man stout-hearted enough to venture on another expedition in search of it, and that was Captain Smith. He decided to go to Werewocomoco once more, and if he found the new-made Emperor rebellious, to promptly make him prisoner and carry away his stores of corn by force.

While the Captain and his men were making ready to start on the expedition, to their great surprise messengers arrived from Powhatan inviting Captain Smith to visit Werewocomoco again if he would bring with him men to build a house and give the Emperor a grindstone, fifty swords, some firearms, a hen and rooster, and much beads and copper, for which he would be given corn.

Immediately forty-six Englishmen set out on a snowy December day, in two barges and a pinnace, for Werewocomoco. The first night they spent at the Indian village of Warrasqueake, where a friendly chief warned Captain Smith not to go further.

"You shall find Powhatan to use you kindly," he said, "but trust him not, and be sure he have no opportunity to seize on your arms, for he hath sent for you only to cut your throats."

On hearing these words many of his comrades would have turned back, but the Captain spoke to them in such courageous words that in spite of the warning all continued on their way.

While they were journeying on toward their destination, Pocahontas, at Werewocomoco, was daily with her father, watching him with alert ears and eyes, for she saw that the old ruler was brooding over some matter of grave import, and she drew her own inference. Only when planning to wage war on an alien tribe or plotting against the Jamestown settlers did he so mope and muse and fail to respond to her overtures. Late one evening, when she saw two of his loyal warriors steal to his side, in order to hear their conversation better she climbed a near-by tree and listened to their muttered words. Her suspicions were confirmed. There was need of her intervention again. From that moment until she had foiled Powhatan's design, she was on guard day and night watching and waiting for the coming of the Englishmen, often lying sleepless in her wigwam to listen for some unwonted noise in the hushed forest.

When the party from Jamestown reached the Indian village the river was frozen over for a half-mile from shore. With his usual impetuous courage the Captain broke the ice by jumping into the frozen stream, and swam ashore, followed by the others, who were ashamed to be less courageous than he. It was nearly night, and they took possession of a deserted wigwam in the woods near the shore and sent word to Powhatan that they were in immediate need of food, as their journey had been a long one, and asked if he would not send provisions at once. In response an Indian runner came to their wigwam bearing bread, turkeys, and venison, much to the delight of the half-starved colonists. Refreshed by a good meal, they slept heavily in the still forest, and early the next morning went to pay their respects to Powhatan, who was in his "Chief Place of Council" awaiting their visit in his gala robe of luxurious skins and elaborate feather head-dress. His greeting was courteous, but he at once turned to Captain Smith and asked:

"When are you going away? I did not invite you to come."

Although taken by surprise, quick-witted Captain Smith did not show his feelings, but pointing to a group of Indian warriors standing near, he said:

"There are the very men who came to Jamestown to invite us here!"

At this Powhatan gave a guttural laugh and changed the subject at once, by asking to see the articles which Captain Smith had brought for exchange. Then began a long and hot discussion in which neither the Captain nor the wily Emperor gained a point. Powhatan refused to trade unless the white men left their firearms on their barges and would barter corn only for the coveted articles. Captain Smith would not accede to his demands even to get the much-needed corn, and was on his guard because of the warning he had received, knowing that Powhatan was only waiting for the right moment to kill him.

The debate went on for hours, during which there had been only one trade made when Smith exchanged a copper kettle for forty bushels of corn. Annoyed at this, he determined to take matters into his own hand. Beckoning to some friendly Indians, he asked them to go to the river bank and signal to his men on the barges to come ashore with baskets to take back the corn for which he had traded the kettle. Meanwhile he kept up a brisk conversation with the old Werowance to divert his attention, assuring him that on the next day he and his men would leave their firearms on the ships, trusting to Powhatan's promise that no harm should come to them.

Powhatan was too clever to be fooled by any such delightful promise; he knew the quick-witted Captain was probably playing the same game that he was, and feared lest the white man should be quicker than he at it. He slyly whispered a command to a young warrior, and at a sign from him two gaily decorated squaws darted forward and, squatting at the feet of the Captain, began to sing tribal songs to the beating of drums and shaking of rattles, and while they sang Powhatan silently drew his fur robe about him and stole away to a forest retreat long prepared for an hour of danger. Before him went a supply of provisions, and with him some women and children, but not Pocahontas. Meeting her father in his hasty flight, she listened to his request that she go with him, but with a laughing gesture of refusal she fled through the woods to the place where the white men were grouped. The old Chief's power over his daughter had been greatly weakened by the coming of the colonists to Jamestown, and who knows what a fire of envy that may have kindled in his heart?

As soon as the Emperor reached his hiding-place, he sent an old Sachem in war paint and feathers back to Captain Smith, bearing a valuable bracelet as an offering, and saying that his chief had fled because he feared the white man's weapons, but if they could be laid aside, he, Powhatan, would return to give the colonists an abundance of corn. Captain Smith, with arms folded and flashing eyes, refused the bracelet and the request, and the Sachem went back to carry the news to Powhatan.

Pocahontas had watched the interview with breathless interest, and when she saw the old warrior turn away, and knew that Captain Smith had foiled her father's intent, she knew that the brave *Caucarouse* was in great danger. That night, while all the Englishmen except their leader were out hunting, the Captain sat alone in his wigwam musing on ways and means to gain his end. There was a sound in the still forest—a crackling of underbrush—he roused at a light touch on his arm. Pocahontas stood by his side, alone in the darkness; swiftly she whispered her message and he understood its gravity only too well.

"My father is going to send you food, and, if you eat it, you will die," she said. "It is not safe for you to stay here any longer. Oh, go! I beg you, go!"

She was shivering in her fear for his safety, and the Captain was deeply moved by her emotion. Raising her hand to his lips in his wonted fashion, he thanked her and offered her the choicest beads in his store for a remembrance, but she would not accept them!

"He would want to know where I got them, and then he would kill me, too," she said, and vanished as silently and swiftly as she had come.

As she had reported, soon there came warriors from Powhatan bearing huge vessels filled with food, smoking hot. The Chief had returned to Werewocomoco, they said, and wished to show his good-will to the white men. Would they partake of a feast which he had sent?

They set down their burden of tempting food, and the Captain's eyes gleamed; with a profound bow he thanked Powhatan for his courtesy, but he said:

"When we English make a feast for any one, we ourselves first taste each dish before we offer it to our guests. If you would have me eat what you have brought, you must first taste of each dish yourselves."

His manner was defiant as he stood waiting for them to accept his challenge, and, seeing they made no move to touch what they had brought, he said, still more defiantly:

"Tell your Chief to come and attack us. We are ready for you!"

So soldierly was he, that the frightened Indians turned and fled, while the colonists hastily threw away the food Powhatan had sent. The old ruler had again been checkmated by his daughter's loyalty to the white men and the Captain's courage.

Early the next morning, when the tide was right, the white men were able to leave Werewocomoco, and all on board the barges drew sighs of relief as they sailed away from the Emperor's stronghold.

While they had been absent from Jamestown a party had set out for a neighboring island, but a great storm having come up, their boat had been swamped and all on board drowned. As they were the men who had been left in charge of the colony during Smith's absence, it was necessary to send him word immediately, and one of the survivors, Richard Wyffin, was sent on the errand. When he arrived at Werewocomoco the colonists had left, and Powhatan was in a sullen fury against them for having outwitted him. Wyffin's life was in danger, and he must escape as quickly as possible. Pocahontas hurried to his rescue and at a moment when there were no Indians to see, she took him to a forest hiding-place where he could safely spend the night. Later, under cover of the darkness, she crept to the spot, awakened him and led him to the edge of the woods, directing him to take the opposite trail from that on which her father's braves were watching to capture him. And so he escaped and joined the other colonists at Pamunkey, where they had gone from Werewocomoco, Captain Smith being determined either to get corn from Opechancanough or to burn his storehouses, for he, like Powhatan, had promised to trade with the white men. But he proved treacherous, too, and Captain Smith, exasperated and desperate, sprang on him and "in a fierce encounter nearly knocked the breath out of his huge body, then jammed him up against the wall, placed the muzzle of his gun at his breast, and, seizing him by his scalp-lock, dragged him out into full view of his assembled subjects and gave him the alternative—

"'Your corn or your life!'

"Under the circumstances Opechancanough promptly decided to give the corn, and with a ship full of the much-needed provisions the settlers sailed triumphantly back to Jamestown."

When this was reported to Powhatan it greatly increased his respect for the pale-faced *Caucarouse*, but he was still enraged at the failure of his plan to kill him, and he commanded his warriors to capture him as soon as possible; but meanwhile events occurred which worked for the Captain's good. A Chickahominy Indian had stolen various articles from the settlers, among them a pistol. He escaped, but his two brothers, who were known to be his accomplices, were captured and one held in the Jamestown fort, while the other was told to go for the pistol, and if he did not return with it in twelve hours his brother would be hung. Away went the Indian—while the Captain took pity on the poor naked wretch imprisoned in the cold cell and sent him some food and charcoal for a fire—the fumes from which suffocated him. When his brother came back with the pistol he lay senseless on the ground. Captain Smith at once hurried to the spot and worked so hard to revive him that he recovered, and the next morning was well enough to leave the fort with his brother, both of them having been given substantial presents of copper. The story was told among the tribe as a miracle, and the belief became current that to his other virtues the brave Captain added that of being able to raise men from the dead. Then one of Powhatan's warriors secretly secured a bag of gunpowder and pretended that he could use it as the English did. His dusky comrades crowded around to watch him manage the strange article, but in some way it caught fire, and blew him, with one or two more, to death. This happening so awed and terrified those Indians who saw the accident that they began to be superstitious about the knowledge of the settlers, who could make such powerful things obey their will. It was better to be a friend than foe of the white man, so even Powhatan concluded, and warriors from all the neighboring tribes came to Jamestown bringing presents, also stolen articles, and begging for friendly relations instead of attempting to capture Captain Smith.

Then came an event which forever changed the life of Pocahontas, the Captain's staunch admirer. He, after having adventured up the James River to visit a struggling colony there, was sailing down the river feeling weary and discouraged, as he had many enemies working against him at Jamestown, and was so disheartened that he determined to leave Virginia forever. As he lay musing and trying to sleep in the stern of the ship, a bag of gunpowder exploded, wounding him so badly that he leaped into the water to cool the burning agony of his flesh. He was rescued and the ship sailed for Jamestown with all possible haste. His wounds were dressed, but he was in a dangerous condition and there was no skilled surgeon to care for him, so his plight was pitiable. An Indian carried the sad news to Pocahontas, who at once deserted her comrades for solitary brooding in the forest. Then she took the long wood trail to Jamestown. Hours later one of the settlers found her standing outside the stockade, peering through the cracks between the logs as though it were some comfort to see into the village where her Captain lay—that Captain who held her heart in his keeping. She would have stood there less quietly had she known that an enemy of his had stolen into his cabin and at that very moment was holding a pistol to the wounded man's bosom, trying to nerve himself to do a deed he had been bribed to do! But his courage failed, his hand dropped, and he crept out into the silent night, leaving the wounded man unharmed. While Pocahontas stood on tiptoe outside the stockade, straining her eager eyes for a glimpse of the Captain's cabin, there were footsteps beside her—a hand was laid on her shoulder, and a voice asked:

"Why are you here at such an hour, Pocahontas?"

It was one of the colonists who was Captain Smith's loyal friend. Pocahontas turned to him, gripping her slender hands together in an agony of appeal.

"He is not dead?" she asked. The man shook his head and a glad light flashed into the girl's eyes.

"He has many enemies," she said. "Can you do nothing to nurse him back to health?"

Tears stood in her black eyes, and her appeal would have softened a heart less interested in the Captain's welfare than was her hearer's. Promising to watch over the brave Captain and care for him as his own kin, the white man soothed and comforted Pocahontas, and at last induced her to leave her place at the fort and go back to Werewocomoco, and never did the Captain know of her long vigil for his sake that night.

Reaching the Indian village without her absence having been discovered, she went about her daily routine of work and play as if nothing had happened, but every sound in the still forest caused her heart to beat fast, and she was always listening for an approaching footstep bringing news of her beloved. Then a warrior brought the tidings—Captain Smith was dead. Dead! She could not, would not believe it! *Dead!* He who was so full of life and vigor was not dead—that was too absurd. And yet even as she reasoned with herself, she accepted the fact without question with the immobility of her race; and no one guessed the depth of her wound, even though all the tribe had known of her devotion to the pale-faced *Caucarouse* whose life she had saved.

From that day she went no more to Jamestown, nor asked for news of the settlers, and soon the gay voice and the laughing eyes of the "little romp" were missing, too, from Werewocomoco. Pocahontas could not bear the sights and sounds of that village whose every tree and trail was dear to her because of its association with her Captain. She had relatives among the Potomacks, and to them she went for a long visit, where in different surroundings she could more easily bear the loneliness which overpowered her, child of a savage and unemotional race though she was. It may have been also that Powhatan was beginning to distrust her friendship with the white men. At all events, she, who was fast blossoming into the most perfect womanhood of her race, remained away from home for many months. Had she dreamed that Captain Smith was not dead, but had sailed for England that he might have proper care for his injury, and also because of the increasing enmity against him in the colony, she would have gone about her work and play with a lighter heart. But she thought him dead, and in the mystic faith of her people saw him living in every tree and cloud and blossoming thing.

Powhatan had respected Captain Smith, but for the white men as a race he had more enmity than liking, and now he and his neighbors, the Chickahominies, again refused to send any provisions to Jamestown, and again the colonists faced a famine. Captain Argall, in command of an English ship, suggested once more going to Werewocomoco to force Powhatan into giving them corn, and soon sailed up the Potomac toward the Indian village. One night on the way up, while the ship lay at anchor near shore, an Indian came aboard with the news that the Emperor's dearest daughter, Pocahontas, was staying among the Potomacks visiting a chief named Japazaws. The unscrupulous Captain had an idea. If he could capture Pocahontas and hold her for a ransom he would surely be able to gain anything he demanded from Powhatan. No thought of the kindness and loyalty of the Indian maiden to the white man interfered with his scheming. Corn he must have, and here was a way to obtain it. He quickly arranged with the Indian for an interview with the Chief Japazaws, who proved to be quite as unscrupulous as Captain Argall, and for a copper kettle promised to deliver Pocahontas into the Captain's hands—in fact, to bring her aboard his vessel on the following day.

Having taken his wife into his confidence, Japazaws told her in the presence of Pocahontas that the white Captain had invited her to visit his ship. She retorted that she would like to accept, but would not go unless Pocahontas would go too. Japazaws pretended to be very angry at this:—

"I wish you to go," he exclaimed; "if you do not accept I will beat you until you do."

But the squaw was firm.

"I will not go without Pocahontas," she declared.

Pocahontas was very kind-hearted, as the chief and his wife knew, so at once she said:

"Stop beating her; I will do as she wishes!"

Captain Argall gave them a cordial greeting and had a lavish feast prepared in their honor, and while they were talking together he asked Pocahontas if she would not like to see the gun-room. She assented, entirely unsuspicious of any treachery, and was horrified when she heard the door fastened behind her, and knew that for some reason she was a prisoner. Terror-stricken,—brave girl though she was,—she pounded violently on the door and cried as she had never cried before in all her care-free life, begging "Let me out!" but in vain. She could hear Japazaws and his wife weeping even more violently than she on the other side of the door, and begging for her release, but it was only a pretense. The door remained locked, and as soon as the couple were given the copper kettle and a few trinkets, they left the ship contentedly. After that there was an ominous silence on the vessel, except for the sobbing of the Indian girl, who was still more frightened as she felt the motion of the ship and knew they were getting under way.

But as they sailed down the river to Jamestown, the captain unlocked the door and the girl was allowed to come out of her prison. She faced him with a passionate question:

"What wrong have I done that I should be so treated—I who have been always the loyal friend of the English?"

So noble was she in her youth and innocence, that the captain was horrified at the deed he had done and could do no less than tell her the truth. He assured her that she had done no wrong, that he well knew that she was the white man's friend, and that no harm should befall her, but that it was necessary to take firm measures to secure provisions for the starving colonists. Hearing this, she was less frightened and became quiet, if not in spirit, at least in manner, giving no cause for trouble as they entered the harbor. But her heart was filled with sadness when she again saw that fort to which she had so often gone with aid for her vanished friend whose name now never passed her lips.

Indian girls mature rapidly, and the maiden who had first attracted Captain Smith's attention was no less lovely now, but she was in the full flower of womanliness and her charm and dignity of carriage compelled respect from all.

Powhatan was in his Place of Council when a messenger from Jamestown demanded audience with him and gave his message in quick, jerky sentences:

"Your daughter Pocahontas has been taken captive by the Englishmen," he said. "She will be held until you send back to Jamestown all the guns, tools, and men stolen from them by your warriors."

The old chief, terrified, grief-stricken, and in a dilemma, knew not what to say, for though he loved his daughter, he was determined to keep the firearms taken from the English. For a long time he was deep in thought. Finally he replied:

"The white men will not harm my child, who was their very good friend. They know my wrath will fall on them if they harm a hair of her head. Let her remain with them until I shall have made my decision."

Not another word would he say, but strode out from the Council Hall and was lost in the forest.

Three months went by without the Englishmen receiving a word from him, and Pocahontas meanwhile became their inspiration and joy, giving no sign that she feared her captors or objected to her captivity. Then Powhatan sent seven white men who had been held by the Indians to the settlement, carrying a gun which had been spoiled for use. Their leader brought this message from the Indian Emperor:

"If you will send back my daughter I will send you five hundred bushels of corn and be your friend forever. I have no more guns to return, as the remainder have been lost."

Prompt was the retort:

"Tell your Chief that his daughter will not be restored to him until our demand has been complied with. We do not believe that the guns have been lost."

The runner took back the message, and again nothing more was heard from Powhatan for several months, during which time the colonists became so deeply attached to the young captive that they dreaded to think of the settlement without her cheery presence. Especially did John Rolfe, a young widower, who was by report "an English gentleman of approved behavior and honest carriage," feel a special interest in the charming young savage; in fact he fell in love with her, but felt that he must convert her to the Christian religion before asking her to become his wife. So he devoted much time to instructing her in the doctrines of the white man's faith. Pocahontas accepted the new religion eagerly, and little did John Rolfe guess that to her it was the religion of Captain John Smith,—a new tie binding her to the man who she believed had gone forever beyond her sight, but who would be forever dearest to her loyal heart, untutored girl of the forest though she was. It is doubtful, too, whether John Rolfe would ever have made any headway in her affection had she not believed her beloved Captain to be dead. However that may have been, she became a convert to Christianity, and John Rolfe asked her to marry him.

When almost a year had gone by with no word from Powhatan, the colonists were very angry and decided to force the issue. A party in command of Sir Thomas Dale, who had come from England to be the leader of the Jamestown settlement, sailed for Werewocomoco, taking Pocahontas with them, hoping that when Powhatan heard of the presence of his dearest daughter at his very door he would relent and yield to their demands.

But Powhatan was not at Werewocomoco. Anticipating just such a visit, he was in a safe retreat, and his warriors who thronged to the river bank to meet the white men at once attacked them, and there was lively skirmishing until two brothers of Pocahontas heard of her arrival. Hurrying to the river bank, they quelled the turmoil and hastily paddled out to the ship, where they were soon standing beside their sister, seeing with joy that despite her captivity she was well and happy, with the same merry light in her black eyes as she had in her forest days. Their feeling deepened into awe when with downcast eyes and flushed cheeks she told them of John Rolfe's love for her and of her attachment for him. Their sister girl of the forest, kin of the red men,— going to marry an Englishman from that marvelous land across the sea, of which one of their tribe who had visited it had brought back the report: "Count the stars in the sky, the leaves on the trees, and the sand upon the seashore—such is the number of the people of England!" Pocahontas, their little sister, going to marry an Englishman!—the stalwart Indian boys could scarcely believe the tale, and on leaving the ship they hurried to their father's forest retreat to tell their wondrous tale. The old Chief listened with inscrutable reserve, but his eyes gleamed with exultation and in his heart he rejoiced. His daughter, child of an Indian Werowance, to become wife of a white man,—the two races to be united? Surely this would be a greater advantage than all the firearms that could be bought or stolen!

But if he expected that the breach between the white men and the red would be at once healed, he was mistaken. Although Pocahontas greeted her brothers so cordially, she would have nothing to do with her father or any of his braves, and when Powhatan desired to see her she sent back the imperious message:

"Tell him if he had loved his daughter he would not have valued her less than old swords, pieces, and axes; wherefore will I still dwell with the Englishmen who love me!"

And back to Jamestown she presently sailed with those men of the race to which she had been loyal even in her captivity.

That Powhatan did not resent her refusal to see him after his long silence, but probably admired her for her determination, was soon shown. Ten days after the party reached Jamestown an Indian warrior, Opachisco, uncle of Pocahontas, and two of her brothers, arrived there, sent by Powhatan to show his approval of his daughter's alliance with an Englishman, although nothing would have induced him to visit the white man's settlement himself, even to witness the marriage of his dearest daughter.

Having become a convert to the white man's faith, Pocahontas was baptized according to the ritual of the Christian church, taking the name of Rebecca, and as she was the daughter of an Emperor, she was afterwards called "Lady Rebecca;" but to those who had known her in childhood she would ever be Pocahontas, the "little romp."

And now the Indian maiden, who by her loyalty to the white race had changed the course of her life, was about to merge her identity in that of the colonists:—

"On a balmy April day, with sunshine streaming through the open windows of the Jamestown chapel, the rude place of worship was filled to overflowing with colonists, all eagerly interested in the wedding of John Rolfe with the dusky princess who was the first Christian Indian in Virginia."

The rustic chapel had been decorated with woodland blossoms, and its windows garlanded with vines. Its columns were pine-trees cut from the forest, its rude pews of sweet-smelling cedar, and its simple Communion table covered with bread made from wheat grown in neighboring fields, and with wine from the luscious wild grapes picked in near-by woods.

There, in the beauty and fragrance of the spring day, up the aisle of the chapel passed the young Indian bride on the arm of John Rolfe, who looked every inch an English gentleman in his cavalier's costume. And very lovely was the new-made Lady Rebecca in her gown of white muslin with its richly embroidered over-dress given by Sir Thomas Dale. Her head-dress of birds' plumage was banded across her forehead, Indian fashion, with a jeweled fillet, which also caught her floating veil, worn in the English way, which emphasized her dark beauty. On her wrists gleamed many bracelets, and in her deep eyes was the look of one who glimpses the future and fears it not.

Slowly they advanced up the aisle, and halted before the altar, a picturesque procession; the grave, dignified Englishman, who now and again cast adoring glances at his girlish bride, of an alien forest race; the old Chief of a savage tribe, in his gay ceremonial trappings and head-dress; the two stalwart, bronzed young braves, keenly interested in this great event in their sister's life, all in a strange commingling of Old World and New, auguring good for the future of both Indians and colonists.

The minister of the colony repeated the simple service, and Lady Rebecca, in her pretty but imperfect English, repeated her marriage vows and accepted the wedding-ring of civilized races as calmly as if she had not been by birth a free forest creature. Then, the service ended, down the aisle, in the flickering sunlight, passed the procession, and there at the chapel door, surrounded by the great forest trees which had been her lifelong comrades, and with the wide sky spreading over her in blue benediction, we have a last glimpse of the "little romp," for Pocahontas, the Indian maiden, had become Lady Rebecca, wife of John Rolfe, the Englishman.

Three years later Pocahontas, for so we still find it in our hearts to call her, visited England with her husband and little son Thomas, to see with her own eyes that land across the sea where her husband had been brought up, and of which she had heard such wonderful tales. One can well imagine the wonder of the girl of the forest when she found herself out of sight of land, on the uncharted ocean of which she had only skirted the shores before, and many a night she stole from her cabin during that long voyage to watch the mysterious sea in its majestic swell, and the star-sown heavens, as the ship moved slowly on to its destination.

London, too, was a revelation to her with its big buildings, its surging crowds of white men, its marks of civilization everywhere, and, girl of the outdoors that she had ever been, her presentation at Court, with all that went before and after of the frivolities and conventionalities of city life, must have been a still greater marvel to her. But the greatest surprise of all awaited her. One day at a public reception a new-comer was announced, and without warning she found herself face to face with that Captain of her heart's youthful devotion! There was a moment's silence, a strained expression in the young wife's dark eyes, then Captain John Smith bent over the hand of John Rolfe's wife with the courtly deference he had given in Virginian days to the little Indian girl who was his loyal friend.

"They told me you were dead!"

It was Pocahontas who with quivering lips broke the silence, then without waiting for a reply she left the room and was not seen for hours. When she again met and talked with the brave Captain, she was as composed as usual, and no one could say how deeply her heart was touched to see again the friend of her girlhood days. Perhaps the unexpected sight of him brought with it a wave of home-sickness for the land of her birth and days of care-free happiness, perhaps she felt a stab of pain that the man to whom she had given so much had not sent her a message on leaving the country, but had let her believe the rumor of his death—perhaps the heart of Pocahontas was still loyal to her first love, devoted wife and mother though she was. Whatever may have been the truth, Lady Rebecca was proud and calm in the presence of the Captain after that first moment, and had many conversations with him which increased his admiration for the gracious forest Princess, now a lady of distinction in his own land.

The climate of England did not agree with Pocahontas, her health failed rapidly, and in the hope that a return to Virginia would save her life, her husband took passage for home. But it was too late; after a sickness of only a few hours, she died, and John Rolfe was left without the vivid presence which had been his blessing and his joy.

Pocahontas was buried at Gravesend on the 21st of March, 1617, and as night fell, and John Rolfe tossed on a bed of anguished memories, it is said that a man muffled in a great cloak stole through the darkness and knelt beside the new-made grave with bowed head and clasped hands.

It was Captain Smith who came to offer reverent tribute to the girl who had given him so much, asking nothing in return, a girl of savage lineage, yet of noble character and great charm, whose blossoming into the flower of civilization had no parallel. Alone there, in the somber night, the silent figure knelt—the brave Captain of her loyal devotion paying tardy homage to Pocahontas, the girl of the Virginia forest, the white man's steadfast friend.

DOROTHY QUINCY: THE GIRL OF COLONIAL DAYS WHO HEARD

THE FIRST GUN FIRED FOR INDEPENDENCE

A small, shapely foot clad in silken hose and satin slipper of palest gray was thrust from under flowing petticoats of the same pale shade, as Dorothy Quincy stepped daintily out of church on a Sabbath Day in June after attending divine service.

John Hancock, also coming from church, noted the small foot with interest, and his keen eye traveled from the slipper to its owner's lovely face framed in a gray bonnet, in the depths of which nestled a bunch of rosebuds. From that moment Hancock's fate as a man was as surely settled as was his destiny among patriots when the British seized his sloop, the *Liberty*.

But all that belongs to a later part of our story, and we must first turn back the pages of history and become better acquainted with that young person whose slippered foot so diverted a man's thoughts from the sermon he had heard preached on that Lord's Day in June.

Pretty Dorothy was the youngest daughter of Edmund Quincy, one of a long line of that same name, who were directly descended from Edmund Quincy, pioneer, who came to America in 1628. Seven years later the town of Boston granted him land in the town that was afterward known as Braintree, Massachusetts, where he built the mansion that became the home of succeeding generations of Quincys, from whom the North End of the town was later named.

As his father had been before him, Dorothy's father was a judge, and he spent a part of each year in his home on Summer Street, Boston, pursuing his profession. There in the Summer Street home Dorothy was born on the tenth of May, 1747, the youngest of ten children. Evidently she was sent to school at an early age, and gave promise of a quick mind even then, for in a letter written by Judge Quincy, from Boston to his wife in the country, he writes:

Daughter Dolly looks very Comfortable, and has gone to School, where she seems to be very high in her Mistresses' graces.

But the happiest memories of Dorothy's childhood and early girlhood were not of Boston, but of months spent in the rambling old mansion at Quincy, which, although it had been remodeled by her grandfather, yet retained its quaint charm, and boasted more than one secret passage and cupboard, as well as a "haunted chamber" without which no house of the period was complete.

There we find the child romping across velvety lawns, picking posies in the box-bordered garden, drinking water crystal clear drawn from the old well, and playing many a prank and game in the big, roomy home which housed such a lively flock of young people. Being the baby of the family, it was natural that Dorothy should be a great pet, not only of her brothers and sisters, but of their friends, especially those young men—some of whom were later the principal men of the Province—who were attracted to the old mansion by Judge Quincy's charming daughters. So persistent was little Dolly's interest in her sisters' friends, that it became a jest among them that he who would woo and win fascinating Esther, sparkling Sarah, or the equally lovely Elizabeth or Katherine Quincy, must first gain the good-will of the little girl who was so much in evidence, many times when the adoring swain would have preferred to see his lady love alone. Dorothy used to tell laughingly in later years of the rides she took on the shoulders of Jonathan Sewall, who married Esther Quincy, of the many small gifts and subtle devices used by other would-be suitors as bribes either to enlist the child's sympathies in gaining their end, or as a reward for her absence at some interesting and sentimental crisis.

Mrs. Quincy, who before her marriage was Elizabeth Wendall, of New York, was in full sympathy with her light-hearted, lively family of boys and girls. Although the household had for its deeper inspiration those Christian principles which were the governing factors in family life of the colonists, and prayers were offered morning and night by the assembled family, while the Sabbath was kept strictly as a day for church-going and quiet reflection, yet the atmosphere of the home was one of hospitable welcome. This made it a popular gathering-place not only for the young people of the neighborhood, but also for more than one youth who came from the town of Boston, ten miles away, attracted by the bevy of girls in the old mansion.

Judge Quincy was not only a devout Christian and a respected member of the community, he was also a fine linguist. He was so well informed on many subjects that, while he was by birth and tradition a Conservative, giving absolute loyalty to the mother country, and desirous of obeying her slightest dictate, yet he was so much more broad-minded than many of his party that he welcomed in his home even those admirers of his daughters who were determined to resist what they termed the unjust commands of the English Government. Among these patriots-to-be who came often to the Quincy home was John Adams, in later days the second President of the

United States, and who was a boy of old Braintree and a comrade of John Hancock, whose future history was to be closely linked with the new and independent America. Hancock was, at the time of his first visit to the old Quincy mansion, a brilliant young man, drawn to the Judge's home by an overwhelming desire to see more of pretty Dorothy, whose slippered foot stepping from the old meeting-house had roused his interest. Up to the time when he began to come to the house, little Dorothy was still considered a child by her brothers and sisters, her aims and ambitions were laughed at, if she voiced them, and she was treated as the family pet and plaything rather than a girl rapidly blossoming into very beautiful womanhood.

As she saw one after another of her sisters become engaged to the man of her choice, watched the happy bustle of preparation in the household, then took part in the wedding festivities, and saw the bride pass out of the old mansion to become mistress of a home of her own, Dorothy was quick to perceive the important part played by man in a woman's life, and, young as she was, she felt within herself that power of fascination which was to be hers to so great a degree in the coming years. Dorothy had dark eyes which were wells of feeling when she was deeply moved, her hair was velvet smooth, and also dark, and the play of feelings grave and gay which lighted up her mobile face when in conversation was a constant charm to those who knew the vivacious girl. When she first met John Hancock she had won an enviable popularity by reason of her beauty and grace, and was admired and sought after even more than her sisters had been; yet no compliments or admiration spoiled her sweet naturalness or her charm of manner.

In those days girls married when they were very young, but Dorothy withstood all the adoration which was poured at her feet beyond the time when she might naturally have chosen a husband, because her standards were so high that not one of her admirers came near to satisfying them. But in her heart there was an Ideal Man who had come to occupy the first place in her affection.

As she had sat by her father's side, night after night, listening while John Adams spoke with hot enthusiasm of his friend John Hancock, the boy of Braintree, now a rising young citizen of Boston, the resolute advocate of justice for the colonies, who stood unflinchingly against the demands of the mother country, where he thought them unfair,—the conversation had roused her enthusiasm for this unknown hero, until she silently erected an altar within her heart to this ideal of manly virtues.

Then John Hancock came to the old mansion to seek the girl who had attracted his attention on that Sabbath Day in June, little dreaming that in those conversations which Dorothy had heard between her father and John Adams she had pieced together a complete biography of her Hero. She knew that in 1737, when the Reverend John Hancock was minister of the First Church in the North Precinct of Braintree (afterward Quincy), he had made the following entry in the parish register of births:

John Hancock, my son, January 16, 1737.

Dorothy also knew that there in the simple parsonage the minister's son grew up, and together with his brother and sister enjoyed the usual life of a child in the country. When he was seven years old his father died, leaving very little money for the support of the widow and three children. Thomas Hancock, his uncle, was at that time the richest merchant in Boston, and had also married a daughter of a prosperous bookseller who was heir to no small fortune herself. The couple being childless, at the death of John Hancock's father they adopted the boy, who was at once taken from the simple parsonage to Thomas Hancock's mansion on Beacon Hill, which must have seemed like a fairy palace to the minister's son, as he "climbed the grand steps and entered the paneled hall with its broad staircase, carved balusters, and a chiming clock surmounted with carved figures, gilt with burnished gold." There were also portraits of dignitaries on the walls of the great drawing-room, which were very impressive in their lace ruffles and velvet costumes of the period, and many articles of furniture of which the country boy did not even know the names.

As a matter of course, he was sent to the Boston Public Latin School, and later to Harvard College, from which he graduated on July 17, 1754, when he was seventeen years old—at a time when pretty Dorothy Quincy was a child of seven.

From the time of his adoption of his nephew, Thomas Hancock had determined to have him as his successor in the shipping business he had so successfully built up, and so, fresh from college, the young man entered into the business life of Boston, and as the adopted son of a rich and influential merchant, was sought after by mothers with marriageable daughters, and by the daughters themselves, to whose charms he was strangely indifferent.

For six years he worked faithfully and with a good judgment that pleased his uncle, while at the same time he took part in the amusements of the young people of Boston who belonged to the wealthy class, and who copied their diversions from those in vogue among young folk in London. The brilliant and fine-looking young man was in constant demand for riding, hunting, and skating parties, or often in winter for a sleigh-ride to some country tavern, followed by supper and a dance; or in summer for an excursion down the harbor, a picnic on the islands, or a tea-party in the country and a homeward drive by moonlight. Besides these gaieties there were frequent musters of militia, of which Hancock was a member, and he was very fond of shooting and fishing; so with work and play he was more than busy until he was twenty-three years old. Then his uncle sent him to London to give him the advantages of travel and of mingling with "foreign lords of trade and finance," and also to gain a knowledge of business conditions in England. And so, in 1760, young Hancock arrived in London, where he found "old Europe passing into the modern. Victory had followed the English flag in every quarter of the globe, and a new nation was beginning to evolve out of chaos in the American wilderness, which was at that time England's most valuable dependency."

While he was in London George the Second died, and his grandson succeeded to the throne. The unwonted sight of the pomp and splendor of a royal funeral was no slight event in the life of the young colonist, and the keen eyes of John Hancock lost no detail of the imposing ceremonial. He wrote home:

I am very busy in getting myself mourning upon the Occasion of the Death of his late Majesty King George the 2d, to which every person of any Note here Conforms, even to the deepest Mourning.... Everything here is now very dull. All Plays are stopt and no diversions are going forward, so that I am at a loss how to dispose of myself....

A later letter is of interest as it shows something of the habits of a wealthy young man of the period. "Johnny," as his uncle affectionately calls him, writes:

I observe in your Letter you mention a Circumstance in Regard to my dress. I hope it did not Arise from your hearing I was too Extravagant that way, which I think they cant Tax me with. At same time I am not Remarkable for the Plainness of my Dress, upon proper Occasions I dress as Genteel as anyone, and cant say I am without Lace.... I find money some way or other goes very fast, but I think I can Reflect it has been spent with Satisfaction, and to my own honor.... I endeavor to be in Character in all I do, and in all my Expences which are pretty large I have great Satisfaction in the Reflection of their being incurred in Honorable Company and to my Advantage.

Throughout his life good fortune followed John Hancock in matters small and great, and it was a piece of characteristic good luck that he should have been able to remain to see the new King's coronation. He was also presented at Court, as a representative young colonist of high social standing, and was given a snuff-box by His Majesty as a token of his good-will to one of his subjects from across the sea.

Before leaving for home he learned all he could in regard to the commercial relations between England and her colonies, and after hearing the great orator Pitt make a stirring speech against unjust taxation, he realized how much more daring in word and act were some loyal British subjects than the colonists would have thought possible. Doubtless to Pitt the young patriot-to-be owed his first inspiration to serve the colonies, though it bore no fruit for many months.

October of 1761 found young Hancock again in Boston, and a year later he was taken into partnership with his uncle. This gave him a still greater vogue among the Boston belles who admired him for his strength of character and for his fine appearance, as he was noted for being the best dressed young man in Boston at that time. It is said that "his taste was correct, his judgment of quality unsurpassed, and his knowledge of fashions in London aided by recent residence there." We are told that "a gold-laced coat of broadcloth, red, blue or violet; a white-satin waistcoat embroidered; velvet breeches, green, lilac or blue; white-silk stockings and shoes flashing with buckles of silver or gold; linen trimmed with lace," made the prosperous young merchant outshine others of his position, "and made it appear that by birth at least he belonged to the wealthy and fashionably conservative class."

His uncle was indeed such a strong Conservative that he was unwilling to have his adopted son show any leaning to the radical party. But when on the first of August, 1764, Thomas Hancock died of apoplexy, leaving his Beacon Hill mansion and fifty thousand dollars to his widow, Lydia Hancock, and to John his warehouses, ships, and the residue of his estate, in the twinkling of an eye the young man became a prominent factor in the business world of the day, as the sole owner of an extensive export and import trade. But more important to him than the fortune which he had inherited was the knowledge that he was now at liberty to speak and act in accordance with his own feelings in regard to matters about which his views were slowly but surely changing.

He was now twenty-seven years old, and on paying a flying visit to his friend John Adams, in the home of his early childhood, attended divine service in his father's old church, and thrilled at the glimpse he had of Judge Quincy's youngest daughter, Dorothy, demurely leaving the meeting-house. Dolly was then seventeen years of age, and as lovely in her girlish beauty as any rose that ever bloomed, and John Hancock's feeling of interest in her was far too keen to allow that glimpse to be his last.

He and John Adams visited the Quincy homestead, and young Hancock listened respectfully to the Judge's reminiscences of his father; but at the same time he watched pretty Dorothy, who flitted in and out of the room, giving no hint of her emotion at having an opportunity to listen to the deep voice and note the clear-cut features and brilliant eyes of the Hero of her dreams. She only cast her eyes down demurely, glancing from under her long lashes now and again, when a remark was addressed to her. She was quick to see that her father, while as cordial to his visitor as good breeding demanded, yet wished him to feel that he was not in sympathy with the radical views now openly expressed by the young Boston merchant. Judge Quincy, as we have seen, was a broad-minded, patriotic man, yet being by birth a staunch Conservative, he felt it his duty to show the younger generation what real loyalty to the mother country meant, and that it did not include such rebellion against her commands as they were beginning to express. However, he chatted pleasantly with Hancock and his friend Adams, and when they took their leave, Hancock was invited both to call on the family in Boston and to return to the Quincy homestead. Dorothy seconded the invitation with a momentary lifting of her eyes to his, then became demure, but in the glance that passed between them something was given and taken which was to last for all time, and to add its deepest joy to the future life of pretty Dorothy.

It was certainly love at first sight for John Hancock, and to the young girl his love soon became the one worth-while thing in life.

Not many months after that first visit of John Hancock's to Dorothy's home, he paid Judge Quincy a formal visit in Boston and asked for the hand of his youngest daughter in marriage. As a matter of course, the Judge was flattered, for who was a more eligible match than this rich and handsome young Bostonian? On the other hand, he was sorry to include one of England's rebellious subjects in his family, and he declared so plainly. John Hancock was polite but positive, as he was about everything, and let it be clearly understood that no objection to his suit would make any difference in its final outcome. He and Dorothy loved each other—that was all that really mattered. He sincerely hoped that her father would come to approve of the match, for he would ever consider, he said, Dorothy's happiness before his own. But he clearly stated that he should stand by those words and deeds of the radical party which he believed best for the colonies, despite any effort which might be made to change any of his opinions; also he was going to marry Dorothy. Evidently his determination won the Judge's consent, and in giving it he smothered his objections, for there was no further opposition to the match, and no courtship ever gave clearer evidence of an intense devotion on both sides than that of Hancock and Dorothy, who, being ten years younger than her Hero, looked up to him as to some great and superior being worthy of her heart's supreme devotion.

Political events of vital importance to the colonies happened in swift succession, and Dorothy's Hancock quickly took his place in the front rank of those who were to be the backbone in the colonies' struggle for liberty, although at that time his activity against English injustice was largely due to his wish to protect his own business interests. In 1765 the Stamp Act was passed, and John Hancock openly denounced it and declared he would not use the stamps.

"I will not be made a slave without my consent," he said. "Not a man in England, in proportion to estate, pays the tax that I do."

And he stood by that declaration, becoming generally recognized as a man of ability and of great power, on whom public duties and responsibilities could be placed with assurance that they would be successfully carried out. While he was deeply occupied with colonial affairs Dorothy Quincy was busy in her home with those duties and diversions which formed the greater part of a young woman's daily life in those days, but always in spirit she was with her lover, and she thrilled with pride at each new proof of his fearlessness and growing patriotism.

In September, 1768, when it was rumored that troops had been ordered from Halifax, in an attempt of England to quell the spirit of independence rife among her colonists, Samuel Adams, John Hancock, John Adams, and James Otis waited upon the Governor to ask if the report were true, and to request him to call a special meeting of the Assembly. He declined to do it, and a meeting of protest was held in Faneuil Hall, with representatives from ninety-six towns present, at which meeting it was resolved that "they would peril their lives and their fortunes to defend their rights:" "That money cannot be granted nor a standing army kept up in the province but by their own free consent."

The storm was gathering, and ominous clouds hung low over the town of Boston on a day soon after the meeting in Faneuil Hall, when seven armed vessels from Halifax brought troops up the harbor to a wharf at which they landed, and tramped by the sullen crowd of spectators with colors flying, drums beating—as if entering a conquered city. Naturally the inhabitants of Boston would give them no aid in securing quarters, so they were obliged to camp on the Common, near enough to Dorothy Quincy's home on Summer Street to annoy her by the noise of their morning drills, and to make her realize in what peril her lover's life would be if he became more active in public affairs at this critical period.

If any stimulus to John Hancock's growing patriotism was needed it was given on the tenth of June, when one of his vessels, a new sloop, the *Liberty*, arrived in port with a cargo of Madeira wine, the duty on which was much larger than on other wines. "The collector of the port was so inquisitive about the cargo, that the crew locked him below while it was swung ashore and a false bill of entry made out, after an evasive manner into which importers had fallen of late. Naturally enough, when the collector was released from the hold, he reported the outrage to the commander of one of the ships which had brought troops from Halifax, and he promptly seized the *Liberty* and moved it under his ship's guns to prevent its recapture by Bostonians." This was one of the first acts of violence in the days preceding the struggle for Independence in Massachusetts.

While John Hancock was so fully occupied with public matters, he yet found time to see his Dolly frequently, and her sorrow was his when in 1769 Mrs. Quincy died, and Dorothy, after having had her protecting love and care for twenty-two years, was left motherless. The young girl was no coward, and her brave acceptance of the sorrow won her lover even more completely than before, while his Aunt Lydia, who had become deeply attached to pretty Dorothy, and was eager to have her adopted son's romance end happily, lavished much care and affection on the girl and insisted that she visit her home on Beacon Hill frequently. Possibly, too, Aunt Lydia may have been uneasy lest Judge Quincy, left without the wise counsels of his wife, might insist that his daughter sever her connection with such a radical as Hancock had become. In any case, after her mother's death, Dorothy spent much of her time with her lover's Aunt Lydia, and Hancock was much envied for the charms of his vivacious bride-to-be. In fact, it has been said that "not to have been attracted to Dorothy Quincy would have argued a heart of steel," of which there are but few. To her lover she was all and more than woman had ever been before, in charm and grace and beauty, and he who among men was noted for his stern resolve and unyielding demeanor was as wax in the hands of the young woman, who ruled him with gentle tyranny.

To Dorothy her lover was handsome and brilliant beyond even the Hero of her girlish dreams; her love was too sacred for expression, even to him who was its rightful possessor. He appealed to her in a hundred ways, she delighted in his "distinguished presence, his inborn courtesy, his scrupulous toilets;" she adored him for "his devotion to those he loved, his unusual generosity to friends and inferiors," and she thrilled at the thought of his patriotism, his rapid advancement. And if, as has been said, crowds were swayed by his magnetism, what wonder that it touched and captivated Dorothy Quincy, the object of his heart's deepest devotion?

On the fifth of March, 1770, British soldiers fired on a crowd in the streets of Boston, and the riot that ensued, in which the killing of six and the injury to a half-dozen more, was dignified by the name of a "Massacre." Blood was now at boiling-point, and the struggle between the mother country and her colonists had commenced. Private meetings were beginning to be held for public action, and John Adams, Samuel Adams, John Hancock, and Josiah Quincy, a nephew of Dorothy's father, and an ardent believer in American liberty, were among the leading spirits who took notice of every infringement of rights on the part of the government and its agents. In the House of Representatives they originated almost every measure for the public good, and the people believed them to be the loyal guardians of their rights and privileges.

John Hancock, who at first had stood out against taxation without representation because of his own business interests, now stood firmly for American Independence for the good of the majority, with little left of the self-seeking spirit which had animated his earlier efforts. Occupied as he now was with the many duties incident on a public life, it is said he was never too busy to redress a wrong, and never unwilling to give lavishly where there was need, and Dorothy Quincy rejoiced as she noted that many measures for the good of the country were stamped with her lover's name.

On the very day of the so-called "Boston Massacre" Great Britain repealed an Act recently passed which had placed a heavy duty on many articles of import. That tax was now lifted from all articles except tea, on which it was retained, to maintain the right of Parliament to tax the colonies, and to show the King's determination to have his way.

"In resistance of this tax the Massachusetts colonists gave up drinking their favorite beverage and drank coffee in its place. The King, angry at this rebellion against the dictates of Parliament, refused to lift the tax, and tea was shipped to America as if there were no feeling against its acceptance. In New York, Philadelphia, and Charleston mass-meetings of the people voted that the agents to whom it had been shipped should be ordered to resign their offices. At Philadelphia the tea-ship was met and sent back to England without being allowed to come to anchor. At Charleston the tea was landed, but as there was no one there to receive it, or pay the duty, it was thrown into a damp cellar and left there to spoil. In Boston things were managed differently. When the *Dartmouth*, tea-laden, sailed into the harbor, the ship, with two others which soon arrived and anchored near the *Dartmouth*, was not allowed to dock."

A meeting of citizens was hastily called, and a resolution adopted that "tea on no account should be allowed to land." The tea-ships were guarded by a committee of Boston patriots who refused to give permits for the vessels to return to England with their cargoes. Then came what has been called Boston's "picturesque refusal to pay the tax." As night fell Samuel Adams rose in a mass-meeting and said, "This meeting can do nothing more to save the country." As the words fell from his lips there was a shout in the street and a group of forty men disguised as "Mohawks" darted past the door and down to the wharves, followed by the people. Rushing on board the tea-ships, the disguised citizens set themselves to cleaning the vessels of their cargoes. As one of them afterward related: "We mounted the ships and *made tea in a trice*. This done, I mounted my team and went home, as an honest man should."

Twilight was gathering when the Indian masqueraders began their work, and it was nearly three hours later when their task was done. Boston Harbor was a great teapot, with the contents of three hundred and forty-two chests broken open and their contents scattered on the quiet water. A sharp watch was kept that none of it should be stolen, but a few grains were shaken out of a shoe, which may be seen to-day in a glass jar in Memorial Hall, Boston. And this was the famous "Boston Tea-Party"!

Men's passions were now aroused to fever heat, and the actions of the patriots were sharply resented by the conservatives who upheld the government, while the radicals were fighting for the rights of the people. In all the acts of overt rebellion with which John Hancock's name was constantly connected he was loyally and proudly upheld by his Dorothy, who, despite her inborn coquetry, daily became better fitted to be the wife of a man such as John Hancock.

But though she stood by him so bravely in all his undertakings, and would not have had him recede one step from the stand he had taken, yet there was much to alarm her. Because of his connection with the Boston Tea-Party, and other acts of rebellion, the soldiers of the crown had distributed royalist hand-bills broadcast, with this heading:

"TO THE SOLDIERS OF HIS MAJESTY'S TROOPS IN BOSTON"

There followed a list of the authors of the rebellion, among whom were Samuel Adams, John Hancock, and Josiah Quincy. The hand-bill also announced that "it was probable that the King's standard would soon be erected," and continued: "The friends of our king and country and of America hope and expect it from you soldiers the instant rebellion happens, that you will put the above persons immediately to the sword, destroy their houses and plunder their effects. It is just they should be the first victims to the mischiefs they have brought upon us."

Reason enough for Hancock's Dorothy to be apprehensive, beneath her show of bravery!

In January, 1775, the patriots made an effort to show that they were still loyal subjects, for they sent a petition from the Continental Congress to the King, wherein they asked "but for peace, liberty and safety," and stated that "your royal authority over us, and our connection with Great Britain, we shall always carefully and zealously endeavor to support and maintain."

Despite this the oppressions increased, and the persistent roughness of the British troops continued unchecked. In March an inhabitant of Billerica, Massachusetts, was tarred and feathered by a party of his majesty's soldiers. A remonstrance was sent to General Gage, the king's chosen representative in the colony, in which was this clause:

"We beg, Your Excellency that the breach, now too wide, between Great Britain and this province may not, by such brutality of the troops, still be increased.... If it continues, we shall hereafter use a different style from that of petition and complaint."

In reply from London came the news that seventy-eight thousand guns and bayonets were on their way to America. Also came a report that orders had gone out to arrest John Hancock, William Otis, and six other head men of Boston. The informant, a friend of Hancock's, added: "My heart aches for Mr. Hancock. Send off expresses immediately to tell him that they intend to seize his estate, and have his fine house for General...."

April of 1775 came, and the Provincial Congress met at Concord, Massachusetts, and took upon itself the power to make and carry out laws. Immediately General Gage issued a proclamation stating that the Congress was "an unlawful assembly, tending to subvert government and to lead directly to sedition, treason, and rebellion.

"And yet even in the face of such an ominous outlook the indefatigable Massachusetts patriots continued to struggle for their ideal of independence. John Adams, himself a patriot of the highest class, asserted that Samuel Adams, John Hancock, and James Otis were the three most important characters of the day, and Great Britain knew it. Certainly all four men were feared in the mother country, and Hancock's independence of the government brought several suits against him." Like those of his co-workers for freedom from tyranny, his nerves were now strung to the highest tension, and he spent many a sleepless night planning how best to achieve his high purposes and grim resolves, while his love for pretty Dorothy was the one green spot in the arid desert of colonial strife.

Boston was no longer a safe place for those who could change it for a more peaceful place of residence. Judge Quincy, who had been keeping a close watch over his own business affairs, now decided to leave for Lancaster, where his married daughter, Mrs. Greenleaf, lived. All homes were completely disorganized, and by the time the Judge decided to leave most of his friends had already gone, taking their household goods with them out of harm's way. All social life was ended, and it was indeed a suitable prelude to a grim period of American history.

When the Judge decided to take refuge in Lancaster, the question was, should Dorothy go, too? Her lover was in Concord, where the Provincial Congress was in session. Knowing the condition of affairs in Boston, he had not returned to his home during the intermissions of the session, finding it more convenient to stay in Concord and spend his Sundays in Lexington, where he and John Adams were warmly welcomed at the home of the Rev. Jonas Clark, a Hancock cousin.

Now, when Hancock heard of Judge Quincy's plan to leave Boston for Lancaster, he wrote immediately to his Aunt Lydia and made an appeal calculated to touch a much more stony heart than hers. Would she take his Dolly under her protection until the state of colonial affairs should become more peaceful? Boston was no place for a woman who could be out of it; but on the other hand, neither was a town as far away as Lancaster a suitable retreat for a girl with a lover who might get only occasional glimpses of her there. Would his *dear* aunt please call on Judge Quincy, and, after putting the matter squarely before him, try to bring his Dolly away to Lexington with her? The Rev. Mr. Clark would welcome them as warmly as he and Adams had been received, and give them a comfortable home as long as necessary. Would his aunt not do this for him? As a final appeal he added that if General Gage should carry out his intention of seizing Adams and himself, he might have a few more chances to see the girl he loved.

Aunt Lydia was quick in her response. Of course she would do as he wished. It would be far better for the motherless girl to be under her protection at this time than with any one else, and she could understand perfectly her nephew's desire to be under the same roof even for a brief time with his dear Dolly. She would see the Judge immediately.

At once her stately coach was ordered out, and soon it rolled up before the Quincy door to set down Aunt Lydia, intent on achieving her end. And she did. Although the Judge was not altogether pleased with the idea of being separated from Dorothy, he saw the wisdom of the plan and assented to it. Dorothy, with a girl's light-heartedness at the prospect of a change, especially one which meant seeing her lover, hastily packed up enough clothing for use during a brief visit. Then she said an affectionate farewell to her father, little dreaming what an eventful separation it was to be, and rode away by the side of Aunt Lydia, who was delighted that she had been able to so successfully manage the Judge, and that she was to have cheerful Dorothy for a companion during days of dark depression.

To Lexington they went, and as John Hancock had predicted, the Rev. Mr. Clark gave them a cordial welcome. Hancock was there to greet them, and with great satisfaction the elder woman saw the lovers' rapturous meeting, and knew that her diplomacy had brought this joy to them.

When the excitement of the meeting had somewhat subsided, they talked long and earnestly of the critical situation, and Dorothy, with her hand clasped close in her lover's, heard with sudden terror of a rumor that General Gage intended to seize Adams and Hancock at the earliest opportunity. But roses bloomed in her cheeks again as she declared, proudly: "I have no fear! You will be clever enough to evade them. No cause as worthy as yours will have as a reward for its champion such a fate as to be captured!"

Seeing her flashing eyes and courageous thrusting aside of possibilities, that he might not count her a coward, John Hancock loved her better than before, and tenderly raised her hand to his lips with a simple: "God bless you, dear. I hope you may be right!"

And now, in quiet Lexington, Dorothy and Aunt Lydia occupied themselves with such daily tasks as they were able to accomplish in the minister's home, and the girl was bewildering in her varied charms as John Hancock saw them displayed in daily life during their brief but precious meetings. Dorothy enjoyed an occasional letter from a cousin, Helena Bayard, who was still in Boston, and who gave lively accounts of what was happening there.

As Mrs. Bayard lived in a boarding-house, she saw many persons who knew nothing of her relatives, and one day, after returning from a visit, she found the parlor full of boarders, who eagerly asked her if she had heard the news. She said she had not, and in a letter to Dorothy later, she gives this spicy account of what she heard:

I was told that Linsee was coming, and ten thousand troops, which was glorious news for the Congress. Mr. Hancock was next brought on the carpet, and as the company did not suspect I had the least acquaintance with him, I can't think they meant to affront me.

However, as Mr. Hancock has an elegant house and well situated, and this will always be a garrison town, it will do exceedingly well for a fort, ... "I wonder how Miss ... will stand affected? I think he defers marrying until he returns from England." At this speech I saw a wink given, and all was hush!—myself as hush as the grave, for reasons. "Mr. Hancock has a number of horses. Perhaps he would be glad to dispose of them, as the officers are buying up the best horses in town"—Mrs. Bayard, don't look so dull! You will be taken the greatest care of! Thought I,—if you knew my heart, you would have the most reason to look dull. However, a little time will decide that.

21

I am, you will say, wicked, but I wish the small-pox would spread. Dolly, I could swell my letter into a balloon, but lest I should tire you, I will beg my sincere regards to Mr. Hancock, and beg the favor of a line from my dear Dolly,

Your affectionate Coz

Helena Bayard.

Dorothy's eyes flashed as she read this, and laying it down she exclaimed: "We will see whether the British come off victorious or not! If I mistake not, there is more ability in the finger-tip of John Hancock than in those of all the generals in the English army. You will be taken the greatest care of, indeed—We shall see what we shall see!" with which sage remark pretty Dolly, head held high, walked out of the room and gave vent to her feelings in vigorous exercise.

The issue was to be confronted sooner than they knew, and it was peaceful Lexington where the first alarm of war sounded.

According to advice, a messenger had been sent to Concord to warn Hancock of his possible danger, but neither he nor Adams attached much importance to the report, after their first alarm was over, and they were enjoying the quiet village life of Lexington with the two women guests at the parsonage, when on the eighteenth of April, General Gage really did order a force to march on Concord, not so much to seize the few military supplies stored there, as to capture the rebellious enemies of the crown.

Just how a small group of men in Boston, calling themselves the "Sons of Liberty," who had constituted themselves a volunteer committee to watch over the movements of the enemy, knew of the plan of the British to march to Concord, and on the way to arrest Hancock and Samuel Adams, will never be known. It is enough to know that they had received the information, and knew that the British were determined not to have a report of the march reach the enemy until it had been successfully accomplished. The question was how to carry the news to Lexington and Concord ahead of the British troops. There was no time to waste in lengthy discussions, and in a very short time Paul Revere was ready for his historic ride. The signals agreed on before affairs had reached this climax were: if the British went out by water, *two* lanterns would be swung in the North Church steeple; if they went by land, *one* would be shown, and a friend of Paul Revere's had been chosen as the man to set the signal.

Now, on the night of the eighteenth of April, 1775, *two* lanterns swung high in the historic steeple, and off started Paul Revere on the most famous ride in American history. As Longfellow has so vividly expressed it:

A hurry of hoofs in a village street, A shape in the moonlight, a bulk in the dark, And beneath, from the pebbles, in passing, a spark Struck out by a steed flying fearless and fleet; That was all! And yet through the gloom and the light The fate of a nation was riding that night; And the spark struck out by that steed, in his flight, Kindled the land into flame with its heat.

With clank of spur and brave use of whip, on he dashed, to waken the country and rouse it to instant action—and as he passed through every hamlet heavy sleepers woke at the sound of his ringing shout:

"The Regulars are coming!"

Then on clattered horse and rider, scattering stones and dirt, as the horse's hoofs tore into the ground and his flanks were flecked with foam. Midnight had struck when the dripping steed and his breathless rider drew up before the parsonage where unsuspecting Dorothy and Aunt Lydia were sheltered, as well as the two patriots. The house was guarded by eight men when Paul Revere dashed up to the door, and they cautioned him not to make a noise.

"Noise!" exclaimed Revere. "You'll have noise enough before long. The Regulars are coming out!"

John Hancock, ever on the alert for any unwonted sounds, heard the commotion and recognizing Revere's voice opened a window and said:

"Courier Revere, we are not afraid of you!"

Revere repeated his startling news.

"Ring the Bell!" commanded Hancock. In a few moments the church bell began to peal, according to pre-arranged signal, to call men of the town together. All night the tones of the clanging bell rang out on the clear air and before daylight one hundred and fifty men had mustered for defense, strong in their desire for resistance and confident of the justice of it.

John Hancock was determined to fight with the men who had come together so hurriedly and were so poorly equipped for the combat. With a firm hand he cleaned his gun and sword and put his accoutrements in order, refusing to listen to the plea of Adams that it was not their duty to fight, that theirs it was, rather, to safeguard their lives for the sake of that cause to which they were so important at this critical time. Hancock was deaf to all appeals, until Dorothy grasped his hands in hers and forced him to look into her eyes:—

"I have lost my mother," she said; "to lose you, too, would be more than I could bear, unless I were giving you for my country's good. But you can serve best by living rather than by courting danger. You must go, and go now!"

And Hancock went.

Meanwhile a British officer had been sent in advance of the troops to inquire for "Clark's parsonage." By mistake he asked for Clark's tavern, which news was brought to Hancock as he was debating whether to take Dorothy's advice or not. He waited no longer. With Adams he immediately took refuge in a thickly wooded hill back of the parsonage. An hour later Paul Revere returned to the house to report that after he left there, with two others, he had been captured by British officers. Having answered their questions evasively about the whereabouts of the patriots, he finally said: "Gentlemen, you have missed your aim; the bell's ringing, the town's alarmed. You are all dead men!" This so terrified the officers that, not one hundred yards further on, one of them mounted Revere's horse and rode off at top speed to give warning to the on-coming troops, while Revere went back to report to Hancock and Adams.

It was evidently unsafe for them to remain so near the scene of the struggle, and at daylight they were ready to start for the home of the Rev. Mr. Marrett in Woburn. Dorothy and Aunt Lydia were to remain in Lexington, and although they had kept well in the background through all the excitement of the fateful night, Aunt Lydia now went down to the door, not only to see the last of her beloved nephew, but to try to speak to some one who could give her more definite news of the seven hundred British soldiers who had arrived in town and were drawn up in formidable array against the motley company of colonists. The British officers at once commanded the colonists to lay down their arms and disperse. Not a single man obeyed. All stood in silent defiance of the order. Then the British regulars poured into the "minute-men" a fatal volley of shots; and about that time Aunt Lydia descended to the parsonage door, and excited Dorothy threw open her window that she might wave to her lover until he was out of sight. As she drew back, she saw something whiz through the air past her aunt's head, striking the barn door beyond, and heard her aunt exclaim:

"What was that?"

It was a British bullet, and no mistake! As Dorothy told later: "The next thing I knew, two men were being brought into the house, one, whose head had been grazed by a bullet, insisted that he was dead; but the other, who was shot in the arm, behaved better."

Dorothy Quincy had seen the first shot fired for independence!

Never was there a more gallant resistance of a large and well-disciplined enemy force than that shown by the minute-men on that day at Lexington, and when at last the British retreated under a hot fire from the provincials at whom they had sneered, they had lost two hundred and seventy-three, killed, wounded, and missing, while the American force had lost only ninety-three.

As soon as the troops were marching on their way to Concord, a messenger brought Dorothy a penciled note from Hancock: "Would she and his aunt come to their hiding-place for dinner, and would they bring with them the fine salmon which was to have been cooked for dinner at the parsonage?" Of course they would—only too eagerly did they make ready and allow the messenger to guide them to the patriot's place of concealment. There, while the lovers enjoyed a tête-à-tête, Adams and Aunt Lydia made the feast ready, and they were all about to enjoy it, when a man rushed in crying out wildly:

"The British are coming! The British are coming! My wife's in eternity now."

This was grim news, and there was no more thought of feasting. Hurriedly Mr. Marrett made ready and took the patriots to a safer hiding-place, in Amos Wyman's house in Billerica. There, later in the day, they satisfied their appetites as best they could with cold pork and potatoes in place of the princely salmon, while Dorothy and Aunt Lydia, after eating what they had heart to consume of the feast, returned to Parson Clark's home, where they waited as quietly as possible until the retreat of the British troops. Then Dorothy had the joy of being again clasped in her lover's arms—and as he looked questioningly into her dear eyes, he could see lines of suffering and of new womanliness carved on her face by the anxiety she had experienced during the last twenty-four hours. Then, at a moment when both were seemingly happiest at being together, came their first lovers' quarrel.

When she had somewhat recovered from the fear of not seeing Hancock again, Dorothy announced that she was going to Boston on the following day—that she was worried about her father, who had not yet been able to leave the city, that she must see him. Hancock listened with set lips and grim determination:

"No, madam," he said, "you shall not return as long as there is a British bayonet in Boston."

Quick came the characteristic reply: "Recollect, Mr. Hancock, I am not under your control yet! I shall go to my father to-morrow."

23

Her determination matched his own, and Hancock saw no way to achieve his end, yet he had not thought of yielding. As usual, he turned to Aunt Lydia for advice. She wisely suggested retiring, without settling the mooted question, as they were all too tired for sensible reflection on any subject. Then, after defiant Dorothy had gone to her room, the older woman stole to the girl's bedside, not to advise,—oh no!—merely to suggest that there was more than one girl waiting to step into Dorothy's place should she flout the handsome young patriot. Also, she suggested, how terrible it would be if Hancock should be killed, or even captured while the girl he worshiped was away from his side! There was no reply, and the older woman stole from the room without any evidence that she had succeeded in her mission. But she smiled to herself the next morning when Dorothy announced that she had never had any real intention of leaving for Boston, and gracefully acknowledged to an entranced lover that *he* had been right, after all!

The next question was, where should the women take refuge until the cloud of war should have passed over sufficiently to make it safe for them to return to their homes? Hancock advised Fairfield, Connecticut, a beautiful town where there would be small chance of any danger or discomfort. His suggestion met with approval, and Mrs. Hancock and her pretty ward at once set off for the Connecticut town, while Adams and Hancock journeyed cautiously toward Worcester, where they were to meet and go with other delegates to the Continental Congress at Philadelphia. They were detained at Worcester three days, which gave Hancock a chance to see his Dorothy again on her way to the new place of refuge. Theirs was a rapturous though a brief visit together; then the patriots went on toward New York, and Dorothy and Aunt Lydia proceeded to Fairfield, where they were received in the home of Mr. Thaddeus Burr, an intimate friend of the Hancocks, and a leading citizen, whose fine colonial house was a landmark in the village.

Judge Quincy, meanwhile, had at last been able to take flight from Boston, and after a long, uncomfortable trip, had arrived at his daughter's home in Lancaster, where he heard that "Daughter Dolly and Hancock had taken dinner ten days before, having driven over from Shirley for the purpose." He writes to his son Henry of this, and adds, "As I hear, she proceeded with Mrs. Hancock to Fairfield; I don't expect to see her till peaceable times are restored."

The two patriots reached New York safely, and Hancock at once wrote to Dorothy:

New York, *Sabbath Even'g, May 7, 1775.*

My dear Dolly:—

I Arrived well, tho' fatigued, at King's Bridge at Fifty Minute after Two o'clock yesterday, where I found the Delegates of Massachusetts and Connect' with a number of Gentlemen from New York, and a Guard of the Troop. I dined and then set out in the Procession for New York,—the Carriage of your Humble servant being first in the procession (of course). When we Arrived within three Miles of the City, we were Met by the Grenadier Company and Regiment of the City Militia under Arms,—Gentlemen in Carriages and on Horseback, and many thousand of Persons on foot, the roads fill'd with people, and the greatest cloud of dust I ever saw. In this Situation we Entered the City, and passing thro' the Principal Streets of New York amidst the Acclamations of Thousands were set down at Mr. Francis's. After Entering the House three Huzzas were Given, and the people by degrees dispersed.

When I got within a mile of the City my Carriage was stopt, and Persons appearing with proper Harnesses insisted upon Taking out my Horses and Dragging me into and through the City, a Circumstance I would not have Taken place on any consideration, not being fond of such Parade.

I beg'd and entreated that they would suspend the Design, and they were at last prevail'd upon and I proceeded....

After having Rode so fast and so many Miles, you may well think I was much fatigued, but no sooner had I got into the Room of the House we were Visited by a great number of Gentlemen of the first Character of the City, who took up the Evening.

About 10 o'clock I Sat down to Supper of Fried Oysters &, at 11 o'clock went to Capt Sear's and Lod'g. Arose at 5 o'clock, went to the House first mentioned, Breakfasted, Dress'd and went to Meeting, where I heard a most excellent Sermon....

The Grenadier Company of the City is to continue under Arms during our stay here and we have a guard of them at our Doors Night and Day. This is a sad mortification for the Tories. Things look well here.... I beg you will write me. Do acquaint me every Circumstance Relative to that Dear Aunt of Mine; write Lengthy and often.... People move slowly out, they tell me, from Boston.... Is your Father out? As soon as you know, do acquaint me, and send me the letters and I will then write him. Pray let me hear from you by every post. God bless you, my Dr. Girl, and believe me most Sincerely

Yours most affectionately

John Hancock.

One can fancy the flutter of pride in Dorothy's heart at the reading of such honors to her lover, and she settled down to await the turn of events with a lighter heart, while Hancock and Adams, with the other delegates, went on toward Philadelphia, their trip being a triumphal progress from start to finish.

On the ninth of May they arrived at their destination, and on the following day the Continental Congress met, when John Hancock was unanimously elected President of the Congress.

While her lover was occupied with matters of such vital importance, he always found time to pour out his hopes and fears and doings in bulky letters which reached his lady love by coach, every fortnight, and which—"shortened absence" to her impatient desire for the one man in the world who meant all to her. But even where Dorothy's heart was so seriously engaged, she could no more help showering coquettish smiles and pretty speeches on those residents of Fairfield whom she came to know, than she could help bewitching them by her charm and beauty. The more sober-minded men of the town were delighted by her conversation, which was sparkling, and by her keen comment on public affairs—comment far beyond the capability of most of her sex and age, while it became the fashion to pay court to vivacious Dorothy, but the moment an adorer attempted to express his sentimental feelings he found himself checkmated by a haughty reserve that commanded admiration, but forced an understanding that Mistress Dolly wished no such attentions.

Of this John Hancock knew nothing, as Dolly was the most tantalizingly discreet of correspondents, and poor Hancock looked and longed in vain for written evidence of her devotion, despite which, however, he continued to write long letters to her:

In one, written on June 10, 1775, he says pathetically:

I am almost prevailed on to think that my letters to my aunt and you are not read, for I cannot obtain a reply. I have asked a million questions and not an answer to one.... I really take it extremely unkind. Pray, my dear, use not so much ceremony and reservedness.... I want long letters.... I beg my dear Dolly, you will write me often and long letters. I will forgive the past if you will mend in future. Do ask my aunt to make me up and send me a watch-string, and do you make up another. I want something of your doing....

I have sent you in a paper Box directed to you, the following things for your acceptance & which I do insist you wear, if you do not, I shall think the Donor is the objection.

2 pair white silk, 4 pair white thread stockings which I think will fit you, 1 pr Black Satin Shoes, 1 pr Black Calem Do, the other shall be sent when done, 1 very pretty light Hat, 1 neat airy Summer Cloak ... 2 caps, 1 Fann.

I wish these may please you, I shall be gratified if they do, pray write me, I will attent to all your Commands.

Adieu my Dr. Girl, and believe me with great Esteem and Affection

Yours without Reserve

John Hancock.

Surely such an appeal could not have failed of its purpose, and we can imagine Dorothy in the pretty garments of a lover's choosing, and her pride and pleasure in wearing them. But little coquette that she was, she failed to properly transmit her appreciation to the man who was so eager for it, and at that particular time her attention was entirely taken up by other diversions, of which, had Hancock known, he would have considered them far more important than colonial affairs.

To the Fairfield mansion, where Dolly and her aunt were staying, had come a visitor, young Aaron Burr, a relative of Thaddeus Burr, a brilliant and fascinating young man, whose cleverness and charming personality made him very acceptable to the young girl, whose presence in the house added much zest to his visit, and to whom he paid instant and marked attention. This roused Aunt Lydia to alarm and apprehension, for she knew Dorothy's firmness when she made up her mind on any subject, and feared that the tide of her affection might turn to this fascinating youth, for Dorothy made no secret of her enjoyment of his attentions. This should not be, Aunt Lydia decided.

With determination, thinly veiled by courtesy, she walked and talked and drove and sat with the pair, never leaving them alone together for one moment, which strict chaperonage Dolly resented, and complained of to a friend with as much of petulancy as she ever showed, tossing her pretty head with an air of defiance as she told of Aunt Lydia's foolishness, and spoke of her new friend as a "handsome young man with a pretty property."

The more devoted young Burr became to her charming ward, the more determined became Aunt Lydia that John Hancock should not lose what was dearer to him than his own life. With the clever diplomacy of which she was evidently past mistress, she managed to so mold affairs to her liking that Aaron Burr's visit at Fairfield came to an unexpectedly speedy end, and, although John Hancock's letters to his aunt show no trace that he knew of a dangerous rival, yet he seems to have suddenly decided that if he were to wed the fair Dolly it were well to do it quickly. And evidently he was still the one enshrined in her heart, for in the recess of Congress between August first and September fifth, John Hancock dropped the affairs of the colony momentarily, and journeyed to Fairfield, never again to be separated from her who was ever his ideal of womanhood.

On the 28th day of August, 1775, Dorothy Quincy and the patriot, John Hancock, were married, as was chronicled in the *New York Gazette* of September 4th:

This evening was married at the seat of Thaddeus Burr, at Fairfield, Conn., by the Reverend Mr. Eliot, the Hon. John Hancock, Esq., President of the Continental Congress, to Miss Dorothy Quincy, daughter of Edmund Quincy, Esq., of Boston. Florus informs us that "in the second Punic War when Hannibal besieged Rome and was very near making himself master of it, a field upon which part of his army lay, was offered for sale, and was immediately purchased by a Roman, in a strong assurance that the Roman valor and courage would soon raise the siege." Equal to the conduct of that illustrious citizen was the marriage of the Honorable John Hancock, Esq., who, with his amiable lady, has paid as great a compliment to American valor by marrying now while all the colonies are as much convulsed as Rome was when Hannibal was at her gates.

The *New York Post* also gave a detailed account of the wedding, and of the brilliant gathering of the "blue blood" of the aristocratic old town as well as of the colonies. Had the ceremony taken place in the old Quincy home, as had originally been intended, in a room which had been specially paneled with flowers and cupids for the auspicious event, it would doubtless have been a more homelike affair, especially to the bride, but it would have lacked the dignified elegance to which the stately Burr mansion lent itself so admirably.

Pretty Dorothy a bride! Mrs. John Hancock at her gallant husband's side, receiving congratulations, with joy shining in her dark eyes, which were lifted now and again to her husband, only to be answered by a responsive glance of love and loyalty. They were a handsome and a happy pair, to whom for a few hours the strife of the colonies had become a dream—to whom, despite the turbulent struggle in which Hancock must soon again play such a prominent part, the future looked rose color, because now nothing but death could part them.

Vivacious Dorothy had not only now become Mrs. John Hancock, but she was also called *Madam* Hancock! Oh, the bliss of the dignified title to its youthful owner! She read with girlish satisfaction the item in a New York paper of September 4th, which reported, "Saturday last, the Honorable John Hancock and his Lady arrived here, and immediately set out for Philadelphia." With still greater pleasure a few days later she set herself to the establishing of a home in that city which was to be her first residence as a married woman. And well did she carry out her design to make John Hancock a worthy comrade, for besides accomplishing all the necessary duties of a housekeeper, she quickly acquired the dignity and reserve needed for the wife of a man filling such a prominent position in the colonies during the war for Independence. There was much lavish living and extravagant elegance of dressing, with which she was obliged to vie, even in the town where the Quakers were so much in evidence; and meeting, as she did, many persons of social and political importance, it was impossible for pretty Dorothy to be as care-free and merry now as she had been in the days when no heavy responsibilities rested on her shoulders.

So well did she fill her position as Madam Hancock that she won golden opinions from the many distinguished men and women who came together under Hancock's hospitable roof-tree; her husband noting with ever increasing pride that his Dolly was more deeply and truly an American woman in her flowering than ever he could have dreamed she would become when he fell in love with her on that Sunday in June. And loyally did he give to her credit for such inspiration as helped to mold him into the man who received the greatest honors in the power of the colonists to bestow.

With the later life of Dorothy Hancock we are not concerned; our rose had bloomed. It matters not to us that Madam Hancock was one of the most notable women of the Revolution, who had known and talked with George Washington, that she and Martha Washington had actually discussed their husbands together. To Dorothy's great pride Mrs. Washington had spoken enthusiastically of Hancock's high position, while at that time her husband was but a general. Then, too, pretty Madam Hancock had known the noble Lafayette—had met in intimate surroundings all those great and patriotic men who had devoted their best endeavors to the establishment of a free and independent America. All that is no concern of ours in this brief story of the girl, Dorothy, nor is it ours to mourn with the mother over the death or her two children, nor ours to wonder why, three years after the death of her beloved husband, a man who had made his mark in the history of his country, she should have married again.

Ours only it is to admire Hancock's Dolly as we see her in her girlish beauty, as we follow her through the black days of fear and of tension preceding the outbreak of that war in which her lover played such a prominent part; ours to enjoy her charming manner and sparkling wit, and to respect with deep admiring a brave girl of the Massachusetts colony who watched a great nation in its birth-throes, and whose name is written in history not alone as Madam Hancock, but as Dorothy Quincy, the girl who saw the first gun fired for Independence.

An inspiration and an example for the girls of to-day, at a time when all good Americans are united in a firm determination to make the world safe for democracy.

MOLLY PITCHER: THE BRAVE GUNNER OF THE BATTLE OF MONMOUTH

"Oh, but I would like to be a soldier!"

The exclamation did not come from a man or boy as might have been expected, but from Mary Ludwig, a young, blue-eyed, freckled, red-haired serving-maid in the employ of General Irving's family, of Carlisle, Pennsylvania. Molly, as they called her, had a decided ability to do well and quickly whatever she attempted, and her eyes of Irish blue and her sense of humor must have been handed down to her somewhere along the line of descent, although her father, John George Ludwig, was a German who had come to America with the Palatines.

Having been born in 1754 on a small dairy farm lying between Princeton and Trenton, New Jersey, Molly's early life was the usual happy one of a child who lived in the fields and made comrades of all the animals, especially of the cows which quite often she milked and drove to pasture. Like other children of her parentage she was early taught to work hard, to obey without question, and never to waste a moment of valuable time. In rain or shine she was to be found on the farm, digging, or among the live stock, in her blue-and-white cotton skirt and plain-blue upper garment, and she was so strong, it was said, that she could carry a three-bushel bag of wheat on her shoulder to the upper room of the granary. This strength made her very helpful in more than one way on the farm, and her parents objected strongly when she announced her determination to leave home and earn her living in a broader sphere of usefulness, but their objections were without avail.

The wife of General Irving, of French and Indian war fame, came to Trenton to make a visit. She wished to take a young girl back to Carlisle with her to assist in the work of her household, and a friend told her of Molly Ludwig. At once Mrs. Irving saw and liked the buxom, honest-faced country girl, and Molly being willing, she was taken back to the Irvings' home. There she became a much respected member of the family, as well as a valuable assistant, for Molly liked to work hard. She could turn her hand to anything, from fine sewing, which she detested, to scrubbing floors and scouring pots and pans, which she greatly enjoyed, being most at home when doing something which gave her violent exercise. Meals could have been served off a floor which she had scrubbed, and her knocker and door-knobs were always in a high state of polish.

But though she liked the housework which fell to her lot, it was forgotten if by any chance the General began to talk of his experiences on the battle-field. One day, when passing a dish of potatoes at the noon meal, the thrilling account of a young artilleryman's brave deed so stirred Molly's patriotic spirit that she stood at breathless attention, the dish of potatoes poised on her hand in mid-air until the last detail of the story had been told, then with a prodigious sigh she proclaimed her fervent desire to be a soldier.

The General's family were not conventional and there was a hearty laugh at the expense of the serving-maid's ambition, in which Molly good-naturedly joined. Little did she dream that in coming days her wish was to be fulfilled, and her name to be as widely known for deeds of valor as that of the artilleryman who had so roused her enthusiasm.

So wholesome and energetic in appearance was Molly that she had many admirers, some of them fired with a degree of practical purpose, beyond their sentimental avowals. Molly treated them one and all with indifference except as comrades until John Hays, the handsome young barber of the town, much sought after by the girls of Carlisle, began to pay her attention, which was an entirely different matter. Molly grew serious-minded, moped as long as it was possible for one of her rollicking nature to mope—even lost her appetite temporarily—then she married the adoring and ecstatic Hays, and gave her husband a heart's loyal devotion.

Of a sudden the peaceful Pennsylvania village was stirred to its quiet center by echoes of the battle of Lexington, and no other subject was thought of or talked about. All men with a drop of red blood in their veins were roused to action, and Hays was no slacker. One morning he spoke gently to his wife, with intent to hurt her as little as possible.

"I am going, Molly," he said; "I've joined the Continental army."

Then he waited to see the effect of his words. Although he knew that his wife was patriotic, he was utterly unprepared for the response that flamed in her eager eyes as she spoke.

"God bless you!" she exclaimed; "I am proud to be a soldier's wife. Count on me to stand by you."

And stand by she did, letting no tears mar the last hours with him, and waving as cheerful a farewell when he left her as though he were merely going for a day's pleasuring. From the firing of the first gun in the cause of freedom her soul had been filled with patriotic zeal, and now she rejoiced in honoring her country by cheerfully giving the man she loved to its service, although she privately echoed her wish of long ago when she had exclaimed, "Oh, how I wish I could be a soldier!"

Like a brave and sensible young woman, Molly stayed on with the Irvings, where she scrubbed and scoured and baked and brewed and spun and washed as vigorously as before, smiling proudly with no sharp retort when her friends laughingly predicted that she "had lost her pretty barber, and would never set eyes on him again." She was too glad to have him serving his country, and too sure of his devotion, to be annoyed by any such remarks, and kept quietly on with her work as though it were her sole interest in life.

Months went by, and hot July blazed its trail of parched ground and wilted humanity. One morning, as usual, Molly hung her wash on the lines, then she took a pail and went to gather blackberries on a near-by hillside. As she came back later with a full pail, she saw a horseman, as she afterward said, "riding like lightning up to General Irving's house." Perhaps he had brought news from her husband, was her instant thought, and she broke into a run, for she had received no tidings from him for a long time, and was eager to know where he was and how he fared. She had been right in her instinct, the messenger had brought a letter from John Hays, and it contained great news indeed, for he wrote:

"When this reaches you, take horse with bearer, who will go with you to your father's home. I have been to the farm and seen your parents, who wish you to be with them now. And if you are there, I shall be able to see you sometimes, as we are encamped in the vicinity."

Molly might have objected to such a peremptory command, but the last sentence broke down any resistance she might have shown. Hastily she told Mrs. Irving of the letter and its tidings, and although that lady was more than sorry to lose Molly at such short notice, she not only made no objections to her departure, but helped her with her hurried preparations and wished her all possible good fortune. In less time than it takes to tell it, Molly had "unpegged her own clothing from the lines," then seeing they were still wet, she made the articles into a tight bundle which she tied to the pommel, the messenger sprang into the saddle, with Molly behind him, and off they started from the house which had been Molly's home for so long, journeying to the farm of her childhood's memories.

Although she missed the kind-hearted Irving family who had been so good to her, it was a pleasure to be with her parents again, and Molly put on her rough farm garments once more, and early and late was out among the cattle, or working in the fields. And she had a joyful surprise when her husband paid her a flying visit a few days later. After that, he came quite frequently, though always unexpectedly, and if proof was wanting that she was the kind of a wife that John Hays was proud to have his fellow-soldiers see, it lies in the fact that he allowed Molly to visit him in camp more than once. She saw him at Trenton, and at Princeton, before the Continental army routed the British there, on January 3, 1777.

In order to surprise the three British regiments which were at Princeton at that time, General Washington, Commander-in-chief of the Continental force, quietly left Trenton with his troops, and crept up behind the unsuspecting British at Princeton, killing about one hundred men and taking three hundred prisoners, while his own losses were only thirty men. Then, anxious to get away before Lord Cornwallis could arrive with reinforcements for the British, he slipped away with his men to Morristown, New Jersey, while the cannon were still booming on the battle-field, their noise being mistaken in Trenton for thunder. With the Continental troops went John Hays, gunner, and as soon as Molly heard of the engagement, and the retirement of General Washington's troops, she hastened to the field of action to seek out any wounded men whom she could care for or comfort in their last hours. Picking her way across the littered field, she brought a drink of water here, lifted an aching head there, and covered the faces of those who had seen their last battle. As she passed slowly on, she saw a friend of her husband's, Dilwyn by name, lying half buried under a pile of debris. She would have passed him by but for a feeble movement of his hand under the rubbish, seeing which, she stooped down, pushed aside his covering, and felt for his pulse to see whether he were still alive. As she bent down her quick eye saw a cannon near where the wounded man lay, a heavy, cumbersome gun which the Continentals had evidently left behind as being of a type too heavy to drag with them on their hasty march to Morristown. Beside the cannon Molly also saw a lighted fuse slowly burning down at one end. She had a temptation as she looked at the piece of rope soaked in some combustible, lying there ready to achieve its purpose. She stooped over Dilwyn again, then she rose and went to the cannon, fuse in hand. In a half-second the booming of the great gun shook the battle-field—Molly had touched it off, and at exactly the right moment, for even then the advance guard of Lord Cornwallis and his men was within range!

At the sound of the cannon they halted abruptly, in alarm. The foe must be lurking in ambush dangerously near them, for who else would have set off the gun? They spent an hour hunting for the concealed Continentals, while Molly picked Dilwyn up and laid him across her shoulder as she had carried the wheat-bags in childhood, and coolly walked past the British, who by that time were swarming across the battle-field, paying no attention to the red-headed young woman carrying a wounded soldier off the field, for what could she have to do with discharging a gun!

Molly meanwhile bore her heavy burden across the fields for two miles until she reached the farm, where she laid the wounded man gently down on a bed which was blissfully soft to his aching bones, and where he was cared for and nursed as if he had been Molly's own kin. When at last he was well again and able to ride away from the farm, he expressed his admiration for his nurse in no measured terms, and there came to her a few days later a box of fine dress goods with the warmest regards of "one whose life you saved." As she looked at the rich material, Molly smoothed it appreciatively with roughened hand, then she laid the bundle away among her most cherished possessions, but making use of it never entered her mind—it was much too handsome for that!

Every hour the British troops were delayed at Princeton was of great advantage to the Continental forces, and by midnight they had come to the end of their eighteen-mile march, to their great rejoicing, as it had been a terrible walk over snow and ice and in such bitter cold that many a finger and ear were frozen, and all had suffered severely. The men had not had a meal for twenty-four hours, had made the long march on top of heavy fighting, and when they reached their destination they were so exhausted that the moment they halted they dropped and fell into a heavy sleep.

While they were marching toward Morristown, Lord Cornwallis was rushing his troops on to New Brunswick to save the supplies which the British had stored there. To his great relief he found them untouched, so he gave up the pursuit of Washington's fleeing forces, and the Continental army, without resistance, went into winter quarters at Morristown, as their Commander had planned to do. While John Hays, with the American army, was following his Commander, Molly, at the farm, had become the proud mother of a son, who was named John Hays, Jr., and who became Molly's greatest comfort in the long months when she had no glimpse or tidings of her husband. Then came news—General Washington's troops were again on the march, passing through New Jersey toward New York. There would be a chance to see her husband, and Molly determined to take it, whatever risk or hardship it might entail, for not only did she long to see Hays, but she could not wait longer to tell him of the perfections of their son. And so Molly went to the scene of the battle of Monmouth.

It was Sunday, the 28th of June, 1778, a day which has come down in history, not only because of the battle which marks its date, but because of its scorching heat. The mercury stood near the 100 mark, and man and beast were well-nigh overcome.

History tells us that the British had remained at Philadelphia until early in June, when they had evacuated that city and crossed the Delaware River on June the eighteenth, with an intention to march across New Jersey to New York. Having heard of this movement of the British, General Washington, with a force nearly equal to that of the enemy, also crossed into New Jersey, with the purpose of retarding the British march and, if opportunity offered, bring on a general engagement. By the 22d of June the whole of the American force was massed on the east bank of the Delaware in a condition and position to give the enemy battle. Despite some opposition on the part of General Lee and other officers, Lafayette and Greene agreed with General Washington in his opinion that the time to strike had come, and soon orders were given which led to the battle of Monmouth.

Lafayette was detached with a strong body of troops to follow up the British rear and act, if occasion presented. Other riflemen and militia were in advance of him and on his flanks, making a strong body of picked troops. To protect his twelve-mile baggage-train from these troops, Sir Henry Clinton placed them with a large escort under Knyphausen, while he united the rest of his force in the rear to check the enemy, if they came too close. The distance between Knyphausen's force and that which brought up the rear suggested the idea to Washington to concentrate his assault on the rear force, and to hasten the attack before the British should reach the high ground of Middletown, about twelve miles away, where they would be comparatively safe.

At once General Lee was sent forward to join Lafayette, with instructions to engage the enemy in such action as was possible until the remainder of the troops should arrive. Lee carried out his part of the command in such a half-hearted way as to bring severe censure on him later, and when General Greene arrived on the scene of action, Lee and his men were in retreat.

A sharp reproof from General Washington brought Lee partially to his senses; he turned about and engaged in a short, sharp conflict with the enemy, and retired from the field in good order. At that time Greene's column arrived, and as a movement of the British threatened Washington's right wing, he ordered Greene to file off from the road to Monmouth and, while the rest of the army pushed forward, to fight his way into the wood at the rear of Monmouth Court-House. Greene was obeying orders when, foreseeing that by the flight of Lee

Washington would be exposed to the whole weight of the enemy's attack, he suddenly wheeled about and took an advantageous position near the British left wing.

As he hoped, this diverted the enemy's attention from the fire of the American army. A furious attack followed, but was met by a cool resistance which was the result of the army's discipline at Valley Forge.

The artillery of Greene's division, well posted on a commanding position, was in charge of General Knox, and poured a most destructive fire on the enemy, seconded by the infantry, who steadily held their ground. Repeated efforts of the British only increased their losses.

Colonel Monckton's grenadiers, attempting to drive back the American forces, were repulsed by General Knox's artillery with great slaughter. A second attempt was made, and a third, when Colonel Monckton received his death-blow and fell from his horse. General Wayne then came up with a force of farmers, their sleeves rolled up as if harvesting, and they forced the British back still farther, leaving the bodies of their wounded and dead comrades on the field.

Through the long hours of the desperate fighting on that June day, the mercury rose higher and higher, and many of the men's tongues were so swollen with the heat that they could not speak, and they fell exhausted at their posts. Seeing this, Molly, who was with her husband on the field of battle, discovered a bubbling spring of water in the west ravine, and spent her time through the long hours of blistering heat tramping back and forth carrying water for the thirsty men, and also for her husband's cannon. She used for her purpose "the cannon's bucket," which was a fixture of the gun of that time, and she told afterward how every time she came back with a brimming bucket of the sparkling water, the men would call out:

"Here comes Molly with her pitcher!"

As the battle grew fiercer and her trips to the spring became more frequent, the call was abbreviated into, "Molly Pitcher!" by which name she was so generally known from that day that her own name has been almost forgotten.

Higher and higher rose the sun in a cloudless sky, and up mounted the mercury until the suffering of the soldiers in both armies was unspeakable, although the British were in a worse state than the Americans, because of their woolen uniforms, knapsacks, and accoutrements, while the Continental army had no packs and had laid off all unnecessary clothing. Even so, many of both forces died of prostration, despite Molly's cooling drinks which she brought to as many men as possible. John Hays worked his cannon bravely, while perspiration streamed down his face and heat blurred his vision. Suddenly all went black before him—the rammer dropped from his nerveless hand, and he fell beside his gun. Quickly to his side Molly darted, put a handkerchief wet with spring water on his hot brow, laid her head on his heart to see whether it was still beating. He was alive! Beckoning to two of his comrades, Molly commanded them to carry him to the shade of a near-by tree. And soon she had the satisfaction of seeing a faint smile flicker over his face as she bent above him. At that moment her keen ears heard General Knox give a command.

"Remove the cannon!" he said. "We have no gunner brave enough to fill Hays's place!"

"No!" said Molly, hastening to the General's side and facing him with a glint of triumph in her blue eyes. "The cannon shall not be taken away! Since my brave husband is not able to work it, I will do my best to serve in his place!"

Picking up the rammer, she began to load and fire with the courage and decision of a seasoned gunner, standing at her post through long hours of heat and exhaustion. When at a late hour the enemy had finally been driven back with great loss, and Washington saw the uselessness of any renewal of the assault, General Greene strode over to the place where Molly Pitcher was still manfully loading the cannon, and gripped her hand with a hearty:

"I thank you in the name of the American army!"

One can fancy how Molly's heart throbbed with pride at such commendation, as she picked her way over the bodies of the dead and wounded to the spot where her husband was propped up against a tree, slowly recovering from his prostration, but able to express his admiration for a wife who had been able to take a gunner's place at a moment's notice and help to rout the British.

"That night the American army slept upon their arms; Greene, like his Commander, taking his repose without couch or pillow, on the naked ground, and with no other shelter than a tree beneath the broad canopy of heaven. But this shelter was not sought, nor sleep desired, until every wounded and hungry soldier had been cared for and fed with the best food the camp could supply. Rising at dawn, Washington found the enemy gone! They had stolen silently away with such rapidity as would, when their flight became known, put them beyond the chance of pursuit—and so the American army had been victorious at Monmouth, and Molly Pitcher had played an important part in that victory."

She, too, had slept that night under the stars, and when morning came she was still in the dusty, torn, powder-stained clothing she had worn as cannonier, and afterward while working over the wounded. Her predicament was a bad one when a messenger arrived from General Washington requesting an interview with her. She, Molly Pitcher, to be received by the Commander-in-chief of the American forces in such a garb as that! How could she make herself presentable for the interview? With her usual quick wit, Molly borrowed an artilleryman's coat, which in some measure hid her grimy and torn garments. In this coat over her own petticoats, and a cocked hat with a feather, doubtless plucked from a straying hen, she made no further ado, but presented herself to Washington as requested, and from the fact that she wore such a costume on that June day has come the oft-repeated and untrue story that she wore a man's clothing on the battle-field.

General Washington's eyes lighted with pleasure at the sight of such a brave woman, and he received her with such honor as he would have awarded one of his gallant men. Molly was almost overcome with his words of praise, and still more so when he conferred on her the brevet of Captain, from which came the title, "Captain Molly," which she was called by the soldiers from that day. General Washington also recommended that she be given a soldier's half-pay for life, as a reward for her faithful performance of a man's duty at the battle of Monmouth.

That was enough to make John Hays, now completely recovered from his prostration, the proudest man in the army; but added to that he had the satisfaction of seeing Molly given a tremendous ovation by the soldiers, who cheered her to the echo when they first saw her after that fateful night. To cap the climax, the great French General Lafayette showed his appreciation of her courage by asking Washington if his men "might have the pleasure of giving Madame a trifle."

Then those French officers who were among the American regiments formed in two long lines, between which Captain Molly passed in her artilleryman's coat, cocked hat in hand, and while lusty cheers rang out, the hat was filled to overflowing with gold crowns.

And so it was that Molly Pitcher, a country girl of New Jersey, played a prominent part in the battle of Monmouth and won for herself an enviable place in American history.

It is of little importance to us that when the war was over, Molly with her husband and child lived quietly in Carlisle, John Hays going back to his trade, Molly doing washing and enjoying her annuity of forty dollars a year from the government.

After John Hays's death Molly married again, an Irishman named McCauley, and it would have been far better for her to have remained a widow, for her life was unhappy from that time until her death in 1833, at the age of seventy-nine.

But that does not interest us. Ours it is to admire the heroic deeds of Molly Pitcher on the battle-field, to thrill that there was one woman of our country whose achievements have inspired poets and sculptors in the long years since she was seen

loading, firing that six-pounder,—

when, as a poet has said,

Tho' like tigers fierce they fought us, to such zeal had Molly brought us That tho' struck with heat and thirsting, yet of drink we felt no lack; There she stood amid the clamor, swiftly handling sponge and rammer While we swept with wrath condign, on their line.

At Freehold, New Jersey, at the base of the great Monmouth battle monument are five bronze tablets, each five feet high by six in width, commemorating scenes of that memorable battle. One of these shafts is called the "Molly Pitcher," and shows Mary Hays using that six-pounder; her husband lies exhausted at her feet, and General Knox is seen directing the artillery. Also forty-three years after her death, on July 4, 1876, the citizens of Cumberland County, Pennsylvania, placed a handsome slab of Italian marble over her grave, inscribed with the date of her death and stating that she was the heroine of Monmouth.

In this, our day, we stand at the place where the old and the new in civilization and in humanity stand face to face. Shall the young woman of to-day, with new inspiration, fresh courage, and desire to better the world by her existence, face backward or forward in the spirit of patriotism which animated Molly Pitcher on the battle-field of Monmouth? Ours "not to reason why," ours "but to do and die," not as women, simply, but as citizen-soldiers on a battle-field where democracy is the golden reward, where in standing by our guns we stand shoulder to shoulder with the inspired spirits of the world.

Molly Pitcher stood by her gun in 1778—our chance has come in 1917. Let us not falter or fail in expressing the best in achievement and in womanhood.

ELIZABETH VAN LEW: THE GIRL WHO RISKED ALL THAT SLAVERY MIGHT BE ABOLISHED AND THE UNION PRESERVED

I

It was the winter of 1835. Study hour was just over in one of Philadelphia's most famous "finishing schools" of that day, and half a dozen girls were still grouped around the big center-table piling their books up preparatory to going to their rooms for the night. Suddenly Catherine Holloway spoke.

"Listen, girls," she said; "Miss Smith says we are to have a real Debating Club, with officers and regular club nights, and all sorts of interesting subjects. Won't it be fun? And what do you suppose the first topic is to be?"

Books were dropped on the table, and several voices exclaimed in eager question, "What?"

"'Resolved: That Slavery be abolished.' And Betty Van Lew is to take the negative side!"

There was a chorus of suppressed "Oh-h-hs!" around the table, then some one asked, "Who is going to take the other side?"

The speaker shook her head. "I don't know," she said. "I hope it will be me. My, but it would be exciting to debate that question against Betty!"

"You would get the worst of it," said a positive voice. "There isn't a girl in school who knows what she thinks on any subject as clearly as Betty knows what she believes about slavery."

The speaker tossed her head. "You don't know much about it, if you think that!" she declared. "We Massachusetts colonists are just as sure on our side as she is on hers—and you all ought to be if you are not! Father says it is only in the cotton-raising States that they think the way Betty does, and we Northerners must stand firm against having human beings bought and sold like merchandise. I just hope I will be chosen on that debate against Betty."

She was, but she came off vanquished by the verbal gymnastics of her opponent, to whom the arguments in favor of slavery were as familiar as the principles of arithmetic, for Betty had heard the subject discussed by eloquent and interested men ever since she was able to understand what they were talking about.

Never did two opponents argue with greater fire and determination for a cause than did those two school-girls, pitted against each other in a discussion of a subject far beyond their understanding. So cleverly did the Virginia girl hold up her end of the debate against her New England opponent, and so shrewdly did she repeat all the arguments she had heard fall from Southern lips, that she sat down amid a burst of applause, having won her case, proudly sure that from that moment there would be no more argument against slavery among her schoolmates, for who could know more about it than the daughter of one of Richmond's leading inhabitants? And who could appreciate the great advantages of slavery to the slaves themselves better than one who owned them?

But Betty had not reckoned with the strength of the feeling among those Northerners with whose children she was associated. They had also heard many telling arguments at home on the side against that which Betty had won because she had complied so fully with the rules of debate; and she had by no means won her friends over to her way of thinking. Many a heated argument was carried on later in the Quaker City school over that question which was becoming a matter of serious difference between the North and the South.

Before the war for Independence slavery existed in all the States of the Union. After the war was over some of the States abolished slavery, and others would have followed their example had it not been for the invention of the cotton-gin, which made the owning of slaves much more valuable in the cotton-growing States. East of the Mississippi River slavery was allowed in the new States lying south of the Ohio, but forbidden in the territory north of the Ohio. When Missouri applied for admission into the Union, the question of slavery west of the Mississippi was discussed and finally settled by what was afterward called "The Missouri Compromise of 1820."

In 1818, two years before this Compromise was agreed upon, Elizabeth Van Lew was born in Richmond. As we have already seen, when she was seventeen, she was in the North at school. Doubtless Philadelphia had been chosen not only because of the excellence of the school to which she was sent, but also because the Quaker City was her mother's childhood home, which fact is one to be kept clearly in mind as one follows Betty Van Lew's later life in all its thrilling details.

For many months after her victory as a debater Betty's convictions did not waver—she was still a firm believer that slavery was right and best for all. Then she spent a vacation with a schoolmate who lived in a New England village, in whose home she heard arguments fully as convincing in their appeal to her reason as those to which she had listened at home from earliest childhood. John Van Lew, Betty's father, had ever been one of those Southerners who argued that in slavery lay the great protection for the negro—in Massachusetts Betty heard impassioned appeals for the freedom of the individual, of whatever race, and to those appeals her nature slowly responded as a result partly of her inheritance from her mother's Northern blood, and partly as a result of that keen sense of justice which was always one of her marked traits.

At the end of her school days in the North, Betty's viewpoint had so completely changed that she went back to her Richmond home an unwavering abolitionist, who was to give her all for a cause which became more sacred to her than possessions or life itself.

Soon after her return to Virginia she was visited by the New England friend in whose home she had been a guest, and to the Massachusetts girl, fresh from the rugged hills and more severe life of New England, Richmond was a fascinating spot, and the stately old mansion, which John Van Lew had recently bought, was a revelation of classic beauty which enchanted her.

The old mansion stood on Church Hill, the highest of Richmond's seven hills. "Across the way was St. John's, in the shadow of whose walls Elizabeth Van Lew grew from childhood. St. John's, which christened her and confirmed her, and later barred its doors against her." Behind the house at the foot of the hill stood "The Libby," which in years to come was to be her special care.... But this is anticipating our story. Betty Van Lew, full of the charm and enthusiasm of youth, had just come home from school, and with her had come the Northern friend, to whom the Southern city with its languorous beauty and warm hospitality was a wonder and a delight.

The old mansion stood close to the street, and "from the pavement two steep, curving flights of stone steps, banistered by curious old iron railings, ascended to either end of the square, white-pillared portico which formed the entrance to the stately Van Lew home with its impressive hall and great high-ceilinged rooms. And, oh! the beauty of the garden at its rear!"

Betty's friend reveled in its depths of tangled color and fragrance, as arm in arm the girls wandered down broad, box-bordered walks, from terrace to terrace by way of moss-grown stone stairs, deep sunk in the grassy lawn, and now and again the New England girl would exclaim:

"Oh, Betty, I can't breathe, it is all so beautiful!"

And indeed it was. "There were fig-trees, persimmons, mock orange, and shrubs ablaze with blossoms. The air was heavy with the sweetness of the magnolias, loud with the mocking-birds in the thickets, and the drone of insects in the hot, dry grass. And through the branches of the trees on the lower terrace one could get frequent glimpses of the James River, thickly studded with black rocks and tiny green islands." No wonder that the girl from the bleak North found it in her heart to thrill at the beauty of such a gem from Nature's jewel-casket as was that garden of the Van Lews'!

And other things were as interesting to her in a different way as the garden was beautiful. Many guests went to and from the hospitable mansion, and the little Northerner saw beautiful women and heard brilliant men talk intelligently on many subjects of vital import, especially on the all-important subject of slavery; of the men who upheld it, of its result to the Union. But more interesting to her than anything else were the slaves themselves, of whom the Van Lews had many, and who were treated with the kindness and consideration of children in a family.

"Of course, it is better for them!" declared Betty. "Everybody who has grown up with them knows that they simply *can't* take responsibility,—and yet!" There was a long pause, then Betty added, softly: "And yet, all human beings have a right to be free; I know it; and all the States of the Union must agree on that before there is any kind of a bond between them."

She spoke like an old lady, her arm leaning on the window-sill, with her dimpled chin resting in her hand, and as the moonlight gleamed across the window-sill, young as she was, in Betty Van Lew's face there was a gleam of that purpose which in coming years was to be her consecration and her baptism of fire, although a moment later the conversation of the girls had drifted into more frivolous channels, and a coming dance was the all-important topic.

As we know, when Missouri applied for admission into the Union, the slavery question was discussed and finally settled by the so-called "Missouri Compromise" in 1820. Now, in 1849, a new question began to agitate both North and South. Before that time the debate had been as to the abolishing of slavery, but the question now changed to "Shall slavery be extended? Shall it be allowed in the country purchased from Mexico?" As this land had been made free soil by Mexico, many people in the North insisted that it should remain free. The South insisted that the newly acquired country was the common property of the States, that any citizen might go there with his slaves, and that Congress had no power to prevent them. Besides this, the South also insisted that there ought to be as many slave States as free States. At that time the numbers were equal—fifteen slave States and fifteen free. Some threats were made that the slaveholding States would leave the Union if Congress sought to shut out slavery in the territory gained from Mexico.

That a State might secede, or withdraw from the Union, had long been claimed by a party led by John C. Calhoun, of South Carolina. Daniel Webster had always opposed this doctrine and stood as the representative of those who held that the Union could not be broken. Now, in 1850, Henry Clay undertook to end the quarrel between the States, and as a result there was a famous debate between the most notable living orators, Webster, Calhoun, and Clay, and a new compromise was made. It was called the Compromise of 1850, and it was confidently hoped would be a final settlement of all the troubles growing out of slavery. But it was not. With slow and increasing bitterness the feeling rose in both North and South over the mooted question, and slowly but surely events moved on toward the great crisis of 1860, when Abraham Lincoln was elected President of the United States.

"The Southern States had been hoping that this might be prevented, for they knew that Lincoln stood firmly for the abolition of slavery in every State in the Union, and that he was not a man to compromise or falter when he believed in a principle. So as soon as he was elected the Southern States began to withdraw from the Union, known as the United States of America. First went South Carolina, then Georgia, Florida, Alabama, Mississippi, and Louisiana. Then delegates from these States met in Montgomery, Alabama, and formed a new Union which they called the 'Confederate States of America,' with Jefferson Davis as its President. Then Texas joined the Confederacy, and events were shaping themselves rapidly for an inevitable culmination.

"When South Carolina withdrew there was within her boundary much property belonging to the United States, such as lighthouses, court-houses, post-offices, custom-houses, and two important forts, Moultrie and Sumter, which guarded the entrance to Charleston harbor, and were held by a small band of United States troops under the command of Major Robert Anderson.

"As soon as the States seceded a demand was made on the United States for a surrender of this property. The partnership called the Union, having been dissolved by the secession of South Carolina, the land on which the buildings stood belonged to the State, but the buildings themselves, being the property of the United States, should be paid for by the State, and an agent was sent to Washington to arrange for the purchase.

"Meanwhile, scenting grave trouble, troops were being enlisted and drilled, and Major Anderson, fearing that if the agent did not succeed in making the purchase the forts would be taken by force, cut down the flagstaff and spiked the guns at Fort Moultrie, and moved his men to Fort Sumter, which stood on an island in the harbor and could be more easily defended, and so the matter stood when Mr. Lincoln was inaugurated, March 4, 1861."

Fort Sumter was now in a state of siege. Anderson and his men could get no food from Charleston, while the troops of the Confederacy had planted cannon with which they could at any time fire on the fort. Either the troops must very soon go away or food must be sent them. Mr. Lincoln decided to send food. But when the vessels with food, men and supplies reached Charleston, they found that the Confederates had already begun to fire on Fort Sumter. Then, as Major Anderson related: "Having defended the Fort for thirty-four hours, until the quarters were entirely burned, the main gates destroyed by fire ... the magazine surrounded by flame, and its doors closed from the effects of heat, four barrels and three cartridges only being available, and no provisions remaining but pork, I accepted terms of evacuation offered by General Beauregard ... and marched out of the Fort, Sunday the 14th instant, with colors flying and drums beating."

When the news of the fall of Sumter reached the North, the people knew that all hope of a peaceable settlement of the dispute with the South was gone. Mr. Lincoln at once called for 75,000 soldiers to serve for three months, and the first gun of the Civil War had been fired.

While these momentous events were stirring both North and South, Betty Van Lew, in her Richmond home, was experiencing the delights of young womanhood in a city celebrated for its gaiety of social life. "There were balls and receptions in the great house, garden-parties in the wonderful garden, journeyings to the White Sulphur Springs, and other resorts of the day, in the coach drawn by six snowy horses," and all sorts of festivities for the young and light-hearted. Even in a city as noted for charming women as was Richmond, Betty Van Lew enjoyed an enviable popularity. To be invited to the mansion on the hill was the great delight of her many acquaintances, while more than one ardent lover laid his heart at her feet; but her pleasure was in the many rather than in the one, and she remained heart-whole while most of her intimate friends married and went to homes of their own. It is said that as she grew to womanhood, she was "of delicate physique and a small but commanding figure, brilliant, accomplished and resolute, with great personality and of infinite charm." At first no one took her fearless expression of opinion in regard to the slavery question seriously, coming as it did from the lips of such a charming young woman, but as time went on and she became more outspoken and more diligent in her efforts to uplift and educate the negroes, she began to be less popular, and to be spoken of as "queer and eccentric" by those who did not sympathize with her views.

Nevertheless, Richmond's first families still eagerly accepted invitations to the Van Lew mansion, and it was in its big parlor that Edgar Allan Poe read his poem, "The Raven," to a picked audience of Richmond's elect, there Jenny Lind sang at the height of her fame, and there as a guest came the Swedish novelist, Fredrika Bremer, and in later years came Gen. Ulysses S. Grant, whose admiration of Elizabeth Van Lew was unbounded because of her service to the Union.

Betty's father having died soon after she came from school, and her brother John being of a retiring disposition, Mrs. Van Lew and Betty did the honors of the stately house on the hill in a manner worthy of Southern society women, and as years went by and Betty became a woman, always when they had brilliant guests she listened carefully, saying little, but was fearlessly frank in her expression of opinion on vital subjects, when her opinion was asked.

"And now, Sumter had been fired on. Three days after the little garrison marched out of the smoking fort, Virginia seceded from the Union, and Richmond went war-mad. In poured troops from other States, and the beautiful Southern city became a vast military camp. Daily the daughters of the Confederacy met in groups to sew or knit for the soldiers, or to shoot at a mark with unaccustomed hands. One day a note was delivered at the Van Lew mansion, and opened by Mrs. Van Lew, who read it aloud to her daughter:

"'Come and help us make shirts for our soldiers. We need the immediate assistance of all our women at this critical time....'"

The silence in the room was unbroken except for the heart-beats of the two women facing a sure future, looking sadly into each other's eyes. Suddenly Elizabeth threw back her head proudly.

"Never!" she said. "Right is right. We must abide by the consequences of our belief. We will work for the Union or sit idle!"

The testing of Elizabeth Van Lew had come. Fearlessly she made her choice—fearlessly she took the consequences. From that moment her story is the story of the Federal Spy.

II

"Out in the middle of the turbulent river James lay Belle Isle Prison surrounded by its stockade. In the city of Richmond, at the foot of Church Street, almost at Betty Van Lew's door, was the Libby, with its grim, gray walls; only a stone's throw farther away were Castle Lightning on the north side of Cary Street, and Castle Thunder on the south side. In July of 1861 the battle of Bull Run was fought, and the Confederate army defeated and put to flight by the Union soldiers. The Libby, Belle Isle and Castle Thunder all were overflowing with scarred and suffering human beings,—with sick men, wounded men, dying men, and Northern prisoners." Here was work to do!

Down the aisles of the hastily converted hospitals and into dim prison cells came almost daily a little woman with a big smile, always with her hands full of flowers or delicacies, a basket swinging from her arm. As she walked she hummed tuneless airs, and her expression was such a dazed and meaningless one that the prison guards and other soldiers paid little heed to the coming and going of "Crazy Bet," as she was called. "Mis' Van Lew—poor creature, she's lost her balance since the war broke out. She'll do no harm to the poor boys, and maybe a bit of comfortin'. A permit? Oh yes, signed by General Winder himself,—let her be!" Such was the verdict passed from sentry-guard to sentry in regard to "Crazy Bet," who wandered on at will, humming her ditties and ministering to whom she would.

One day a cautious guard noticed a strange dish she carried into the prison. It was an old French platter, with double bottom, in which water was supposed to be placed to keep the food on the platter hot. The dish roused the guard's suspicions, and to a near-by soldier he muttered something about it. Apparently unheeding him, "Crazy Bet" passed on beyond the grim, gray walls, carrying her platter, but she had heard his words. Two days later she came to the prison door again with the strange dish in her hand wrapped in a shawl. The sentry on guard stopped her.

"I will have to examine that," he said.

"Take it!" she said, hastily unwrapping it and dropping it into his hands. It contained no secret message that day, as it had before—only water scalding hot, and the guard dropped it with a howl of pain, and turned away to nurse his burned hands, while "Crazy Bet" went into the prison smiling a broad and meaningless smile.

Well did the Spy play her rôle, as months went by; more loudly she hummed, more vacantly she smiled, and more diligently she worked to obtain information regarding the number and placing of Confederate troops, which information she sent on at once to Federal headquarters. Day by day she worked, daring loss of life, and spending her entire fortune for the sake of the cause which was dearer to her than a good name or riches—the preservation of the Union and the abolishing of slavery.

From the windows of the Libby, and from Belle Isle, the prisoners could see passing troops and supply-trains and give shrewd guesses at their strength and destination, making their conjectures from the roads by which they saw the Confederates leave the town. Also they often heard scraps of conversations between surgeons or prison guards, which they hoarded like so much gold, to pass on to "Crazy Bet," and so repay her kindness and her lavish generosity, which was as sincere as her underlying motive was genuine. Meals at the Van Lew mansion grew less and less bountiful, even meager,—not one article did either Elizabeth Van Lew or her loyal mother buy for themselves, but spent their ample fortune without stint on the sick and imprisoned in their city, while there was never an hour of her time that the Federal Spy gave to her own concerns. If there was nothing else to be done, she was writing a home letter for some heart-sick prisoner from the North, and secretly carrying it past the censors to be sure that it should reach the anxious family eagerly awaiting news of a loved one.

"Crazy Bet" loaned many books to the prisoners, which were returned with a word or sentence or a page number faintly underlined here and there. In the privacy of her own room, the Spy would piece them together and read some important bit of news which she instantly sent to Federal headquarters by special messenger, as she had ceased using the mails in the early stages of the war. Or a friendly little note would be handed her with its hidden meaning impossible to decipher except by one who knew the code. Important messages were carried back and forth in her baskets of fruit and flowers in a way that would have been dangerous had not "Crazy Bet" established such a reputation for harmless kindness. She had even won over Lieutenant Todd, brother of Mrs. Lincoln, who was in charge of the Libby, by the personal offerings she brought him of delectable buttermilk and gingerbread. Clever Bet!

So well did she play her part now, and with such assurance, that she would sometimes stop a stranger on the street and begin a heated argument in favor of the Union, while the person who did not know her looked on the outspoken little woman with a mixture of admiration and contempt. At that time her lifelong persecution, by those who had before been her loyal friends, began. Where before she had been met with friendly bows and smiles, there were now averted glances or open insults. She encountered dislike, even hatred, on every side, but at that time it mattered little to her, for her heart and mind were occupied with bigger problems.

What she did mind was that from time to time her permit to visit the hospitals and prisons was taken away, and she was obliged to use all the diplomacy of which she was mistress, to win it back again from either General Winder or the Secretary of War. At one time the press and people became so incensed against the Northern prisoners that no one was allowed to visit the prisons or do anything for their relief. Among the clippings found among Betty Van Lew's papers is this:

Rapped Over the Knucks.

One of the city papers contained Monday a word of exhortation to certain females of Southern residence (and perhaps birth) but of decidedly Northern and Abolition proclivities. The creatures thus alluded to were not named.... If such people do not wish to be exposed and dealt with as alien enemies to the country, they would do well to cut stick while they can do so with safety to their worthless carcasses.

On the margin in faded ink there is written: "These ladies were my mother and myself. God knows it was but little we could do."

Spring came, and McClellan, at the head of the Army of the Potomac, moved up the peninsula. "On to Richmond!" was the cry, as the troops swept by. It is said that the houses in the city shook with the cannonading, and from their roofs the people could see the bursting of shells. "Crazy Bet," watching the battle with alternate hope and fear, was filled with fierce exultation, and hastily prepared a room in the house on the hill with new matting and fresh curtains for the use of General McClellan. But the Federal forces were repulsed by the Confederate troops under General Lee and "drew away over the hills." General McClellan had failed in his attempt to take Richmond, and within that room freshly prepared for his use bitter disappointment and dead hope were locked.

There was great rejoicing in Richmond in this repulse of the Federal army, and even those old friends who were now enemies of Elizabeth Van Lew, could afford to throw her a smile or a kind word in the flush of their triumph. She responded pleasantly, for she was a big enough woman to understand a viewpoint which differed from her own. Meanwhile, she worked on tirelessly through the long days and nights of an unusually hot summer, meeting in secret conferences with Richmond's handful of Unionists, to plot and scheme for the aid of the Federal authorities. "The Van Lew mansion was the fifth in a chain of Union Secret Service relaying stations, whose beginning was in the headquarters tent of the Federal army. Of this chain of stations the Van Lew farm, lying a short distance outside of the city, was one. It was seldom difficult for Betty Van Lew to get passes for her servants to make the trip between the farm and the Richmond house, and this was one of her most valuable methods of transmitting and receiving secret messages. Fresh eggs were brought in from the farm almost every day to the house on Church Hill, and no one was allowed to touch them until the head of the house had counted them, with true war-time economy, and she always took one out, for her own use in egg-nog, so she said. In reality that egg was but a shell which contained a tiny scroll of paper, a message from some Union general to the Federal Spy. An old negro brought the farm products in to Richmond, and he always stopped for a friendly chat with his mistress, yes, and took off his thick-soled shoes that he might deliver into her hands a cipher despatch which she was generally awaiting eagerly! Much sewing was done for the Van Lews at that time by a little seamstress, who worked at both farm and city home, and in carrying dress goods and patterns back and forth she secreted much valuable information for the Spy, on whom the Union generals were now depending for the largest part of their news in regard to Confederate plans and movements of troops." And she did not disappoint them in the slightest detail.

She must have a disguise in which she could go about the city and its environs without fear of detection, and she must also gain more valuable and accurate information from headquarters of the Confederacy. This she resolved, and then set to work to achieve her end. At once she wrote to a negro girl, Mary Elizabeth Bowser, who had been one of the Van Lews' slaves, but who had been freed and sent North to be educated, inviting her to visit the stately mansion where she had grown up, and the invitation was eagerly accepted. On her arrival in Richmond, she was closeted a long time with her one-time mistress, to whom she owed her liberty, and when the interview ended the girl's eyes were shining, and she wore an air of fixed resolve only equaled by that of Betty Van Lew.

A waitress was needed in the White House of the Southern Confederacy. Three days after Mary Bowser arrived at the Van Lews', she had applied for the position and become a member of Jefferson Davis's household. Another link had been forged in the long chain of details by which the Spy worked her will and gained her ends.

Despite the suspicion and ill-will felt in Richmond for the Van Lews, more than one Confederate officer and public official continued to call there throughout the war, to be entertained by them. The fare was meager in comparison to the old lavish entertaining, but the conversation was brilliant and diverting, and so cleverly did Betty lead it that "many a young officer unwittingly revealed much important information of which he never realized the value, but which was of great use to 'Crazy Bet' when combined with what she already knew.

"And when night fell over the city Betty would steal out in her disguise of a farm-hand, in the buckskin leggins, one-piece skirt and waist of cotton, and the huge calico sunbonnet, going about her secret business, a little lonely, unnoticed figure, and in a thousand unsuspected, simple ways she executed her plans and found out such things as she needed to know to aid the Federal authorities."

History was in the making in those stirring days of 1862, when, having failed to take Richmond, General McClellan had returned North by sea, when the Confederates under General Lee prepared to invade the North, but were turned back after the great battle of Antietam. Thrilling days they were to live through, and to the urge and constant demand for service every man and woman of North and South instantly responded. But none of the women gave such daring service as did Elizabeth Van Lew. Known as a dauntless advocate of abolition and of the Union, suspected of a traitor's disloyalty to the South, but with that stain on her reputation as a Southerner unproved from the commencement of the war until its close, her life was in continual danger. She wrote a year later, "I was an enthusiast who never counted it dear if I could have served the Union—not that I wished to die." For four long years she awoke morning after morning to a new day of suspense and threatening danger, to nights of tension and of horrible fear. "No soldier but had his days and weeks of absolute safety. For her there was not one hour; betrayal, friends' blunders, the carelessness of others; all these she had to dread." All these she accepted for the sake of a cause which she believed to be right and just.

As her system of obtaining information in regard to movements of the Confederates became more perfect, she was connected more closely with the highest Federal authorities,—so closely connected, in fact, that flowers which one day grew in her Richmond garden stood next morning on General Grant's breakfast table.

"One day she received a letter from General Butler, which was to be delivered to a Confederate officer on General Winder's staff. In the letter this officer was asked to 'come through the lines and tell what he knew,' and there were promises of rewards if it should be done successfully. The Spy sat quietly thinking for some time after receiving this letter. If it should fall into Confederate hands it would be the death-warrant of its bearer. Who could be trusted to take it to the officer for whom it was intended? Coolly Elizabeth Van Lew arose, went out, and walked straight to the office of General Winder, took the letter from her bosom, and handed it to the officer for whom it was intended, watching him closely as he read it.

"In the next room were detectives and armed guards, the whole machinery of the Confederate capital's secret police. The officer had but to raise his voice and her game would be up; she would pay the penalty of her daring with her life. She had been suspicious of the officer for some weeks, had marked him as a traitor to his cause. Was she right?

"His face whitened, his lips were set as he read, then, without a quiver of a muscle, he rose and followed her out of the room; then he gave way and implored her to be more prudent. If she would never come there again he would go to her, he said. And so she gained another aid in her determined purpose of 'striking at the very heart of the Confederacy.'

"Another day there was a message of vital importance to send to General Grant, who had asked her to make a report to him of the number and placing of forces in and about Richmond. The cipher despatch was ready, but if it were to reach Grant in time there was not an hour to lose in finding a messenger. At that time no servant of hers could leave the city, and no Federal agent could enter it. Hoping for an inspiration, she took her huge market-basket on her arm, the basket which was so familiar by this time as a part of 'Crazy Bet's' outfit, and with it swinging at her side, humming a tuneless song, she passed down the street, smiling aimlessly in return for mocking glances—and all the while in her hand she held the key to Richmond's defenses!

"As she walked a man passed her and whispered, 'I'm going through to-night!' then walked on just ahead of her. She gave no sign of eagerness, but she was thinking: Was he a Federal agent to whom she could intrust her message, or was he sent out by the police to entrap her as had often been attempted? The cipher despatch in her hand was torn into strips, each one rolled into a tiny ball. Should she begin to drop them, one by one? In perplexity she glanced up into the man's face. No! Her woman's instinct spoke loud and clear, made her turn into a side street and hurry home. The next day she saw him marching past her house for the front with his Confederate regiment, in the uniform of a junior officer, and knew that once again she had been saved from death."

But although she had many such escapes and her wit was so keen that it was a powerful weapon in any emergency, yet as the conflict between the North and the South deepened the need of caution became more necessary than ever, for Confederate spies were everywhere. In her half-destroyed diary which for many months lay buried near the Van Lew house, over and over again the writer emphasizes her fear of discovery. She says:

"If you spoke in your parlor or chamber, you whispered,—you looked under the lounges and beds. Visitors apparently friendly were treacherous.... Unionists lived ever in a reign of terror. I was afraid even to pass the prison; I have had occasion to stop near it when I dared not look up at the windows. I have turned to speak to a friend and found a detective at my elbow. Strange faces could sometimes be seen peeping around the columns and pillars of the back portico.... Once I went to Jefferson Davis himself to see if we could not obtain some protection.... His private Secretary told me I had better apply to the Mayor.... Captain George Gibbs had succeeded Todd as keeper of the prisoners; so perilous had our situation become that we took him and his family to board with us. They were certainly a great protection.... Such was our life—such was freedom in the Confederacy. I speak what I know." The diary also tells of Mrs. Van Lew's increasing dread of arrest, dear, delicate, loyal lady—for that was constantly spoken of, and reported on the street, while some never hesitated to say she should be hanged.

Another summer came and wore away, and the third year of the war was drawing to a close in the terrible winter of 1863-4. The Union army in the East had twice advanced against the Confederates, to be beaten back at Fredericksburg and at Chancellorsville. In June and July of 1863 Lee began a second invasion of the North, but was defeated at Gettysburg, Pennsylvania. In July, 1863, Vicksburg and Port Hudson were captured and the Mississippi River was in Union hands, but in the following autumn the Confederates of the West defeated the Union army at Chickamauga, after which General Grant took command and was victorious near Chattanooga, and so with alternate hope and despair on both sides the hideous war went on.

Through cipher despatches "Crazy Bet" learned of an intended attempt of Federal officers to escape from Libby Prison, and at once a room in the Van Lew mansion was made ready to secrete them if they achieved their purpose. The room was at the end of one of the big parlors, and dark blankets were hung over its windows; beds were made ready for exhausted occupants, and a low light kept burning day and night in readiness for their possible arrival.

Meanwhile the prisoners in the Libby, desperate because of the horrible conditions in the buildings where they were quartered, were busily constructing a tunnel which ran from the back part of the cellar called "Rat-Hell" to the prison yard. The work was carried on under the direction of Colonel Rose, and his frenzied assistants worked like demons, determined to cut their way through the walls of that grim prison to the light and life of the outer world. At last the tunnel was ready. With quivering excitement over their great adventure added to their exhaustion, the men who were to make their escape, one after another disappeared in the carefully guarded hole leading from the cellar of the prison into a great sewer, and thence into the prison yard. Of this little company of adventurous men eleven Colonels, seven Majors, thirty-two Captains, and fifty-nine Lieutenants escaped before the daring raid was discovered. The news spread like wild-fire through the ranks of the prisoners who were still in the building and among those on duty. Immediately every effort was made by those in charge to re-capture the refugees and bring them back, and as a result, between fifty and sixty of them were once again imprisoned in the squalid cells of the Libby.

Just at that time John Van Lew, Betty's brother, was conscripted into the Confederate army, and although unfit for military duty because of his delicate health, he was at once sent to Camp Lee. As he was a keen sympathizer with his sister's Union interests, as soon as he was sent to the Confederate camp he deserted and fled to the home of a family who lived on the outskirts of the city, who were both Union sympathizers and friends of his sister's. They hid him carefully, and Betty at once came to aid in planning for his escape from the city. Unfortunately it was the night of the escape of the Federal prisoners from the Libby, so a doubly strong guard was set over every exit from Richmond, making escape impossible. Here was a difficult situation! Betty Van Lew knew that some way out of the dilemma must be found; for the house where her brother was secreted would surely be searched for the escaped refugees, and it would go hard with those who were concealing him if they were discovered harboring a deserter.

With quick wit she immediately presented herself at General Winder's office, where she used her diplomatic powers so successfully that the general was entirely convinced of John Van Lew's unfit physical condition for military service, and promised to make every effort toward his exemption. When all efforts proved unavailing, the general took him into his own regiment, and "the Union sympathizer never wore a Confederate uniform, and only once shouldered a Confederate musket, when on a great panic day he stood, a figurehead guard at the door of a government department. At last, in 1864, when even General Winder could not longer protect him from active service at the front, Van Lew deserted again, and served with the Federal Army until after the fall of Richmond."

Meanwhile the old Van Lew house, in its capacity of Secret Service station, was a hive of industry, which was carried on with such smooth and silent secrecy that no one knew what went on in its great rooms. And watching over all those who came and went on legitimate business, or as agents of the Federal Government on secret missions, was a woman, alert of body, keen of mind, standing at her post by day and by night. After all members of her household were safely locked in their rooms for the night, the Spy would creep down, barefooted, to the big library with its ornamented iron fireplace. On either side of this fireplace were two columns, on each of which was a small, carved figure of a lion. Possibly by accident—probably by design, one of these figures was loosened so that it could be raised like a box-lid, and in the darkness of the night the swift, silent figure of the Spy would steal into the big room, lift the carved lion, deftly slip a message in cipher into the cavity beneath the figure and cautiously creep away, with never a creaking board to reveal her coming or going.

With equal caution and swift dexterity, early the next morning an old negro servant would steal into the room, duster and broom in hand, to do his cleaning. Into every corner of the room he would peer, to be sure there were no watching eyes, then he would slip over to the fireplace, lift the lion, draw out the cipher message, place it sometimes in his mouth, sometimes in his shoe, and as soon as his morning chores were done he would be seen plodding down the dusty road leading to the farm, where some one was eagerly waiting for the tidings he carried. Well had the Spy trained her messengers!

The old mansion had also hidden protection for larger bodies than could be concealed under the recumbent lion by the fireplace. Up under the sloping roof, between the west wall of the garret and the tiles, was a long, narrow room, which was probably built at the order of Betty Van Lew, that she might have a safe shelter for Union refugees. All through the war gossip was rife concerning the Van Lews and their movements, and there were many rumors that the old mansion had a secret hiding-place, but this could never be proved. Besides those whom it sheltered from time to time, and the one whose thought had planned it, only one other person knew of the existence of that garret room, and for long years she was too frightened to tell what she had seen in an unexpected moment.

Betty Van Lew's niece was visiting in the old house during the blackest period of the struggle between the North and South. She was a little girl, and her bump of curiosity was well developed. After tossing restlessly in bed on a hot night, she opened her door in order to get some air. To her surprise she saw Aunt Betty tiptoeing through the other end of the dark hall, carrying something in her hand. With equal stealth the curious child followed the creeping figure up through the dark, silent house into the garret—saw a hand reach behind an old chest of drawers standing against the wall in the garret, and with utter amaze saw a black hole in the wall yawn before her eyes. There stood her aunt before the opening of the wall, shading with cautious hand the candle she carried, while facing her stood a gaunt, hollow-eyed, bearded man in uniform reaching out a greedy hand for the food on the plate. The man saw the child's eyes burning through the darkness back of the older woman, but she put a chubby finger on her lip, and ran away before he had a chance to realize that she was flesh and blood and not an apparition. Panting, she ran swiftly down the long staircase and, with her heart beating fast from fright, flung herself on the bed and buried her head in the pillows, lying there for a long time, so it seemed to her.

Then, scarcely daring to breathe, for fear of being discovered, she stole out of bed again, opened her door, and once more crept up through the silent mansion, this time alone. In a moment she stood outside the place where the hole in the wall had opened before her amazed vision. Not a sound in the great, dark garret! Putting her mouth close to the partition she called softly to the soldier, and presently a deep voice told her how to press the spring and open the secret door. Then, a shivering but determined little white-robed figure, she stood before the yawning chasm and talked with the big, Union soldier, who seemed delighted at the sound of his own voice, and years afterward she remembered how he had looked as he said:

"My! what a spanking you would have got if your aunt had turned around!" She did not dare to stand there talking to him long, for she was old enough to realize that there must be a reason for his being in hiding, and that if the secret room should be discovered it might bring unhappiness to her aunt. So in a very few moments the little white-gowned figure flitted silently, swiftly down-stairs again, and no one knew until years later of that midnight excursion of hers—or of the secret room, for which the old house was thoroughly searched more than once.

The winter of 1863-4 was one full of tense situations and of many alarms for both Confederates and Unionists. In February, after the daring escape of the Federal officers from the Libby, there were several alarms, which roused young and old to the defense of the city. The enemy made a movement to attack the city on the east side, but were driven back. Again on the 29th of the month, the bells all rang to call men to service. The city battalions responded, while General Wilcox ordered all men who were in the city on furlough, and all who could bear arms, out to protect the city, for Kilpatrick was attempting a raid on Richmond, along Brook turnpike. "But while he was dreaming of taking Richmond, Gen. Wade Hampton suddenly appeared with his troops and routed him, taking three hundred and fifty prisoners, killing and wounding many, and capturing a large number of horses."

Then came an event for which the Federal sympathizers, and especially those in the Union Secret Service, had prepared with all the caution and secrecy possible, trying to perfect every detail to such a degree that failure would be impossible. To release all Federal prisoners in Richmond—this was but a part of the audacious scheme in which Betty Van Lew and a Union sympathizer called "Quaker," for purposes of disguise, played an important part.

On the 28th of February, 1864, Col. Ulric Dahlgren left Stevensburg with a company of men, selected from brigades and regiments, as a picked command to attempt a desperate undertaking. At Hanovertown he crossed with his men, all dressed in Confederate uniforms, confidently expecting to get into Richmond by stealth. Unfortunately their movements were discovered, and when they rode along through the woods near the road at Old Church, in their disguise, a party of Confederates in ambush opened fire on them, captured ninety white men and thirty-five negroes, and killed poor little crippled Dahlgren, a small, pale young officer, who "rode with crutches strapped to his saddle, and with an artificial leg in the stirrup, as he had lost a limb a few months before. His death was as patriotic as was his desperate attempt, for bravely his eager band rode into the ambush—there was a volley of shots from the thicket by the roadside, and the young colonel fell from his horse, dead. Some of his men managed to escape, but most of them were captured."

In Dahlgren's pocket was found an order to all of his men and officers. To the officers he said:

"We will have a desperate fight, but stand up to it. When it does come, all will be well. We hope to release the prisoners from Belle Isle first, and having seen them fairly well started, we will cross James River into Richmond, destroying the bridges after us, and exhorting the released prisoners to destroy and burn the hateful city, and do not allow the rebel leader Davis and his traitorous crew to escape."

To his guides and runners he said:

"Be prepared with oakum, turpentine, and torpedoes. Destroy everything that can be used by the rebels. Shoot horses and cattle, destroy the railroads and the canal, burn the city, leave only the hospitals, and kill Jeff Davis and his Cabinet."

A dangerous plan indeed! Small wonder that when its details became known in their diabolical cruelty, the people of Richmond cried out for revenge, and the hanging of the prisoners; but this was not heeded by the officials, who had a saner judgment.

The raid had failed! Ulric Dahlgren had lost his life in a daring attempt to which he was evidently urged by Betty Van Lew and the so-called Quaker. Bit by bit the reasons for its failure filtered through to the Spy, chief of which was the treachery of Dahlgren's guide, by which the forces of the raiders, after separating in two parts for the attack, lost each other and were never able to unite. The brave, crippled young commander riding fearlessly on to within five miles of the city into the ambush, his command falling under the volley of shots from a hidden enemy—when these details reached Betty Van Lew her anguish was unbearable, for she had counted on success instead of failure. And now, there was work to do! Pacing the floor, she made her plans, and with swift daring carried them out.

Dahlgren was buried on the very spot where he fell; but a few days later the body was taken to Richmond by order of the Confederate government, where it lay for some hours at the York River railroad station. Then, at midnight, it was taken away by the city officials and buried, no one knew where. But Betty Van Lew says in her diary: "The heart of every Unionist was stirred to its depths ... and to discover the hidden grave and remove his honored dust to friendly care was decided upon."

Admiral Dahlgren, father of the unfortunate colonel, sent one hundred dollars in gold to Jefferson Davis, asking that the body of his son be sent to him. The order was at once given to the chief of police, with the added command to have the body placed in a decent coffin; but when the police went to carry out the order, taking with them the soldiers who had buried Dahlgren, the grave was empty!

Through the daring act of Secret Service agents, doubtless, and of Betty Van Lew's assistants, on a bitter cold and stormy night, two Union sympathizers went out to the grave, the location of which had been cleverly discovered by the Unionists. The body of young Dahlgren was quickly taken up and carried to a work-shop belonging to Mr. William Rowley, who lived a short distance in the country. He watched over the remains all night, and during the hours of darkness more than one Union sympathizer stole out to the shop to pay their last respects to the pathetic young victim of the attempted raid. At dawn the body was placed in a metallic coffin and put on a wagon, under a load of young peach-trees, which entirely concealed the casket. Then Mr. Rowley, who was a man of iron nerves and great courage, jumped to the driver's seat and bravely drove the wagon with its precious freight out of Richmond, past the pickets, without the visible trembling of an eye-lash to betray his dangerous mission.

"As he had feared, at the last picket post, he was stopped and challenged. His wagon must be searched. Was his brave hazard lost? As he waited for the search to be made which would sign his death warrant, one of the guards recognized him as an old acquaintance, and began a lively conversation with him. Other wagons came up, were searched, and went on. Presently the Lieutenant came from his tent and called to the guard to 'Search that man and let him go!'

"The guard looked with interest at the well-packed load, and remarked that it would be a shame to tear up those trees.

"Rowley gave no sign of fear or nervousness. Nonchalantly he said that he had not expected them to be disturbed, but that he knew a soldier's duty.

"Another wagon drove up, was searched, and sent on. Again the Lieutenant gave an order to 'search the man so that he can go!' Could anything save him now? Rowley wondered. If he had not been a born actor he would have shown some sign of the terrible strain he was under as he waited for the discovery of his hidden burden.

"A moment of agonizing suspense, then the guard said, in a low voice, 'Go on!' and Rowley, without search, went on with his concealed burden.

"Meanwhile, two accomplices had flanked the picket, and they presently joined Rowley and showed him the way to a farm not far away, where a grave was hastily dug and the coffin lowered into it. Two loyal women helped to fill it in, and planted over it one of the peach-trees which had so successfully prevented discovery. So ended the Dahlgren raid—and so the Spy had been foiled in one of the most daring and colossal plots with which she was connected. Because of the stealing of the young Colonel's body, Admiral Dahlgren's wish could not be complied with until after the war."

The raid had failed, and with the return of spring, the Union Army was closing in around Richmond, which made it an easier matter for Betty Van Lew to communicate with the Union generals, especially with General Grant, through his Chief of Secret Service. As the weary months wore away, more than once the Spy was in an agony of suspense, when it seemed as if some one of her plots was about to bring a revelation of her secret activities; as if disclosure by some traitor was inevitable; but in every case she was saved from danger, and was able to continue her work for the Union.

And now the Confederate forces were ransacking the South in search of horses, of which they were sorely in need. The Spy quickly hid her one remaining animal in the smoke-house, but it was not safe there. Confederate agents were prowling about the city, searching every building in which a horse could be secreted. In the dead of night Betty Van Lew led her steed, with feet wrapped in cloths to prevent noise, from the smoke-house into the old mansion itself, and stabled it in the study, where she had covered the floor with a thick layer of straw to deaden any sound of stamping hoofs. And the horse in his palatial residence was not discovered.

General Grant was now at the head of all the armies of the United States, and to him was given the duty of attacking Lee. General Sherman was at the head of a large force in the West, and his duty was to crush the force of General Johnston.

On the fourth of May, 1864, each general began his task. Sherman attacked Johnston, and step by step drove him through the mountains to Atlanta, where Johnston was removed, and his army from that time was led by

General Hood. After trying in vain to beat Sherman, he turned and started toward Tennessee, hoping to draw Sherman after him. But he did not succeed; Sherman sent Thomas, the "Rock of Chickamauga," to deal with Hood, and in December he destroyed Hood's army in a terrible battle at Nashville. Meanwhile Sherman started to march from Atlanta to the sea, his army advancing in four columns, covering a stretch of country miles wide. They tore up the railroads, destroyed the bridges, and finally occupied Savannah. There Sherman stayed for a month, during which his soldiers became impatient. Whenever he passed them they would shout: "Uncle Billy, I guess Grant is waiting for us in Richmond!" And on the first of February they resumed their march to North Carolina.

Grant, meanwhile, had begun his attack on Lee, on the same day that Sherman had marched against Johnston. Starting from a place called Culpepper Court House, Grant's army entered the Wilderness, a tract of country covered with a dense growth of oak and pine, and after much hard fighting closed in around Richmond, laying siege to Petersburg. Bravely Lee and his gallant men resisted the Union forces until April, 1865, when, foreseeing the tragic end ahead, Lee left Richmond and marched westward. Grant followed, and on the ninth of April Lee surrendered his army at Appomattox Court House. Johnston surrendered to Sherman near Raleigh, in North Carolina, about two weeks later, and in May Jefferson Davis was taken prisoner.

This ended the war. The Confederacy fell to pieces, and the Union was saved. "In the hearts of all Union sympathizers was a passionate exultation that the United States was once again under one government; but what a day of sorrowing was that for loyal Southerners!"

It is said that on Sunday, the second of April, when the end was in sight, children took their places in the Sunday Schools, and congregations gathered as usual in the churches, united in their fervent prayers for their country and their soldiers. The worshipping congregation of St. Paul's Church was disturbed by the sight of a messenger who walked up the middle aisle to the pew where Jefferson Davis was sitting, spoke hastily to him, then went briskly out of the church. What could it mean?

"Ah!" says an historian, "the most sadly memorable day in Richmond's history was at hand ... the day which for four long years had hung over the city like a dreadful nightmare had come at last. The message had come from General Lee of the order to evacuate Richmond! Beautiful Richmond to be evacuated! It was like the knell of doom.

"President Davis and the other officers of the Confederate government hastily prepared to leave, and to carry such records and stores as they were able. The officers of the State government and the soldiers were preparing to march. The news of the evacuation swept over the city, spreading dismay and doom as it went. The people began to collect their valuables and hide them or pack them to carry to a place of safety, if any such place could be found; and throughout the city there were scenes of indescribable confusion. The streets were blocked with furniture and other goods which people were trying to move. All government store-houses were thrown open, and what could not be carried away was left to be plundered by those who rushed in to get bacon, clothing, or whatever they could take. The Confederate troops were rapidly moving toward the South.... At one o'clock it became known that under the law of the Confederate Congress all the tobacco and cotton in the city had been ordered burned to keep it out of the hands of the enemy. In vain the Mayor sent a committee to remonstrate against burning the warehouses. No heed was paid to the order, and soon tongues of lurid flame were leaping from building to building, until the conflagration was beyond all control. Men and women were like frenzied demons in their efforts to save property; there was terrific looting. Wagons and carts were hastily loaded with goods; some carried their things in wheel-barrows, some in their arms. Women tugged at barrels of flour, and children vainly tried to move boxes of tobacco. The sidewalks were strewn with silks, satins, bonnets, fancy goods, shoes, and all sorts of merchandise. There was no law and there were no officers; there was only confusion, helpless despair on every side. Before sunrise there was a terrific explosion which shook the whole city; the magazine back of the poorhouse was blown up.... At six o'clock in the morning the evacuation was complete, and the railroad bridges were set on fire."

The conflagration was at its height when the vanguard of the Federal army entered the city, the cavalry galloping at full speed.

"Which is the way to the Capitol?" they shouted, then dashed up Governor Street, while a bitter wail rose from the people of Richmond. "The Yankees! The Yankees! Oh, the Yankees have taken our city!"

As the cry went up, a United States flag was unfurled over the Capitol. At once General Weitzel took command and ordered the soldiers to stop all pillaging and restore order to the city; but it was many hours before the command could be fully carried out. Then and only then did the exhausted, panic-stricken, heart-sick people fully realize the hideous disaster which had come to their beloved city; only when they saw the destruction and desolation wrought by the fire did they fully grasp the awful meaning of the cry, "On to Richmond!" which for four long years had been the watch-word of the Union forces.

And how fared it with the Federal Spy during those hours of anguish for all true Southerners? Betty Van Lew, who had been in close touch with the Union generals, had for some time foreseen the coming climax of the four years' struggle, and weeks earlier she had sent north to General Butler for a huge American flag, eighteen feet long by nine wide, which in some unknown way was successfully carried into Richmond without detection by the picket guard, and safely secreted in the hidden chamber under the Van Lew roof.

And now General Lee had surrendered. Virginia was again to be a State of the Union; came a messenger fleet of foot, cautious of address, bringing breathless tidings to the Spy: "Your house is to be burned—the Confederate soldiers say so. What can you do to prevent it?"

Even as she listened to his excited words, Betty Van Lew's heart was throbbing with joyful excitement, despite the uproar in the city from the constant explosion of shells, the sound of the blowing up of gun-boats in the harbor, and of the powder magazines, which was shaking the foundations of the city, as red flames leaped across the black sky. Even then there was in the heart of the Spy a wild exultation. "Oh, army of my country, how glorious was your welcome!" she exclaims in her diary.

She heard the news that her home was about to be burned. With head erect and flashing eyes she went out alone and stood on the white-pillared portico, a fearless little figure, defying the mob who were gathering to destroy the old mansion which was so dear to her.

"I know you—and you—and you!" she cried out, calling them each by name, and pointing at one after another. "General Grant will be in this city within an hour; if this house is harmed your house shall be burned by noon!" At the fearless words, one by one they turned, muttering, and slunk away, and the Van Lew house was neither burned nor harmed in any way.

The Union troops were coming near now, marching to the center of the city. As the long, dusty line of men in blue swung into Main Street, Betty Van Lew ran up to the secret room under the garret roof, drew out the great flag for which she had sent in anticipation of this day, and when the Union soldiers marched past the historic old mansion, the Stars and Stripes were waving proudly over its portico. The Confederacy was no more!

Despite her bravery, Betty Van Lew's life was now in danger. There was urgent need of special protection for her. Feeling against the northern victors was at fever height in poor, desolated, defeated Richmond, and it is small wonder that one born in their city, who yet stood openly and fearlessly against all that the Southerners held sacred, should have been despised, and worse than that. Realizing her danger, and knowing the priceless service she had rendered the Union generals in the four long years of the war, Colonel Parke, with a force of men, was sent to protect the Spy. To the General's utter amazement they did not find her in the old house. She was found in the deserted Capitol, ransacking it for documents which she feared might be destroyed and which would be a loss to the Government.

As "Crazy Bet" and as a Union Spy, Betty Van Lew's long and remarkable service of her country was ended. The Confederacy was dissolved, and again the flag of the United States of America could rightfully wave from every building in the land. At the beginning of the war, when Betty took on herself the rôle of Federal Secret Service agent, she was light of heart, alert of body and mind. Now, for four years, she had born a heavy burden of fear and of crushing responsibility, for the sake of a cause for which she was willing to sacrifice comfort, wealth and other things which the average woman counts dear, and her heart and brain were weary.

Two weeks after the inauguration of Grant as President of the United States, as a reward for her faithful service, he appointed Betty Van Lew postmistress of Richmond. Well she knew that her enemies would declare the appointment a reward for her services against the Confederacy, and that it would but make her more of an alien in Richmond than ever she had been before. But she was desperately poor, so she accepted the position and for eight years filled it efficiently. When she came in contact with old friends from time to time in a business way, they were politely cold, and in her diary she writes:

"I live, as entirely distinct from the citizens as if I were plague-stricken. Rarely, very rarely, is our door-bell ever rung by any but a pauper or those desiring my service." She adds: "September, 1875, my Mother was taken from me by death. We had not friends enough to be pall-bearers."

When Grant had been succeeded by Hayes as President of the United States, the one-time Spy was obliged to ask for his aid:

"I am hounded down"—she wrote to his private Secretary. "I never, never was so bitterly persecuted; ask the President to protect me from this unwarranted, unmerited, and unprecedented persecution."

From her own point of view, and from that of those who fought for the abolition of slavery and the preservation of the Union, Betty Van Lew's persecution was indeed "unwarranted and unmerited." But there was another side to the matter. Elizabeth Van Lew, although the child of a Northern mother, was also the daughter of John Van Lew, one of Richmond's foremost citizens. The loyalty of the Southerners to the Confederacy and to one another, from their viewpoint, was praiseworthy, and there is every reason why they should have shunned one of Richmond's daughters, who not only approved the cause of the hated Yankees, but who aided the Union generals in their determination to sweep "On to Richmond, to the defeat of the Confederacy."

What to one was loyalty, to the other was treason—what to the Spy was a point of honor, to her old friends was her open and lasting disgrace, and never can the two viewpoints be welded into one, despite the symbol of Union which floats over North and South, making the United States of America one and "indivisible, now and forever!"

Betty Van Lew remained postmistress of Richmond for eight years, then she was removed, and there were black years of poverty and loneliness for her, as she had not laid by a dollar for a day of want, but had given lavishly to all in need, especially to the negroes. She was not able to sell her valuable but unproductive real estate, and was reduced to actual need. "I tell you really and solemnly," she confesses to her diary, "I have suffered for necessary food. I have not one cent in the world. I have stood the brunt alone of a persecution that I believe no other person in the country has endured.... I honestly think that the Government should see that I was sustained."

At last she was given a clerkship in the Post-Office Department at Washington, but after two years this was taken from her, probably for political reasons, and it was recommended that she be given a clerkship of a lower grade. This was done, and although she was cut by the injustice of the act, she clung patiently to her only means of support. Two weeks later, it is said that a Northern newspaper contained an editorial which spoke sneeringly of "A Troublesome Relic," and ended with, "We draw the line at Miss Van Lew." Even though she had not a penny in the world, she could not bear the sting of that, and she wrote her resignation, and went back to the great, lonely house on Church Hill a heart-broken, pitiable woman, who had given her all for what she believed to be the cause of right and justice.

But she could not live in the old mansion alone, and without food or money. In despair she wrote a letter to a friend in the North, a relative of Col. Paul Revere, whom she had helped when he was a prisoner in the Libby. She had to borrow a stamp from an old negro to send the letter, and even worse to her than that was the necessity of revealing her desperate plight. But she need not have felt as she did. As soon as the letter reached its destination there was a hurried indignation meeting of those Boston men who knew what she had done for the Union, and immediately and gladly they provided an ample annuity for her, which placed her beyond all need for the remaining years of her life. This was, of course, a great relief; but even so, it could not ease the burden of her lonely isolation.

"No one will walk with us on the street," she writes; "no one will go with us anywhere.... It grows worse and worse as the years roll on...."

And so the weary months and years went by, and at last, in the old mansion with its haunting memories, nursed by an aged negress to whom she had given freedom years before, Elizabeth Van Lew died. Among her effects there was found on a torn bit of paper this paragraph:

"If I am entitled to the name of 'Spy' because I was in the Secret Service, I accept it willingly, but it will hereafter have to my mind a high and honorable significance. For my loyalty to my country, I have two beautiful names; here I am called 'Traitor,' farther North a 'Spy,' instead of the honored name of Faithful."

And well may she be called "Faithful" by both friend and enemy, for she gave freely of youth and strength, of wealth and her good name, of all that human beings hold most sacred, for that which was to her a consecrated and a just cause.

In the Shockhoe Hill Cemetery of Richmond, there is to be seen a bronze tablet, erected to the noble woman who worked tirelessly and without fitting reward for a cause which she believed to be righteous. The inscription on the tablet reads:

Elizabeth L. Van Lew
1818   1900.

She risked everything that is dear to man—friends,
fortune, comfort, health, life itself;
all for the one absorbing desire of her
heart—that slavery might be abolished and
the Union preserved.

This Boulder

from the Capitol Hill in Boston, is a tribute
from Massachusetts friends.

44

Elizabeth Van Lew was indeed a Spy working against the city of her birth, and the friends of her love and loyalty,—a traitor in one sense of the word; but above all was she tireless in working for her highest ideals, and so is she worthy of respect and honor wherever the Stars and Stripes float free over united America.

IDA LEWIS: THE GIRL WHO KEPT LIME ROCK BURNING; A

HEROIC LIFE-SAVER

"Father has the appointment! We are going to live on the island, and you must all row over to see me very often. Isn't it wonderful?"

A bright-faced young girl, surrounded by a group of schoolmates, poured out her piece of news in such an eager torrent of words that the girls were as excited as the teller of the tale, and there was a chorus of: "Wonderful! Of course we will! What fun to live in that fascinating place! Let's go and see it now!"

No sooner decided than done, and in a very short time there was a fleet of rowboats led by that of Ida Lewis, on their way to the island in Baker's Bay, where the Lime Rock Light stood, of which Captain Hosea Lewis had just been appointed keeper.

Ida, Captain Hosea's daughter, was born at Newport, Rhode Island, on the 25th of February, 1841, and was sent to school there as soon as she was old enough. She was a quick-witted, sure-footed, firm-handed girl from her earliest childhood, and a great lover of the sea in all its changing phases. Often instead of playing games on land with her mates she would beguile some old fisherman to take her out in his fishing dory, and eagerly help him make his hauls, and by the time she was fourteen years old she was an expert in handling the oars, and as tireless a swimmer as could be found in all Newport.

And now her father had been appointed keeper of the Lime Rock Light, the "Ida Lewis" light, as it came to be known in later years, and the girl's home was no longer to be on *terra firma*, but on the rock-ribbed island where the lighthouse stood, whose beacon-light cast strong, steady rays across Baker's Bay, to the greater Narragansett Bay, of which it is only an arm.

The flock of girls in their boats rowed hard and fast across the silvery water with a steady plash, plash of the dipping oars in the calm bay, and ever Ida Lewis was in the lead, heading toward the island with a straight course, and keeping a close watch for the rocks of which the Bay was full. She would turn her head, toss back her hair, and call out in ringing tones to the flock, "'Ware, shoals!" and obediently they would turn as she turned, follow where she led. Soon her boat ran its sharp bow against the rocky ledge to which they had been steering, and with quick confidence Ida sprang ashore, seized the painter, and drew her boat to a mooring, while the rest of the fleet came to the landing and one after another the girls jumped ashore. Then up the rocky path to the lighthouse filed Ida and her friends, eager to inspect the queer place which was to be Ida's home.

"How perfectly lovely! How odd! Oh, how I wish I were going to live here! Ida, you are lucky—But just think how the wind will howl around the house in a storm! Will your father ever let you tend the light, do you think?"

The questions were not answered, and those who asked them did not expect a response. They all chattered on at the same time, while they inspected every nook and corner of their friend's new home. It was a small place, that house on Lime Rock, built to house the light-keeper's family, but one which could well answer to the name of "home" to one as fond of the sea as was Ida Lewis. On the narrow promontory, with the waves of the quiet bay lapping its rocky shores, the two-story white house stood like a sea-gull poised for flight. A living-room, with wide windows opening out on the bay it had, and simple bedrooms where one could be lulled to sleep by the lapping of waters on every side, while at the front of the house stood the tower from which the light sent its searching beams to guide mariners trying to enter the Newport harbor.

The girls climbed the spiral staircase leading up to the light, and looked with wonder not unmixed with awe at the great lamp which was always filled and trimmed for immediate use—saw the large bell which tolled continuously during storm or fog; then they went down again to the sunshiny out of doors, and were shown the boat-house, not so far back of the light that it would be difficult to reach in a storm.

It was all a fairy residence to those young girls, and little could they imagine that bright-eyed Ida, who was about to become a lighthouse-keeper's daughter, was to be known in later years as the Grace Darling of America, because of her heroic life on that small promontory in Baker's Bay!

The Lewis family settled in the lighthouse as speedily as possible, and when their simple household goods were arranged, the island home was a pretty and a comfortable place, where the howling winds of winter or the drenching, depressing fogs of all seasons would have no chance to take from the homelike cheer inside, no matter how severe they were. Books, pictures, a large rag rug, a model of a sloop, made by Captain Hosea, family portraits belonging to his wife—whose girlhood had been spent on Block Island as the daughter of Dr. Aaron C. Wiley, and to whose ears the noise of wind and waves was the music of remembered girlhood—all these added to the simple interior of the lighthouse, while out of doors there was, as Ida said, "All the sea, all the sky, all the joy of the great free world, and plenty of room to enjoy it!"

And enjoy it she certainly did, although she had to rise early and eat the plainest of fare, for the pay of a lighthouse-keeper would not allow of many luxuries. At night she was in bed and fast asleep before her friends on land had even thought of leaving their amusements or occupations for sleep. It was a healthy life, and Ida grew broad of shoulders, heavier in weight and as muscular as a boy. Every morning she inspected her boat, and if it needed bailing out or cleaning she was at work on it before breakfast; then at the appointed hour she was ready to row her younger brothers and sisters to the mainland to school. Like a little housekeeper, after dropping them, she went to market in Newport for her mother, and sometimes her boat would be seen crossing the bay more than once a morning, if there were many supplies to be carried over; then the children must be rowed back after school hours. Small wonder that Ida came to know every rock in the bay, and was able to steer her boat safely in and out among the many obstructions which were a peril to less intelligent mariners.

Towering over all neighboring buildings, the Lime Rock Light stood on its rocky ledge, clearly seen by men on vessels entering or leaving Narragansett Bay, and by officers and men at Fort Adams, as well as by those who lived within sight of the light, and it came to be a daily word, "Watch for the girl," for Ida sturdily rowed across the bay, no matter how furious the storm, how dense the fog.

Late one afternoon, after visiting a friend, she was rowing from Newport at the hour when a snub-nosed schooner sailed slowly into the harbor on its way from New York to Newport with every sign of distress visible among its crew, for not even the Captain knew where lay the channel of safety between the perilous rocks, and the fog was thick.

Ida saw the schooner, and guessed its dilemma. Rowing as close to it as she could, she signaled to the captain to follow her, and her words were carried to him on the heavy air:

"Come on! Don't be afraid!"

Obediently he went on, as the girl directed, and reached the dock of his destination in safety, where he shook hands heartily with his bright-eyed guide before she pushed off again for her island home. Later he spread the news among his mates that there was a "boss in Baker's Bay who knew what she was about," and his advice was, "In danger look for the dark-haired girl in a row-boat and follow her."

This came to be the accepted fashion among captains of the schooners which in that day plied so frequently between New York and Newport, and many a letter of thanks, or a more substantial remembrance, did she receive from some one she had piloted across the angry bay.

Soldiers trying to reach the fort, or sailors anxious to row out to their ships, always found a ready ferry-woman in Ida, and before the Lewis family had been in the lighthouse for many months she was one of the most popular young persons on land or sea within many miles—for who had ever before seen such a seaworthy young mariner as she, or where could such a fund of nautical wisdom be discovered as was stored in her clear head? This question was asked in affectionate pride by more than one good seaman who had become Ida's intimate friend at the close of her first year on Lime Rock, while all the skippers had an intense admiration for the girl who not only handled her life-boat with a man's skill, but who kept the light filled and trimmed and burning to save her father steps, now that he was crippled with rheumatism.

The heat of summer had given place to the crisp coolness of a glorious October day as Ida was just starting to row to the mainland to do an errand for her mother. She looked out of the window, across the bay, to see if there was any prospect of a shower, and her keen eyes glimpsed a sight that made her hurry for the glass. Looking through it, she gave a sharp cry and rushed to the door.

"What is it, daughter?" the captain queried.

But Ida was already out of the house. So he hobbled slowly to the window and, with the use of the glass Ida had dropped, saw his energetic child push the life-boat out of its shelter, drag it to the shore, jump in and row rapidly to the middle of the bay where a pleasure-boat had capsized. There were four men in the water, struggling with the high waves which momentarily threatened to overcome them. When Ida reached them in her life-boat, two were clinging to the overturned craft, and two were making a desperate effort to swim toward shore. The watching captain, through his glass, saw Ida row close to the capsized boat and with strong, steady hands pull and drag one after another of the men into her boat. When they were all in, she rowed with sure

46

strokes back across the stormy water, carrying her load of human freight to shore and receiving their thanks as modestly as if she had not done a remarkable deed for a girl of seventeen. A very fine piece of work was Ida's first rescue, but by no means her last. She loved to row out in a storm and dare the winds and waves to do their worst, and she grew to think her mission a clear one, as life-saver of the light.

A year after her first experience as life-saver, her father, who had recently been paralyzed, died, and so capable was his eighteen-year-old daughter in doing his duties that she was allowed to continue in the care of the light until her father's successor should be appointed. When the news came to her, Ida's eyes gleamed, as if in anticipation of some happy event, and to her devoted Newfoundland dog she exclaimed: "We love it too well to give it up to anybody; don't we, doggie dear? We will succeed to ourselves!" And she did succeed to herself, being finally made keeper of the light by special act of Congress—the appointment being conferred upon her in 1879 by General Sherman as a compliment to her ability and bravery; doubtless because of the recommendation of those fishermen and seamen whose respect for the brave girl was great and who did not wish the government to remove her. In any case, she was chosen for the responsible position as successor to her father, and to herself, as she quaintly put it, and more and more she became devoted to every stone of the small promontory, and to every smallest duty in connection with her work and her island home.

Winter and summer passed in the regular routine of her daily duties as keeper of the light, and every time she lighted the big lamp whose beams shone out over the waters with such comforting gleams for watching mariners she was filled with assurance that hers was the greatest and most interesting mission in the world.

Winter came with its howling winds and frozen bay. A terrific storm was blowing from the north; snow was driving from every direction and it was hardly possible to stand on one's feet because of the fury of the gale. Ida lighted her beacon of warning to ships at sea, and rejoiced as she saw its glowing rays flash out over the turbulent waters. Then she went down into the cozy kitchen and speedily ate a simple supper prepared by her mother. How the wind shrieked around the little house on the island! Ida hastily raised the curtain, to see how heavily it was storming, and she gave an exclamation of surprise; then ran up the spiral stairway to the tower, where in the rays of the steady light she could see more clearly. Far out on the waves, beyond the frozen surface of the inner bay, she saw a light skiff bobbing up and down, the toy of wind and wave; in it by the aid of her powerful glass she could see a stiff, still figure. A man had been overcome by the cold—he would die if he were not rescued at once. Quick as a flash she was down-stairs, in the boat-house, had pulled out the boat, although it was a hard task in such a storm even for one as strong as she, and soon was on her way across that part of the bay which was not frozen. Up and down on the storm-tossed waves her craft tossed, now righting itself, now almost submerged—but Ida pulled on with strong sure strokes, and drew alongside of the bobbing skiff—took hold of it, drew it to the side of her own boat, and, looking into the face of the man in it, saw that he must be rowed to land as quickly as possible if he were to be saved. She saved him. When he regained consciousness he found himself propped up before the warm fire in the lighthouse kitchen, with the most delicious feeling of languor stealing through his whole frame, instead of the cruel numbness which had been the last sensation before he became unconscious. And it added materially to his enjoyment that a bright-eyed, dark-haired young woman hovered around him, ministering to his wants in a delightful way.

The young lighthouse-keeper's next rescue was of a soldier from the Fort Adams garrison who, in trying to cross the harbor in a small boat, was thrown into the bay by the force of the waves, and would have been drowned, as he was not a good swimmer, had not Ida's keen eyes seen him and she gone instantly to his rescue. He was a heavy man, and Ida tried in vain to lift him into her boat, but was not strong enough. What should she do? The great waves were lashing against the boats in such a fury that what was done must be done quickly. With ready wit she threw a rope around his body under the arm-pits, and towed him to shore as hard and fast as she could, at the same time watching closely that his head did not go under water. It was a man-sized job, but Ida accomplished it, and, seeing his exhaustion when she reached shore, she called two men, who aided in resuscitating him.

"Who towed him in?" asked one of them, who was a stranger to Ida.

"I did," she replied.

"Ah, go on!" he said, incredulously. "A girl like you doing that! Tell me something I can believe!"

Ida laughed and turned to the other man. "He will tell you what I have done and what I can do, even if I am a girl!" she said; and the seaman, just landed from a coastwise steamer, looked at her with admiration tinged with awe. "She's the boss of these parts," said his companion, "and the prettiest life-saver on the coast. Just try it yourself and see!"

As the man did not seem to care about risking his life to have it saved, even by Ida Lewis, he went his way, but whenever his steamer touched at Newport after that he always paid his respects to the "prettiest life-saver on the coast."

Twelve months went by, with ever-increasing fame for the girl keeper of Lime Rock Light who had become one of the features of the vicinity, to meet and talk with whom many a tourist lengthened a stay in Newport, and Ida enjoyed meeting them and showing them her light and her home and her boat and her dog and all her other treasures, while in return they told her many interesting things about the great world beyond the beams of her light.

Up in the tower one day—it was in the autumn of 1867—she was looking out over the bay, fearing trouble for some vessel, as a furious storm was raging, and the wind was blowing snow in such white sheets that few captains could make their way among the rocks of the harbor without difficulty, while any one foolish enough to set out in a rowboat would find it impossible to reach the shore.

Out flashed the rays of the beacon-light, and far off on the tempestuous waves Ida saw what seemed to be two men in a boat with a load of sheep. The wind was howling, and borne on its shrieking Ida fancied she could hear the moans of the men and the frightened beasts.

One quick look at her light, to make sure that it was all right to leave, then down ran the life-saver to her self-appointed work. Never was there such a gale blowing in Narragansett Bay, and in the smaller bay white-capped waves and gusts of wind and rain added to biting, stinging cold made it almost impossible even for sturdy Ida to struggle out from the boat-house, to launch her rowboat on the stormy sea. But she never gave in to any obstacles, and soon her little boat could be seen making slow headway across the bay, in the direction of the drifting men and their cargo of sheep.

Now the wind drove her back, now it blew her small craft to one side and the other, but steadily, though slowly, she gained on herself, and at last she reached the men, who could make no headway in the teeth of such a gale, and were simply drifting and watching Ida's acts with incredulous wonder. A young girl—come to rescue them in such a storm as this! Quickly she helped them to climb into her boat, and took up her oars. One man protested. "But the sheep," he said.

"Leave them to me!" commanded Ida, sternly, rowing as fast as she could, her dark hair streaming over her shoulders and her cheeks rose-red from the stinging cold of the air. Neither man ventured another word. Reaching the rocky coast of the island, Ida sprang out after them, pointed out the kitchen door, and said:

"Stay in there and get warm till I come back."

"But—" began one.

Ida was already out of hearing, and the men whose lives had been saved did as they had been told, and in the warm kitchen awaited the coming of their rescuer. In an hour there were footsteps outside, the door opened, and a glowing girl stepped in out of the bitter gale, stamping her almost frozen feet and holding out her benumbed hands to the glowing fire.

"Well, they are all safe on land," she said. "I think they had better be left in the boat-house overnight. The wind is in the right quarter for a clear day to-morrow; then you can put out again."

There was no reply. A girl like this keeper of the Lime Rock Light left no room for pretty compliments, but made a man feel that if she could do such deeds with simple courage, what could he not do with such a spirit as hers! No one ever paid Ida Lewis higher praise than these two rough men when, on leaving, they each gripped her hand and the spokesman said:

"Whenever I see your light shining, I'll put up a prayer for its keeper, and thanking you for what you did for us, ma'am—if my little one's a girl, she will be Ida Lewis!"

Up spoke his comrade: "My daughter's twelve year old come September next, and I hope she'll be your kind. It'd make a new kind of a world to have such!"

While such praise did not turn Ida's very level head, or make her vain, it gave her a deep satisfaction and a tremendous sense of responsibility in her beloved occupation.

Two years went by, and Ida Lewis was a name which commanded respect throughout Rhode Island because of her work for the government, and there was scarcely a day when she did not direct some wandering boatman or give valuable aid to a distressed seafarer, but from the day she brought the men and their load of sheep to shore it was a year before there was any need of such aid as she had given them. Then on a day never to be forgotten by those to whose rescue she went, she saw two of the soldiers who were stationed at Fort Adams rowing toward the fort from Newport. A young lad was at the oars, and he showed that he was not in any way experienced as a boatman. A sudden squall overtook the small boat in mid-bay, and, as Ida Lewis looked at it, it capsized. At the moment Ida happened to be without hat or coat, or even shoes. Rushing to the boat-house, she took her staunch friend to the shore, and launched out in the wild squall under an inky-black sky; and she had to row against a wind that drove her back time after time. Finally she reached the wreck, only to find the boy had gone under. The soldiers were clinging to the bobbing keel of the boat, and Ida grasped them with a firm, practised hand, while at the same time managing to keep her own boat near enough so that when a wave washed them together she was able to help the exhausted soldiers to climb into it. They were unable to speak, and one of them was so exhausted that she feared she could not get him to land in time to resuscitate him.

With wind-blown hair, and eyes dark with determination, she rowed as she had never rowed before, and at last her boat touched the rocky home ledge. Out she jumped, and in less time than it takes to tell it, she had the men before her fire, wrapped in blankets. One of them was unconscious for such a long time that his rescuer was wondering what was best to do—to take the risk of leaving him and row to the mainland for a doctor, or to take the risk of doing for him with her own inexperienced hands. Just then his blue eyes opened, and after a drink of stimulant he slowly revived, and at last was able to talk coherently. The storm was still raging and the men remained on the lighthouse ledge with the girl rescuer, for whom they showed open admiration; then, when the clouds lifted and the moon shone wanly through the rift, they took their own boat and rowed off to the fort. But they were staunch friends of Ida Lewis from that day, and she enjoyed many a chat with them, and had more than one pleasant afternoon on the mainland with them when they were off duty.

At another time she was out in her boat in a bad storm, when through the dense darkness she heard cries of, "Help! help!" and, rowing in the direction from which the cries came, she found three men in the water clinging to the keel of an overturned boat. With her usual promptness in an emergency, she dragged them all into her boat and took them to shore. Another day, from the lighthouse tower, she saw the slender figure of a man clinging to a spindle which was a mile and a half from the lighthouse. In a very short time he would be too exhausted to hold on any longer. She must hurry, hurry! With flying feet she made her boat ready; with firm strokes she rowed out to the spindle, rescued the man and bore him safely to shore.

At this time Ida Lewis was so well known as being always on hand in any emergency that it was taken as a matter of course to have her appear out of the sky, as one's preserver, and the man, though extremely grateful, did not seem as astonished as he might have otherwise been to be saved from such a death by a young girl who apparently dropped from the skies just to rescue him.

In all of these experiences, when she was able to save men's lives at the risk of her own, and was successful by reason of her quick wit and self-forgetful courage, despite the grave chances she took, she never had a single fright about her own safety, but simply flew across the bay at any time of day or night at the sight of a speck on the water which to her trained eye was a human being in danger.

Winter's hand had laid its glittering mantle of ice on Baker's Bay, and on a glorious sunlit morning Ida was ready to start to Newport to make some necessary purchases. When she was just about to push her boat off the rocks she looked over the bay with the intent, piercing glance for which she was famous among fisher-folk, who declared she could "see out of the back of her head," and caught a glimpse of uniforms, of struggling figures in that part of the bay which was so shallow as to be always frozen in mid-winter, and which the soldiers all knew to be dangerous to cross. But there were two of them, waving their arms in frantic appeal for help, as they tried to keep from going under in the icy water of the bay.

There was not a moment to lose. Ida put out from shore, rowed swiftly to a point as near the drowning and freezing men as was possible, then with her oars broke the ice sufficiently to make a channel for her boat. As she came near to them she found that the insecure ice, melted by the strong sun, had given way under them, while they were evidently trying to take a short cut to Fort Adams from Newport.

It was hard work and quick work for Ida's experienced hands to get them into the life-boat; and so nearly frozen were they that she was obliged to rest on her oars, at the same time rubbing their numb limbs as well as she could. Then she rowed for shore faster than she had ever rowed but once before, and, as she told afterward:

"I flew for restoratives and hot water, and worked so hard and so fast, rubbing them and heating them, that it was not long before they came to life again and were sitting up in front of the fire, apologizing for their folly, and promising that they would never again give me such a piece of work to do, or cross the bay in winter at a point where they knew it was a risk." She added, naïvely: "They were as penitent as naughty children, so I took advantage of it and gave them a lecture on things soldiers ought not to do, among them drinking whisky—even with the good excuse of being cold—and showing them quite plainly that this scare they had had came from that bad habit. They seemed very sorry, and when they got up to go, they saluted me as if I were their captain. Then off they went to the fort."

Several days later she received a letter of thanks from the officers at Fort Adams, and a gold watch from the men she had rescued "in grateful appreciation of a woman's heroism."

On through the long years Ida Lewis, with hair growing slowly a little grayer, and with arms a little less equal to the burden of rowing a heavy boat through fierce winter gales, was faithful to her duties as keeper of the light, now never spoken of as the Lime Rock Light, but always as the Ida Lewis Light; and, although she was always averse to notoriety, yet she was forced to accept the penalty of her brave deeds, and welcome the thousands of tourists who now swarmed daily over the promontory and insisted on a personal talk with the keeper of the light. Had it not been for Mrs. Lewis, both aged and feeble, but able to meet and show the visitors over the island, Ida would have had no privacy at all and no time for her work.

Although she always disliked praise or publicity, yet she accepted official recognition of her faithful work with real appreciation, and it was touching to see her joy when one day she received a letter bearing the signature of the Secretary of the Treasury, notifying her that the gold life-saving medal had been awarded to her—and stating that she was the only woman in America upon whom the honor had been conferred! At a later date she also received three silver medals: gifts from the State of Rhode Island, and from the Humane Society of Massachusetts, and also from the New York Life-Saving Association. All these recognitions of her achievements Ida Lewis received with shining eyes and wonder that such praise should have come to her for the simple performance of her duty. "Any one would rescue a drowning man, of course," she said. "I just happen to be where I see them first!"

But although she was so modest, and although so many honors were heaped upon her, none ever meant to her what the first expression of public appreciation meant, shown by the citizens of Rhode Island.

An invitation had been sent to her, asking her to be present at the Custom-House at Newport on a certain day in 1869. She accepted the invitation, and went at the appointed hour without much thought about the matter. When she reached the Custom-House, to her surprise a committee of prominent Newport residents met her and escorted her to a seat on the platform, from which she looked down on a vast audience, all staring with evident curiosity at the slight, dark-haired woman in whose honor the throng had come together. There were speeches so filled with praise of her deeds that Ida Lewis would have liked to fly from the sight of the applauding crowd; but instead must sit and listen. The speeches at an end, there was a moment's pause; then she found herself on her feet, amid a chorus of cheers, being presented with a magnificent new life-boat, the *Rescue*, a gift from the citizens of Newport as a slight recognition of her acts of bravery.

Ida never knew all she said in response to the presentation speech; she only knew that tears streamed down her cheeks as she gripped a man's hand and said, "Thank you, thank you—I don't deserve it!" over and over again, while the audience stood up and applauded to the echo. As if that were not enough to overcome any young woman, as she left the building, James Fisk, Jr., approached her and, grasping her hand warmly, told her that there was to be a new boat-house built back of the light, large enough for her beautiful new boat.

It was late that night before Ida fell asleep, lulled at last by the wind and the lapping of the waves, and thinking with intense happiness not of her own achievements, but of the pride and joy with which her mother received the account of her daughter's ovation and gift, and her words rang in Ida's ears above the noise of the waters, "Your father would be so proud, dear!"

For fifty-three years Ida Lewis remained the faithful keeper of her beloved light, and because of her healthy, out-of-door life we catch a glimpse of the woman of sixty-five which reminds us strongly of the girl who led the way to the lighthouse point on that day in 1841, to show her new home to her schoolmates. In the face of howling winds and winter gales she had snatched twenty-three lives from the jaws of death, and in her sixty-fifth year she was at her old work.

A woman had rowed out to the light from Newport, and when her boat had almost reached the pier which had been erected recently on the island shore, she rashly stood on her feet, lost her balance and fell overboard. Ida Lewis, who was rowing in near the pier, instantly came to the rescue, helped the struggling and much frightened woman into her own boat, and then picked up the other one, which was drifting away.

Sixty-five years young, and heroic from earliest girlhood to latest old age! We add our tribute to those heaped on her head by many who knew her in person and others who were acquainted only with her heroic acts, and we rejoice to know that in this year of American crisis we, too, can reflect the heroism of the keeper of Lime Rock Light, for in our hands are greater opportunities for wide service and greater variety of instruments by which to mold the destiny of nations and save life. Proud are we that we, too, are American, as was Ida Lewis, and we can give interest as consecrated and sincere to the work at our hand to-day as she gave, whose daily precepts were work and thrift, and who said, in her quaint way, of the light which had been her beacon of inspiration for so many years of service:

"The light is my child and I know when it needs me, even if I sleep. This is home to me, and I hope the good Lord will take me away when I have to leave it."

Her wish was granted. In the last week of October, 1911, she fell asleep in the lighthouse on Lime Rock, which had been her home for so long, lulled into an eternal repose by the wind and waves, which had for many years been her beloved companions—and as she slept the beacon-light which she had for so long kept trimmed and burning sent out its rays far beyond the little bay where Ida Lewis lay asleep.

Patriotism, faithfulness, service—who can reckon their value? The gleam of Ida Lewis's light flashes inspiration and determination to our hearts to-day.

CLARA BARTON: "THE ANGEL OF THE BATTLEFIELDS"

For several weeks the sound of hammer and saw had been heard on the Barton farm where a new barn was being built. The framework was almost up, and David Barton and his little sister Clara, with a group of friends, were eagerly watching the carpenters, who were just fixing the high rafters to the ridge-pole.

"I dare you to climb to the top, Dave!" suddenly challenged a boy in the group.

David Barton, who was known as the "Buffalo Bill" of the neighborhood, always took a dare. Almost before the challenge had been given his coat was off and he had started toward the new building amid a chorus of cries: "Good for you, Dave!" from the group of young spectators who were always thrilled by his daring exploits. Only the little sister Clara protested.

"Don't, David," she exclaimed. "It isn't safe."

Her warning was not heeded. Up went the sure-footed athlete until he had almost reached the topmost peak of the barn. Crash! a board gave way under his feet, and down to the ground he was hurled, landing on his back on a pile of heavy boards. Limp and lifeless he lay there, a strange contrast to the vigorous young man who had climbed up the building only a few moments earlier, and the accident seemed to paralyze the faculties of those who saw it happen. It was not the builders or the older persons present who spoke first, but small, dark-eyed, determined Clara, who idolized her brother.

"Get mother, and go for the doctor, quick!" she commanded, and in less time than it takes to tell it the entire Barton family had been summoned to the scene of the disaster, and a doctor was bending over the unconscious man.

Dorothy and Sally, the grown-up sisters, hastily obeyed the doctor's orders, and made a room in the farm-house ready for their injured brother, while Stephen Barton and one of the workmen carried him in as gently as possible and laid him on the bed which he was not to leave for many weary months. Examination proved that the injury was a serious one, and there was need of careful and continuous nursing. To the surprise of the whole family, who looked on eleven-year-old Clara, the youngest of them all, as still a baby, when Mrs. Barton made ready to take charge of the sick-room, she found a resolute little figure seated by the bedside, with determination to remain there showing on every line of her expressive face.

"Let me take care of him! I can do it—I want to. Please, oh, please!" pleaded Clara.

At first the coveted permission was denied her, for how could a girl so young take care of a dangerously injured man? But as the weary days and nights of watching wore away and it seemed as if there would be no end to them, from sheer exhaustion the older members of the family yielded their places temporarily to Clara. Then one day when the doctor came and found her in charge, the sick-room was so tidy and quiet, and the young nurse was so clear-minded and ready to obey his slightest order, that when she begged him to let her take care of her brother he gave his hearty permission, and Clara had won her way.

From that time on, through long months, she was the member of the family whose entire thought and care was centered in the invalid. David was very sick for such a long time that it seemed as if he could never rally, and his one great comfort was having Clara near him. Hour after hour, and day after day, she sat by his bedside, his thin hand clasped in her strong one, with the patience of a much older, wiser nurse. She practically shut herself up in that sick-room for two whole years, and it seemed as if there was nothing too hard for her to do well and quickly, if in any way it would make David more comfortable. Finally a new kind of bath was tried with success. David was cured, and Clara Barton had served her earliest apprenticeship as a nurse.

Let us look back and see what went into the making of an eleven-year-old child who would give two years of her life to a task like that.

On Christmas Day of the year 1821, Clarissa Harlowe, as she was named, or "Clara" Barton, as she was always called, was born in her father's home near the town of Oxford, Worcester County, Massachusetts. Her oldest sister Dorothy was seventeen at that time, and her oldest brother Stephen, fifteen, while David was thirteen and Sally ten years old; so it was a long time since there had been a baby in the family, and all were so delighted over the event that Clara Barton says in her *Recollections*, "I am told the family jubilation upon the occasion was so great that the entire dinner and tea sets had to be changed for the serving of the noble guests who gathered."

The house in which the Christmas child was born was a simple farm-house on a hill-top, and inside nearly everything was home-made, even the crib in which the baby was cradled. Outside, the flat flagstone in front of the door was marked by the hand tools of the father. Stephen Barton, or Captain Barton as he was called, was a man of marked military tastes, who had served under "Mad Anthony" Wayne in campaigns against the Indians. In his youngest daughter Clara he found a real comrade, and, perched on his knee, she early gained a passionate love of her country and a child's simple knowledge of its history through the thrilling tales he told her. In speaking of those days she says:

"I listened breathlessly to his war stories. Illustrations were called for, and we made battles and fought them. Every shade of military etiquette was regarded. Colonels, captains, and sergeants were given their proper place and rank. So with the political world; the President, Cabinet, and leading officers of the government were learned by heart, and nothing gratified the keen humor of my father more than the parrot-like readiness with which I lisped these difficult names." That they did not mean much even to such a precocious child as Clara Barton is shown by an incident of those early days, when her sister Dorothy asked her how she supposed a Vice-President looked.

"I suppose he is about as big as our barn, and green!" was the quick reply.

But though the child did not understand all that was poured into her greedy little mind by an eager father, yet it bore fruit in later years, for she says: "When later I ... was suddenly thrust into the mysteries of war, and had to take my place and part in it, I found myself far less a stranger to the conditions than most women, or even ordinary men, for that matter. I never addressed a colonel as captain, got my cavalry on foot, or mounted my infantry!"

When she was not listening to her father's stories or helping her mother with the housework, which, good housewife that Mrs. Barton was, she took great pains to teach her youngest daughter how to do well, Clara was as busy as possible in some other way. In that household there were no drones, and the little girl was not even allowed to waste time in playing with dolls, although she was given time to take care of her pets, of which she had an ever-increasing collection, including dogs, cats, geese, hens, turkeys, and even two heifers which she learned to milk.

Dorothy, Sally and Stephen Barton were teachers, and as Clara early showed her quick mentality, they all took great interest in educating her according to their different ideas. As a result, when the little girl was three years old she could read a story to herself, and knew a little bit about geography, arithmetic and spelling. That decided the family. Such a bright mind must be developed as early as possible. So on a fine, clear winter morning Stephen lifted her to his shoulders with a swing of his strong arms, and in that way she rode to the school taught by Col. Richard C. Stone, a mile and a half from the Barton farm. Although the new pupil was such a very little girl, and so shy that often she was not able even to answer when she was spoken to or to join the class in reciting Bible verses or in singing songs, yet Colonel Stone was deeply interested in her, and his manner of teaching was so unusual that the years with him made a lasting impression on his youngest scholar's mind. To Clara it was a real loss when, at the end of five years, the Colonel left the school, to be succeeded by Clara's sisters in summer and by her brother Stephen in winter.

David was Clara's favorite brother. So athletic was he, and so fond of all forms of out-of-door life and exercise, that he was no less than a hero to the little sister, who watched him with intense admiration, and in her secret heart determined that some day and in some way she, too, would be brave and daring.

Having decided this in her own mind, when David suggested teaching her to ride, she was delighted, and, hiding her fear, at once took her first lesson on one of the beautiful blooded colts which were a feature of her father's farm. In her *Story of My Childhood* she says: "It was David's delight to take me, a little girl five years old, to the field, seize a couple of those beautiful grazing creatures, broken only to the halter and bit, and, gathering the reins of both bridles in one hand, throw me on the back of one colt, spring on the other himself, and, catching me by the foot and bidding me 'cling fast to the mane,' gallop away over field and fen, in and out among the other colts, in wild glee like ourselves. They were merry rides we took. This was my riding-school. I never had any other, but it served me well.... Sometimes in later years when I found myself on a strange horse, in a troop saddle, flying for life or liberty in front of pursuit, I blessed the baby lessons of the wild gallops among the colts."

And so it was that the child grew strong in body and alert in mind, while the routine of daily farm duties, when she was not at school or galloping over the fields with David, developed her in concentration and in inventive ability. Housekeeping at that time was crude, and most of the necessary articles used were made at home. There were no matches. The flint snapped by the lock was the only way of lighting a fire. Garments were homespun, and home-made food was dried, canned and cooked in large quantities by the busy housekeeper. Although there was always a fire blazing on the hearth of the home, it was thought to be a religious duty to have the meeting-house unheated on the Sabbath day. Little Clara, who was particularly susceptible to cold, bore the bitter chill of the building as bravely as she could, each week in the long winter, but one Sunday as she sat in the big pew, not daring to swing her feet, they grew more and more numb until at last, when she was obliged to stand on them, she fell over—her poor little feet were frozen, and she had to be carried home and thawed out!

When she was eight years old her father left his hill farm and moved down to the Learned house, a much bigger farm of three hundred acres, with the brook-like French river winding through its broad meadows, and three great barns standing in the lowlands between the hill and the house. Stephen and David remained on the hill to work their small farms there, and the other sisters stayed there, but Clara was not lonesome in the new home in the valley, for at that time she had as playmates the four children of Captain Barton's nephew, who had recently died. With them Clara played hide-and-seek in the big hay-mows, and other interesting games. Her most marked characteristic then and for many years afterward was her excessive shyness, yet when there was anything to do which did not include conversation she was always the champion. At times she was so bashful that even speaking to an intimate friend was often an agony to her, and it is said she once stayed home from meeting on Sunday rather than tell her mother that her gloves were too worn out to wear!

Inside the new house she found many fascinating things to do, and did them with eager interest. The house was being redecorated, and Clara went from room to room, watching the workmen, and even learned to grind and mix paints. Then she turned her attention to the paperers, who were so much amused with the child's cleverness that they showed her how to match, trim and hang paper, and in every room they good-naturedly let her paste up some piece of the decoration, so she felt that the house was truly hers, and never lost her affection for it in any of her later wanderings or changes of residence.

When the new home was completed inside Clara turned her attention to out-of-door matters and found more than one opportunity for daring feats. With shining eyes and bated breath, she learned to cross the little winding French river on teetering logs at its most dangerous depths. When this grew tame, she would go to the sawmill and ride out on the saw carriage twenty feet above the stream, and be pulled back on the returning log, and oh the joy of such dangerous sport!

By the time she was eleven years old her brothers had been so successful with their hill farms that they followed their father down to the valley of the river, where they bought the sawmill and built new dams and a grain-mill, and Sally and Stephen, who both married, settled in homes near the Barton farm. Then came the building of the new barn and David's accident. Eleven-year-old Clara, a child in years but mature mentally, proved equal to the emergency and took up her rôle of nurse in the same vigorous way she went about everything—but she had to pay a high price for her devotion.

David was strong and well again, but the little sister who had been his constant companion through the weary months was far from normal. The family had been so occupied with the invalid that no thought had been given to his young nurse. Now with grave concern Captain Barton talked with his wife.

"She has not gained an ounce in weight in these two years," he said, "and she isn't an inch taller. If anything, she seems to be more morbidly self-conscious and shy than ever. What shall we do with her?"

That was the question. The years shut up in the sick-room had completely unfitted Clara for ordinary life; she seemed to be more afraid of speaking to any one, more afraid of being seen or talked to than ever before. All took a hand at helping her to forget herself. Sally, who knew what an imaginative nature her small sister had, interested her in reading poetry, which was a delight to Clara. At the same time her father and brothers kept her out-of-doors as much as possible, and her father gave her a fine horse of her own. She named him Billy, and at once jumped on his back to get acquainted. From that time the slim, graceful animal with his youthful rider became one of the features of the neighborhood as they galloped across country. But, despite all that was done to make her healthy and happy, her self-consciousness and shyness remained, and another way of curing her was tried. She was sent to the boarding-school which was kept by her old teacher, Colonel Stone. He was delighted to have her in the school, and her quick mind was an amazement to him; but she was so homesick that often it was impossible for her to study or to recite, while being with one hundred and fifty girls of her own age made her more bashful than ever. In despair, Colonel Stone advised her father to take her home before she became seriously sick, and soon she found herself again in her beloved haunts. After that time her brother Stephen taught her mathematics; and later, when two fine teachers came to Oxford, she studied Latin, philosophy and chemistry with them, besides literature, history and languages—finding herself far ahead of the other scholars of her age, although she had been buried in a sick-room for two years.

As long as she was busy she was contented, but when vacation came she was again miserable. Her active mind and body demanded constant work; when she did not have it she was simply wretched, and made those around her so.

One day, when she was in her brother's mill watching the busy weavers, she had a sudden desire to work a loom herself. When she mentioned this at home her mother was horrified, but Stephen, who understood her restless nature better, took Clara's side and a few days later she proudly took her place before her loom and with enthusiastic persistence mastered the mysteries of the flying shuttle. How long she would have kept on with the work cannot be guessed, for on the fifteenth day after she began work the mill burned down, and she was again on the look-out for new employment for her active brain and body.

That she was a real girl was shown when, having discovered that she had no summer hat, she decided she must have one. Walking through the rye-fields, she had an idea. With quick interest in a new accomplishment, she cut a number of green rye stalks, carried them into the house and scalded them, then laid them out in the sun to bleach, and when they were white, she cut them into even lengths, pulled them apart with her teeth, braided them in eleven strands and made the first straw bonnet she ever owned.

Somehow or other the months of vacation wore away; then the question was, what to do next? Her nature demanded constant action. She was far ahead of others of her own age in the matter of studies, and Mrs. Barton was in real bewilderment as to what to do with her youngest child. A phrenologist, who was a keen observer of child nature, was visiting the Bartons at that time, and Clara, who had the mumps and was lying on the lounge in the adjoining room, heard her mother tell their guest of her daughter's restlessness and self-consciousness and ask his advice. Listening eagerly, she heard his reply:

"The sensitive nature will always remain," he said. "She will never assert herself for herself; she will suffer wrong first. But for others she will be perfectly fearless. Throw responsibility upon her. Give her a school to teach."

The very words, "give her a school to teach," sent a shiver of fear through Clara's frame, as she lay there listening, but at the same time she felt a thrill of pleasure at the idea of doing something so important as teaching. If her mother was so much troubled about her peculiar traits as to be obliged to talk them over with a stranger, they must be very hard to bear. She would set to work to be something quite different, and she would begin at once!

And so it happened that when Clara Barton was fifteen years old she followed in the footsteps of her brother and sisters and became a teacher. As soon as she decided to take the step, she was given District School No. 9, up in "Texas village," and in May, 1836, "after passing the teachers' examination with a mark of 'excellent,' she put down her skirts and put up her hair and walked to the little schoolhouse, to face and address her forty scholars." That was one of the most awful moments of her life. When the rows of pupils were ranged before her, and she was supposed to open the exercises by reading from the Bible, she could not find her voice, and her hand trembled so visibly that she was afraid to turn the pages and so disclose her panic. But no one knew. With perfect outward calmness, she kept her eyes on the open book until her pulse beat less fast, then she looked straight ahead and in a steady voice asked them to each read a verse in turn. This was a new and delightful plan to her pupils, who were still more pleased when the reading was over to have the new teacher question them in a friendly way about the meaning of the verses they had just read in the "Sermon on the Mount."

That first day proved her marked ability as a teacher, and so kindly and intimate was she with her scholars that they became more her comrades than her pupils. When the four rough boys of the school "tried her out" to see how much she could endure, to their astonishment, instead of being able to lock her out of the building as they had done with the previous teacher, she showed such pluck and physical strength that their respect was won and kept. After that, almost daily, at recess time she would join them in games such as no teacher had ever played with them before. And with her success Clara gained a new assurance and a less shy manner, although she never entirely lost her self-consciousness.

So successful was she with that first school that it was the preface to sixteen years of continuous teaching, winter and summer. Her two most interesting experiences as a teacher were in North Oxford and in Bordentown, New Jersey. North Oxford was the mill village where her brother's factories were, and where there were hundreds of children. When her popularity as the teacher in No. 9, Texas village, spread to North Oxford, she was asked to go there to start a school for operatives. This was a piece of work to her liking, and for ten years she says: "I stood with them in the crowded school-room summer and winter, without change or relaxation. I saw my little lisping boys become overseers, and my stalwart overseers become business men and themselves owners of mills. My little girls grew to be teachers and mothers of families." Here was satisfying work for the busy brain and active body! But even that did not take up all of her time; she found long hours in which to read and study, and also acted as Stephen's bookkeeper in the mill, during those years in North Oxford.

At the end of the ten years she broke away from the routine of teaching and became a pupil herself in Clinton Liberal Institute in New York, as there were no colleges for women at that time. The year of study refreshed her in mind and body, and, as her mother died during the year and her father decided to live with his married children, Clara was free to seek the work of the world wherever it should claim her.

From the seminary she went to Hightstown to teach, and while there rumors of her ability to cope with conditions and unruly scholars reached the village of Bordentown, ten miles away from Hightstown. Many attempts had been made to start a public school there, but without success. As a result the children of the poor ran wild in the streets, or when an attempt was made to open a school they broke up the sessions by their lawless behavior. When she heard this, Clara Barton was so greatly interested that she went to Bordentown to talk it over with the town officials, who told her that it was useless to think of making the experiment again.

Clara Barton's eyes flashed with determination. "Give me three months, and I will teach free!" she said.

As a result of her generous offer, she was allowed to rent a tumble-down, unoccupied building, and opened her school with six pupils! Every one of the six became so enthusiastic over a teacher who was interested in each individual that their friends were eager to be her pupils, too, and parents were anxious to see what the wonderful little bright-eyed, friendly woman could do for their children. At the end of five weeks the building was too small for her scholars, and the roll-call had almost six hundred names on it. To a triumphant teacher who had volunteered her services to try an experiment, a regular salary was now offered and an assistant given her. And so Clara Barton again proved her talent for teaching.

But Bordentown was her last school. When she had been there for two years and perfected the public-school system, her voice gave out as a result of constant use, and she went to Washington for a rest. But it did not take her long to recuperate, and soon she was eagerly looking out for some new avenue of opportunity to take the place of teaching. Government work interested her, and she heard rumors of scandals in the Patent Office, where some dishonest clerks had been copying and selling the ideas of inventors who had filed patents. This roused her anger, for she felt the inventors were defrauded and undefended individuals who needed a protector. As her brother's bookkeeper, she had developed a clear, copper-plate handwriting, which would aid her in trying to get the position she determined to try for. Through a relative in Congress she secured a position in the Patent Office, and when it was proved that she was acceptable there, although she was the first woman ever appointed independently to a clerkship in the department, she was given charge of a confidential desk, where she had the care of such papers as had not been carefully enough guarded before. Her salary of $1,400 a year was as much as was received by the men in the department, which created much jealousy, and she had many sneers and snubs and much disagreeable treatment from the other clerks; but she went serenely on her way, doing her duty and enjoying the new line of work with its chances for observation of the government and its working.

War clouds were now beginning to gather over both North and South, and signs of an approaching conflict were ominously clear in Washington, where slavery sentiments swayed all departments. Clara Barton saw with keen mental vision all the signs of the times, and there was much to worry her, for from the first she was clearly and uncompromisingly on the unpopular side of the disturbing question, and believed with Charles Sumner that "Freedom is national; slavery is sectional." She believed in the Union and she believed in the freedom of the individual. So eager was she to help the government in the coming national crisis that she offered her services as a clerk, to do the work of two dishonest men; for this work she was to receive the salary of one clerk, and pay back into the Treasury that of the other, in order to save all the money possible for an emergency. No deed gives a clearer insight into the character of Clara Barton than that. As it was in the case of the school in Bordentown, so was it now. If public service was the question, she had no thought of self or of money—the point was to achieve the desired end. And now she was nearer the goal of her own personal service to the world than she dreamed.

Fort Sumter was fired on. President Lincoln called for seventy-five thousand troops, and all those who were at the seat of government knew that the hour for sacrifice of men and money had come. Massachusetts responded to the call for troops with four regiments, one of which, the Sixth, set out for Washington at once. As they marched through the streets of Baltimore they were attacked by a furious mob who succeeded in killing four soldiers and wounding many more, but the troopers fought them off as bravely as possible and marched on to the station, where they entrained for Washington, many of them arriving there in a pitiable condition. When they detrained at the national capital they were met by a large number of sympathetic women, among them Clara Barton, who recognized some of her old friends and pupils among those who were limping, or with injured arms, or carried on stretchers, and her heart went out to them in loyalty and pride, for they were giving their services to their country in an hour of need.

The men who had not been injured were temporarily quartered at the Capitol, while the wounded were taken to the Infirmary, where their wounds were dressed at once, any material on hand being used. When the supply of handkerchiefs gave out, Clara Barton, as well as other impromptu nurses, rushed to their homes and tore up sheets for bandages, and Miss Barton also filled a large box full of needles, pins, buttons, salves and other necessities, and carried it back to the Infirmary, where she had her first experience in caring for wounded soldiers. When she could leave the Infirmary, she went to the Capitol and found the poor fellows there famished, for they had not been expected and their commissary stores had not yet been unloaded. Down to the market hurried the energetic volunteer nurse, and soon came back carrying a big basketful of supplies, which made a feast for the hungry men. Then, as she afterward wrote in a letter to a friend, "the boys, who had just one copy of the *Worcester Spy* of the 22nd, were so anxious to know its contents that they begged me to read it to them, which I did—mounting to the desk of the President of the Senate, that they all might hear."

In her letter she says, "You would have smiled to see *me* and my *audience* in the Senate Chamber of the U. S. A." and adds: "God bless the noble fellows who leave their quiet happy homes at the call of their country. So far as our poor efforts can reach, they shall never lack a kindly hand or a sister's sympathy if they come."

Eager to have the soldiers given all the comforts and necessities which could be obtained, Miss Barton put an advertisement in the *Worcester Spy*, asking for supplies and money for the wounded and needy in the Sixth Regiment, and stating that she herself would receive and give them out. The response was overwhelming. So much food and clothing was sent to her that her small apartment overflowed with supplies, and she was obliged to rent rooms in a warehouse to store them.

And now Clara Barton was a new creature. She felt within herself the ability to meet a great need, and the energy which for so long had been pent up within her was poured out in a seemingly unending supply of tenderness and of help for suffering humanity. There was no time now for sensitiveness, or for shyness; there was work to do through the all-too-short days and nights of this struggle for freedom and unity of the nation. Gone was the teacher, gone the woman of normal thought and action, and in her place we find the "Angel of the Battlefields," who for the remainder of her life was to be one of the world's foremost figures in ministrations to the suffering, where suffering would otherwise have had no alleviation.

"On the 21st of July the Union forces were routed at Bull Run with terrific loss of life and many wounded. Two months later the battle of Ball's Bluff occurred, in which there were three Massachusetts regiments engaged, with many of Clara Barton's lifelong friends among them. By this time the hospitals and commissaries in Washington had been well organized, and there was no desperate need for the supplies which were still being shipped to Miss Barton in great quantities, nor was there need of her nursing. However, she went to the docks to meet the wounded and dying soldiers, who were brought up the Potomac on transports." Often they were in such a condition from neglect that they were baked as hard as the backs of turtles with blood and clay, and it took all a woman's swift and tender care, together with the use of warm water, restoratives, dressings, and delicacies to make them at all comfortable. Then their volunteer nurse would go with them to the hospitals, and back again in the ambulance she would drive, to repeat her works of mercy.

But she was not satisfied with this work. If wounds could be attended to as soon as the men fell in battle, hundreds of deaths could be prevented, and she made up her mind that in some way she was going to override public sentiment, which in those early days of the war did not allow women nurses to go to the front, for she was determined to go to the very firing-line itself as a nurse. And, as she had got her way at other times in her life, so now she achieved her end, but after months of rebuffs and of tedious waiting, during which the bloody battle of Fair Oaks had been fought with terrible losses on each side. The seven days' retreat of the Union forces under McClellan followed, with eight thousand wounded and over seventeen hundred killed. On top of this came the battle of Cedar Mountain, with many Northerners killed, wounded and missing.

One day, when Assistant Quartermaster-General Rucker, who was one of the great-hearts of the army, was at his desk, he was confronted by a bright-eyed little woman, to whose appeal he gave sympathetic attention.

"I have no fear of the battle-field," she told him. "I have large stores, but no way to reach the troops."

Then she described the condition of the soldiers when they reached Washington, often too late for any care to save them or heal their wounds. She *must* go to the battle-front where she could care for them quickly. So overjoyed was she to be given the needed passports as well as kindly interest and good wishes that she burst into tears as she gripped the old soldier's hand, then she hurried out to make immediate plans for having her supplies loaded on a railroad car. As she tersely put it, "When our armies fought on Cedar Mountain, I broke the shackles and went to the field." When she began her work on the day after the battle she found an immense amount of work to do. Later she described her experience in this modest way:

"Five days and nights with three hours' sleep—a narrow escape from capture—and some days of getting the wounded into hospitals at Washington brought Saturday, August 30th. And if you chance to feel that the positions I occupied were rough and unseemly for a woman, I can only reply that they were rough and unseemly for men. But under all, lay the life of a nation. I had inherited the rich blessing of health and strength of constitution such as are seldom given to women, and I felt that some return was due from me and that I ought to be there."

The famous army nurse had served her novitiate now, and through the weary years of the war which dragged on with alternate gains and losses for the Union forces, Clara Barton's name began to be spoken of with awe and deep affection wherever a wounded man had come under her gentle care. Being under no society or leader, she was free to come or go at will. But from the first day of her work at the front she was encouraged in it by individual officers who saw the great value of what she accomplished.

At Antietam, when the fighting began, her wagons were driven through a field of tall corn to an old homestead, while the shot whizzed thick around them. In the barnyard and among the corn lay torn and bleeding men—the worst cases, just brought from the places where they had fallen. All was in confusion, for the army medical supplies had not yet arrived, and the surgeons were trying to make bandages of corn husks. The new army nurse immediately had her supplies unloaded and hurried out to revive the wounded with bread soaked in wine. When her bread gave out there were still many to be fed. All the supplies she had were three cases of unopened wine.

"Open the wine, and give that," she commanded, "and God help us."

Her order was obeyed, and as she watched the cases being unpacked her eyes fell on the packing around the bottles of wine. It was nicely sifted corn-meal. If it had been gold dust it could not have been more valuable. The wine was unpacked as quickly as possible; kettles were found in the farm-house, and in a twinkling that corn-meal was mixed with water, and good gruel for the men was in the making. Then it occurred to Miss Barton to see what was in the cellar of the old house, and there three barrels of flour and a bag of salt were found, stored by the rebels and left behind when they marched away. "What wealth!" exclaimed the woman, who was frantically eager to feed her flock. All that night Clara Barton and her workers carried buckets of hot gruel up and down the long lines to the wounded and dying men. Then up to the farm-house went the army nurse, where, in the dim light of a lone flickering candle, she could dimly see the surgeon in charge, sitting in apparent despair by the table, his head resting in his hands. She tiptoed up to him and said, quietly, "You are tired, doctor."

Looking up, he exclaimed: "Tired? Yes, I am tired! Tired of such heartlessness and carelessness! And," he added, "think of the condition of things. Here are at least one thousand wounded men; terribly wounded, five hundred of whom cannot live till daylight without attention. That two-inch of candle is all I have, or can get. What can I do? How can I bear it?"

A smile played over Clara Barton's clear-cut face. Gently but firmly she took him by the elbow and led him to the door, pointing toward the barn, where dozens of lanterns gleamed like stars.

"What is it?" he exclaimed.

"The barn is lighted," she said, "and the house will be directly."

"Who did it?"

"I, doctor."

"Where did you get them?"

"Brought them with me."

"How many have you?"

"All you want, four boxes."

For a moment he stared at her as if to be sure he was not in a dream. Then he turned away without a word, and never spoke of the matter again, but his deference to Clara Barton from that time was the greatest a man can pay a woman.

Not until all her stores were exhausted and she was sick with a fever would Clara Barton leave the battle-field of Antietam; then, dragging herself to the train, she went back to Washington to be taken care of until she was better. When at last she was strong enough to work again she went to see her friend Quartermaster-General Rucker, and told him that if she had had five wagons she would have had enough supplies for all the wounded at Antietam. With an expression of intense admiration on his soldierly face as he watched the brave volunteer nurse, he declared:

"You shall have enough next time!"

The promise was made good. Having recognized the value of her efficient services, the Government assisted in every way, making it possible for her to carry on her work on the battle-fields and in military camps and hospitals in the best way.

Clara Barton!—Only the men who lay wounded or dying on the battle-field knew the thrill and the comfort that the name carried. Again and again her life was in danger—once at Antietam, when stooping to give a drink of water to an injured boy, a bullet whizzed between them. It ended the life of the poor lad, but only tore a hole in Clara Barton's sleeve. And so, again and again, it seemed as if a special Providence protected her from death or injury. At Fredericksburg, when the dead, starving and wounded lay frozen on the ground, and there was no effective organization for proper relief, with swift, silent efficiency Clara Barton moved among them, having the snow cleared away and under the banks finding famished, frozen figures which were once men. She rushed to have an old chimney torn down and built fire-blocks, over which she soon had kettles full of coffee and gruel steaming.

As she was bending over a wounded rebel, he whispered to her: "Lady, you have been kind to me ... every street of the city is covered by our cannon. When your entire army has reached the other side of the Rappahannock, they will find Fredericksburg only a slaughter-pen. Not a regiment will escape. Do not go over, for you will go to certain death."

She thanked him for the kindly warning and later told of the call that came to her to go across the river, and what happened. She says:

"At ten o'clock of the battle day when the rebel fire was hottest, the shells rolling down every street, and the bridge under the heavy cannonade, a courier dashed over, and, rushing up the steps of the house where I was, placed in my hand a crumpled, bloody piece of paper, a request from the lion-hearted old surgeon on the opposite shore, establishing his hospitals in the very jaws of death:

"'Come to me,' he wrote. 'Your place is here.'

"The faces of the rough men working at my side, which eight weeks before had flushed with indignation at the thought of being controlled by a woman, grew ashy white as they guessed the nature of the summons, ... and they begged me to send them, but save myself. I could only allow them to go with me if they chose, and in twenty minutes we were rocking across the swaying bridge, the water hissing with shot on either side.

"Over into that city of death, its roofs riddled by shell, its every church a crowded hospital, every street a battle-line, every hill a rampart, every rock a fortress, and every stone wall a blazing line of forts.

"Oh, what a day's work was that! How those long lines of blue, rank on rank, charged over the open acres, up to the very mouths of those blazing guns, and how like grain before the sickle they fell and melted away.

"An officer stepped to my side to assist me over the débris at the end of the bridge. While our hands were raised in the act of stepping down, a piece of an exploding shell hissed through between us, just below our arms, carrying away a portion of both the skirts of his coat and my dress, rolling along the ground a few rods from us like a harmless pebble in the water. The next instant a solid shot thundered over our heads, a noble steed bounded in the air and with his gallant rider rolled in the dirt not thirty feet in the rear. Leaving the kind-hearted officer, I passed on alone to the hospital. In less than a half-hour he was brought to me—dead."

She was passing along a street in the heart of the city when she had to step aside to let a regiment of infantry march by. At that moment General Patrick saw her, and, thinking she was a frightened resident of the city who had been left behind in the general exodus, leaned from his saddle and said, reassuringly:

"You are alone and in great danger, madam. Do you want protection?"

With a rare smile, Miss Barton said, as she looked at the ranks of soldiers, "Thank you, but I think I am the best-protected woman in the United States."

The near-by soldiers caught her words and cried out:

"That's so! That's so!" and the cheer they gave was echoed by line after line, until the sound of the shouting was like the cheers after a great victory. Bending low with a courtly smile, the general said:

"I believe you are right, madam!" and galloped away.

"At the battles of Cedar Mountain, Second Bull Run, Antietam, during the eight months' siege of Charleston, in the hospital at Fort Wagner, with the army in front of Petersburg and in the Wilderness and the hospitals about Richmond, there was no limit to the work Clara Barton accomplished for the sick and dying, but among all her experiences during those years of the war, the Battle of Fredericksburg was most unspeakably awful to her. And yet afterward she saw clearly that it was this defeat that gave birth to the Emancipation Proclamation.

"And the white May blossoms of '63 fell over the glad faces—the swarthy brows, the toil-worn hands of four million liberated slaves. 'America,' writes Miss Barton, 'had freed a race.'"

As the war drew to an end, President Lincoln received hundreds of letters from anxious parents asking for news of their boys. There were eighty thousand missing men whose families had no knowledge whether they were alive or dead. In despair, and believing that Clara Barton had more information of the soldiers than any one else to whom he could turn, the President requested her to take up the task, and the army nurse's tender heart was touched by the thought of helping so many mothers who had no news of their boys, and she went to work, aided by the hospital and burial lists she had compiled when on the field of action.

For four years she did this work, and it was a touching scene when she was called before the Committee on Investigation to tell of its results. With quiet simplicity she stood before the row of men and reported, "Over thirty thousand men, living and dead, already traced. No available funds for the necessary investigation; in consequence, over eight thousand dollars of my own income spent in the search."

As the men confronting her heard the words of the bright-eyed woman who was looked on as a sister by the soldiers from Maine to Virginia, whose name was a household one throughout the land, not one of them was ashamed to wipe the tears from his eyes! Later the government paid her back in part the money she had spent in her work; but she gave her time without charge as well as many a dollar which was never returned, counting it enough reward to read the joyful letters from happy, reunited families.

While doing this work she gave over three hundred lectures through the East and West, and as a speaker she held her audiences as if by magic, for she spoke glowingly about the work nearest to her heart, giving the proceeds of her lectures to the continuance of that work. One evening in the winter of 1868, when speaking in one of the finest opera-houses in the East, before one of the most brilliant assemblages she had ever faced, her voice suddenly gave out, as it had in the days when she was teaching. The heroic army nurse and worker for the soldiers was worn out in body and nerves. As soon as she was able to travel the doctor commanded that she take three years of absolute rest. Obeying the order, she sailed for Europe, and in peaceful Switzerland with its natural beauty hoped to regain normal strength; for her own country had emerged from the black shadow of war, and she felt that her life work had been accomplished, that rest could henceforth be her portion.

But Clara Barton was still on the threshold of her complete achievement. When she had been in Switzerland only a month, and her broken-down nerves were just beginning to respond to the change of air and scene, she received a call which changed the color of her future. Her caller represented the International Committee of the Red Cross Society. Miss Barton did not know what the Red Cross was, and said so. He then explained the nature of the society, which was founded for the relief of sick and wounded soldiers, and he told his eager listener what she did not know, that back of the Society was the Geneva Treaty, which had been providing for such relief work, signed by all the civilized nations except her own. From that moment a new ambition was born in Clara Barton's heart—to find out why America had not signed the treaty, and to know more about the Red Cross Society.

Nearly a year later, while still resting in quiet Switzerland, there broke one day upon the clear air of her Swiss home the distant sounds of a royal party hastening back from a tour of the Alps. To Miss Barton's amazement it came in the direction of her villa. Finally flashed the scarlet and gold of the liveries of the Grand Duke of Baden. After the outriders came the splendid coach of the Grand Duchess, daughter of King Wilhelm of Prussia, so soon to be Emperor William of Germany. In it rode the Grand Duchess. After presenting her card through the footman, she herself alighted and clasped Miss Barton's hand, hailing her in the name of humanity, and said she already knew her through what she had done in the Civil War. Then, still clasping her hand in a tight grip of comradeship, she begged Miss Barton to leave Switzerland and aid in Red Cross work on the battle-fields of the Franco-Prussian War, which was in its beginnings. It was a real temptation to once again work for suffering humanity, yet she put it aside as unwise. But a year later, when the officers of the International Red Cross Society came again to beg that Miss Barton take the lead in a great systematic plan of relief work such as that for which she had become famous during the Civil War, she accepted. In the face of such consequences as her health might suffer from her decision, she rose, and, with head held high and flashing eyes, said:

"Command me!"

Clara Barton was no longer to be the Angel of the American battle-fields only—from that moment she belonged to the world, and never again could she be claimed by any one country. But it is as the guardian angel of our soldiers in the United States that her story concerns us, although there is reason for great pride in the part she played in nursing the wounded at Strassburg, and later when her presence carried comfort and healing to the victims of the fight with the Commune in Paris.

As tangible results of her work abroad, she was given an amethyst cut in the shape of a pansy, by the Grand Duchess of Baden, also the Serbian decoration of the Red Cross as the gift of Queen Natalie, and the Gold Cross of Remembrance, which was presented her by the Grand Duke and Duchess of Baden together. Queen Victoria, with her own hand, pinned an English decoration on her dress. The Iron Cross of Germany, as well as the Order of Melusine given her by the Prince of Jerusalem, were among an array of medals and pendants— enough to have made her a much-bejeweled person, had it been her way to make a show of her own rewards.

Truly Clara Barton belonged to the world, and a suffering person had no race or creed to her—she loved and cared for all.

When at last she returned to America, it was with the determination to have America sign the Geneva Treaty and to bring her own country into line with the Red Cross movement, which she had carefully watched in foreign countries, and which she saw was the solution to efficient aid of wounded men, either in the battle-field or wherever there had been any kind of disaster and there was need of quick aid for suffering. It was no easy task to convince American officials, but at last she achieved her end. On the 1st of March, 1882, the Geneva Treaty was signed by President Arthur, ratified by the Senate, and immediately the American National Red Cross was formed with Clara Barton as its first president.

The European "rest" trip had resulted in one of the greatest achievements for the benefit of mankind in which America ever participated, and its birth in the United States was due solely to the efforts of the determined, consecrated nurse who, when eleven years old, gave her all to a sick brother, and later consecrated her life to the service of a sick brotherhood of brave men.

On the day after her death, on April 12, 1912, one editor of an American newspaper paid a tribute to her that ranks with those paid the world's greatest heroes. He said:

"On the battle-fields of the Rebellion her hands bound up the wounds of the injured brave.

"The candles of her charity lighted the gloom of death for the heroes of Antietam and Fredericksburg.

"Across the ocean waters of her sweet labors followed the flag of the saintly Red Cross through the Franco-Prussian war.

"When stricken Armenia cried out for help in 1896, it was Clara Barton who led the relief corps of salvation and sustenance.

"A woman leading in answering the responsibility of civilization to the world!

"When McKinley's khaki boys struck the iron from Cuba's bondage it was Clara Barton, in her seventy-seventh year, who followed to the fever-ridden tropics to lead in the relief-work on Spanish battle-grounds.

"She is known wherever man appreciates humanity."

Hers was the honor of being the first president of the American Red Cross, but she was more than that—she *was* the Red Cross at that time. It was, as she said, "her child," and she furnished headquarters for it in her Washington home, dispensing the charities of a nation, amounting to hundreds of thousands of dollars, and was never requested to publish her accounts, an example of personal leadership which is unparalleled.

In 1897 we find the Red Cross president settled in her home at Glen Echo, a few miles out of Washington, on a high slope overlooking the Potomac, and, although it was a Red Cross center, it was a friendly lodging as well, where its owner could receive her personal friends. Flags and Red Cross testimonials from rulers of all nations fluttered from the walls, among them a beautiful one from the Sultan of Turkey. Two small crosses of red glass gleamed in the front windows over the balcony, but above the house the Red Cross banner floated high, as if to tell the world that "the banner over us is love." And to Glen Echo, the center of her beloved activity, Clara Barton always loved to return at the end of her campaigns. To the many thousands who came to visit her home as one of the great humane centers of the world, she became known as the "Beautiful Lady of the Potomac," and never did a title more fittingly describe a nature.

To the last she was a soldier—systematic, industrious, severely simple in her tastes. It was a rule of the household that every day's duties should be disposed of before turning in for the night, and at five o'clock the next morning she would be rolling a carpet-sweeper over the floor. She always observed military order and took a soldier's pride in keeping her quarters straight.

Hanging on the wall between her bedroom and private sitting-room was a small mirror into which her mother looked when she came home as a bride.

Her bed was small and hard. Near it were the books that meant so much to her—the Bible, Pilgrim's Progress, the stories of Sarah Orne Jewett, the poems of Lucy Larcom, and many other well-worn, much-read classics.

That she was still feminine, as in the days of girlhood when she fashioned her first straw bonnet, so now she was fond of wearing handsome gowns, often with trains. Lavender, royal purple, and wine color were the shades she liked best to wear, and in which her friends most often remember her. Despite her few extravagant tastes, Clara Barton was the most democratic woman America ever produced, as well as the most humane. She loved people, sick and well, and in any State and city of the Union she could claim personal friends in every walk of life.

When, after ninety-nine years of life and fifty of continuous service to suffering human nature, death laid its hand upon her on that spring day, the world to its remotest corner stopped its busy barter and trade for a brief moment to pay reverent tribute to a woman, who was by nature of the most retiring, bashful disposition, and yet carried on her life-work in the face of the enemy, to the sound of cannon, and close to the firing-line. She was on the firing-line all her life. That is her life story.

Her "boys" of all ages adored her, and no more touching incident is told of her than that of a day in Boston, when, after a meeting, she lingered at its close to chat with General Shafter. Suddenly the great audience, composed entirely of old soldiers, rose to their feet as she came down the aisle, and a voice cried:

"Three cheers for Clara Barton!"

They were given by voices hoarse with feeling. Then some one shouted:

"Tiger!"

Before it could be given another voice cried:

"No! *Sweetheart!*"

Then those grizzled elderly men whose lives she had helped to save broke into uproar and tears together, while the little bent woman smiled back at them with a love as true as any sweetheart's.

To-day we stand at the parting of the ways. Our nation is in the making as a world power, and in its rebirth there must needs be bloodshed and scalding tears. As we American girls and women go out bravely to face the untried future and to nurse under the banner of the Red Cross, we shall do our best work when we bear to the battle-field the same spirit of high purpose and consecration that inspired Clara Barton and made her the "Angel of the Battle-fields." Let us, as loyal Americans, take to heart part of a speech she once made on Memorial Day, when she stood with the "Boys in Blue" in the "God's-acre" of the soldier, and declared:

"We cannot always hold our great ship of state out of the storms and breakers. She must meet and buffet with them. Her timbers must creak in the gale. The waves must wash over her decks, she must lie in the trough of the sea as she does to-day. But the Stars and Stripes are above her. She is freighted with the hopes of the world. God holds the helm, and she's coming to port. The weak must fear, the timid tremble, but the brave and stout of heart will work and hope and trust."

VIRGINIA REED: MIDNIGHT HEROINE OF THE PLAINS IN PIONEER

DAYS OF AMERICA

On a lovely April morning in 1846 there was an unusual stir in the streets of Springfield, Illinois, for such an early hour. From almost every house some one was hurrying, and as neighbor nodded to neighbor the news passed on:

"The wagons are ready—they are going!"

As the sun mounted slowly in the cloudless sky, from all parts of town there still flocked friends and relatives of the small band of emigrants who were about to start on their long trip across the plains, going to golden California.

California—magic word! Not one of those who were hurrying to wish the travelers God-speed, nor any of the band who were leaving their homes, but felt the thrilling promise and the presage of that new country toward which the emigrants were about to turn their faces.

The crowd of friends gathered at the Reeds' home, where their great prairie-wagons and those of the Donners were drawn up in a long line before the door; the provision wagons, filled to overflowing with necessities and luxuries, the family wagons waiting for their human freight. Mr. James F. Reed, who had planned the trip, was one of Springfield's most highly respected citizens, and the Donner brothers, who lived just outside of the town, had enthusiastically joined him in perfecting the details of the journey, and had come in to town the night before, with their families, to be ready for an early start. And now they were really going!

All through the previous winter, in the evening, when the Reeds were gathered before their big log fire, they had talked of the wonderful adventure, while Mrs. Reed's skilful fingers fashioned such garments as would be needed for the journey. And while she sewed, Grandma Keyes told the children marvelous tales of Indian massacres on those very plains across which they were going to travel when warmer days came. Grandma told her breathless audience of giant red men, whose tomahawks were always ready to descend on the heads of unlucky travelers who crossed their path—told so many blood-curdling stories of meetings between white men and Indian warriors that the little boys, James and Thomas, and little black-eyed Patty and older Virginia, were spellbound as they listened.

To Virginia, an imaginative girl, twelve years old, the very flames, tongueing their way up the chimney in fantastic shapes, became bold warriors in mortal combat with emigrants on their way to the golden West, and even after she had gone to bed it seemed to her that "everything in the room, from the high old-fashioned bedposts down to the shovel and tongs, was transformed into the dusky tribe in paint and feathers, all ready for a war-dance" as they loomed large out of shadowy corners. She would hide her head under the clothes, scarcely daring to wink or breathe, then come boldly to the surface, face her shadowy foes, and fall asleep without having come to harm at the hands of the invisibles.

Going to California—oh the ecstatic terror of it! And now the day and the hour of departure had come!

The Reeds' wagons had all been made to order, and carefully planned by Mr. Reed himself with a view to comfort in every detail, so they were the best of their kind that ever crossed the plains, and especially was their family wagon a real pioneer *car de luxe*, made to give every possible convenience to Mrs. Reed and Grandma Keyes. When the trip had been first discussed by the Reeds, the old lady, then seventy-five years old and for the most part confined to her bed, showed such enthusiasm that her son declared, laughingly: "I declare, mother, one would think you were going with us."

"I am!" was the quick rejoinder. "You do not think I am going to be left behind when my dear daughter and her children are going to take such a journey as that, do you? I thought you had more sense, James!"

And Grandma did go, despite her years and her infirmities.

The Reeds' family wagon was drawn by four yoke of fine oxen, and their provision wagons by three. They had also cows, and a number of driving and saddle horses, among them Virginia's pony Billy, on whose back she had been held and taught to ride when she was only seven years old.

The provision wagons were filled to overflowing with all sorts of supplies. There were farming implements, to be used in tilling the land in that new country to which they were going, and a bountiful supply of seeds. Besides these farm supplies, there were bolts of cotton prints and flannel for dresses and shirts, also gay handkerchiefs, beads, and other trinkets to be used for barter with the Indians. More important still, carefully stowed away was a store of fine laces, rich silks and velvets, muslins and brocades, to be exchanged for Mexican land-grants. The family wagon, too, had been fitted up with every kind of commodity, including a cooking-stove, with its smoke-stack carried out through the canvas roof of the wagon, and a looking-glass which Mrs. Reed's friends had hung on the canvas wall opposite the wagon door—"so you will not forget to keep your good looks, they said!"

And now the party was ready to start. Among its number were Mrs. Reed and her husband, with little Patty, the two small boys, James and Thomas, and the older daughter, Virginia; the Donners, George and Jacob, with their wives and children; Milton Elliott, driver of the Reed family wagon, who had worked for years in Mr. Reed's big sawmill; Eliza Baylis, the Reeds' domestic, with her brother and a number of other young men, some of them drivers, others merely going for adventure. In all, on that lovely April morning, it was a group of thirty-one persons around whom friends and relatives clustered for last words and glimpses, and it was a sad moment for all. Mrs. Reed broke down when she realized that the moment of parting had really come, while Mr. Reed, in response to the good wishes showered on him, silently gripped hand after hand, then he hurried into the house with Milt Elliott, and presently came out carrying Grandma, at the sight of whom her friends cheered lustily. She waved her thin hand in response as she was lifted gently into the wagon and placed on a large feather-bed, where she was propped up with pillows and declared herself to be perfectly comfortable.

And indeed her resting-place was very much like a room, for the wagon had been built with its entrance at the side, like an old-fashioned stage-coach, and from the door one stepped into a small square room. At the right and left were spring seats with high backs, which were comfortable for riding, and over the wheels for the length of the wagon, a wide board had been placed, making what Virginia called a "really truly second story" on which beds were made up. Under this "second story" were roomy compartments in which were stowed away stout bags holding the clothing of the party, each bag plainly marked with a name. There was also a full supply of medicines, with lint and bandages for an emergency, and Mr. Reed had provided a good library of standard books, not only to read during the journey, but knowing they could not be bought in the new West. Altogether, from provision wagon to family caravan, there was a complete equipment for every need, and yet when they arrived in California, as one of the party said, "We were almost destitute of everything!"

The wagons were loaded, Grandma was safely stowed away in her warm bed, with little Patty sitting on its end where she could hold back the door flap that the old lady might have a last glimpse of her old home—the hard farewells had been said, and now Mr. Reed called in as cheery a voice as he could command, "All aboard!"

Milton Elliott cracked his whip, and the long line of prairie-wagons, horses and cattle started. Then came a happy surprise. Into saddles and vehicles sprang more than a score of friends and relatives who were going to follow the party to their first night's encampment, while many of Virginia's schoolmates ran at the side of the wagon through the principal streets of the town until one by one they dropped back from fatigue, Virginia waving a continued farewell from the wagon while they were in sight.

The first day's trip was not a long one, as it was thought wise to make the start easy for man and beast. Most of the way Virginia rode on Billy, sometimes beside the wagon, then again galloping ahead with her father. A bridge was seen in the distance, and Patty and the boys cried out to Milton, "Please stop, and let us get out and walk over it; the oxen may not take us across safely!" Milt threw back his head and roared with laughter at such an idea, but he halted to humor them, then with a skilful use of his loud-voiced "Gee! and Haw!" made the huge beasts obey his will.

On the line of great wagons wound its way beyond the town, until the sun was sinking in the west, when they stopped for the night on the ground where the Illinois State House now stands. The oxen were then unhitched and the wagons drawn up in a hollow circle or "corral," within the protection of which cattle and horses were set free for the night, while outside the corral a huge camp-fire soon blazed, around which the party gathered for their first evening meal together, and their last one with those friends who had come thus far on their way with them. It was a determinedly merry group around the fire, and stories were told and songs sung, which to the radiant Virginia were a foretaste of such coming adventure as was beyond her wildest dreams.

As she sat in the glow of the camp-fire, with sleepy Patty's head pillowed on her lap, she felt even more than before the thrill of this wonderful adventuring. To keep a record of her travels,—that was the thing to do! Full of the idea, she pinned together sheets of wrapping-paper into a bulky blank-book, on the outside of which she printed:

Going to California. 1846.

From that time she kept a faithful though not a continuous record of the experiences of what came to be known later as "the ill-fated Donner party of martyr pioneers." And from that record she later wrote her story of their journeying to the golden West.

By the eleventh day of May the band of emigrants had reached the town of Independence, Missouri, and Virginia's record says:

"Men and beasts are in fine condition. There is nothing in all the world so fascinating as to travel by day in the warm sunshine and to camp by night under the stars. Here we are just outside the most bustling town I ever saw and it is good news to find a large number of inhabitants with their wagons, ready to cross the prairie with us. Who knows, perhaps some new friendships will be made as we all go on together! They all seem to feel as eager to go as we are, and everybody is glad. I will get acquainted with as many as I can now, and bring cheerful ones to visit Grandma, for she feels rather homesick, except when Patty and I make her laugh."

Again, "The first few days of travel through the Territory of Kansas were lovely. The flowers were so bright and there were so many birds singing. Each day father and I would ride ahead to find a place to camp that night. Sometimes when we galloped back we would find the wagons halting at a creek, while washing was done or the young people took a swim. Mother and I always did our wash at night, and spread it on the bushes to dry. All this is such a peaceful recital that I began to think I need not keep a diary at all, till one hot day when I was in the wagon helping Patty cut out some doll's dresses, Jim came running up to the wagon, terribly excited and crying out:

"'Indians, Virginia! Come and see! They have to take us across the river!' Out he rushed and I after him, with every story Grandma ever told us dancing through my brain. Now there was going to be an adventure! But there wasn't. We had reached the Caw River, where there were Indians to ferry us across. They were real and red and terrifying, but I never flinched. If they brought out tomahawks in midstream, I would be as brave as a pioneer's daughter should be. But would you believe me, those Indians were as tame as pet canaries, and just shot us across the river without glancing at us, and held out their big hands with a grunt, for the coins! That was one of the greatest disappointments of my life."

All went well with the travelers during those first weeks of the trip, and no one enjoyed it more than Grandma Keyes after she got over being homesick. But when they reached the Big Blue river, it was so swollen that they had to lie by and wait for it to go down, or make rafts to cross it on. As soon as they stopped traveling Grandma began to fail, and on the 29th of May, with scarcely any pain, she died. Virginia's diary says: "It was hard to comfort mother until I persuaded her that to die out in that lovely country, and with most of your family around you, was far better than living longer at home. Besides, she might have died in Springfield. So mother cheered up a little, while all the party helped us in making the sad preparations. A coffin was made from a cotton-wood tree, and a young man from home found a gray stone slab and cut Grandma's name, birthplace, and age on it. A minister of the party made a simple address, and with the sunlight filtering through the trees we buried her under an oak-tree and covered the grave with wild flowers. Then we had to go on our way and leave dear Grandma in the vast wilderness, which was so hard for mother that for many days I did not take my rides on Billy, but just stayed with her. But the landscape was so comfortingly beautiful that at last she cheered up and began to feel that Grandma was not left alone in the forest, but was with God. Strange to say, that grave in the woods has never been disturbed; around it grew up the city of Manhattan, Kansas, and there it is in the city cemetery of to-day."

The river did not go down, as the men had hoped, so they began to cut down trees and split them into twenty-five-foot logs which were hollowed out and joined together by cross timbers, these were firmly lashed to stakes driven into the bank, and ropes were tied to each end to pull the rafts back and forth across the river. It was no easy matter to get the heavy wagons down the steep bank to the rafts, and they had to be held back by the ropes and let down slowly so the wheels would run into the hollowed logs. The women and children stayed in the wagons, and talked and laughed gaily, that they might not show the fear they felt as they balanced above the swollen river. But it was crossed safely and then on the oxen jogged over a rough road until the great Valley of the Platte was reached, where the road was good and the country beautiful beyond expression. Virginia says: "Our party was now so large that there was a line of forty wagons winding its way like a serpent through the valley. There was no danger of any kind, and each day was happier than the one before. How I enjoyed galloping over the plains on Billy!" she exclaims, adding, "At night we young folks would sit around the camp-fire, chatting merrily, and often a song would be heard, or some clever dancer would give us a barn-door jig on the hind gate of a wagon!"

The caravan wound its slow way westward, making from fifteen to twenty miles a day, and always at night, when the party camped, a corral was formed to protect the cattle from thieving Indians, who, says Virginia, sadly, "are not like grandma's Indians. They treat us kindly except for taking our things, which is annoying but not terrifying." And she adds, "We have fine fare for those who like to eat game, as we have so many good riflemen in the party who are always bringing it in." She then confesses, "I certainly never thought I would be relishing antelope and buffalo steaks, but they are good food when one has grown used to them. Often I ride with father in a buffalo hunt, which is very thrilling. We all help Eliza, who has turned into a fine camp cook. As soon as we reach the place where we are to spend the night all hands get to work, and, my, but things taste good when that meal is ready! When we drove into the South Fork of the Platte, Eliza had the cream ready to churn, and while we were fording the stream she worked so hard that she turned out several pounds of butter."

The diary gives quite a long narrative here as follows:

"By the Fourth of July we were near Fort Laramie in Dakota, and what a sight I saw as we approached the fort. 'Grandma's Indians!' I exclaimed, as I saw bands of horses grazing on the plains and Indians smeared with war-paint and armed with hunting-knives, tomahawks, bows and arrows, moving about in the sunlight. They did not seem to notice us as we drove up to the strongly fortified walls around the buildings of the American Fur Company, but by the time we were ready to leave, the red men and their squaws were pressing close to the wagons to take trinkets which we had ready for them. Little Patty stood by me and every now and then she squeezed my arm and cried, 'Look! Look!' as the Indians crowded around us. Many of the squaws and papooses were gorgeous in white doeskin suits gaily trimmed with beads, and were very different from us in our linsey dresses and sunbonnets.

"As soon as father met the manager of the Fur Company, he advised us to go right on as soon as we could, because he said the Sioux were on the war-path, going to fight the Crows or Blackfeet, and their march would be through the country which we had to cross, and they might treat us badly, or rob us, as they were in an ugly humor. This greatly frightened some of the women, and to calm them the men cleaned and loaded their rifles and did everything they could to hurry away from the fort. We were there only four days, and when we drove away we met the mounted Indians, about three hundred of them, tomahawks, war-paint, and all! They looked very handsome and impressive as they advanced in a stately procession, two abreast, and rode on before our train, then halted and opened ranks. As our wagons passed between their lines they took green twigs from between their teeth and tossed them to us in token of friendship. Then, having shown their good faith, they crowded around our wagons and showed great curiosity at the funny little smoke-stack sticking through the top of our family wagon. A brave caught a glimpse of his war-paint and feathers in our looking-glass, which hung opposite the door, and he was fascinated. Beckoning to his comrades, he pointed to it, and to the strange reflection of himself, and they all fairly pushed to the front, to see themselves, in the glass. Unfortunately at that time I rode up on Billy, and at once the Indians forgot everything except their admiration of my pony. They swarmed around me, grunting, nodding, and gesturing, and brought buffalo robes and tanned buckskin, also pretty beaded moccasins and robes made of grass, and signed to me that they would give all these in exchange for Billy. I shook my head as hard as I could shake it, but they were determined to have Billy. They made signs that they would give their ponies for mine, but again I shook my head. They talked together awhile, then one of them triumphantly brought me an old coat which had evidently belonged to a soldier, and seemed much surprised that its brass buttons were not enough of an inducement to make me give up the coveted prize. Though both father and I continued to refuse their request as positively as ever, they still swarmed around us and looked at me in a most embarrassing way. I did not mind much, but father seemed angry and he said, sternly: 'Virginia, you dismount at once and let one of the men take Billy. Get into the wagon now.' When father spoke in that way I was never slow to obey, so I climbed into the wagon, and, being anxious to get a better look at the Indians, I took a field-glass out of the rack where it hung and put it to my eyes. The glass clicked as I took it from the rack and like a flash the Indians wheeled their ponies and scattered, taking the noise for the click of firearms. I turned to mother and laughed.

"'You see you need not be afraid, mother dear,' I said; 'I can fight the whole Sioux tribe with a spy-glass! If they come near the wagon again just watch me take it up and see them run!'"

64

Those were happy days of adventuring in a new and smiling country, and all were in high spirits when on the 19th of July they reached the Little Sandy River, where they encamped, and all gathered together to talk over whether to take a new route which had been opened up by Mr. Lansford Hastings, called the Hastings Cut-off. This route passed along the southern shore of the Great Salt Lake, then joined the Old Fort Hall emigrant road on the Humboldt River. The new route was said to shorten the trip by about three hundred miles, and Virginia says in her diary, "Father was so eager to reach California quickly, that he was strongly in favor of taking the Cut-off, while others were equally firm in their objections to taking such a risk. At that time our party had grown to be a large one, for so many families had joined us on our way across the plains, and all had to have their say about the matter.

"There was a long discussion of the merits of the two routes, and as a result, at last we decided to split up, for a number of the party preferred not to risk taking the new route, while eighty-seven of us, including our family and the Donners, decided to take the Cut-off.

"On the 20th of July we broke camp and left the little Sandy, the other division of the party taking the old trail to Fort Hall, and the rest of us, who were called 'the Donner party' from that time, taking the new one.

"When we reached Fort Bridger, we were told that Mr. Hastings, whom we had expected to find there, had gone ahead to pilot a large emigrant train, and had left word that all later bands were to follow his trail; that they would find an abundant supply of wood, water, and pasturage along the whole line of road except for one forty-mile drive; that there were no difficult cañons to pass; and that the road was mostly good. This was encouraging and we traveled on comfortably for a week, when we reached the spot where Webber River breaks through the mountains into a cañon. There, by the side of the road, was a forked branch with a note stuck in its cleft, left by Hastings, saying, 'I advise all parties to encamp and wait for my return. The road I have taken is so rough that I fear wagons will not be able to get through to the Great Salt Lake Valley.' He mentioned another and better route which avoided the cañon altogether, and at once father, Mr. Stanton and William Pike said they would go ahead over this road, and if possible meet Hastings and bring him back to pilot us through to the valley.

"While the men went off to try to find Hastings, we encamped and waited for them to come back. In five days father came alone, having become separated from his companions, who he feared might have been lost. They had met Hastings, but he had refused to leave his party for their sake. Finally, however, father had insisted that he go with them to a high peak of the Wahsatch Mountains and from there point out to them the direction our party ought to take. Coming down from the peak, father lost sight of Stanton and Pike and was forced to come on alone, taking notes and blazing trees to help him in retracing his path when he should have us to guide. Searchers were at once sent out after the lost men, while we broke camp and started on our risky journey. It was easy enough traveling at first, but the following day we were brought to a sudden stop by a patch of dense woodland which it took a whole day's chopping to open up enough for our wagons to pass through. From there we chopped and pushed our way through what seemed an impassable wilderness of high peaks and rock-bound cañons, and then faced a great rough gulch. Believing it would lead out to the valley, our men again set to work vigorously, and for six long days they chopped until they were almost exhausted. Then a new party of emigrants caught up with us and, aided by three fresh men, the eight-mile road through the gulch was finished. It did not lead to the opening we had expected, but into a pretty mountain dell, but we were happy, because we found the searchers there with Mr. Stanton and Mr. Pike. They reported that we must go back on the newly made road and cross a more distant range of mountains in order to strike the trail to the valley. That was a moment of terror, even to the most courageous of our valiant band, but everyone forced a smile and a cheerful word as we started to retrace our way. We had five days more of traveling and road-making, and climbed a mountain so steep that six yoke of oxen had to pull each wagon up the steep ascent. Then we crossed the river flowing from Utah Lake to Great Salt Lake and at last found the trail of the Hastings party, thirty days after we set out for the point we had expected to reach in ten or twelve days.

"While we rested we took an inventory of our provisions, and found the supply was not sufficient to last until we should reach California. Here was a predicament! Mr. Donner called for volunteers to ride ahead on horseback to Sutter's Fort, to tell of our sorry plight and ask Captain Sutter to send back provisions by them for us, as we traveled toward them. Mr. Stanton and Mr. McCutchen said they would go to the fort, and rode away on their errand of mercy.

"Our wagons, meanwhile, wound their slow way along, far behind the horsemen, who were soon out of our sight, and two days later we found a lovely green valley where there were twenty wells of clear, sparkling water to cool our parched throats, which were only used to the alkaline pools from which we had been obliged to drink. Close beside the largest well we found a rough board, stuck in the ground with strips of white paper pinned to it, and around the board pieces of the paper were strewn on the turf, as if they had been torn off the board. 'There has been some message written on that paper. We must piece the bits together,' declared Mrs. Donner. No sooner said than done. Laying the board on her lap, she began to patch the scraps together, while we eagerly watched her. At last the words could be read: '2 days—2 nights—hard driving—cross—desert—reach water.' This was evidently meant as a warning to us, and the thought of two days' hard driving through the desert was anything but cheering. In fact, it would be such a strain on our cattle that we remained where we were, with the fine water to drink and good pasturage for three days. Then we filled our water casks, made all other preparations for the forty-mile drive, and started off again. We traveled for two days and nights, suffering from heat and thirst by day and from bitter cold by night. At the end of the second day we still saw the vast desert ahead of us as far as we could look. There was no more fodder for our cattle, our water-casks were empty, and the burning rays of the sun scorched us with pitiless and overpowering heat. Father rode on ahead in search of water, and scarcely had he left us than our beasts began to drop from exhaustion and thirst. Their drivers instantly unhitched them and drove them ahead, hoping to meet father and find wells where the thirsty beasts could be refreshed. They did find father and he showed them the way to wells he had found where the beasts could drink, then he traveled back to us, reaching our camp at dawn. We waited all that day in the desert, with the sun beating down on us with cruel heat, and still drivers and cattle had not come back. It was a desperate plight, for another night without water would mean death. We must set out on foot and try to reach some of the other wagons, whose owners had gone ahead." Virginia adds, "Never shall I forget that night, when we walked mile after mile in the darkness, every step seeming to be the very last we could take, each of us who were older and stronger, taking turns in carrying the younger children. Suddenly out of the black night came a swift, rushing noise of one of the young steers, who was crazed by thirst and rushing madly toward us. Father snatched up little Patty, and commanded the rest of us to keep close to his side, while he drew his pistol. We could hear the heavy snorting of the maddened beast, when he turned and dashed off into the darkness, leaving us weak and shivering with fright and relief. And still we were obliged to drag our weary feet on, for ten long miles, when we reached the Jacob Donner wagons. The family were all asleep inside, so we lay down on the ground under the protecting shadow of the family wagon. A bitter wind was howling across the desert, and it so chilled us that we crept close together, and if all five of our dogs had not snuggled up close to us, warming us with the heat from their big bodies, we would probably had died from cold.

"At dawn father rushed off to find his cattle, but in vain. He met the drivers, who told him that as the frenzied beasts were being driven toward the wells, they had broken loose and been lost in the darkness. At once all the men of the company turned out to help father to search for them, but none were ever found except one ox and a cow, and in that plight we were left stranded on the desert, eight hundred miles from California! To turn back to Fort Bridger was an impossibility—to go forward meant such hardship as blanched even my sun-reddened cheeks, and I shuddered at the thought that mother must live through greater privations than those we had already encountered. Well it was that the future was hidden from our eyes on that day in the desert!

"Two oxen were loaned father, which, yoked together with our one cow and ox, would draw one wagon, but not the family one, which had grown to be so home-like to us in our journeyings. It was decided to dig a trench, and *cache* all of our things except those which we could take in the one wagon. A *cache* is made by digging a hole in the ground and sinking in it the bed of a wagon, in which articles are packed; the hole is then covered with boards and earth, so they are completely hidden, and when we buried ours we hoped some day to return and take them away."

Having *cached* so many of their treasures, on the party went as bravely as possible until they reached Gravelly Ford on the Humboldt, where on the 5th of October there was such a tragic occurrence that Virginia says, "I grew up into a woman in a night, and life was never the same again, although for the sake of mother and the children I hid my feelings as well as I could."

Here her record is detailed, and as concise as possible. She writes:

"I will tell it as clearly and quickly as I can. We had reached a short sandy hill, and as the oxen were all tired, it was the custom at such places for the drivers to double up teams and help one another up the hill. A driver named Snyder, for some unaccountable reason, decided to go up alone. His oxen could not pull their load, and Snyder, angry at them, began to beat them. Father, who had gone on ahead, looking for the best road, came back, and in trying to make Snyder stop abusing his beasts, roused his anger to the point of frenzy. Father said, 'We can settle this, John, when we get up the hill.' 'No,' said Snyder. 'We will settle it now!' and, jumping on the tongue of his wagon, he struck father a hard blow over the head with his heavy whip-stock. One blow followed another, and father was stunned, as well as blinded by the blood streaming down from the gashes in his head. The whip was about to drop again when mother sprang between the two men. Father saw the uplifted whip and had only time to cry 'John! John!' when down came the blow on mother's head. Quick as a flash father's hunting-knife was out and Snyder fell, mortally wounded, and fifteen minutes later died. Then father realized, too late, what he had done. Dashing the blood from his eyes, he knelt over the dying man, who had been his friend, with remorse and agony in his expression.

66

"Camp was pitched at once, our wagon being some distance from the others, and father, whose head was badly cut, came to me.

"'Daughter,' he asked, 'do you think you can dress these wounds in my head? Your mother is not able and they must be attended to.' I said, promptly: 'Yes, if you will tell me what to do.' Then we went into the wagon, where we would not be disturbed, and I washed and dressed his wounds as best I could. When I had done what he told me to do, I burst out crying, and father clasped me in his arms, saying: 'I should not have asked so much of you!' I told him it was pity for him that made me cry. Then he talked to me quietly until I had controlled my feelings and was able to go back to the tent where mother was lying, weak and dazed by the happenings of the day. And there were worse things to come. In our party there was a man who had been in the habit of beating his wife until father told him he must either stop it or measures be taken to make him. He did not dare abuse her again, but he hated father from that time, and now he had his chance for revenge. After Snyder had been buried, and father had sadly watched the last clod of earth piled on the grave, the men of the party held a conference from which our family were excluded. We waited a short distance away, in terrified suspense to know the outcome of it, as we were sure it concerned father. And it did. His plea of self-defense was not acceptable to them, they said, and we shivered as we saw such bitterness on the men's faces as seemed sure would lead to lynching. Father saw it, but he was no coward. Baring his neck, he stepped forward, and proudly said, 'Come on, gentlemen!' No one moved, and presently he was told that he must leave the party, an exile— must go out in the wilderness alone without food or weapons. It was a cruel sentence, for it might result either in starvation or in murder by the Indians, and it is no wonder that mother was beside herself with fright, that we children knew not what to do or where to turn for help. Father heard the sentence in silence, then facing the group of old-time friends, with brave eyes, he said: 'I will not go. My act was one of self-defense, and as such is justified before God and man.'

"Meanwhile, my mother had been thinking, as she told me later, and she begged father to accept the sentence and leave the party, thinking it would be less dangerous than to remain among men who had become his enemies. He firmly refused until she pleaded that the whole party were now practically destitute of food, and if he remained, as an outcast, he would be obliged to see his children starve, while by going he might be able to meet them with food which he had procured somewhere. After a fearful struggle with his own desires, father consented, but not until the men of the party had promised to care for his innocent wife and children. Then, after he had held mother in his arms for a long agonized moment, he turned to me, and I forced my eyes to meet his with such fearless trust that he looked less despairing as he picked up Patty for a last hug and gripped the boys with an emotion too deep for any words; then he went off, an exile in the desert.

"I had no idea what I was going to do about it, but I knew I must do something. Through the long hours of the day, while I was busy soothing and comforting mother, who felt it keenly that we were left as much alone as if we were lepers, I was thinking busily. Our wagon was drawn up apart from the others, and we ate our scanty evening meal in silence. Milt Elliott and some others tried to talk with us, and show their friendliness, but mother would only answer in monosyllables and commanded the children to do the same. We were an utterly desolate, frightened group as darkness fell over us. I was busy helping the children get to bed, and then I found mother in such a state of collapse that I could think of nothing but comforting and quieting her.

"At last she fell asleep, and I crept to my bed, but I could not sleep. I must act. At last, I made a decision. I was strong and fearless, and father had no food or light or supplies, out there alone in the trackless wilderness. I stole to my mother's side and she roused at my light touch.

"'Mother, dear,' I whispered, 'I am going out to find father and take him some food, and his gun, and ammunition.' She roused and exclaimed:

"'What do you mean, child? You cannot find your father!'

"'I'm not going alone,' I replied 'I've asked Milt and he says he'll go with me.'

"Without giving her a chance to say I must not go, I hurried to the supply-chest and found some crackers, a small piece of bacon, some coffee and sugar. I took a tin cup, too, and a dipper for father to make coffee in, and packed his gun, pistols, and ammunition with them. His lantern was on the shelf, and I put a fresh piece of candle in it and matches in my pocket—then I was ready to start.

"Everything had to be done very quickly and quietly, for there would be a great risk if the children knew what I was going to do, or if any others of the party discovered my intention. So I did everything on tip-toe, and holding my breath for fear of being discovered.

"Mother called, 'Virginia!' and I went to her side. 'How will you find him in the darkness?'

"'I shall look for his horse's tracks and follow them,' I whispered. At that moment Milton's cautious step was heard at the side of the wagon, and with a last hug mother released me, and Milt and I stole off on our dangerous expedition.

"Out into the darkness we crept. Stealthily we hid in the shadows cast by the wagons in the flickering light of the dying camp-fire—cautiously we stole up behind the unsuspicious sentinel who was wearily tramping back and forth, and we held our breath for fright as he suddenly looked over the sleeping camp, then peered out into the mysterious darkness of the desert, but he did not see us. For safety we lay down on the ground, and silently dragged our bodies along until we were well out of his sight and hearing; then we pushed our feet along without lifting them, to be sure they did not fall into some unseen hole or trap, and now and again we were startled by some noise that to our excited senses seemed to mean that a wild animal was near us. My eyes had been searching the darkness around and before us, and at last I whispered:

"'Stop, Milt. Let us light the lantern!'

"Then stooping down, I spread out my skirts so that not the slightest flash of a match or gleam of light could be seen by the sentinel or by any one in the encampment. Milton lighted the lantern. I took it in one hand, and with the other held my skirts up in such a way as to shield its beams, and in its feeble light I searched the ground still frantically for some trace of the footprints of father's horse. Although I was nervous and excited enough to fly on the wings of lightning, I did not let the feeling get the better of me, but made a deliberate search of every inch of ground, making a complete circle around the outskirts of the camp, for I was determined to find those tracks. At last! There they were, unmistakable and clear. I gave a smothered cry and showed them to Milt. Then, still with the lantern carefully covered, so that no unguarded flash might bring a death-dealing shot from the sentinel's rifle, I followed where they led, Milt close behind, carrying the gun and provisions. Mile after mile we followed—followed, now seeing the tracks, now losing them. Oh what an agony was compressed in those awful hours!

"Suddenly on the midnight air came the wild howl of coyotes. From the distance echoed an even more hideous cry—that of the panther, seeking for prey. At that sound Milton's hair literally stood on end, and if I had shown one sign of weakening he would gladly have given up the search. But I went on, closing my ears to the dreaded sounds. All of a sudden my heart beat so wildly that I was obliged to press my hand over it to quiet its hammering. What I heard or saw or felt I can never explain, but I know that all the terror of my thirteen years of life seemed to be condensed into one moment of dread. And yet go on I must, praying to God to protect us and let me find father. I pushed ahead, with panic holding me in its wild grip as I pictured a horrible death if we should be captured by Indians. Then suddenly with wide-strained eyes and fluttering heart, I forgot all weariness and fear. In the far distance a dim, flickering light. Gripping Milt's arm, I whispered:

"'Father!'

"No sooner had I said it than I thought, 'Perhaps it is an Indian camp-fire.' But common sense put that aside, for I was sure I had seen father's horse's hoofprints, and certainly they would lead to him. But suppose he had been captured by Indians, and this fire we were coming to should lead to horrible disclosures. All this went through my mind, but I said nothing of it to Milton. I just went walking steadily on. Oh, how far away the light was! Would we never reach it? It seemed as if the more we walked the farther from it we were. But no, it was he—it was—it was! With a glad cry of, 'Oh, father! father!' I rushed forward and flung myself in his arms.

"'My child, my Virginia!' he exclaimed, when surprise had let him find his voice. 'You should not have come here!'

"'But I *am* here,' I cried, 'and I've brought you some food and your gun, and a blanket, and a little coffee, and some crackers! And here's a tin cup, too, and your pistols, and some powder and caps. Oh, and here are some matches, too!' I exclaimed, holding out one after another of the precious articles to his astonished gaze, and laughing and crying as I talked.

"It was almost pitiful to see father's astonishment at the thought that some one had come to help him in his terrible plight, and as he took the things I had brought he kissed and fondled me like a little child, and said that, God helping him, he would hurry on to California and secure a home for his beloved family—and it seems conceited to mention it, but he called me his 'brave daughter' over and over again, until I was glad of the darkness to hide my burning cheeks. Then in the protecting darkness, with Milton to stand guard, we sat together and talked of mother and Patty and the boys, and of what we should do while we were parted from him. Father was the first to remember that dawn would soon flush the east, and rising, he kissed me again and tried to say farewell.

"'But I'm not going back!' I cried. 'I'm going with you. Milt will go back, but I am going on with you.' Seeing his stern, set face, I pleaded, piteously: 'Oh, don't send me back—I can never bear to see those cruel men again. Let me go with you?' He turned a white, drawn face to mine.

"'For mother's sake, dear,' he said, 'go back and take care of her. God will care for me.' Before I could cry out or make a move to go with him, he had gathered up the articles I had brought him, jumped on his horse, and ridden away into the solitude of the Western desert. Milton and I were left alone to find our way back to the encampment where mother was watching and waiting for me with an eager, aching heart. When my straining eyes had seen the last of that solitary figure riding off into the black desert, I turned abruptly away, and Milt and I crept back over the vast desert. Before there was a glimmer of dawn I was safely clasped in mother's arms, repeated my comforting news over and over again that we had found father, that he was well and on his way to that land toward which our own faces were turned."

In this simple, direct fashion has Virginia Reed told of a heroic deed in the history of brave pioneer girls—but as the story comes from her pen, it is scarcely possible to realize the anxiety, the torturing fear, the hideous danger of such an expedition as that one of hers when at midnight, on the great plains, she set out to find her father.

"After that," she says, "though we were obliged to travel on, and though the party tried to be friendly with us, our hearts were sore and our thoughts were centered on father, journeying on alone. But as we went on we found welcome surprises by the way. A note written by him, stuck on a forked twig by the wayside, feathers scattered over the path to show that he had killed a bird and was not hungry. When we had found such evidence of his being alive and well, mother would be light-hearted for a whole day. Then the signs ceased, and mother's despair was pitiful to see. Had he been killed by the Indians or perhaps died of starvation? Patty and I were afraid we would lose mother, too. But starvation was menacing the whole party, and she was roused to new strength in a desire to protect her children from that fate. And even more ominous in their portent of disaster, before us rose the snow-capped Sierra Nevada mountains, which we must cross before the heavy snows fell, and the question was, could we do it? We left our wagon behind, which was too heavy for the mountain trip, placed in it every article we could do without, packed what we needed in another, and struggled on as best we could until the 19th of October, when we had a great joy. As we were wearily traveling along the Truckee, up rode Mr. Stanton and with him were seven mules loaded with provisions! No angel from the skies could have been more welcome, and, hungry though we were, better than food was the news that father was alive and pushing on to the west. Mr. Stanton had met him near Sutter's Fort, and had given him provisions and a fresh horse. Oh, how relieved mother was! I think she could not have eaten a mouthful, hungry as she was, without the glad tidings. Father had asked Mr. Stanton to personally conduct us across the Sierras before snow came, which he had promised to do, so with new courage we hurried on, keeping a close watch on those gaunt peaks ahead of us, which we must climb before realizing our dreams. Although it was so early in the season, all trails were covered with snow, but we struggled on, mother riding one mule with Tommy in her lap, Patty and Jim on another, behind two Indians who had accompanied Mr. Stanton, and I riding behind our leader. But though we did all in our power to travel fast, we were obliged to call a halt before we reached the summit, and camp only three miles this side of the crest of the mountain range.

"That night," says Virginia, "came the dreaded snow. Around the camp-fires under the trees great feathery flakes came whirling down. The air was so full of them that one could see objects only a few feet away. The Indians knew we were doomed and one of them wrapped his blanket about him and stood all night under a tree. We children slept soundly on our cold bed of snow, which fell over us so thickly that every few moments my mother would have to shake the shawl—our only covering—to keep us from being buried alive. In the morning the snow lay deep on mountain and valley, and we were forced to turn back to a lake we had passed, which was afterward called 'Donner Lake,' where the men hastily put up some rough cabins—three of them known as the Breen cabin, the Murphy cabin, and the Reed-Graves cabin. Then the cattle were all killed, and the meat was placed in the snow to preserve it, and we tried to settle down as comfortably as we could, until the season of snow and ice should be over. But the comfort was a poor imitation of the real thing, and now and then, in desperation, a party started out to try to cross the mountains, but they were always driven back by the pitiless storms. Finally, a party of fifteen, known in later days as the 'Forlorn Hopes,' started out, ten men and five women, on snow-shoes, led by noble Mr. Stanton, and we heard no more of them until months afterward.

"No pen can describe the dreary hopelessness of those who spent that winter at Donner Lake," says Virginia. "Our daily life in that dark little cabin under the snow would fill pages and make the coldest heart ache. Only one memory stands out with any bright gleam. Christmas was near, and there was no way of making it a happy time. But my mother was determined to give us a treat on that day. She had hidden away a small store of provisions—a few dried apples, some beans, a bit of tripe, and a small piece of bacon. These she brought out, and when we saw the treasures we shouted for joy, and watched the meal cooking with hunger-sharpened eyes. Mother smiled at our delight and cautioned:

"'Children, eat slowly, for this one day you can have all you wish!' and never has any Christmas feast since driven out of my memory that most memorable one at Donner Lake.

"Somehow or other the cold dark days and weeks passed, but as they went by our store of supplies grew less and less, and many died from cold and hunger. Frequently we had to cut chips from the inside of our cabin to start a fire, and we were so weak from want of food that we could scarcely drag ourselves from one cabin to the other, and so four dreadful months wore away. Then came a day when a fact stared us in the face. We were starving. With an almost superhuman strength mother roused. 'I am going to walk across the mountains,' she said; 'I cannot see my children die for lack of food.' Quickly I stood beside her. 'I will go, too,' I said. Up rose Milt and Eliza. 'We will go with you,' they said. Leaving the children to be cared for by the Breens and Murphys, we made a brave start. Milt led the way on snow-shoes and we followed in his tracks, but Eliza gave out on the first day and had to go back, and after five days in the mountains, we, too, turned back and mother was almost exhausted, and we went back just in time, for that night there was the most fearful storm of the winter, and we should have died if we had not had the shelter of our cabins. My feet had been badly frozen, and mother was utterly spent from climbing one high mountain after another, but we felt no lasting bad effects from the venture. But we had no food! Our cabins were roofed over with hides, which now we had to take down and boil for food. They saved life, but to eat them was like eating a pot of glue, and I could not swallow them. The roof of our cabin having been taken off, the Breens gave us a shelter, and when Mrs. Breen discovered what I had tried to hide from my own family, that I could not eat the hide, she gave me little bits of meat now and then from their fast-dwindling store.

"One thing was my great comfort from that time," says Virginia. "The Breens were the only Catholics in the party, and prayers were said regularly every night and morning in their little cabin, Mr. Breen reading by the light of a small pine torch, which I held, kneeling by his side. There was something inexpressibly comforting to me in this simple service, and one night when we had all gone to bed, huddled together to keep from freezing, and I felt it would not be long before we would all go to sleep never to wake again in this world, all at once I found myself on my knees, looking up through the darkness and making a vow that if God would send us relief and let me see my father again, I would become a Catholic. And my prayer was answered.

"On the evening of February 19th, we were in the cabin, weak and starving, when we heard Mr. Breen's voice outside, crying:

"'Relief, thank God! Relief!'

"In a moment, before our unbelieving eyes, stood seven men sent by Captain Sutter from the fort, and they had brought an ample supply of flour and jerked beef, to save us from the death which had already overtaken so many of our party. There was joy at Donner Lake that night, for the men said: 'Relief parties will come and go until you have all crossed the mountains safely.' But," Virginia's diary says: "mingled with one joy were bitter tears. Even strong men sat and wept as they saw the dead lying about on the snow, some even unburied, as the living had not had strength to bury them. I sorrowed most for Milt Elliott—our faithful friend, who seemed so like a brother, and when he died, mother and I dragged him out of the cabin and covered him with snow, and I patted the pure white snow down softly over all but his face—and dragged myself away, with a heart aching from the pain of such a loss.

"But we were obliged to turn our thoughts to the living and their future, and eagerly listened to the story of the men, who told us that when father arrived at Sutter's Fort, after meeting Mr. Stanton, he told Captain Sutter of our desperate plight and the captain at once furnished horses and supplies, with which father and Mr. McCutchen started back, but were obliged to return to the fort, and while they were conferring with Captain Sutter about their next move, the seven living members of the 'Forlorn Hope' party who had left us the first part of the winter, arrived at the fort. Their pale, worn faces told the story and touched all hearts. Cattle were killed and men were up all night drying beef and making flour by hand-mills for us; then the party started out to our rescue and they had not reached us one moment too soon!

"Three days later, the first relief started from Donner Lake with a party of twenty-three men, women, and children, and our family was among them. It was a bright, sunny day and we felt happy, but we had not gone far when Patty and Tommy gave out. As gently as possible I told mother that they would have to go back to the lake and wait for the next expedition. Mother insisted that she would go back with them, but the relief party would not allow this, and finally she gave in and let the children go in care of a Mr. Hover. Even the bravest of the men had tears in their eyes when little Patty patted mother's cheek and said, 'I want to see papa, but I will take good care of Tommy, and I do not want you to come back.' Meanwhile we traveled on, heavy-hearted, struggling through the snow single file. The men on snow-shoes broke the way and we followed in their tracks. At night we lay down on the snow to sleep, to awake to find our clothing all frozen. At break of day we were on the road again.... The sunshine, which it would seem would have been welcome, only added to our misery. The dazzling reflection made it very trying to our eyes, while its heat melted our frozen clothing and made it cling to our bodies. Jim was too small to step in the tracks made by the men, and to walk at all he had to place his knee on the little hill of snow after each step, and climb over it. Mother and I coaxed him along by telling him that every step he took he was getting nearer papa and nearer something to eat. He was the youngest child that walked over the Sierra Nevada.

"On their way to our rescue the relief party from Sutter's Fort had left meat hanging on a tree for our use as we came out. What was their horror when we reached the spot to find that it had been taken by wild animals. We were starving again—where could we get food? As we were trying to decide on our next move, one of the men who was in the lead ahead stopped, turned, and called out:

"'Is Mrs. Reed with you? If she is, tell her Mr. Reed is here!' There before us stood father! At the sight, mother, weak with joy, fell on her knees with outstretched arms, while I tried to run to meet him, but found myself too much exhausted, so I just held out my arms, too, and waited! In a moment he was where we could touch him and know that he was flesh and blood and not just a beautiful dream. He had planned to meet us just where we were, and had brought with him fourteen men and a generous supply of bread.

"As he knelt and clasped mother in his arms she told him that Patty and Tommy were still at the lake, and with a horrified exclamation, he started to his feet. 'I must go for them at once,' he said. 'There is no time to lose.' With one long embrace off he went as if on winged feet, traveling the distance which had taken us five days to go in two, we afterward heard. He found the children alive, to his great joy, but, oh, what a sight met his gaze! The famished little children and the death-like look of all at the lake made his heart ache. He filled Patty's apron with biscuits, which she carried around, giving one to each person. He also had soup made for the infirm, and rendered every possible assistance to the sufferers, then, leaving them with provisions for seven days, he started off, taking with him seventeen who were able to travel, and leaving at the lake three of his men to aid those who were too weak to walk.

"Almost as soon as father's party started out, they were caught in a terrible snow-storm and hurricane, and his description of the scene later was heart-breaking, as he told about the crying of the half-frozen children, the lamenting of the mothers and suffering of the whole party, while above all could be heard the shrieking of the storm king. One who has never seen a blizzard in the Sierras can have no idea of the situation, but we knew. All night father and his men worked in the raging storm, trying to put up shelters for the dying women and children, while at times the hurricane would burst forth with such fury that he felt frightened on account of the tall timber surrounding the camp. The party was almost without food, having left so much with the sufferers at the lake. Father had *cached* provisions on his way to the lake, and had sent three men forward to get it before the storm set in, but they could not get back. At one time the fire was nearly gone; had it been lost, all would have perished. For three days and three nights they were exposed to the fury of that terrible storm; then father became snow-blind, and would have died if two of his faithful comrades had not worked over him all night, but from that time all responsibility of the relief work was taken from him, as he was physically unfit.

"At last the storm abated, and the party halted, while father with Mr. McCutchen and Mr. Miller went on ahead to send back aid for those who were exhausted from the terrible journeying. Hiram Miller carried Tommy, while Patty started bravely to walk, but soon she sank on the snow and seemed to be dying. All gathered around in frantic efforts to revive the child, and luckily father found some crumbs in the thumb of his woolen mitten which he warmed and moistened between his own lips, and fed Patty. Slowly she came to life again, and was carried along by different ones in the company, so that by the time the party reached Woodworth's Camp she was quite herself again, and as she sat cozily before a big camp-fire she fondled and talked to a tiny doll which had traveled with her all the way from Springfield and which was her chosen confidante.

"As soon as father's party reached Woodworth's Camp a third relief party started back to help those who were slowly following, and still another party went on to Donner Lake to the relief of those who were still living. But many of that emigrant band lie sleeping to-day on the shore of that quiet mountain lake, for out of the eighty-three persons who were snowed in there, forty-two died, and of the thirty-one emigrants who left Springfield on that lovely April morning of 1846, only eighteen lived to reach California. Among them were our family, who, despite the terrible hardships and hideous privations we had suffered, yet seemed to have been especially watched over by a kind Providence, for we all lived to reach our goal, and were the only family who were not obliged at some part of the journey to subsist on human flesh to keep from perishing. God was good to our family, and I, Virginia, testify to the heroic qualities which were developed in even the youngest of us, and for my own part, I gratefully recognize the blessings which came to me from an unqualified faith in God and an unfaltering trust that He would take care of us—which He did.

"Mother, Jimmy and I reached California and were taken at once to the home of the mayor, Mr. Sinclair, where we were given a warm welcome and where nothing was left undone for our comfort. But we were still too anxious to be happy, for we knew that father's party had been caught in the storm." Virginia says: "I can see mother now as she stood leaning against the door for hours at a time, looking at the mountains. At last—oh wonderful day—they came, father, Patty and Tommy! In the moment of blissful reunion tears and smiles intermingled and all the bitterness and losses and sorrows of the cruel journey were washed away, leaving only a tender memory of those noble souls who had fared forth, not to the land of their dreams, but to a far country whose maker and builder is God.

"And for us, it was spring in California!"

LOUISA M. ALCOTT: AUTHOR OF "LITTLE WOMEN"

In a pleasant, shady garden in Concord, Massachusetts, under a gnarled old apple-tree, sat a very studious looking little person, bending over a sheet of paper on which she was writing. She had made a seat out of a tree stump, and a table by laying a board across two carpenter's horses, whose owner was working in the house, and no scholar writing a treatise on some deep subject could have been more absorbed in his work than was the little girl in the garden.

For a whole long hour she wrote, frequently stopping to look off into the distance and bite the end of her pencil with a very learned look, then she would bend over her paper again and write hard and fast. Finally, she laid down her pencil with an air of triumph, jumped up from the stump and rushed toward the house.

"Mother! Anna! I've written a poem about the robin we found this morning in the garden!" Dashing into the library she waved the paper in the air with a still more excited cry: "Listen!" and dropped on the floor to read her poem to a much thrilled audience of two. With great dramatic effect she read her lines, glancing up from time to time to see that she was producing the proper effect. This is what she read:

TO THE FIRST ROBIN

Welcome, welcome, little stranger, Fear no harm and fear no danger, We are glad to see you here, For you sing "Sweet Spring is near."

 Now the white snow melts away, Now the flowers blossom gay, Come, dear bird, and build your nest, For we love our robin best.

She finished with an upward tilt of her voice, while her mother excitedly flourished the stocking she was darning over her head, crying: "Good! Splendid!" and quiet Anna echoed the words, looking with awe at her small sister, as she added, "It's just like Shakespeare!"

The proud mother did not say much more in praise of the budding poetess's effort, for fear of making her conceited; but that night, after the verses had been read to a delighted father, and the young author had gone happily off to bed, the mother said:

"I do believe she is going to be a genius, Bronson!"

Yet, despite the prediction, even an appreciative parent would have been more than surprised had she been able to look into the future and had seen her daughter as one of the most famous writers of books for young people of her generation. The little girl who sat under the apple-tree on that day in early spring and wrote the verses was no other than Louisa May Alcott, and her tribute to the robin was to be treasured in after years as the first evidence of its writer's talent.

Louisa, the second daughter of Amos Bronson and Abba May Alcott, was born in Germantown, Pa., on the 29th of November, 1832, and was fortunate in being the child of parents who not only understood the intense, restless and emotional nature of this daughter, but were deeply interested in developing it in such a way that her marked traits would be valuable to her in later life. To this unfailing sympathy of both father and mother the turbulent nature owed much of its rich achievement, and Louisa Alcott's home surroundings and influences had as much to do with her success as a writer as had her talent, great as that was.

At the time of her birth her father was teaching school in Germantown, but he was a man whose ideas were original and far in advance of his time, and his way of teaching was not liked by the parents of his pupils, so when Louisa was two years old and her older sister, Anna, four, the family went to Boston, where Mr. Alcott opened his famous school in Masonic Temple, and enjoyed teaching by his own new methods, and when he was happy his devoted wife was equally contented.

Louisa was too young to go to school then, except as a visitor, but her father developed her young mind at home according to his own theories of education, and during the remainder of the all-too short days the active child was free to amuse herself as she chose. To play on the Common was her great delight, for she was a born investigator, and there she met children of all classes, who appealed to her many-sided nature in different ways. Louisa was never a respecter of class distinctions—it did not matter to her where people lived, or whether their hands and faces were dirty, if some personal characteristic attracted her to them, and from those early days she was unconsciously studying human nature, and making ready for the work of later years.

In her own sketch of those early days, she says:

"Running away was one of my great delights, and I still enjoy sudden flights out of the nest to look about this very interesting world and then go back to report!"

On one of her investigating tours, she met some Irish children whose friendliness delighted her, and she spent a wonderful day with them, sharing their dinner of cold potatoes, salt fish and bread crusts. Then—delightful pastime—they all played in the ash-heaps for some time, and took a trip to the Common together. But when twilight came, her new friends deserted her, leaving her a long way from home, and little Louisa began to think very longingly of her mother and sister. But as she did not know how to find her way back she sat down on a door-step, where a big dog was lying. He was so friendly that she cuddled up against his broad back and fell asleep. How long she slept she did not know, but she was awakened by the loud ringing of a bell, and a man's deep voice calling:

"Little girl lost! Six years old—in a pink frock, white hat and new green shoes. Little girl lost! Little girl lost!"

It was the town crier, and as he rang his bell and gave his loud cry, out of the darkness he heard a small voice exclaim:

"Why, dat's *me*!"

With great difficulty the crier was able to persuade the child to unclasp her arms from the neck of the big friendly dog, but at last she left him, and was taken to the crier's home and "feasted sumptuously on bread and molasses in a tin plate with the alphabet round it," while her frantic family was being notified. The unhappy ending to that incident is very tersely told by Louisa, who says: "My fun ended the next day, when I was tied to the arm of the sofa to repent at leisure!"

That the six years spent in Boston were happy ones, and that the budding spirit of Louisa was filled with joy at merely being alive, was shown one morning, when, at the breakfast table, she suddenly looked up with an all-embrasive smile and exclaimed:

"I love everybody in *dis* whole world!"

Despite the merriment which was always a feature of the Alcott home, as they were all blessed with a sense of humor which helped them over many a hard place, there was an underlying anxiety for Mr. and Mrs. Alcott, as the school was gradually growing smaller and there was barely enough income to support their family, to which a third daughter, Elizabeth, the "Beth" of *Little Women*, had been added recently. During those days they lived on very simple fare, which the children disliked, as their rice had to be eaten without sugar and their mush without butter or molasses. Nor did Mr. Alcott allow meat on his table, as he thought it wrong to eat any creature which had to be killed for the purpose. An old family friend who lived at a Boston hotel sympathized strongly with the children's longing for sweets, and every day at dinner she saved them a piece of pie or cake, which Louisa would call for, carrying a bandbox for the purpose. The friend was in Europe for years, and when she returned Louisa Alcott had become famous. Meeting her on the street one day, Louisa greeted her old friend, eagerly:

"Why, I did not think you would remember me!" said the old lady.

"Do you suppose I shall ever forget that bandbox!" was the quick reply.

As time went on, Mr. Alcott's school dwindled until he had only five scholars, and three of them were his own children. Something new had to be tried, and quickly, so the family moved out of the city, into a small house at Concord, Mass., which had an orchard and a garden, and, best of all, the children had a big barn, where they gave all sorts of entertainments; mostly plays, as they were born actors. Their mother, or "Marmee," as the girls called her, loved the fun as well as they did, and would lay aside her work at any moment to make impossible costumes for fairies, gnomes, kings or peasants, who were to take the principal parts in some stirring melodrama written by the girls themselves, or some adaptation of an old fairy tale. They acted Jack the Giant-killer in fine style, and the giant came tumbling headlong from a loft when Jack cut down the squash-vine running up a ladder and supposed to represent the immortal beanstalk. At other performances Cinderella rolled away in an impressive pumpkin, and one of their star plays was a dramatic version of the story of the woman who wasted her three wishes, in which a long black pudding was lowered by invisible hands and slowly fastened onto her nose.

But though the big barn often echoed with the sound of merry voices, at other times the girls dressed up as pilgrims, and journeyed over the hill with scrip and staff, and cockle shells in their hats; fairies held their revels among the whispering birches, and strawberry parties took place in the rustic arbor of the garden.

And there we find eight-year-old Louisa writing her verses to the robin, with genius early beginning to burn in the small head which later proved to be so full of wonderful material for the delight of young people.

"Those Concord days were the happiest of my life," says Miss Alcott. "We had charming playmates in the little Emersons, Channings, Goodwins and Hawthornes, with the illustrious parents and their friends to enjoy our pranks and share our excursions.... My wise mother, anxious to give me a strong body to support a lively brain, turned me loose in the country and let me run wild, learning of Nature what no books can teach, and being led—as those who truly love her seldom fail to be—'through Nature up to Nature's God.'"

The Alcott children were encouraged to keep diaries in which they wrote down their thoughts and feelings and fancies, and even at that early age Louisa's journal was a record of deep feelings and of a child's sacred emotions. In one of her solemn moods, she makes this entry:

"I had an early run in the woods before the dew was off the grass. The moss was like velvet, and as I ran under the arch of yellow and red leaves I sang for joy, my heart was so bright and the world so beautiful. I stopped at the end of the walk and saw the sunshine out over the wide 'Virginia meadows.'

"It seemed like going through a dark life or grave into heaven beyond. A very strange and solemn feeling came over me as I stood there, with no sound but the rustle of the pines, no one near me, and the sun so glorious, as for me alone. It seemed as if I *felt* God as I never did before, and I prayed in my heart that I might keep that happy sense of nearness all my life."

To that entry there is a note added, years later: "*I have*, for I most sincerely think that the little girl 'got religion' that day in the wood, when dear Mother Nature led her to God."—L. M. A. 1885.

That deep religious note in Louisa Alcott's nature is very marked and is evident in all of her work, but, on the other hand, she had a sparkling wit and such a keen sense of humor that in her blackest moods she could always see something funny to amuse her, and frequently laughed at her own expense.

That her conscience was as active as her mind and her body is shown by one of her "private plays," which she makes Demi describe in *Little Men*. He says:

"I play that my mind is a round room, and my soul is a little sort of creature with wings that lives in it. The walls are full of shelves and drawers, and in them I keep my thoughts, and my goodness and badness and all sorts of things. The goods I keep where I can see them, and the bads I lock up tight, but they get out, and I have to keep putting them in and squeezing them down, they are so strong. The thoughts I play with when I am alone or in bed, and I make up and do what I like with them. Every Sunday I put my room in order, and talk with the little spirit that lives there, and tell him what to do. He is very bad sometimes and won't mind me, and I have to scold him."

Truly a strange game for a child to play, but the Alcotts were brought up to a reverent knowledge of their souls as well as their bodies, and many a sober talk at twilight did mother or father have with the daughters to whom the experience of the older generation was helpful and inspiring. A very happy family they were, despite frequent lack of luxuries and even necessities, but loyalty and generosity as their marked characteristics. No matter how little money or food an Alcott had, it was always shared with any one who had less, and the largest share was usually given away.

On Louisa's fourth birthday, she tells of a feast given in her honor in her father's school-room in Masonic Temple. All the children were there, and Louisa wore a crown of flowers and stood upon a table to give a cake to each child as they all marched around the table. "By some oversight," says Louisa, "the cakes fell short, and I saw that if I gave away the last one, *I* should have none. As I was queen of the revel, I felt that I ought to have it, and held on to it tightly, until my mother said: 'It is always better to give away than to keep the nice things; so I know my Louy will not let the little friend go without.'" She adds: "The little friend received the dear plummy cake, and I ... my first lesson in the sweetness of self-denial—a lesson which my dear mother illustrated all her long and noble life."

At another time a starving family was discovered, when the Alcotts, forming in a procession, carried their own breakfast to the hungry ones. On one occasion, when a friend had unexpected guests arrive for dinner, too late to secure any extra provisions, the Alcotts with great glee lent their dinner to the thankful hostess, and thought it a good joke. Again, on a snowy Saturday night, when their wood-pile was extra low, and there was no way of getting any more that week, a poor child came to beg a little, as their baby was sick and the father on a spree with all his wages. At first Mrs. Alcott hesitated, as it was bitterly cold and Abba May, the little baby sister, was very young, but Mr. Alcott decided the matter with his usual kindly optimism.

"Give half our stock and trust in Providence; the weather will moderate or wood will come," he declared. And the wood was lent, Mrs. Alcott cheerily agreeing: "Well, their need is greater than ours. If our half gives out we can go to bed and tell stories!"

A little later in the evening, while it was still snowing heavily, and the Alcotts were about to cover their fire to keep it, a farmer who was in the habit of supplying them with wood knocked at the door and asked anxiously:

"Wouldn't you like me to drop my load of wood here? It would accommodate me, and you need not hurry to pay for it. I started for Boston with it but the snow is drifting so fast, I want to go home."

"Yes," answered Mr. Alcott, and as the man went away, he turned to his wife and exclaimed: "Didn't I tell you that wood would come if the weather didn't moderate?"

Again, a tramp asked Mr. Alcott to lend him five dollars. As he had only a ten-dollar bill, the dear man at once offered that, asking to have the change brought back as soon as possible. Despite the disbelief of his family in the tramp's honesty, the man did bring the five-dollar bill soon with profuse thanks, and the gentle philosopher's faith in human nature was not crushed.

Still another experiment in generosity proved a harder one in its results to the Alcotts, when Mrs. Alcott allowed some poor emigrants to rest in her garden while she treated them to a bountiful meal. Unfortunately for their generous benefactor, in return they gave small-pox to the entire family, and, although the girls had light cases, Mr. and Mrs. Alcott were very sick and, as Miss Alcott records later: "We had a curious time of exile, danger and trouble." She adds: "No doctors and all got well."

When Louisa Alcott was almost ten years old, and Anna twelve, Mr. Alcott took a trip to England, hoping to interest the people there in his new theories of education and of living. So enthusiastically and beautifully did he present his theories that he won many converts, and one of them, a Mr. Lane, returned to America with him to help him found a colony on the new ideas, which were more ideal than practical, and so disapproved of by Mr. Alcott's friends, who thought him foolish to waste time and money on them.

However, after months of planning, Mr. Alcott, Mr. Lane and other enthusiasts decided to buy an estate of one hundred acres near Harvard Village, Mass., and establish the colony. The place was named "Fruitlands," in anticipation of future crops, and the men who were to start the community were full of hope and enthusiasm, in which Mrs. Alcott did not share, as she knew her husband's visionary nature too well not to fear the result of such an experiment. However, she aided in making the plan as practical as she could, and drew such a rosy picture of their new home to the children that they expected life at Fruitlands to be a perpetual picnic.

Alas for visions and for hopes! Although life at Fruitlands had its moments of sunshine and happiness, yet they were far overbalanced by hard work, small results and increasing worry over money matters, and at last, after four years of struggle to make ends meet, Mr. Alcott was obliged to face the fact that the experiment had been an utter failure, that he had exhausted his resources of mind, body and estate. It was a black time for the gentle dreamer, and for a while it seemed as if despair would overwhelm him. But with his brave wife to help him and the children's welfare to think of, he shook off his despondency bravely, and decided to make a fresh start. So Mrs. Alcott wrote to her brother in Boston for help, sold all the furniture they could spare, and went to Still River, the nearest village to Fruitlands, and engaged four rooms. "Then on a bleak December day the Alcott family emerged from the snowbank in which Fruitlands, now re-christened *Apple Stump* by Mrs. Alcott, lay hidden. Their worldly goods were piled on an ox-sled, the four girls on the top, while father and mother trudged arm in arm behind, poorer indeed in worldly goods, but richer in love and faith and patience, and alas, experience."

After a winter in Still River they went back to Concord, where they occupied a few rooms in the house of a sympathetic friend—not all their friends were sympathetic, by any means, as most of them had warned Mr. Alcott of this ending to his experiment. But all were kindly as they saw the family take up life bravely in Concord again, with even fewer necessities and comforts than before. Both Mr. and Mrs. Alcott did whatever work they could find to do, thinking nothing too menial if it provided food and clothing for their family. Naturally the education of the children was rather fragmentary and insufficient, but it developed their own powers of thinking. Through the pages of their diaries in which they wrote regularly, and which were open to their mother and father, they learned to express their thoughts clearly on all subjects. Also they were encouraged to read freely, while only the best books were within their reach. Louisa's poetic and dramatic efforts were not ridiculed, but criticized as carefully as if they had been masterpieces, so she had no fear of expressing her deepest thoughts, but acted out her own nature freely and fearlessly.

In fact the four daughters were happy, wholesome, hearty girls, whose frolics and pastimes took such unique forms that people wondered whether they were the result of Mr. Alcott's theories, and Miss Alcott tells of one afternoon when Mr. Emerson and Margaret Fuller were visiting her mother and the conversation drifted to the subject of education. Turning to Mr. Alcott, Miss Fuller said:

"Well, Mr. Alcott, you have been able to carry out your methods in your own family; I should like to see your model children."

A few moments later, as the guests stood on the door-step, ready to leave, there was a wild uproar heard in the near distance and round the corner of the house came a wheel-barrow holding baby May, dressed as a queen; Miss Alcott says: "I was the horse, bitted and bridled, and driven by my sister Anna, while Lizzie played dog and barked as loud as her gentle voice permitted.

"All were shouting and wild with fun, which, however, came to a sudden end, for my foot tripped and down we all went in a laughing heap, while my mother put a climax to the joke by saying with a dramatic wave of the hand:

"'Here are the model children, Miss Fuller!'"

When Mrs. Alcott's father, Colonel May, died, he left his daughter a small property, and she now determined to buy a house in Concord with it, so that whatever the varying fortunes of the family might be in future they would at least have a roof over their heads. An additional amount of five hundred dollars was added by Mr. Emerson, who was always the good angel of the family, and the place in Concord known as "Hillside" was bought, where life and work began in earnest for Louisa and her sisters, for only too clearly they saw the heavy weight that was being laid on their mother's shoulders.

Louisa was growing in body and spirit in those days, stretching up physically and mentally, and among the sources of her finest inspiration was the gentle reformer, philosopher and writer, Ralph Waldo Emerson, who was ever her father's loyal friend and helper. Louisa's warm little heart enshrined the calm, great-minded man who always understood things, and after she had read Goethe's correspondence with Bettine, she, like Bettine, placed her idol on a pedestal and worshipped him in a truly romantic fashion. At night, after she had gone to her room, she wrote him long passionate letters, expressing her devotion, but she never sent the letters—only told him of them in later years, when they laughed together over her girlish fancy. Once, she confessed to having sat in a tall cherry-tree at midnight and sung to the moon until the owls scared her to bed; and of having sung Mignon's song under his window in very bad German, and strewed wild flowers over his door-step in the darkness. This sounds very sentimental and silly, but Louisa was never that. She had a deep, intense nature, which as yet had found no outlet or expression, and she could have had no safer hero to worship than this gentle, serene, wise man whose friendship for her family was so practical in its expression. Also at that period, which Louisa herself in her diary calls the "sentimental period," she was strongly influenced by the poet and naturalist, Thoreau. From him she learned to know Nature in a closer and more loving intimacy. Thoreau was called a hermit, and known as a genius, and more often than not he could be found in his hut in the woods, or on the river bank, where he learned to look for the bright-eyed "Alcott girl," who would swing along his side in twenty-mile tramps, eager and inquisitive about everything, learning new facts about flowers and trees and birds and insects from the great man at her side. Truly a fortunate girl was Louisa, with two such friends and teachers as the great Emerson and Thoreau. Hawthorne, too, fascinated her in his shy reserve, and the young girl in her teens with a tremendous ability to do and to be something worth while in life could have had no more valuable preface to her life as a writer than that of the happy growing days at Concord, with that group of remarkable men.

At that time she did not think seriously of having talent for writing, as she had only written a half-dozen pieces of verse, among them one called "My Kingdom," which has been preserved as a bit of girlish yearning for the best in religion and in character, sweetly expressed, and some thrilling melodramas for the "troupe" in the barn to act. These were overflowing with villains and heroes, and were lurid enough to satisfy the most intense of her audience. Later some of them were collected under the title of "Comic Tragedies"—but at best they only serve to show how full of imaginative possibilities the girl's nature was.

Although the Alcotts had their own home in Concord now, it was yet almost impossible to make ends meet, and with the sturdy independence which proved to be one of her marked traits, Louisa determined to earn some money and add to the family income. It was no easy thing to do, for there were few avenues of work open to girls in that day. But she could teach, for it was quite a popular resource to open a small school in some barn, with a select set of pupils. Louisa herself had been to one of these "barn schools," and now she opened one in Mr. Emerson's barn, but it paid very poorly, as did everything which the Alcotts attempted to do. The brave mother was so completely discouraged, that when one day a friend passing through Concord called on her, Mrs. Alcott confessed the state of her financial affairs. As a result of that confession, the family once more migrated to Boston, leaving the Hawthornes as occupants of "Hillside." In the city Mrs. Alcott was given a position as visitor to the poor by a benevolent association, and she also kept an employment agency—a more respectable occupation than it was in later years. Once more there was money in the treasury, and with their usual happy optimism the family cheered up and decided that life was worth living, even under the most trying circumstances. While his wife was busy in that way, Mr. Alcott gradually drew a circle of people around him to whom his theories of life were acceptable, and who paid a small price to attend the "conversations" he held on subjects which interested him to discuss. Being appreciated, even by a small audience, was balm to the wounded spirit of the gentle philosopher, whose "Fruitlands" experiment had been such a bitter one, and now he was as happy as though he were earning large amounts by his work, instead of the meager sum paid by his disciples to hear him talk of his pet theories. But he was contented, and his happiness was reflected by his adoring family. Mrs. Alcott, too, was satisfied with the work she was doing, so for a time all went well with the "Pathetic Family" as Louisa had christened them.

Louisa, meanwhile, was learning many lessons as she traveled slowly up the road to womanhood—learning courage and self-denial, linked with cheerfulness from mother and father, and enjoying a wholesome comradeship in the home life with her sisters.

Anna, the oldest daughter, was much like her father. She never worried about her soul or her shortcomings as Louisa did; she accepted life as it came, without question, and was of a calm nature, unlike turbulent, questioning Louisa, who had as many moods as there were hours in a day and who found ruling her tempestuous nature the hardest piece of work life offered her. She confesses in her diary: "My quick tongue is always getting me into trouble, and my moodiness makes it hard to be cheerful when I think how poor we are, how much worry it is to live, and how many things I long to do—I never can. So every day is a battle, and I'm so tired I don't want to live, only it's cowardly to die till you have done something." Having made this confession to an unresponsive page of her journal, the restless nature gave up the desire to be a coward, and turned to achieving whatever work might come to her hand to do, little dreaming what was before her in the coming years. She was very fine looking, of which she evidently was conscious, for she says in her diary:

"If I look in my glass I try to keep down vanity about my long hair, my well-shaped head, and my good nose." Besides these good points of which she speaks so frankly, she was tall and graceful, with a heavy mass of glossy, chestnut-brown hair. Her complexion was clear and full of color, and her dark-blue eyes were deep-set and very expressive.

During those years in Boston, the Alcotts spent two summers in an uncle's roomy house, where they enjoyed such comforts as had not before fallen to their lot, and calm Anna, sweet retiring Beth, or Betty, as she was called, and artistic May, the youngest of the flock, revelled in having rooms of their own, and plenty of space for their own belongings. May was a pretty, golden-haired, blue-eyed child with decided tastes, and an ability to get what she most wanted in life without much effort—an ability which poor Louisa entirely lacked, for her success always came as the result of exhausting work.

Louisa was now seventeen years old, and Anna nineteen. At that time came the small-pox siege, and after Anna had recovered partially she was obliged to take a rest, leaving her small school in Louisa's charge. There were twenty scholars, and it was a great responsibility for the girl of seventeen, but she took up the work with such enthusiasm that she managed to captivate her pupils, whose attention she held by illustrating many of their lessons with original stories, telling them in a way they would never forget. When Anna came back the school was so flourishing that Louisa continued to help with the teaching, and it seemed probable that she had found her greatest talent, although little did she guess how many interesting avenues of experience were to widen before her wondering eyes before she was to settle down to her life-work.

Meanwhile she kept on helping Anna with her school, and to liven up the daily routine of a rather dull existence she began to write thrilling plays, which she always read to Anna, who criticized and helped revise them with sisterly severity. The plays were acted by a group of the girls' friends, with Anna and Louisa usually taking the principal parts. From creating these wonderful melodramas, which always won loud applause from an enthusiastic audience, and because of her real ability to act, Louisa now decided that she would go on the real stage. "Anna wants to be an actress, and so do I," she wrote in her diary. "We could make plenty of money perhaps, and it is a very gay life. Mother says we are too young, and must wait."

Wise mother, and firm as wise! The girls were obliged to accept her decree, and Louisa was so depressed by it that for a time she made every one miserable by her downcast mood. Then, fortunately, an interested relative showed one of her plays to the manager of the Boston Theater. He read "The Rival Prima Donnas" with kindly eyes, and offered to stage it. Here was good luck indeed! The entire Alcott family held as great a jubilation when they heard the news as if they had fallen heir to a fortune, and Louisa at once forgot her ambition to act, in her ambition to be known as a successful play-wright.

Unfortunately, there was some hitch in the arrangements, and the play was never produced, but the manager sent Louisa a free pass to the theater, which gave her a play-wright's pride whenever she used it, and her enjoyment in anticipating the production had been so great that she was able to bear the actual disappointment with real philosophy. And by that time her mood had changed. Although she always loved to act, and acted well, her own good sense had asserted itself, and she had set aside a dramatic career, realizing that it included too many difficulties and hardships.

Her next adventure was quite different. To her mother's employment office came a gentleman who wished a companion for his old father and sister. The position offered only light work, and seemed a good one in every respect, and impulsive Louisa, who happened to hear the request, asked her mother, eagerly: "Can't I go? Oh, do let *me* take it!" Her mother, thinking the experience would not be harmful, let her accept the position, and as a result she had two of the most disillusioning and hard months of her life. She had her revenge later by writing a story called "How I Went Out to Service," in which she described the experience in a vivid way.

An extract from her "heart journal," as she now called her diary, is a revelation of home life which gave to Louisa much of that understanding of human nature which has made her books so popular. She says: "Our poor little home had much love and happiness in it, and was a shelter for lost girls, abused wives, friendless children and weak or wicked men. Father and mother had no money to give, but gave their time, sympathy, help, and if blessings would make them rich they would be millionaires. This is practical Christianity."

At that time they were living in a small house, with Beth as housekeeper, while Anna and Louisa taught, May went to school, and the mother attended to her own work. Mr. Alcott, too, was doing all he could to add to the family income by his lectures, and by writing articles on his favorite subjects, so all together, they managed to live in some sort of fashion. But Louisa had now made up her mind that she must do more for the comfort of the beloved mother, who was always over-worked and worried, despite her courage and cheery manner, and she decided to try to publish a story.

Full of the intention, one night, she sat down on the floor and searched through the pile of papers which included most of her "scribblings" since her first use of a pen. Plays, poems and many other closely written sheets were thrown aside. At last she found what she was looking for, and read and re-read it three times, then set it aside until morning, when, with the greatest possible secrecy, she put it in an envelope, sealed, addressed and mailed it. From that time she went about her work with the air of one whose mind is on greater things, but she was always wide awake enough when it came time for some one to go for the mail, and her sisters joked her about her eagerness for letters, which she bore good-naturedly enough. Then came a wonderful day when she was handed a letter from a well-known firm of publishers. Her hand shook as she opened it, and she gave a suppressed cry of joy as she read the short note, and looked with amazement at the bit of paper enclosed.

Later in the day, when the housework was done and school was over, she sauntered into the room where the family was gathered in a sewing-bee. Throwing herself into a chair with an indifferent air, she asked:

"Want to hear a good story?"

Of course they did. The Alcotts were always ready for a story, and Louisa read extremely well. Her audience listened to the thrilling tale with eager attention, and at the end there was a chorus of cries: "How fine! How lovely! How interesting!" Then Anna asked: "Who wrote it?" With shining eyes and crimson cheeks Louisa jumped to her feet and, waving the paper overhead, cried:

"*Your sister! I wrote it!* Yes, I really did!"

One can imagine the great excitement of the group who then clustered around the authoress and asked questions all at once.

That first published story was pronounced by its creator to be "great rubbish," and she only received the sum of five dollars for it, but it was a beginning, and from that time in her active brain plots for stories long and short began to simmer, although she still taught, and often did sewing in the evenings, for which she was fairly well paid.

In mid-winter of 1853 Mr. Alcott went West on a lecture tour, full of hope for a financial success. He left the home group as busy as usual, for Mrs. Alcott had several boarders, as well as her employment office. Anna had gone to Syracuse to teach in a school there, Louisa had opened a home school with ten pupils, and the calm philosopher felt that he could leave them with a quiet mind, as they were all earning money, and this was his opportunity to broaden the field in which the seeds of unique ideas were sown.

So off he went, full of eager courage, followed by the good wishes of the girls, who fondly hoped that "father would be appreciated at last." Alas for hopes! On a February night, when all the household were sleeping soundly, the bell rang violently. All were awakened, and Louisa says, "Mother flew down, crying 'my husband!' We rushed after, and five white figures embraced the half-frozen wanderer who came in tired, hungry, cold and disappointed, but smiling bravely, and as serene as ever. We fed and warmed and brooded over him," says Louisa, "longing to ask if he had made any money, but none did till little May said, after he had told all the pleasant things: 'Well, did people pay you?' Then, with a queer look, he opened his pocket-book and showed one dollar, saying with a smile that made our eyes fill: 'Only that! My overcoat was stolen, and I had to buy a shawl. Many promises were not kept, and traveling is costly, but I have opened the way, and another year shall do better.'

"I shall never forget," adds Louisa, "how beautifully mother answered him, though the dear hopeful soul had built much on his success; but with a beaming face she kissed him, saying, 'I call that doing *very* well. Since you are safely home, dear, we don't ask anything more.'

"Anna and I choked down our tears, and took a lesson in real love which we never forgot.... It was half tragic and comic, for father was very dirty and sleepy, and mother in a big night-cap and funny old jacket."

Surely no one ever had a better opportunity to probe to the heart of the real emotions that make up the most prosaic as well as the most heroic daily lives than a member of that generous, happy, loving Alcott family.

And still Louisa kept on doing other things besides the writing, which was such a safety valve for her intense nature. For a short time she worked for a relative in the country, and she also taught and sewed and did housework, and made herself useful wherever her strong hands and willing heart could find some way of earning a dollar.

The seven years spent in Boston had developed her into a capable young woman of twenty-two, who was ready and eager to play her part in the great drama of life of which she was an interested spectator as she saw it constantly enacted around her.

Even then, before she had stepped across the threshold of her career, she unconsciously realized that the home stage is the real background of the supreme world drama, and she shows this by the intimate, tender domestic scenes which made all of her stories bits of real life, with a strong appeal to those whose homes are joyous parts of the present, or sacred memories.

When she was determined to achieve an end, Louisa Alcott generally succeeded, even in the face of obstacles; and now having decided to take on her own broad shoulders some of the burdens which were weighing heavily on her beloved mother, she turned to the talent which had recently yielded her the magnificent sum of five dollars. In the days at Concord she had told many stories about fairies and flowers to the little Emerson children and their friends, who eagerly drank in all the mystic tales in which wood-nymphs, water sprites, giants and fairy queens played a prominent part, and the stories were thrilling, because their teller believed absolutely in the fairy creatures she pictured in a lovely setting of woodland glades and forest dells. These stories, which she had written down and called "Flower Fables," she found among her papers, and as she read them again she felt that they might interest other children as they had those to whom they were told. She had no money to publish them, however, and no publisher would bear the expense of a venture by an untried writer. But it took more than that to daunt Louisa when her mind was made up. With great enthusiasm she told a friend of the family, Miss Wealthy Stevens, of her desire, and she generously offered to pay for publication, but it was decided not to tell the family until the book should come out. Then in radiant secrecy Louisa burned the midnight oil and prepared the little book for the press. One can fancy the proud surprise of Mrs. Alcott when, on the following Christmas morning, among her pile of gifts she found the little volume with this note:

December 25, 1854.

Dear Mother:

Into your Christmas stocking I have put my first-born, knowing that you will accept it with all its faults (for grandmothers are always kind) and look upon it merely as an earnest of what I may yet do; for with so much to cheer me on, I hope to pass in time from fairies and fables to men and realities. Whatever beauty or poetry is to be found in my little book is owing to your interest in, and encouragement of, my efforts from the first to the last, and if ever I do anything to be proud of, my greatest happiness will be that I can thank you for that, as I may do for all the good there is in me, and I shall be content to write if it gives you pleasure.

Jo is fussing about, My lamp is going out.

To dear mother, with many kind wishes for a Happy New Year and Merry Christmas,

I am ever your loving daughter,

Louy.

Recompense enough, that note, for all a loving mother's sacrifices and attempts to give her daughter understanding sympathy and love—and it is small wonder if that Christmas gift always remained one of her most precious possessions.

Six hundred copies of the little "Flower Fables" were published, and the book sold very well, although their author only received the sum of $32 for them, which was in sharp contrast, she says in her journal, "to the receipts of six months only in 1886, being *eight thousand dollars* for the sale of books and no new one; but" she adds, "I was prouder over the thirty-two dollars than the eight thousand."

Louisa Alcott was now headed toward her destiny, although she was still a long way from the shining goal of literary success, and had many weary hills yet to climb.

As soon as *Flower Fables* was published, she began to plan for a new volume of fairy tales, and as she was invited to spend the next summer in the lovely New Hampshire village of Walpole, she thankfully accepted the invitation, and decided to write the new book there in the bracing air of the hill town. In Walpole, she met delightful people, who were all attracted to the versatile, amusing young woman, and she was in great demand when there was any entertainment on foot. One evening she gave a burlesque lecture on "Woman, and Her Position, by Oronthy Bluggage," which created such a gale of merriment that she was asked to repeat it for money, which she did; and so there was added to her store of accomplishments another, from which she was to reap some rewards in coming years.

Her enjoyment of Walpole was so great that her family decided to try its fine air, as they were tired of city life and needed a change of scene. A friend offered them a house there, rent free, and in their usual impromptu way they left Boston and arrived in the country village, bag and baggage. Mr. Alcott was overjoyed to have a garden in which to work, and Mrs. Alcott was glad to be near her niece, whose guest Louisa had been up to that time.

Louisa's comment on their arrival in her diary was:

"Busy and happy times as we settle in the little house in the lane, near by my dear ravine—plays, picnics, pleasant people and good neighbors." Despite the good times, it is evident that she was not idle, for she says, "Finished fairy book in September.... Better than *Flower Fables*. Now, I must try to sell it."

In September Anna had an offer to become a teacher in the great idiot asylum in Syracuse. Her sensitive nature shrank from the work, but with real self-sacrifice she accepted it for the sake of the family, and went off in October. Meanwhile Louisa had been thinking deeply about her future, and her diary tells the story of a decision she made, quite the most important one of her life. She writes:

"November; decided to seek my fortune, so with my little trunk of home-made clothes, $40 earned by stories sent to the *Gazette*, and my MSS., I set forth with mother's blessing one rainy day in the dullest month in the year."

She went straight to Boston, where she writes:

"Found it too late to do anything with the book (the new one she had written at Walpole) so put it away and tried for teaching, sewing, or any honest work. Won't go home to sit idle while I have a head and a pair of hands."

Good for you, Louisa—you are the stuff that success is made of! That her courage had its reward is shown by the fact that her cousins, the Sewalls, generously offered her a home for the winter with them which she gratefully accepted, but insisted on paying for her board by doing a great deal of sewing for them. She says in her diary: "I sew for Mollie and others and write stories. C. gave me books to notice. Heard Thackeray. Anxious times; Anna very home-sick. Walpole very cold and dull, now the summer butterflies have gone. Got $5 for a tale and $12 for sewing; sent home a Christmas box to cheer the dear souls in the snow-banks."

In January she writes: "C. paid $6 for *A Sister's Trial*, gave me more books to notice, and wants more tales." The entries that follow give a vivid picture of her pluck and perseverance in that first winter of fortune-seeking, and no record of deeds could be more graphic than the following entries:

"Sewed for L. W. Sewall and others. Mr. Field took my farce to Mobile to bring out; Mr. Barry of the Boston Theater has the play. Heard Curtis lecture. Began a book for summer, *Beach Bubbles*. Mr. F. of the *Courier* printed a poem of mine on 'Little Nell'. Got $10 for 'Bertha' and saw great yellow placards stuck up announcing it. Acted at the W's. March; got $10 for 'Genevieve'. Prices go up as people like the tales and ask who wrote them.... Sewed a great deal, and got very tired; one job for Mr. G. of a dozen pillow-cases, one dozen sheets, six fine cambric neck-ties, and two dozen handkerchiefs, at which I had to work all one night to get them done, ... I got only $4.00." The brave, young fortune-seeker adds sensibly, "Sewing won't make my fortune, but I can plan my stories while I work."

In May she had a welcome visit from Anna on her way home from Syracuse, as the work there was too hard for her, and the sisters spent some happy days together in Boston. Then they were obliged to go home, as dear little Beth was very sick with scarlet-fever which she caught from some poor children Mrs. Alcott had been nursing. Both Beth and May had the dangerous disease, and Beth never recovered from the effects of it, although she lived for two years, a serene, patient invalid, who shed a benediction on the sorrowing household. That summer was an anxious time for the family. In her usual way Louisa plunged headlong into housework and nursing, and when night came she would scribble one of the stories which the papers were now glad to accept whenever she could send them. So with varying degrees of apprehension and rejoicing, the weary months passed, and as Beth was slowly improving and she was not needed at home, Louisa decided to spend another winter in the city. Her diary says:

"There I can support myself and help the family. C. offers $10 a month and perhaps more.... Others have plenty of sewing; the play may come out, and Mrs. R. will give me a sky-parlor for $3 a week, with fire and board. I sew for her also." With practical forethought, she adds, "If I can get A. L. to governess I shall be all right."

Then in a burst of the real spirit which had animated her ever since she first began to write and sew and teach and act, and make over old clothes given her by rich friends that she need not spend any money on herself, she declares in her diary:

"I was born with a boy's spirit under my bib and tucker. I *can't wait* when I *can work*; so I took my little talent in my hand and forced the world again, braver than before, and wiser for my failures."

That the decision was no light one, and that the winter in Boston was not merely an adventure, is shown by her declaration:

"I don't often pray in words; but when I set out that day with all my worldly goods in the little old trunk, my own earnings ($25) in my pocket, and much hope and resolution in my soul, my heart was very full, and I said to the Lord, 'Help us all, and keep us for one another,' as I never said it before, while I looked back at the dear faces watching me, so full of love, and hope, and faith."

Louisa Alcott's childhood and girlhood, with all the hardships and joys which went into the passing years, had been merged in a triumphant young womanhood—a fitting preface to the years of fame and fortune which were to follow. A brave, interesting girl had become a courageous older woman, who faced the untried future with her small earnings in her pocket, her worldly goods in her trunk, and hopeful determination in her heart to do some worth-while thing in the world, for the sake of those she dearly loved. She had started up the steep slope of her life's real adventuring, and despite the rough paths over which she must still travel before reaching her goal, she was more and more a sympathetic comrade to the weak or weary, ever a gallant soldier, and a noble woman, born to do great deeds. So enthusiastic was she in playing her part in the world's work, that when she was twenty-seven years old, and still toiling on, with a scant measure of either wealth or fame, she exclaimed at a small success:

"Hurrah! My story was accepted and Lowell asked if it was not a translation from the German, it was so unlike other tales. I felt much set up, and my fifty dollars will be very happy money.... I have not been pegging away all these years in vain, and I may yet have books and publishers, and a fortune of my own. Success has gone to my head, and I wander a little.

"Twenty-seven years old and very happy!"

The prediction of "books, publishers and a fortune" came true in 1868, when a Boston firm urged her to write a story for girls, and she had the idea of describing the early life of her own home, with its many episodes and incidents. She wrote the book and called it *Little Women*, and was the most surprised person in the world, when from her cozy corner of Concord she watched edition after edition being published, and found that she had become famous. From that moment Louisa Alcott belonged to the public, and one has but to turn to the pages of her ably edited *Life, Letters and Journals*, to realize the source from which she got the material for her "simple story of simple girls," bound by a beautiful tie of family love, that neither poverty, sorrow nor death could sever. Four little pilgrims, struggling onward and upward through all the difficulties that beset them on their way, in Concord, Boston, Walpole and elsewhere, had provided human documents which the genius of Louisa Alcott made into an imperishable story for the delight and inspiration of succeeding generations of girls.

Little Women was followed by *Little Men, Old Fashioned Girl, Eight Cousins, Rose in Bloom, Under the Lilacs,* and a long line of other charming books for young people. And, although the incidents in them were not all taken from real life as were those of her first "immortal," yet was each and every book a faithful picture of every-day life. That is where the genius of Louisa Alcott came in. From the depicting of fairies and gnomes, princes and kings, she early turned to paint the real, the vital and the heroic, which is being lived in so many households where there is little money and no luxury, but much light-hearted laughter, tender affection for one another, and a deep and abiding love of humanity.

Well may all aspiring young Americans take example from the author of *Little Women*, and when longing to set the world on fire in the expression of their genius, learn not to despise or to turn away from the simple, commonplace details of every-day life.

And for successful life and work, there is no better inspiration than the three rules given Louisa Alcott in girlhood for her daily guidance:

Rule yourself;
Love your neighbor;
Do the duty which lies nearest you.

CLARA MORRIS: THE GIRL WHO WON FAME AS AN ACTRESS

A certain young person who lived in a boarding-house in the city of Cleveland, Ohio, was approaching her thirteenth birthday, which fact made her feel very old, and also very anxious to do some kind of work, as she saw her mother busily engaged from morning to night, in an effort to earn a living for her young daughter and herself.

Spring came in that year with furious heat, and the young person, seeing her mother cruelly over-worked, felt hopelessly big and helpless. The humiliation of having some one working to support her—and with the dignity of thirteen years close upon her, was more than she could bear. Locking herself into her small room, she flung herself on her knees and with a passion of tears prayed that God would help her.

"Dear God," she cried, "just pity me and show me what to do. Please!" Her entreaty was that of the child who has perfect confidence in the Father to whom she is speaking. "Help me to help my mother. If you will, I'll never say 'No!' to any woman who comes to me all my life long!"

In her story of her life, which the young person wrote many years later, she says, in telling of that agonized plea: "My error in trying to barter with my Maker must have been forgiven, for my prayer was answered within a week.... I have tried faithfully to keep my part of the bargain, for no woman who has ever sought my aid has ever been answered with a 'No!'"

Somewhat relieved at having made known her longing to Some One whom she believed would understand and surely help, the young person went through the dreary routine of boarding-house days more cheerfully, to her mother's joy. And at night, when she lay tossing and trying to sleep despite the scorching heat, she seemed to be reviewing the thirteen years of her existence as if she were getting ready to pigeon-hole the past, to make ready for a fuller future.

With clear distinctness she remembered having been told by her mother, in the manner of old-fashioned tellers, that, "Once upon a time, in the Canadian city of Toronto, in the year 1849, on the 17th of March—the day of celebrating the birth of good old St. Patrick, in a quiet house not far from the sound of the marching paraders, the rioting of revelers and the blare of brass bands, a young person was born." Memory carried on the story, as she lay there in the dark, still hours of the night, and she repeated to herself the oft-told tale of those few months she and her mother spent in the Canadian city before they journeyed back to the United States, where in Cleveland the mother tried many different kinds of occupations by which to support the child and herself. It was a strange life the young person remembered in those early days. She and her mother had to flit so often—suddenly, noiselessly. Often she remembered being roused from a sound sleep, sometimes being simply wrapped up without being dressed, and carried through the dark to some other place of refuge. Then, too, when other children walked in the streets or played, bare-headed or only with hat on, she wore a tormenting and heavy veil over her face. At an early age she began to notice that if a strange lady spoke to her the mother seemed pleased, but if a man noticed her she looked frightened, and hurried her away as fast as possible. At first this was all a mystery to the child, but later she understood that the great fear in her mother's eyes, and the hasty flights, were all to be traced to a father who had not been good to the brave mother, and so she had taken her little girl and fled from him. But he always found her and begged for the child. Only too well the young person remembered some of those scenes of frantic appeal on the father's side, of angry refusal by her mother, followed always by another hasty retreat to some new place of concealment. At last—never-to-be forgotten day—there was a vivid recollection of the time when the father asserted brutally that "he would make life a misery to her until she gave up the child"—that "by fair means or foul he would gain his end." Soon afterward he did kidnap the young person, but the mother was too quick for him, and almost immediately her child was in her own arms again.

This necessary habit of concealment, and also the mother's need to earn her own living, made life anything but an easy matter for them both. The mother's terror lest her child be taken from her again made her fear to allow the little girl to walk out alone, even for a short distance, and in such positions as the older woman was able to secure, it was always with the promise that the child should be no nuisance. And so the young person grew up in a habit of self-effacement, and of sitting quietly in corners where she could not be seen or heard, instead of playing with other children of her own age. Then came a great hope, which even as she lay in bed and thought about it, brought the tears to her eyes, she had so longed to have it come true.

When she was six years old, she and her mother had been living in a boarding-house in Cleveland, where there was a good-natured actress boarding, who took such a fancy to the shy little girl who was always sitting in a corner reading a book, that one day she approached the astonished mother with a proposition to adopt her daughter. Seeing surprise on the mother's face, she frankly told of her position, her income and her intention to give the girl a fine education. She thought a convent school would be desirable, from then, say, until the young person was seventeen.

The mother was really tempted by the offer of a good education, which she saw no way to give her daughter, and might have accepted it if the actress had not added:

"When she reaches the age of seventeen, I will place her on the stage."

That ended the matter. The mother was horror-stricken, and could hardly make her refusal clear and decided enough. Even when her employer tried to make her see that by her refusal she might be doing her daughter a great injustice, she said, sharply: "It would be better for her to starve trying to lead an honorable life, than to be exposed to such publicity and such awful temptations." And thus, in ignorance of what the future had in store for her child, did she close the door on a golden opportunity for developing her greatest talent, and the young person's first dream of freedom and a fascinating career had come to grief. As she reviewed her disappointment and the dreary days that followed, a flood of self-pity welled up in the girl's heart, and she felt as if she must do something desperate to quiet her restless nature.

Fortunately the disappointment was followed by a welcome change of scene, for mother and daughter left Cleveland and went to try their fortunes in what was then "the far west." After a long trip by rail and a thirty-mile drive across the prairie, they arrived at their journey's end, and the marvelous quiet of the early May night in the country soothed the older woman's sore heart and filled the child with the joy of a real adventure.

They remained in that beautiful world beyond the prairie for two years, and never did the charm of the backwoods's life pall on the growing girl, who did not miss the city sights and sounds, but exulted in the new experiences as, "with the other children on the farm, she dropped corn in the sun-warmed furrows, while a man followed behind with a hoe covering it up; and when it had sprouted and was a tempting morsel for certain black robbers of the field, she made a very active and energetic young scarecrow."

While the out-of-door life was a fine thing for the young person, still more to her advantage was it that she was now thrown with other children, who were happy, hearty, rollicking youngsters, and, seeing that the stranger was new to farm-life, had rare fun at her expense. For instance, as she later told:

"They led me forth to a pasture, shortly after our arrival at the farm, and, catching a horse, they hoisted me up on to its bare, slippery back. I have learned a good bit about horses since then," she says, "have hired, borrowed and bought them, but never since have I seen a horse of such appalling aspect. His eyes were the size of soup-plates, large clouds of smoke came from his nostrils. He had a glass-enamelled surface, and if he was half as tall as he felt, some museum manager missed a fortune. Then the young fiends, leaving me on my slippery perch, high up near the sky, drew afar off and stood against the fence, and gave me plenty of room to fall off. But when I suddenly felt the world heave up beneath me, I uttered a wild shriek—clenched my hands in the animal's black hair and, madly flinging propriety to any point of the compass that happened to be behind me, I cast one pantalette over the enameled back, and thus astride safely crossed the pasture—and lo, it was not I who fell, but their faces instead! When they came to take me down somehow the animal seemed shrunken, and I hesitated about leaving it, whereupon the biggest boy said I had 'pluck.' I had been frightened nearly to death, but I always could be silent at the proper moment; I was silent then, and he would teach me to ride sideways, for my mother would surely punish me if I sat astride like that. In a few weeks, thanks to him, I was the one who was oftenest trusted to take the horses to water at noon, riding sideways and always bare-back, mounted on one horse and leading a second to the creek, until all had had their drink. Which habit of riding—from balance—" the young person adds, "has made me quite independent of stirrups since those far-away days."

Besides the riding, there were many other delightful pastimes which were a part of life on the farm, and on rainy days, when the children could not play out of doors, they would flock to the big barn, and listen eagerly to stories told by the city girl, who had read them in books. Two precious years passed all too swiftly on the farm, and the young person was fast shooting up into a tall, slender girl, who had learned a love of nature in all its forms, which never left her. She had also grown stronger, which satisfied her mother that the experiment had been successful. But now there was education to be thought of, and when news came of the death of that father, who had been the haunting specter of the mother's life, they went back at once to Cleveland, where the mother obtained employment, and the growing daughter was sent to a public school. But at best it gave a meager course of study to one who had always been a reader of every book on which she could lay her hands. To make the dreary, daily routine less tiresome, she supplemented it by a series of "thinks." These usually took place at night after her candle had been blown out, and the young person generally fell asleep in a white robe and a crown of flowers, before she had gathered up all the prizes and diplomas and things she had earned in the world of reverie, where her dream self had been roving.

And now came the approach of her thirteenth birthday, and her plea that she might be made more useful in the world. And then, came this:

In the boarding-house where she and her mother were living, the mother acting as assistant to the manager, the young person occupied with enduring her monotonous existence and with watching the boarders, there were two actresses, a mother and daughter. The daughter, whose name was Blanche, was only a year or two older than the young person whose eyes followed her so eagerly, because Blanche was one of those marvelous creatures whose real life was lived behind the foot-lights.

Something in the silent, keen-eyed girl who was so near her own age attracted Blanche, and the two became good friends, spending many an hour together when the young person was not in school. In exchange for her thrilling stories of stage life, Blanche's new friend would tell vivid tales which she had read in books, to all of which good-natured Blanche would listen with lazy interest, and at the finish of the narrative often exclaimed:

"You ought to be in a theater. You could act!"

Although this assertion was always met by determined silence, as her friend thought she was being made fun of, yet the young person did not fail to brood over the statement when she was alone. Could there be any truth in the statement, she wondered? Then came a marvelous event. Blanche hurried home from the theater one day to tell her young friend that extra ballet girls were wanted in their company. She must go at once and get engaged.

"But," gasped the young person, "maybe they won't take me!"

"Well," answered Blanche, "I've coaxed your mother, and my mother says she'll look out for you—so at any rate, go and see. I'll take you to-morrow."

To-morrow! "Dimly the agitated and awed young person seemed to see a way opening out before her, and again behind her locked door she knelt down and said 'Dear God! Dear God!' and got no further, because grief has so many words, and joy has so few."

That was Friday, and the school term had closed that day. The next morning, with a heart beating almost to suffocation, the young person found herself on the way to the theater, with self-possessed Blanche, who led the way to the old Academy of Music. Entering the building, the girls went up-stairs, and as they reached the top step Blanche called to a small, dark man who was hurrying across the hall:

"Oh, Mr. Ellsler—wait a moment, please—I want to speak to you."

The man stopped, but with an impatient frown, for as he himself afterward said in relating the story:

"I was much put out about a business matter, and was hastily crossing the corridor when Blanche called me, and I saw she had another girl in tow, a girl whose appearance in a theater was so droll I must have laughed had I not been more than a little cross. Her dress was quite short—she wore a pale-blue apron buttoned up the back, long braids tied at the ends with ribbons, and a brown straw hat, while she clutched desperately at the handle of the biggest umbrella I ever saw. Her eyes were distinctly blue and big with fright. Blanche gave her name, and said she wanted to go in the ballet. I instantly answered that she was too small—I wanted women, not children. Blanche was voluble, but the girl herself never spoke a single word. I glanced toward her and stopped. The hands that clutched the umbrella trembled—she raised her eyes and looked at me. I had noticed their blueness a moment before, now they were almost black, so swiftly had their pupils dilated, and slowly the tears rose in them. All the father in me shrank under the child's bitter disappointment; all the actor in me thrilled at the power of expression in the girl's face, and I hastily added:

"'Oh, well, you may come back in a day or two, and if any one appears meantime who is short enough to march with you, I'll take you on.' Not until I had reached my office did I remember that the girl had not spoken a single word, but had won an engagement—for I knew I should engage her—with a pair of tear-filled eyes."

As a result of his half-promise, three days later, the young person again presented herself at the theater, and was engaged for the term of two weeks to go on the stage in the marches and dances of a play called "The Seven Sisters," for which she was to receive the large sum of fifty cents a night. She, who was later to be known as one of the great emotional actresses of her day, whose name was to be on every lip where the finest in dramatic art was appreciated, had begun to mount the ladder toward fame and fortune.

Very curiously and cautiously she picked her way around the stage at first, looking at the scenes, so fine on one side, so bare and cheap on the other; at the tarletan "glass windows," at the green calico sea lying flat and waveless on the floor. At last she asked Blanche:

"Is everything only make-believe in a theater?"

And Blanche, with the indifference of her lackadaisical nature answered, "Yes, everything's make-believe, except salary day."

Then came the novice's first rehearsal, which included a Zouave drill to learn, as well as a couple of dances. She went through her part with keen relish and learned the drill so quickly that on the second day she sat watching the others, while they struggled to learn the movements. As she sat watching the star came along and angrily demanded, "Why are you not drilling with the rest?"

"The gentleman sent me out of the ranks, sir," she answered, "because he said I knew the manual and the drill."

The star refused to believe this and, catching up a rifle, he cried: "Here, take hold, and let's see how much you know. Now, then, shoulder arms!"

Standing alone, burning with blushes, blinded with tears of mortification, she was put through her paces, but she really did know the drill, and it was no small reward for her misery when her persecutor took the rifle from her and exclaimed:

"Well, saucer-eyes, you do know it! I'm sorry, little girl, I spoke so roughly to you!" Holding out his hand to her, he added, "You ought to stay in this business—you've got your head with you!"

Stay in it! The question was would the manager want her when the fatal night of her first stage appearance had come and gone!

In those days of rehearsals, costumes were one of her most vital interests; for a ballet girl's dress is most important, as there is so little of it, that it must be perfect of its kind. The ballet of which the young person was now a member were supposed to be fairies in one dance. For the second act they wore dancing-skirts, and for the Zouave drill, they wore the regular Fire Zouave uniform.

At last, the first performance of the play came. It was a very hot night, and so crowded was the tiny dressing-room occupied by the ballet corps, that some of the girls had to stand on the one chair while they put their skirts on. The confusion was great, and the new-comer dressed as quickly as possible, escaped down-stairs, and showed herself to Blanche and her mother, to see if her make-up was all right.

To her surprise, after a moment of tense silence they both burst into loud laughter, their eyes staring into her face. In telling of that night later, she said; "I knew you had to put on powder, because the gas made you yellow, and red because the powder made you ghastly, but it had not occurred to me that skill was required in applying the same, and I was a sight to make any kindly disposed angel weep! I had not even sense enough to free my eyelashes from the powder clinging to them. My face was chalk white, and low down on my cheeks were nice round, bright red spots.

"Mrs. Bradshaw said: 'With your round blue eyes and your round white and red face, you look like a cheap china doll. Come here, my dear!'

"She dusted off a few thicknesses of the powder, removed the hard red spots, and while she worked she remarked; 'To-morrow, after you have walked to get a color, go to your glass and see where the color shows itself.... Of course, when you are making up for a character part you go by a different rule, but when you are just trying to look pretty, be guided by Nature.' As she talked, I felt the soft touch of a hare's foot on my burning cheeks and she continued her work until my face was as it should be to make the proper effect.

"That lesson was the beginning and the ending of my theatrical instruction. What I learned later was learned by observation, study, and direct inquiry—but never by instruction, either free or paid for."

And now the moment of stage entry had arrived. "One act of the play represented the back of a stage during a performance. The scenes were turned around with their unpainted sides to the audience. The scene-shifters and gas-men were standing about; everything was supposed to be going up. The manager was giving orders wildly, and then a dancer was late. She was called frantically, and finally, when she appeared on the run, the manager caught her by the shoulders, rushed her across the stage, and fairly pitched her onto the imaginary stage, to the great amusement of the audience. The tallest and prettiest girl in the ballet had been picked out to do this bit of work, and she had been rehearsed day after day with the greatest care for the small part.

"All were gathered together ready for their first entrance and dance, which followed a few moments after the scene already described. The tall girl had a queer look on her face as she stood in her place; her cue came, but she never moved.

"I heard the rushing footsteps of the stage-manager; 'That's you,' he shouted; 'Go on! Go on! Run! Run!' Run? She seemed to have grown fast to the floor....

"'Are you going on?' cried the frantic prompter.

"She dropped her arms limply at her sides and whispered; 'I—I—c-a-n't.'

"He turned, and as he ran his imploring eye over the line of faces, each girl shrank back from it. He reached me. I had no fear, and he saw it.

"'Can you go on there?' he cried. I nodded.

"'Then for God's sake go—go!'

"I gave a bound and a rush that carried me half across the stage before the manager caught me, and so, I made my first entrance on the stage, and danced and marched and sang with the rest, and all unconsciously took my first step on the path that I was to follow through shadow and through sunshine—to follow by steep and stony places, over threatening bogs, through green and pleasant meadows—to follow steadily and faithfully for many and many a year to come."

To the surprise of every one, when salary day came around the new ballet girl did not go to claim her week's pay. Even on the second she was the last one to appear at the box-office window. Mr. Ellsler himself was there, and he opened the door and asked her to come in. As she signed her name, she paused so noticeably that he laughed, and said, "Don't you know your own name?"

The fact was, on the first day of rehearsal, when the stage-manager had taken down all names, he called out to the latest comer, who was staring at the scenery and did not hear him:

"Little girl, what is your name?"

Some one standing near him volunteered: "Her name is Clara Morris, or Morrissey or Morrison, or something like that." At once he had written down *Morris*—dropping the last syllable from her rightful name. So when Mr. Ellsler asked, "Don't you know your name?" it was the moment to have set the matter straight, but the young person was far too shy. She made no reply, but signed up and received two weeks' salary as Clara Morris, by which name she was known ever afterward.

In her story of life on the stage, she says, "After having gratefully accepted my two weeks' earnings, Mr. Ellsler asked me why I had not come the week before. I told him I preferred to wait because it would seem so much more if I got both weeks' salary all at one time. He nodded gravely, and said, 'It was rather a large sum to have in hand at one time,' and though I was very sensitive to ridicule, I did not suspect him of making fun of me. Then he said:

"'You are a very intelligent little girl, and when you went on alone and unrehearsed the other night, you proved you had both adaptability and courage. I'd like to keep you in the theater. Will you come and be a regular member of the company for the season that begins in September next?'

"I think it must have been my ears that stopped my ever-widening smile, while I made answer that I must ask my mother first.

"'To be sure,' said he, 'to be sure! Well, suppose you ask her then, and let me know whether you can or not.'"

She says, "Looking back and speaking calmly, I must admit that I do not now believe Mr. Ellsler's financial future depended entirely upon the yes or no of my mother and myself; but that I was on an errand of life or death every one must have thought who saw me tearing through the streets on that ninety-in-the-shade day.... One man ran out hatless and coatless and looked anxiously up the street in the direction from which I came. A big boy on the corner yelled after me: 'Sa-ay, sis, where's the fire?' But, you see they did not know that I was carrying home my first real earnings, that I was clutching six damp one-dollar bills in the hands that had been so empty all my life!

"I had meant to take off my hat and smooth my hair, and with a proper little speech approach my mother, and then hand her the money. But alas! as I rushed into the house I came upon her unexpectedly, for, fearing dinner was going to be late, she was hurrying things by shelling a great basket of peas as she sat by the dining-room window. At sight of her tired face all my nicely planned speech disappeared. I flung my arm about her neck, dropped the bills on top of the empty pods and cried:

"'Oh, mother, that's mine and it's all yours!'

"She kissed me, but to my grieved amazement put the money back into my hand and said, 'No, you have earned this money yourself—you are to do with it exactly as you please.'"

And that was why, the next morning, a much-excited and very rich young person took a journey to the stores, and as a result bought a lavender-flowered muslin dress which, when paid for, had made quite a large hole in the six dollars. By her expression and manner she plainly showed how proud and happy she was to be buying a dress for the mother who for thirteen years had been doing and buying for two. "Undoubtedly," says Miss Morris, "had there been a fire just then I would have risked my life to save that flowered muslin gown."

Up to that time, the only world Clara Morris had known had been narrow and sordid, and lay chill under the shadow of poverty.... Now, standing humbly at the knee of Shakespeare, she began to learn something of another world—fairy-like in fascination, marvelous in reality. A world of sunny days and jeweled nights, of splendid palaces, caves, of horrors, forests of mystery, and meadows of smiling candor. All people, too, with such soldiers, statesmen, lovers, clowns, such women of splendid honor, fierce ambition, thistle-down lightness, as makes the heart beat fast to think of.

That was the era of Shakesperian performances, and out of twenty-eight stars who played with the support of Mr. Ellsler's company, eighteen acted in the famous classic plays. All stars played a week's engagement, some two, so at least half of the season of forty-two weeks was given over to Shakespeare's plays, and every actor and actress had his lines at their tongues' tips, while there were endless discussions about the best rendering of famous passages.

"I well remember," says Miss Morris, "my first step into theatrical controversy. 'Macbeth' was being rehearsed, and the star had just exclaimed: 'Hang out our banners on the outward walls!' That was enough—argument was on. It grew animated. Some were for: 'Hang out our banners! On the outward walls the cry is still, they come!' while one or two were with the star's reading.

"I stood listening, and looking on, and fairly sizzling with hot desire to speak, but dared not take the liberty. Presently an actor, noticing my eagerness, laughingly said:

"'Well, what is it, Clara? You'll have a fit if you don't ease your mind with speech.'

"'Oh, Uncle Dick,' I answered, my words fairly tripping over one another in my haste, 'I have a picture home, I cut out of a paper; it's a picture of a great castle with towers and moats and things, and on the outer walls are men with spears and shields, and they seem to be looking for the enemy, and, Uncle Dick, the *banner* is floating over the high tower! So, don't you think it ought to be read: "Hang out our banners! On the outward walls"—the outward wall, you know, is where the lookouts are standing—"the cry is still, they come!"'

"A general laugh followed my excited explanation, but Uncle Dick patted me on the shoulder and said:

"'Good girl, you stick to your picture—it's right, and so are you. Many people read that line that way, but you have worked it out for yourself, and that's a good plan to follow.'

"And," says Miss Morris, "I swelled and swelled, it seemed to me, I was so proud of the gentle old man's approval. But that same night I came woefully to grief. I had been one of the crowd of 'witches.' Later, being off duty, I was, as usual, planted in the entrance, watching the acting of the grown-ups and grown-greats. Lady Macbeth was giving the sleep-walking scene, in a way that jarred upon my feelings. I could not have told why, but it did. I believed myself alone, and when the memory-haunted woman roared out:

"'Yet who would have thought the old man to have had so much *blood* in him?' I remarked, under my breath. 'Did you expect to find ink in him?'

"A sharp 'ahem' right at my shoulder told me I had been overheard, and I turned to face—oh, horror! the stage-manager. He glared angrily at me and demanded my ideas on the speech, which in sheer desperation at last I gave, saying:

"'I thought Lady Macbeth was amazed at the *quantity* of blood that flowed from the body of such an old man—for when you get old, you know, sir, you don't have so much blood as you used to, and I only thought that, as the "sleeping men were laced, and the knives smeared and her hands bathed with it," she might perhaps have whispered, "Yet who would have thought the old man to have so *much* blood in him?"' I didn't mean an impertinence. Down fell the tears, for I could not talk and hold them back at the same time.

"He looked at me in dead silence for a few moments, then he said: 'Humph!' and walked away, while I rushed to the dressing-room and cried and cried, and vowed that never, never again would I talk to myself—in the theater, at all events.

"Only a short time afterward I had a proud moment when I was allowed to go on as the longest witch in the caldron scene in 'Macbeth.' Perhaps I might have come to grief over it had I not overheard the leading man say: 'That child will never speak those lines in the world!' And the leading man was six feet tall and handsome, and I was thirteen and a half years old, and to be called a child!

"I was in a secret rage, and I went over and over my lines at all hours, under all circumstances, so that nothing should be able to frighten me at night. And then, with my pasteboard crown and white sheet and petticoat, I boiled up in the caldron and gave my lines well enough for the manager to say low:

"'Good! Good!' and the leading man next night asked me to take care of his watch and chain during his combat scene, and," says Miss Morris, "my pride of bearing was unseemly, and the other girls loved me not at all, for, you see, they, too, knew he was six feet tall and handsome."

The theatrical company of which Clara Morris had become a member was what was called by the profession, a "family theater," in which the best parts are apt to be absorbed by the manager and his family, while all the poor ones are placed with strict justice where they belong. At that time, outside of the star who was being supported, men and women were engaged each for a special line of business, to which "line" they were strictly kept. However much the "family theater" was disliked by her comrades in the profession, it was indeed an ideal place for a young girl to begin her stage life in. The manager, Mr. Ellsler, was an excellent character actor; his wife, Mrs. Ellsler, was his leading woman—his daughter, Effie, though not out of school at that time, acted whenever there was a very good part that suited her. Other members of the company were mostly related in some way, and so it came about that there was not even the "pink flush of a flirtation over the first season," in fact, says Miss Morris, "during all the years I served in that old theater, no real scandal ever smirched it." She adds: "I can never be grateful enough for having come under the influence of the dear woman who watched over me that first season, Mrs. Bradshaw, the mother of Blanche, one of the most devoted actresses I ever saw, and a good woman besides. From her I learned that because one is an actress it is not necessary to be a slattern. She used to say:

"'You know at night the hour of morning rehearsal—then get up fifteen minutes earlier, and leave your room in order. Everything an actress does is commented on, and as she is more or less an object of suspicion, her conduct should be even more correct than that of other women.' She also repeated again and again, 'Study your lines—speak them just as they are written. Don't just gather the idea of a speech, and then use your own words—that's an infamous habit. The author knew what he wanted you to say. If he says, "My lord, the carriage waits," don't you go on and say, "My lord, the carriage is waiting!"'"

These and many other pieces of valuable advice were stored up in Clara Morris's mind, and she made such good use of them that they bore rich fruit in later years.

There was great consternation for mother and daughter, on a certain day when Clara brought home the startling news that the company was to be transferred to Columbus, Ohio, for the remainder of the season. It was a great event in the young actress's life, as it meant leaving her mother and standing alone. But as she confesses: "I felt every now and then my grief and fright pierced through and through with a delicious thrill of importance; I was going to be just like a grown-up, and would decide for myself what I should wear. I might even, if I chose to become so reckless, wear my Sunday hat to a rehearsal, and when my cheap little trunk came, with C. M. on the end, showing it was my very own, I stooped down and hugged it." But she adds with honesty, "Later, when my mother, with a sad face, separated my garments from her own, I burst into sobs of utter forlornness."

The salary of the ballet corps was now raised to $5 a week, and all set to work to try to solve the riddle of how a girl was to pay her board bill, her basket bill, her washing bill, and all the small expenses of the theater— powder, paint, soap, hair-pins, etc.—to say nothing of shoes and clothing, out of her earnings. Clara Morris and the Bradshaws solved the problem in the only possible way by rooming together in a large top-floor room, where they lived with a comparative degree of comfort, and with less loneliness for Clara than she could have felt elsewhere.

During that first season she learned to manage her affairs and to take care of herself and her small belongings, without admonition from any one. At the same time she was learning much of the technique of the profession, and was deeply interested as she began to understand how illusions are produced. She declares that one of the proofs that she was meant to be an actress was her enjoyment of the mechanism of stage effects.

"I was always on hand when a storm had to be worked," she says, "and would grind away with a will at a crank that, turning against a tight band of silk, made the sound of a tremendously shrieking wind. And no one sitting in front of the house, looking at a white-robed woman ascending to heaven, apparently floating upward through the blue clouds, enjoyed the spectacle more than I enjoyed looking at the ascent from the rear, where I could see the tiny iron support for her feet, the rod at her back with the belt holding her securely about the waist, and the men hoisting her through the air, with a painted, sometimes moving sky behind her.

"This reminds me," says Miss Morris, "that Mrs. Bradshaw had several times to go to heaven (dramatically speaking), and as her figure and weight made the support useless, she always went to heaven on the entire gallery, as it is called, a long platform the whole width of the stage, which is raised and lowered by windlass. The enormous affair would be cleaned and hung about with nice white clouds, and then Mrs. Bradshaw, draped in long white robes, with hands meekly crossed upon her breast and eyes piously uplifted, would rise heavenward, slowly, as so heavy an angel should. But alas! There was one drawback to this otherwise perfect ascension. Never, so long as the theater stood, could that windlass be made to work silently. It always moved up or down to a succession of screaks, unoilable, blood-curdling, that were intensified by Mrs. Bradshaw's weight, so that she ascended to the blue tarletan heaven accompanied by such chugs and long-drawn yowlings as suggested a trip to the infernal regions. Her face remained calm and unmoved, but now and then an agonized moan escaped her, lest even the orchestra's effort to cover up the support's protesting cries should prove useless. Poor woman, when she had been lowered again to *terra firma* and stepped off, the whole paint frame would give a kind of joyous upward spring. She noticed it, and one evening looked back and said; 'Oh, you're not one bit more glad than I am, you screaking wretch!'"

Having successfully existed through the Columbus season, in the spring the company was again in Cleveland, playing for a few weeks before disbanding for that horror of all theatrical persons—the summer vacation.

As her mother was in a position, and could not be with Clara, the young actress spent the sweltering months in a cheap boarding-house, where a kindly landlady was willing to let her board bill run over until the fall, when salaries should begin again. Clara never forgot that kindness, for she was in real need of rest after her first season of continuous work. Although her bright eyes, clear skin, and round face gave an impression of perfect health, yet she was far from strong, owing partly to the privations of her earlier life and to a slight injury to her back in babyhood. Because of this, she was facing a life of hard work handicapped by that most cruel of torments, a spinal trouble, which an endless number of different treatments failed to cure.

Vacation ended, to her unspeakable joy she began work again as a member of the ballet corps, and during that season and the next her ability to play a part at short notice came to be such an accepted fact that more than once she was called on for work outside of her regular "line," to the envy of the other girls, who began to talk of "Clara's luck." "But," says Clara, "there was no luck about it. My small success can be explained in two words—extra work." While the others were content if they could repeat a part perfectly to themselves in their rooms, that was only the beginning of work to their more determined companion. "I would repeat those lines," said Miss Morris, "until, had the very roof blown off the theater at night, I should not have missed one." And so it was that the youngest member of the ballet corps came to be looked on as a general-utility person, who could be called on at a moment's notice to play the part of queen or clown, boy or elderly woman, as was required.

Mr. Ellsler considered that the young girl had a real gift for comedy, and when Mr. Dan Setchell, the comedian, played with the company, she was given a small part, which she played with such keen perception of the points where a "hit" could be made, that at last the audience broke into a storm of laughter and applause. Mr. Setchell had another speech, but the applause was so insistent that he knew it would be an anti-climax and signaled the prompter to ring down the curtain. But Clara Morris knew that he ought to speak, and was much frightened by the effect of her business, which had so captured the fancy of the audience, for she knew that the applause belonged to the star as a matter of professional etiquette. She stood trembling like a leaf, until the comedian came and patted her kindly on the shoulder, saying:

"Don't be frightened, my girl—that applause was for you. You won't be fined or scolded—you've made a hit, that's all!"

But even the pleasant words did not soothe the tempest of emotion surging in the young girl's heart. She says:

"I went to my room, I sat down with my head in my hands. Great drops of sweat came out on my temples. My hands were icy cold, my mouth was dry—that applause rang in my ears. A cold terror seized on me—a terror of what? Ah, a tender mouth was bitted and bridled at last! The reins were in the hands of the public, and it would drive me, where?"

As she sat there, in her hideous make-up, in a state of despair and panic, she suddenly broke into shrill laughter. Two women came in, and one said; "Why, what on earth's the matter? Have they blown you up for your didoes to-night? What need you care. You pleased the audience." The other said, quietly: "Just get a glass of water for her; she has a touch of hysteria. I wonder who caused it?" No person had caused it. Clara Morris was merely waking from a sound sleep, unconsciously visioning that woman of the dim future who was to conquer the public in her portrayal of great elemental human emotion.

With incessant work and study, and a firm determination to stop short of nothing less than the perfection of art, those early years of Clara Morris's life on the stage went swiftly by, and in her third season she was more than ever what she herself called "the dramatic scrape-goat of the company," one who was able to play any part at a moment's notice.

"This reputation was heightened when one day, an actor falling suddenly sick, Mr. Ellsler, with a furrowed brow, begged Clara to play the part. Nothing daunted, the challenge was calmly accepted, and in one afternoon she studied the part of King Charles, in 'Faint Heart Never Won Fair Lady,' and played it in borrowed clothes and without any rehearsal whatever, other than finding the situations plainly marked in the book! It was an astonishing thing to do, and she was showered with praise for the performance; but even this success did not better her fortunes, and she went on playing the part of boys and old women, or singing songs when forced to it, going on for poor leading parts even, and between times dropping back into the ballet, standing about in crowds, or taking part in a village dance."

It was certainly an anomalous position she held in Mr. Ellsler's company—but she accepted its ups and downs without resistance, taking whatever part came to hand, gaining valuable experience from every new rôle assigned her, and hoping for a time when the returns from her work would be less meager.

She was not yet seventeen when the German star, Herr Daniel Bandmann, came to play with the company. He was to open with "Hamlet," and Mrs. Bradshaw, who by right should have played the part of Queen Mother, was laid up with a broken ankle. Miss Morris says: "It took a good deal in the way of being asked to do strange parts to startle me, but the Queen Mother did it. I was just nicely past sixteen, and I was to go on the stage for the serious Shakesperian mother of a star. Oh, I couldn't!"

"Can't be helped—no one else," growled Mr. Ellsler; "Just study your lines, right away, and do the best you can."

"I had been brought up to obey," says Miss Morris, "and I obeyed. The dreaded morning of rehearsal came. There came a call for the Queen. I came forward. Herr Bandmann glanced at me, half smiled, waved his arms, and said, 'Not you, not the *Player-Queen*, but GERTRUDE.'

"I faintly answered, 'I'm sorry, sir, but I have to play Gertrude!'

"'Oh no, you won't!' he cried, 'not with me!' Then, turning to Mr. Ellsler, he lost his temper and only controlled it when he was told that there was no one else to take the part; if he would not play with me, the theater must be closed for the night. Then he calmed down and condescended to look the girl over who was to play such an inappropriate rôle.

"The night came—a big house, too, I remember," says Miss Morris. "I wore long and loose garments to make me look more matronly, but, alas, the drapery Queen Gertrude wears was particularly becoming to me and brought me uncommonly near to prettiness. Mr. Ellsler groaned, but said nothing, while Mr. Bandmann sneered out an '*Ach Himmel!*' and shrugged his shoulders, as if dismissing the matter as hopeless."

But it was not. "As Bandmann's great scene advanced to its climax, so well did the young Queen Mother play up to Hamlet, that the applause was rapturous. The curtain fell, and to her utter amaze she found herself lifted high in the air and crushed to Hamlet's bosom, with a crackling sound of breaking Roman pearls and in a whirlwind of German exclamations, kissed on brow, cheeks and eyes. Then disjointed English came forth; 'Oh, you are so great, you *kleine* apple-cheeked girl! You maker of the fraud—you so great, nobody. *Ach*, you are fire—you have pride—you are a Gertrude who have shame!' More kisses, then suddenly realizing that the audience was still applauding, he dragged her before the curtain, he bowed, he waved his hands, he threw one arm around my shoulders. 'He isn't going to do it all over again—out here, is he?' thought the victim of his enthusiasm, and began backing out of sight as quickly as possible."

That amusing experience led to one of the most precious memories of Clara Morris's career, when, a month after the departure of the impetuous German, who should be announced to play with the company but Mr. Edwin Booth. As Clara Morris read the cast of characters, she says, "I felt my eyes growing wider as I saw—

Queen Gertrude............Miss Morris.

"I had succeeded before, oh yes, but this was a different matter. All girls have their gods—some have many of them. My gods were few, and on the highest pedestal of all, grave and gentle, stood the god of my professional idolatry—Edwin Booth. It was humiliating to be forced on any one as I should be forced upon Mr. Booth, since there was still none but my 'apple-cheeked' self to go on for the Queen, and though I dreaded complaint and disparaging remarks from him, I was honestly more unhappy over the annoyance this blemish on the cast would cause him. But it could not be helped, so I wiped my eyes, repeated my childish little old-time 'Now I lay me,' and went to sleep.

"The dreaded Monday came, and at last—the call, 'Mr. Booth would like to see you for a few moments in his room.'

"He was dressed for Hamlet when I entered. He looked up, smiled, and, waving his hand, said in Bandmann's very words: 'No, not you—not the *Player-Queen*—but GERTRUDE.'

"My whole heart was in my voice as I gasped: 'I'm so sorry, sir, but I have to do Queen Gertrude. You see,' I rushed on, 'our heavy woman has a broken leg and can't act. But if you please,' I added, 'I had to do this part with Mr. Bandmann, too, and—and—I'll only worry you with my looks, sir, not about the words or business.'

"He rested his dark, unspeakably melancholy eyes on my face, then he sighed and said: 'Well, it was the closet scene I wanted to speak to you about. When the ghost appears you are to be—' He stopped, a faint smile touched his lips, and he remarked:

"'There's no denying it, my girl, I look a great deal more like your father than you look like my mother—but—' He went on with his directions, and, considerate gentlemen that he was, spoke no single unkind word to me, though my playing of that part must have been a great annoyance to him.

"When the closet scene was over, the curtain down, I caught up my petticoats and made a rapid flight roomward. The applause was filling the theater. Mr. Booth, turning, called after me: 'You—er—Gertrude—er—Queen! Oh, somebody call that child back here!' and somebody roared, 'Clara, Mr. Booth is calling you!' I turned, but stood still. He beckoned, then came and took my hand, saying, 'My dear, we must not keep them waiting too long,' and led me before the curtain with him. I very slightly bent my head to the audience, whom I felt were applauding Hamlet only, but turned and bowed myself to the ground to him whose courtesy had brought me there.

"When we came off he smiled amusedly, tapped me on the shoulder, and said: 'My Gertrude, you are very young, but you know how to pay a pretty compliment—thank you, child!'

"So," says Miss Morris, "whenever you see pictures of nymphs or goddesses floating in pink clouds and looking idiotically happy, you can say to yourself: 'That is just how Clara Morris felt when Edwin Booth said she had paid him a compliment.' Yes, I floated, and I'll take a solemn oath, if necessary, that the whole theater was filled with pink clouds the rest of that night, for girls are made that way, and they can't help it."

The young actress was now rapidly acquiring a knowledge of her ability to act; she also knew that as long as she remained with Mr. Ellsler there would be no advancement for her, and a firm determination took possession of her to take a plunge into the big world, where perhaps there might be a chance not only to earn enough to take care of herself, but also enough so that her mother would no longer be obliged to work, which was Clara's bitter mortification.

While she was considering the advisability of making a change, she received an offer from a Mr. Macaulay, manager of Wood's Museum, at Cincinnati, Ohio. He offered a small salary, but as she was to be his leading woman she decided to accept the offer. "When the matter was apparently settled, he wrote, saying that 'because of the youth of his new star, he wished to reserve a few parts which his wife would act.' Only too well did Clara Morris understand what that meant—that the choicest parts would be reserved. Then an amusing thing happened. She, who was so lacking in self-confidence, suddenly developed an ability to stand up for her rights. By return mail she informed Mr. Macaulay that her youth had nothing to do with the matter—that she would be the leading woman and play all parts or none. His reply was a surprise, as it contained a couple of signed contracts and a pleasant request to sign both and return one at once. He regretted her inability to grant his request, but closed by expressing his respect for her firmness in demanding her rights. Straightway she signed her first contract, and went out to mail it. When she returned she had made up her mind to take a great risk. She had decided that her mother should never again receive commands from any one—that her shoulders were strong enough to bear the welcome burden, that they would face the new life and its possible sufferings together—*together*, that was the main thing." She says:

"As I stood before the glass smoothing my hair, I gravely bowed to the reflection and said, 'Accept my congratulations and best wishes, Wood's leading lady!'—and then fell on the bed and sobbed ... because, you see, the way had been so long and hard, but I had won one goal—I was a leading woman!"

Leaving behind the surroundings of so many years was not a light matter, nor was the parting with the Ellslers, of whose theatrical family she had been a member for so long, easy. When the hour of leave-taking came, she was very sad. She had to make the journey alone, as her mother also was to join her only when she had found a place to settle in. Mr. Ellsler was sick for the first time since she had known him. She said good-by to him in his room, and left feeling very despondent, he seemed so weak. "Judge then," says Miss Morris, "my amazement when, hearing a knock on my door and calling, 'Come in'—Mr. Ellsler, pale and almost staggering, entered. A rim of red above his white muffler betrayed his bandaged throat, and his poor voice was but a husky whisper:

"'I could not help it,' he said. 'You were placed under my care once by your mother. You were a child then, and though you are pleased to consider yourself a woman now, I could not bear to think of your leaving the city without some old friend being by for a parting God-speed.'

"I was inexpressibly grateful, but he had yet another surprise for me. He said, 'I wanted, too, Clara, to make you a little present that would last long and remind you daily of—of—er—the years you have passed in my theater.'

"He drew a small box from his pocket. 'A good girl and a good actress,' he said, 'needs and ought to own a'—he touched a spring, the box flew open—'a good watch,' he finished.

"Literally, I could not speak, having such agony of delight in its beauty, of pride in its possession, of satisfaction in a need supplied, of gratitude and surprise immeasurable. 'Oh!' and again 'Oh!' was all that I could cry, while I pressed it to my cheek and gloated over it. My thanks must have been sadly jumbled and broken, but my pride and pleasure made Mr. Ellsler laugh, and then the carriage was there, and laughter stilled into a silent, close hand-clasp. As I opened the door of the dusty old hack, I saw the first star prick brightly through the evening sky. Then the hoarse voice said, 'God bless you'—and I had left my first manager."

To say that Clara Morris made a success in Cincinnati is the barest truth. Her first appearance was in the rôle of a country girl, *Cicely*, a simple milkmaid with only one speech to make, but one which taxed the ability of an actress to the uttermost to express what was meant. Clara played this part in a demure black-and-white print gown, with a little hat tied down under her chin. On the second night, she played what is called a "dressed part," a bright, light-comedy part in which she wore fine clothes; on the third night hers was a "tearful" part. In three nights she completely won the public, and on the third she received her first anonymous gift, a beautiful and expensive set of pink corals set in burnished gold. "Flowers, too, came over the foot-lights, the like of which she had never seen before, some of them costing more than she earned in a week. Then one night came a bolder note with a big gold locket, which, having its sender's signature, went straight back to him the next morning. As a result it began to be whispered about that the new star sent back all gifts of jewelry; but when one matinée a splendid basket of white camelias came with a box of French candied fruit, it delighted her and created a sensation in the dressing-room. That seemed to start a fashion, for candies in dainty boxes came to her afterward as often as flowers."

On the night of her first appearance, a lawyer of Cincinnati who saw her play the part of Cicely was so delighted with her interpretation of the small rôle that he at once asked: "Who is she? What is her history?"—only to find that, like most happy women, she had none. She came from Cleveland, she lived three doors away with her mother—that was all.

Having seen her a second time, he exclaimed, "That girl ought to be in New York this very moment!" and he added, "I know the foreign theaters—their schools and styles, as well as I know the home theaters and their actors. I believe I have made a discovery!"

After seeing her in the "tearful part," he said firmly: "I shall never rest till this Clara Morris faces New York. She need clash with no one, need hurt no one, she is unlike any one else, and New York has plenty of room for her. I shall make it my business to meet her and preach New York until she accepts the idea and acts upon it."

As a result of that determination, at a later date, he met the object of his interest and roused her to such an enthusiasm in his New York project that she wrote to Mr. Ellsler, begging his aid in reaching New York managers, and one day, shortly afterward, she held in her hand a wee sheet of paper, containing two lines scrawled in an illegible handwriting:

"If you send the young woman to me, I will willingly consider proposal. Will engage no actress without seeing her.—A. Daly."

It was a difficult proposition, for to obtain leave of absence she would be obliged to pay a substitute for at least two performances—would have to stop for one night at a New York hotel, and so spend what she had saved toward a summer vacation. But the scheme was too compelling to be set aside. That very night she asked leave of absence, made all other necessary arrangements, and before she had time to falter in her determination found herself at the Fifth Avenue Hotel in the great bustling city of her dreams. She breakfasted, and took from her bag a new gray veil, a pair of gray gloves and a bit of fresh ruffling. Then, having made all the preparation she could to meet the arbiter of her fate, in her usual custom she said a prayer to that Father in whose protecting care she had an unfaltering trust. Then, she says, "I rose and went forth, prepared to accept success or defeat, just as the good Lord should will."

Having found Mr. Daly, she looked bravely into his eyes and spoke with quick determination to lose no time: "I am the girl come out of the West to be inspected. I'm Clara Morris!"

That was the preface to an interview which ended in his offer to engage her, but without a stated line of business. He would give her thirty-five dollars a week, he said (knowing there were two to live on it), and if she made a favorable impression he would double that salary.

A poor offer—a risky undertaking, exclaimed Clara. "In my pocket was an offer which I had received just before leaving for New York, from a San Francisco manager, with a salary of one hundred dollars, a benefit, and no vacation at all, unless I wished it. This offer was fairly burning a hole in my pocket as I talked with Mr. Daly, who, while we talked, was filling up a blank contract, for my signature. Thirty-five dollars against one hundred dollars. 'But if you make a favorable impression you'll get seventy dollars.' I thought, and why should I *not* make a favorable impression? Yet, if I fail now in New York, I can go West or South not much harmed. If I wait till I am older and fail, it will ruin my life. I slipped my hand in my pocket and gave a little farewell tap to the contract for one hundred dollars; I took the pen; I looked hard at him. 'There's a heap of trust asked for in this contract,' I remarked. 'You won't forget your promise about doubling the contract?'

"'I won't forget anything,' he answered.

"Then I wrote 'Clara Morris' twice, shook hands, and went out and back to Cincinnati, with an engagement in a New York theater for the coming season."

As the tangible results of a benefit performance Clara was able to give her mother a new spring gown and bonnet and send her off to visit in Cleveland, before turning her face toward Halifax, where she had accepted a short summer engagement. At the end of it she went on to New York, engaged rooms in a quiet old-fashioned house near the theater, and telegraphed her mother to come. "She came," says Miss Morris, "and that blessed evening found us housekeeping at last. We were settled, and happily ready to begin the new life in the great, strange city."

From that moment, through the frenzied days of rehearsal with a new company, and with a large number of untoward incidents crowded into each day, life moved swiftly on toward the first appearance of Clara Morris on the New York stage.

With a sort of dogged despair she lived through the worry of planning how to buy costumes out of her small reserve fund. When at last all her gowns were ready, she had two dollars and thirty-eight cents left, on which she and her mother must live until her first week's salary should be paid. Worse than that, on the last awful day before the opening night she had a sharp attack of pleurisy. A doctor was called, who, being intoxicated, treated the case wrongly. Another physician had to be summoned to undo the work of the first, and as a result Daly's new actress was in a condition little calculated to give her confidence for such an ordeal as the coming one. She says, "I could not swallow food—*I could not!* As the hour drew near my mother stood over me while with tear-filled eyes I disposed of a raw beaten egg; then she forced me to drink a cup of broth, fearing a breakdown if I tried to go through five such acts as awaited me without food. I always kissed her good-by, and that night my lips were so cold and stiff with fright that they would not move. I dropped my head for one moment on her shoulder; she patted me silently with one hand and opened the door with the other. I glanced back. Mother waved her hand and called: 'Good luck! God bless you!' and I was on my way to my supreme test."

A blaze of lights, a hum of voices, a brilliant throng of exquisitely gowned, bejeweled women and well-groomed men, in fact a house such as Wood's leading lady had never before confronted! A chance for triumph or for disaster—and triumph it was! Like a rolling snowball, it grew as the play advanced. Again and again Clara Morris took a curtain call with the other actresses. Finally the stage manager said to Mr. Daly, "They want *her*," and Mr. Daly answered, sharply: "I know what they want, and I know what I don't want. Ring up again!"

He did so. But it was useless. At last Mr. Daly said, "Oh, well, ring up once more, and here, you take it yourself."

Alone, Clara Morris stood before the brilliant throng, vibrating to the spontaneous storm of enthusiasm, and as she stood before them the audience rose as one individual, carried out of themselves by an actress whose work was as rare as it was unique—work which never for one moment descended to mere stagecraft, but in its simplest gesture was throbbing with vital human emotion.

As the curtain fell at last, while there was a busy hum of excited voices, the young person whose place on the New York stage was assured slipped into her dressing-room, scrambled into her clothes, and rushed from the theater, hurrying to carry the good news to the two who were eagerly awaiting her—her mother and her dog. "At last she saw the lighted windows that told her home was near. In a moment, through a tangle of hat, veil, and wriggling, welcoming dog, she cried:

"'It's all right, mumsey—a success! Lots and lots of "calls," dear, and, oh, is there anything to eat? *I am so hungry!*'

"So while the new actress's name was floating over many a restaurant supper its owner sat beneath one gas-jet, between mother and pet, eating a large piece of bread and a small piece of cheese, telling her small circle of admirers all about it, and winding up with the declaration, 'Mother, I believe the hearts are just the same, whether they beat against Western ribs or Eastern ribs!'"

Then, supper over, she stumbled through the old-time 'Now I lay me,' and, adding some blurred words of gratitude, she says, "I fell asleep, knowing that through God's mercy and my own hard work I was the first Western actress who had ever been accepted by a New York audience, and as I drowsed off I murmured to myself:

"'And I'll leave the door open, now that I have opened it—I'll leave it open for all the others.'"

She did. Through that open door has passed a long procession from West to East since the day when the young woman from Cleveland brought New York to her feet by her unique ability and dramatic perception. A lover of literature from childhood, a writer of books in later days, Clara Morris moved on through the years of her brilliant dramatic career to a rare achievement, not led by the lure of the foot-lights or the flimsier forms of so-called dramatic art, but by the call of the highest.

Well may the matinée girl of to-day, or the stage-struck young person who responds to the glitter and glare, the applause and the superficial charm of the theatrical world, listen to Miss Morris's story of "Life on the Stage," and realize that laurels only crown untiring effort, success only comes after patient labor, and great emotional actresses come to their own through the white heat of sacrifice, struggle, and supreme desire.

ANNA DICKINSON: THE GIRL ORATOR

A very well-known lawyer of Philadelphia was sitting in his private office one morning when word was brought in to him that a young lady wished to see him. The office-boy had never seen her before, and she had not given her name, but she was very firm in her intention not to be refused an interview.

"Show her in," said the lawyer, pushing back his chair with a bored expression and a resolution to send the stranger away at short notice if she was not a client. What was his surprise when a very young girl, still wearing short dresses, was ushered in, and stood before him with such an earnest expression in her bright eyes that she instantly attracted him. Motioning her to take a seat, he asked her errand.

"I wish some copying to do," was the reply, in such a musical voice that the lawyer became still more interested.

"Do you intend to do it yourself?" he asked.

She bowed assent. "Yes," she said. "We are in need of money and I must help. I write a clear hand."

So pleased was he with her manner and her quiet words, "We are in need of money and I must help," as well as touched by her self-reliance at an age when girls are generally amusing themselves, that he gave her some copying which he had intended to have done in the office. With a grateful glance from her brilliant dark eyes, she thanked him, and, promising to bring the work back as soon as possible, she left the office.

As the door closed behind her the lawyer opened a drawer and took from it a little faded photograph of a young girl with dark eyes and curly hair, looked at it long and sadly, then replaced it in the drawer and went on with his work.

On the following day, when the office-boy announced "the young lady with the copying," she was summoned to his office at once and given a hearty hand-clasp.

"I am glad to see you again," the lawyer said. "I had a daughter you remind me of strongly. She died when she was twelve years old. Be seated, please, and tell me a little about yourself. You are very young to be doing such work as this. Is your father living, and why are you not in school?"

Compelled by his kindly interest, the young girl talked as freely with him as if he were an old friend. Her name, she said, was Anna Elizabeth Dickinson, and she was born in Philadelphia, thirteen years before, on the 28th of October. Her father, John Dickinson, and her mother, who had been Mary Edmundson before her marriage, were both persons who were interested in the vital questions of the day, and Anna had been brought up in an atmosphere of refinement and of high principles. All this her new friend learned by a series of friendly questions, and Anna, having begun her story, continued with a degree of frankness which was little less than surprising, after so short an acquaintance. Her father had been a merchant, and had died when she was two years old, leaving practically no income for the mother to live on and bring up her five children. Both mother and father were Quakers, she said, and she was evidently very proud of her father, for her eyes flashed as she said: "He was a wonderful man! Of course, I can't remember it, but mother has told me that the last night of his life, when he was very sick, he went to an anti-slavery meeting and made a remarkably fine speech. Yes, father was wonderful."

"And your mother?" queried her new friend.

Tears dimmed the young girl's eyes. "There aren't any words to express mother," she said. "That is why I am trying to work at night, or at least part of the reason," she added, with frank honesty. "We take boarders and mother teaches in a private school, too, but even that doesn't give enough money for six of us to live on, and she is so pale and tired all the time." She added, with a toss of her curly head: "And I must have money to buy books, too, but helping mother is more important."

Entirely absorbed in her own narrative now, she continued to pour out a flood of facts with such an eloquence and persuasive use of words that her hearer was lost in amazement over a young girl who was so fluent in her use of language. From her frank tale he gathered that she had been a wayward, wilful, intense, and very imaginative child, who, despite her evident devotion to her mother, had probably given her many hours of worry and unhappiness. It was evident also that as a younger child she had been considered an incorrigible pupil at school, for she seemed to have always rebelled against discipline which she thought unnecessary.

"They could punish me all they liked," she said, with flashing eyes. "I would never obey a rule that had not been explained to me and that wasn't fair—never! Teachers and mothers were always telling good little girls not to play with me, and I was *glad*! Girls the teachers call 'good' sometimes are not that at all; they just know how to hide things from the teachers." As her hearer made no comment, but listened with an amused smile curving his lips, Anna continued: "I *adore* books, but, oh, how I hate school, when the rich girls laugh at my clothes and then at me if I tell them that my mother is poor and we work for all we have! It isn't fair, because we can't help it, and we do the best we can. I never would say it to them in the world—never! In the first school I went to they used to tease the children who were timid, and bother them so much that they would forget their lessons and get punished when it was not their fault. But *I* looked after them," declared Anna, proudly. "I fought their battles for them, until the others left them alone, because they were afraid to fight me, I was so strong. Oh, sir," she cried, "why can't people always be fair and square, I wonder?"

As if mesmerized by the intensity of this remarkable young reformer, the lawyer found himself repeating, "I wonder!" as if he had no opinions on the subject, but at the same time he was doing some thinking in regard to such a unique character as this one before him. When she had finished speaking he rose and put a bundle of work in her hand. "I will help you and your brave mother all I can," he said. "While you are doing that copying I will speak to other lawyers, who, I am sure, will give you more to do. I have looked over what you have done, and can warmly recommend you as a copyist. I hope we shall have many more long talks together."

So with her package under her arm, and a warm feeling of satisfaction in her heart because she had found a new friend who said she could do good work, she hurried home.

Almost from baby days it had been evident that Anna Dickinson was no ordinary child, and how to curb the restless spirit and develop the strong nature into a fine woman was a great problem for the already over-

94

burdened mother. Even as a young child Anna had an iron will, and discipline, of which she later learned the value, so chafed her independent nature that she was generally in a state of rebellion. From her own story it was clear that she must have been a terror to unjust teachers or pupils; but she did not mention the many devoted friends she had gained by her championship of those who were not being treated fairly according to her ideas. Hers was a strong, talented, courageous, fearless nature, which was bound to be a great power for good or evil. The scales were turned in the right direction by her passionate love for her mother and an intense desire to lift some of the burden of financial worry from her shoulders, as she saw Mrs. Dickinson, with tireless industry, struggle to make ends meet, and to feed, clothe, and educate her fatherless children. Her one determination was to have them grow up into noble men and women, but in Anna's early life it seemed as if the tumultuous nature would never be brought to any degree of poise and self-control. She showed a marked love of books, even when she was only seven years old, and would take one of her mother's volumes of Byron's poems and, hiding under a bed, where she would not be disturbed, read for hours.

When she was about twelve years old Anna went to the "Westover Boarding-school of Friends," where she remained for almost two years, and from which she went to the "Friends' Select School" in Philadelphia, where she was still studying when she applied for copying and found a new friend. Both of the schools were free Quaker schools, as her mother could not afford to send her elsewhere, and in both she stood high for scholarship, if not for deportment. In the latter institution she was noted for never failing in a recitation, although she was taking twelve subjects at one time, and was naturally looked upon with awe and admiration by less brilliant pupils. A new scholar once questioned her as to her routine of work, and the reply left her questioner speechless with wonder.

"Oh, I haven't any," said Anna, with a toss of her curly head. "And I don't study. I just go to bed and read, sometimes till one o'clock in the morning—poetry, novels, and all sorts of things; then just before I go to sleep I look my lessons over." Evidently the new-comer was a bit doubtful of being able to follow her leader, for Anna added, reassuringly: "Oh yes, you can, if you try. It's easy when you get the habit!" and went off, leaving a much-amazed girl behind her.

At the time of her visit to the lawyer's office Anna begged to be allowed to leave school to try and add to the family income, but her practical mother persuaded her not to do this for at least a year or so, and, seeing the wisdom of the advice, Anna remained in the "Friends' School." So active was her mind that for weeks at a time she did not sleep over five hours a night; the remaining time she spent in doing all the copying she could get and in reading every book on which she could lay her hands. Newspapers, speeches, tracts, history, biography, poetry, novels and fairy-tales—she devoured them all with eager interest. A favorite afternoon pastime of hers was to go to the Anti-Slavery Office, where, curled up in a cozy corner, she would read their literature or listen to arguments on the subject presented by persons who came and went. At other times she would be seized with a perfect passion for a new book, and would go out into the streets, determined not to return home until she had earned enough to buy the coveted prize. At such a time she would run errands or carry bundles or bags for passengers coming from trains until she had enough money for her book. Then she would hurry to a bookstore, linger long and lovingly over the piles of volumes, and finally buy one, which she would take home and devour, then take it to a second-hand bookshop and sell it for a fraction of what it cost, and get another.

Among her other delights were good lectures, and she eagerly watched the papers to find out when George William Curtis, Wendell Phillips, or Henry Ward Beecher was going to lecture in the city; then she would start out on a campaign to earn the price of a ticket for the lecture.

One day when she had read much about Wendell Phillips, but never heard him, she saw that he was to lecture in Philadelphia on "The Lost Arts." It happened that there was no copying for her to do at that time, and she had no idea how to earn the twenty-five cents which would give her the coveted admittance; but go to the lecture she must. As she walked past a handsome residence she noticed that coal had just been put in and the sidewalk left very grimy. Boldly ringing the bell, she asked if she might scrub the walk, and as a result of her exertion a triumphant young girl was the first person to present herself at the hall that night, and quite the most thrilled listener among the throng that packed the house to hear Wendell Phillips. Although her career was so soon to find her out, little did Anna dream on that night, as she listened spellbound to the orator of the occasion, that not far in the future many of that audience were to be applauding a young girl with dark eyes, curly hair, and such force of character and personal magnetism that she was to sway her audiences even to a greater extent than the man to whom she was listening.

When she was seventeen Anna left school for good, feeling that she could not afford to give any more time to study while her mother needed so many comforts and necessities which money could buy. So she left the "Friends' Select School," and in her unselfish reason for this, and the fact that she was forced to support herself and others at such an early age, when she longed for a more thorough education, lies an appeal for kindly criticism of her work rather than a verdict of superficiality, which some gave who did not understand or appreciate the nature, the inspiration, or the real genius of the young and enthusiastic girl.

She was offered a position as teacher in a school in New Brighton, Beaver County, and accepting it she spent a few months there, but as she did not like it she applied for a district-school position that was vacant in the same town. When she had made all but the final arrangements with the committee she asked, "What salary do you give?"

A committeeman replied: "A man has had the position until now. We gave him twenty-eight dollars a month, but we should not think of giving a *girl* more than sixteen." Something in his manner and words stung Anna like a lash, and, drawing herself up to her full height, she turned to leave the room.

"Sir," she said, "though I am too poor to-day to buy a pair of cotton gloves, I would rather go in rags than degrade my womanhood by accepting anything at your hands!" And off she went, to try her fate in some other place and way, absolutely sure that in some unknown manner she was to wrest success from the future. Young, inexperienced, penniless, and with few friends, she passed weeks looking for a situation in vain. At last she was offered work in a store, but when she found that she must tell what was not true about goods to customers rather than lose a sale, she put on her hat and left at once, and again began her weary quest of work. Everywhere she found that, if she had been a boy, she could have secured better positions and pay than she could as a girl. Also in her wide range of reading she discovered that many of the advantages of life and all of the opportunities, at that time, were given to men rather than to women. Her independent nature was filled with determination to do something to alter this, if she ever had a chance. It came sooner than she would have dared to hope.

One Sunday she was sitting at home, reading a newspaper, when she saw a notice of a meeting to be held that afternoon in a certain hall by the "Association of Progressive Friends," to discuss "Woman's Rights and Wrongs." She would go. Having decided this, she went to the home of a young friend and persuaded her to go, too, and together they walked to the hall and were soon deeply engrossed in the arguments presented by the speakers. The presiding officer of the afternoon was a Doctor Longshore, who announced before the meeting began that at the close of the formal discussion ladies were requested to speak, as the subject was one in which they were especially interested.

"One after another, women rose and gave their views on the question. Then, near the center of the house a girl arose whose youthful face, black curls, and bright eyes, as well as her musical voice and subdued but impressive manner, commanded the attention of the audience. She spoke twice as long as each speaker was allowed, and right to the point, sending a thrill of interest through her listeners, who remembered that speech for many a long day. At the close of the meeting more than one in the audience came forward and spoke to the beaming girl, thanking her for her brilliant defense of her sex, and asking her to surely come to the meeting on the following Sunday." Flushed with triumph and excitement, she received the praise and congratulations and promised to be present the next week. When the time came she again rose and spoke in glowing language of the rights and privileges which should be given to women as well as to men. As soon as she sat down a tall, nervous man, with an air of proud assurance that the world was made for his sex, rose and spoke firmly against Anna's arguments, voicing his belief that men were by right the lords and masters of creation. While he spoke he fixed his eyes on Anna, as if enchanted by the sight of her rapidly crimsoning cheeks and flashing eyes, which showed emotions at white heat. The moment he finished she stood again, and this time, young and inexperienced though she was, with little education and less knowledge of the great world, she held her audience spellbound by the clear ideas which she poured out in almost flawless English, and by her air of conviction which carried belief in her arguments with it. She spoke clearly, steadily, as she summed up all the wrongs she had been obliged to suffer through a struggling girlhood, as well as all she had seen and read about and felt in her soul to be true, although she had no tangible proofs. On flowed the tide of her oratory in such an outburst of real feeling that her hearers were electrified, amazed, by the rare magnetism of this young and unknown girl. As she spoke she drew nearer to the man, whose eyes refused now to meet her keen dark ones, and who seemed deeply confused as she scored point after point in defense, saying, "*You*, sir! said so and so," ... with each statement sweeping away his arguments one by one until he had no ground left to stand on. When her last word had been said and she took her seat amid a storm of applause, he swiftly and silently rose and left the hall, to the great amusement of the audience, whose sympathies were entirely with the young girl who had stated her case so brilliantly.

"Who is she?" was the question asked on every side as the eager crowd pushed its way out of the building, all curious to get a nearer view of the youthful speaker. Doctor Longshore, who had opened the meeting, as on the previous Sunday, was now determined to become acquainted with Anna and find out what had gone into the making of such a remarkable personality, and at the close of the meeting he lost no time in introducing himself to her and making an engagement to go to the Dickinson home to meet her family.

Before the time of his promised call—in fact, before Anna had even mentioned her success as a speaker to her mother—while she was out one day two gentlemen called at the house and inquired if Miss Anna Dickinson lived there. Her mother's cheeks paled with fright, for she feared Anna had been doing some unconventional thing which the strangers had come to report. When they said they had heard her speak at a public meeting and were so much pleased with her speech that they had come to find out something about her home surroundings, Mrs. Dickinson's brow cleared, and, leading them into the house, she spent a pleasant half-hour with them, and was secretly delighted with their comments on her daughter's first appearance in public. When Anna came home Mrs. Dickinson took her to task for not telling her about such a great event, and was surprised to see the real diffidence which the girl showed when she was questioned about the meetings and her speeches. A few days later Doctor Longshore called with her brother, Elwood, and with their flattering assurances that her daughter was a born speaker, and that she had already made some valuable points on a vital subject, Mrs. Dickinson began to feel that all her worry over Anna's turbulent childhood and restless girlhood had not been in vain, that she was born to do great things, and from that time she took a genuine pride in all the achievements of the young girl who came so rapidly into public notice.

The Longshores took Anna into their hearts and home at once, and many of her happiest hours were spent with them. "We felt toward her," Doctor Longshore said, "as if she were our own child. We were the first strangers to show an interest in her welfare and future plans, and she returned our friendship with confidence and love." She was always so buoyant, so full of vitality and gayety, that her visits were eagerly anticipated, and for hours at a time she would entertain her new friends with vivid and droll accounts of her experiences at home and in school and of her attempts to make money. And as she had won her way into the hearts of her audience, at those first meetings, so now she kept the Longshores enthralled, making them laugh at one moment and cry at another. One night she had a horrible dream to relate.

"I had been reading an account of the horrors of the slave system at its worst," she said. "After going to bed, I was long in falling asleep. Finally I slept and dreamed that I was a slave girl, and, oh, the agony of the knowledge! The hot sun scorched my burning skin as I toiled in the fields, with almost no clothing to soften the sun's heat. I was hungry, but there was insufficient food. At last I was dressed in clean, showy clothes and led to the auction-block, where I was auctioned off to the highest bidder. He led me away in triumph to even worse experiences, and when I woke up I could not throw off the horror of the awful nightmare."

Seeing her tremble under the misery of the recollection, Doctor Longshore soothed her by saying that the dream was a natural result of the highly colored account she had been reading before going to sleep, that all slaves were not by any means treated in such a cruel manner, and at last she grew calm. But whenever in future she spoke on the subject of slavery this terrible memory would come back to her so vividly that it would intensify her power to speak with conviction.

For several Sundays she went regularly to the "Progressive Friends'" meeting and spoke with unvarying success. Then she was invited to go to Mullica Hill, New Jersey, to speak on the subject, "Woman's Work." After discussing the matter with her mother and the Longshores, she accepted the invitation and set herself to prepare the lecture which she was to give. Then, on the first Sunday in April, the seventeen-year-old orator went to her trial experience as an invited speaker. By that time her praises had been widely sung, and when she rose and saw her audience there was a sea of upturned, eager faces looking into hers. Speaking from the depths of her own experience, she held the audience in breathless silence for over an hour. There was, it was said, an indescribable pathos in her full, rich voice that, aside from what she said, touched the hearts of her hearers and moved many to tears, while all were spellbound, and at the close of her address no one moved. Finally a man rose and voiced the feeling of the people.

"We will not disperse until the speaker promises to address us again this evening," he said, and a burst of applause greeted his statement. A starry-eyed girl stood and bowed her acknowledgment and agreed to speak again. As the audience dispersed Anna heard some one say, "If Lucretia Mott had made that speech it would be thought a great one."

As she promised, in the evening she spoke again on slavery, with equal success. A collection which was taken up for her amounted to several dollars, the first financial result of what was to be her golden resource.

But Anna had no thought of doing public speaking as her only means of earning her living. She continued to look for positions, but without success. Finally she took a district school in Bucks County, at a monthly salary of twenty-five dollars. So interested was she in the "Progressive Friends'" Sunday meetings that she went home every second week to attend them, and her speeches always won applause from an audience that had learned to anticipate the impassioned statements of the bright-eyed girl who was so much younger and so much more intense than any other speaker.

And now she began to receive invitations to speak in other places. On her eighteenth birthday she spoke in a small village about thirty miles out of Philadelphia, when she fairly electrified her hearers by the force of her arguments and the form in which she presented them. She continued to teach, although during her summer vacation she made many speeches in New Jersey. On one occasion she spoke in the open air, in a beautiful grove where hundreds had come to hear "the girl orator" give her views on temperance and slavery. Her earnestness and conviction of the truth of what she said made a profound impression, and even those who later criticized her speech as being the product of an immature and superficial mind were held as by a spell while she spoke, and secretly admired her while they openly ridiculed her arguments. At another time she was asked to speak at the laying of the corner-stone of a new Methodist church. The clergymen who gathered together were inclined to be severe in their judgment of the remarks of a "slip of a girl." Anna knew that and resolved to speak with more than usual pathos and power. When she began her address amusement was evident on the faces of the dignified men looking at her. Gradually they grew more interested, the silence became intense, and when the men rose to leave they were subdued, and some of them even were not ashamed to be seen wiping away tears. One of them introduced himself to her and with a cordial hand-shake said: "Miss Dickinson, I have always ridiculed Woman's Rights, but, so help me God, I never shall again."

But this time the young orator could not help feeling the power she had to sway great masses of people, and with a thrill of joy she began to believe that perhaps in this work which she loved above anything else in the world she would some day find her vocation, for she was already receiving commendation from men and women of a high order of intelligence and being given larger contributions as a result of her speeches.

The country was at that time in the beginning of its Civil War period, and much was written and said on the issue of the hour. At a Kennett Square meeting, where hot debates were held on the burning question of the day, Anna was one of the speakers, and one of the press notices on the following day said:

"... The next speaker was Miss Anna Dickinson, of Philadelphia, handsome, of an expressive countenance, plainly dressed, and eloquent beyond her years. After the listless, monotonous harangues of the previous part of the day, the distinct, earnest tones of this juvenile Joan of Arc were very sweet and charming. During her discourse, which was frequently interrupted, Miss Dickinson maintained her presence of mind, and uttered her radical sentiments with resolution and plainness. Those who did not sympathize with her remarks were softened by her simplicity and solemnity. Her speech was decidedly the speech of the evening.... Miss Dickinson, we understand, is a member of the Society of Friends, and her speech came in the shape of a retort to remarks which were contrary to her own beliefs. With her usual clear-cut conviction and glowing oratory, Miss Dickinson said that:

"'We are told to maintain constitutions because they are constitutions, and compromises because they are compromises. But what are compromises?' asked the young speaker, 'and what was laid down in these constitutions? Eminent lawgivers have said that certain great fundamental ideas of right are common to the world, and that all laws of man's making which trample on those ideas are null and void—wrong to obey, but right to disobey. The Constitution of the United States sat upon the neck of those rights, recognizes human slavery, and makes the souls of men articles of purchase and sale.'"

So clear of mind and expression was the young orator that her statements sank as deeply into the minds of her hearers as if spoken by a far more learned person, and from that time her intense nature had found its true outlet, and her longing to provide her mother with some of the comforts which had so long been denied her was soon to be realized.

In that same year of her speech at Kennett Square, on an evening in late February, she spoke in Concert Hall, Philadelphia, before an audience of about eight hundred persons. For two hours she spoke, without notes and with easy fluency. There were many well-known men and women there, who were delighted with what they were pleased to call a young girl's notable performance. But Anna herself was far from pleased with her speech. Afterward, on reaching the Longshores', she threw herself into a chair with an air of utter despondency, and, in response to their praise, only shook her head.

"I am mortified," she declared. "I spoke too long, and what I said lacked arrangement, order, and point. And before such an audience!"

This incident shows clearly that, despite all the flattery which was showered on her at that time, she did not lose her sense of balance, but knew with a keen instinct whether she had achieved her end or not.

And now winter was over and spring had come with its spirit of new birth and fulfilment. And, as the buds began to swell and open, the strong will and fresh young spirit of Anna Dickinson asserted itself in a desire for more profitable daily work, for as yet she was not able to give up other employment for the public speaking which brought her in uneven returns. She disliked the confinement and routine of teaching so much that she decided to try a new kind of work, and secured a place in the Mint, where she described her duties vividly to her interested friends.

"I sat on a stool," she said, "from seven o'clock in the morning to six at night for twenty-eight dollars a month. The atmosphere of the room was close and impure, as it was necessary to keep all windows and doors closed in the adjusting-room, for the least draught of air would vary the scales." Not a very congenial occupation for the independent nature of the young orator, but, although she disliked the work, she was very skilful at it, and soon became the fastest adjuster in the Mint. But she could not bear the confinement of the adjusting-room and changed to the coining-room, yet even that was impossible to a spirit which had seen a vision of creative work and of ability to do it. Then, too, she thoroughly disliked the men with whom she was thrown and their beliefs, knowing them to be opposed to principles which she held sacred; so when, in November, she made a speech on the events of the war, in which she stated her views so frankly that when they came to the ears of Government officials who did not agree with her she was dismissed from the Mint, she was rather pleased than troubled.

Through the remainder of the winter she continued to speak in various suburbs of the city, not always to sympathetic audiences, for so radical were some of her assertions, especially coming from the lips of a mere girl, that she was hissed time and again for her assertions. Despite this, she was becoming well known as a speaker of great ability, and as the war went on, with its varying successes for the North and South, she thought with less intensity on the subjects of the future of the negro and the wrongs of women, and became more deeply absorbed in questions of national importance, which was a fortunate thing for her. She was enthusiastic, eloquent, young and pretty, all of which characteristics made her a valuable ally for any cause. Mr. Garrison, the noted Abolitionist, heard her speak twice, and was so delighted with her manner and ability that he asked for an introduction to her, and invited her to visit Boston and make his house her home while there. She thanked him with pretty enthusiasm and accepted, but before going to Boston was persuaded to give the lecture in Philadelphia, for which she had been dismissed from the Mint. A ten-cent admission was charged, and Judge Pierce, one of the early advocates of Woman's Rights, presided and introduced the young speaker. The house was crowded, and this time she was satisfied with her lecture, while the eager Longshores and her mother were filled with a just pride. After all expenses were paid she was handed a check for a bigger sum of money than she had ever owned before. The largest share of it was given at once to her mother, then, after a serious discussion with Doctor Longshore, Anna decided to spend the remainder on her first silk dress. Despite oratory and advanced views, the girl of eighteen was still human and feminine, and it is to be doubted whether any results of her labors ever gave her more satisfaction than that bit of finery for her public appearances.

And now the young orator went to Boston, where through Mr. Garrison's influence she was invited to speak in Theodore Parker's pulpit, as leading reformers were then doing. She also spoke in the Music Hall on "The National Crisis," and that lecture was the hardest trial she ever experienced. For two days before it she could not sleep or eat, and answered questions like one in a dream, and Mr. Garrison and those friends who had been confident of her ability to hold any audience began to feel extremely nervous. If she should make a failure now at the beginning of her career, it would be critical for her future.

The night came, and with ill-concealed nervousness Anna put on the new silk dress, shook her heavy curls into place, and with resolute courage went to the hall, where, on mounting the platform, she noted the most tremendous audience she had ever before faced. Mr. Garrison opened the meeting by reading a chapter of the Bible, then he used up as much time as possible in remarks, in order to make the best of a bad situation, for he felt that she was not in a state of mind or body to hold the coldly critical audience before her. While he read and spoke poor Anna behind him waited to be presented, in an agony of nervousness which she struggled not to show. Then came the singing of the "Negro Boatman's Song of Whittier" by a quartet, accompanied by the organ. At last, with an easy smile, which concealed his real feelings, Mr. Garrison turned to introduce Anna, and she rose and walked forward to the front of the platform, looking more immature and girlish than ever before. Her first sentences were halting, disconnected, her fingers twined and twisted nervously around the handkerchief she held; then she saw a sympathetic upturned face in the front row of the audience staring up at her. Something in the face roused Anna to a determined effort. Throwing herself into her subject, she soon was pouring out a passionate appeal for a broader national life and action. Gone were fear and self-consciousness, gone all but determination to make her audience feel as she felt, believe as she believed, in the interest of humanity and the highest ideals. For over an hour she held that coldly critical mass of New England hearers as if by a magic spell, then the vast audience rose and gave vent to their emotion by the singing of "America," and then persons of distinction and wealth crowded around the speaker of the evening with thanks and praise. To one and all the young orator, whose eyes were still shining with enthusiasm, replied, simply: "I thank you. The subject is very near my heart," and as those who met her turned away they could not hide their amazement at the ability of a young person who looked so immature in her girlish beauty and freshness.

This was the beginning of a period of success. She delivered the Boston lecture in several other New England cities, and had many fine press notices on it, one of which closed with the following sentences:

"Her whole appearance and manner were decidedly attractive, earnest, and expressive. Her lecture was well arranged, logical, and occasionally eloquent, persuasive, and pathetic."

That was the time when every woman with a tender heart and a chance to show it for the benefit of the wounded soldiers served her apprenticeship in some hospital, and Anna was one of them. With keen sympathy she nursed and comforted the sick men, who told her freely about their hardships and sufferings, as well as the motives which led them to go into the army, and she learned their opinion of war and of life on the battle-fields. From this experience she gained much priceless material which she later used most successfully.

She was now beginning to be known as much for her youth and personal charm as for the subject-matter of her lectures, and to her unbounded joy in October, 1862, she received one hundred dollars and many flattering press notices for a speech given before the Boston Fraternity Lyceum. This success encouraged her to plan a series of lectures to be given in various parts of the East, especially in New England, from which she hoped to gain substantial results. But in making her plans she had failed to reckon with the humor of the people who under the stress of war had little interest even in the most thrilling lectures, and she traveled from place to place with such meager returns that she became perfectly disheartened, and, worse than that, she was almost penniless.

When she had filled her last engagement of the series, for which she was to receive the large sum of ten dollars, at Concord, New Hampshire, she realized with a sinking heart that unless she could turn the tide of her affairs quickly she must again seek another occupation. The resolute girl was almost disheartened, and she confessed to a friend later:

"No one knows how I felt and suffered that winter, penniless and alone, with a scanty wardrobe, suffering with cold, weariness, and disappointment. I wandered about on the trains day after day among strangers, seeking employment for an honest living and failing to find it. I would have gone home, but had not the means. I had borrowed money to commence my journey, promising to remit soon; failing to do so, I could not ask again. Beyond my Concord meeting, all was darkness. I had no further plans."

With positive want staring her in the face, in debt for the trip which she had taken on a venture, and shrinkingly sensitive in regard to her inability to aid her mother more lavishly, there was need of quick action. Alone in a boarding-house room, Anna reviewed her resources and the material she had on hand for a new and more taking lecture.

"I have it!" she exclaimed, jumping to her feet, and taking up a pad and pencil she hastily began to write a lecture in which she used the material gained in her hospital experience. She called it "Hospital Life." When she gave it on that night at Concord with a heavy heart it proved to be the pivot on which her success as a lecturer swung to its greatest height. As she drew her vivid pictures of the hospital experience and horrors of war and slavery she melted her audience to tears by her impassioned delivery. The secretary of the New Hampshire Central Committee was in the audience and was enchanted as he heard the young speaker for the first time. At the close of the lecture he said to a friend:

"If we can get this girl to make that speech all through New Hampshire, we can carry the Republican ticket in this State in the coming election."

So impressed was he with Anna's powers of persuasion that he decided to invite her to become a campaign speaker on his own responsibility, if the State Committee did not think well of the idea. But that committee was only too glad to adopt any plan to aid their cause. Anna Dickinson, then only eighteen years old, was invited to become part of the State machinery, to work on the side which appealed to her sense of justice. Elated, excited, and enthusiastic, she accepted the offer and began to speak early in March. What a work that was for the young and inexperienced girl! In the month before election, twenty times she stood before great throngs of eager persons and spoke, rousing great enthusiasm by her eloquent appeals in the name of reason and fair play.

Slight, pretty, and without any of the tricks of the professional political speaker, her march through the State was a succession of triumphs which ended in a Republican victory, and, though many of her enemies called her "ignorant and illogical" as well as "noisy" in mind and spirit, the adverse criticism was of no consequence in comparison to the praise and success which far outweighed it.

The member in the first district, having no faith that a woman could influence politics, sent word to the secretary, "Don't send that woman down here to defeat my election."

The secretary replied, "We have work enough for her to do in other districts without interfering with you!"

When the honorable member saw the furore Anna was creating he changed his mind and begged the secretary to let her speak in his district. The secretary replied: "It is too late; the program is arranged.... You would not have her when you could, now you cannot have her when you will!"

That district was lost by a large majority, while the others went strongly Republican, and it is interesting to note that when the good news reached headquarters the Governor-elect himself personally sent Anna thanks for her eloquent speeches, and to her amazement she was serenaded, feasted, and praised in a way that would have turned the head of a young woman who had been more interested in her own success than in victory for a cause for which she stood. But that and the money she could make and pass on to her mother were Anna's supreme objects in whatever she undertook, and although she would have been less than human if the praise and recognition had not pleased her, yet her real joy lay in the good-sized checks which she could now add to the family treasury.

"Having done such good work in the New Hampshire election, her next field of endeavor was Connecticut, where the Republicans were completely disheartened, for nothing, they said, could prevent the Democrats from carrying the State. The issue was a vital one, and yet so discouraged were the Connecticut politicians that they were about to give up the fight without further effort, when it was decided to try having the successful young girl speaker see what she could do for them. Anna was only too delighted to accept the challenge, and at once started on a round of stump-speaking and speechmaking, with all the enthusiasm of her intense nature added to the inspiration of her recent success in a neighboring State. The results were almost miraculous. Two weeks of steady work not only turned the tide of popular feeling, but created a perfect frenzy of interest in the young orator. Even the Democrats, in spite of scurrilous attacks made on her by some of their leaders, received her everywhere with the warmest welcome, tore off their party badges, and replaced them by her picture, while giving wild applause to all she said. The halls where she spoke were so densely packed that the Republicans stayed away to make room for the Democrats, and the women were shut out to leave room for those who could vote."

Well had her mother's struggle to make a fine woman of her turbulent daughter been repaid. Never was there such a furore over any orator in the history of this country. The critical time of her appearance, the excited condition of the people, her youth, beauty, and remarkable voice, all heightened the effect of her genius. Her name was on every lip. Ministers preached about her, prayed for her as a second Joan of Arc raised up by God to save their State for the loyal party, and through it the nation to freedom and humanity. And through all the excitement and furore the youthful heroine moved with calm poise and a firm determination toward her goal, attempting to speak clearly and truthfully in regard to what were her sacred beliefs.

Election Day was at hand, and missionary work must not slacken even for one moment. On the Saturday night before the fateful day Anna spoke before an audience of over one thousand of the working-men of Hartford, Connecticut. This was the last effort of the campaign, and it was a remarkable tribute to a young woman's powers that the committee of men were willing to rest their case on her efforts. A newspaper account of the meeting said:

"Allyn Hall was packed as it never was before. The aisles were full of men who stood patiently for more than three hours; the window-sills had their occupants, every foot of standing room was taken, and in the rear of the galleries men seemed to hang in swarms like bees. Such was the view from the stage.... To such an audience Miss Dickinson spoke for two hours and twenty minutes, and hardly a listener left the hall during that time. Her power over the audience was marvelous. She seemed to have that absolute mastery of it which Joan of Arc is reported to have had over the French troops. They followed her with that deep attention which is unwilling to lose a word, but greeted her, every few moments, with the most wild applause.... The speech in itself and its effect was magnificent—this strong adjective is the proper one.... The work of the campaign is done. It only remains in the name, we are sure, of all loyal men in this district to express to Miss Dickinson heartfelt thanks for her splendid, inspiring aid. She has aroused everywhere respect, enthusiasm and devotion, let us not say to herself alone, but to the country; while such women are possible in the United States, there isn't a spot big enough for her to stand on that won't be fought for so long as there is a man left."

Even that achievement was not the height of the young orator's attainment. Her next ovation was at Cooper Institute in New York City, where she spoke in May of the same year. Faded newspaper accounts of that meeting fill us with amazement that such a triumph could be, with only a girl's indomitable will, an insufficient education and much reading of books back of it.

"Long before the appointed hour for the lecture the hall was crowded. The people outside were determined to get in at all hazards, ushers were beaten down, those with tickets rushed in, and those without tickets were pushed aside, while thousands went home unable to get standing room even in the lobbies and outer halls.

"On the platform sat some of the most distinguished men of the day: clergymen, lawyers, generals, admirals, leaders of the fashionable set—all eager to do homage to the simple girl of whom the press said:

"'She is medium in height, slight in form, graceful in movement, her head, well poised, adorned with heavy dark hair, displaying to advantage a pleasant face which has all the signs of nervous force and of vigorous mental life. In manner she is unembarrassed, without a shade of boldness; her gestures are simple, her voice is of wonderful power, penetrating rather than loud, as clear as the tone of metal, and yet with a reed-like softness. Her vocabulary is simple, and in no instance has there been seen a straining after effective expressions; yet her skill in using ordinary language is so great that with a single phrase she presents a picture and delivers a poem in a sentence.'"

At the close of the meeting, which had been opened by Henry Ward Beecher, he rose and said, with real emotion, "Let no man open his lips here to-night; music is the only fitting accompaniment to the eloquent utterances we have heard." Then the famous Hutchinson family sang and closed the meeting with the John Brown song, in which the vast audience joined with thrilling effect.

From that Cooper Institute meeting Anna received almost one thousand dollars, an incredible amount for a simple speech to her unmercenary spirit, but one which was to be duplicated many times before her career was over.

After that meeting in New York her reputation as a public speaker was established, despite the carping critics, and she continued to win fresh laurels, not only for herself, but for vital issues. When doing more campaigning in Pennsylvania she had to travel through the mining districts, where her frank words were often ridiculed and she was pelted with stones, rotten eggs, and other unpleasant missiles. But she bore it all like a warrior, and made a remarkable record for speeches in parts of the State where no man dared to go. Despite this and the fact that the victorious party owed its success largely to the young orator, the committee never paid her one cent for her services—to their great discredit, probably having spent all their campaign funds in some other less legitimate way and thinking they could more easily defraud a girl than a more shrewd man.

Nothing daunted, she continued to speak wherever she could get a hearing, and at last came an invitation to make an address in Washington, D. C. Here indeed was a triumph! She hesitated long before accepting the invitation, for it would be a trying ordeal, as among her audience would be the President and many diplomats and high government officials. But with sturdy courage she accepted, and as a result faced, as she later said, the most brilliant audience ever assembled to hear her speak. It was a unique sensation for the dignitaries and men of mark to sit as listeners at the feet of this slender girl, who was speaking on profound questions of the day; but she made a deep impression, even on those who did not agree with her opinions, and it was a proud moment of her life when at the close of the meeting she met the President and his Cabinet. The Chief Executive gladly granted her an interview for the following day, and like other men of lesser rank, was carried out of himself as he watched the play of expression, the light and shade on her mobile face, as they talked together of the vital topics of the day.

Anna Dickinson was now an orator beyond a doubt; in fact, the only *girl* orator the country had ever known. More than that, she made use of her eloquence, her magnetism, her flow of language, not for any minor use, but in presenting to the public the great problems of her day and in pleading for honor and justice, freedom and fullness of joy for the individual, with such intensity of purpose as few men have ever used in pleading a cause.

That she wrote and acted in a play dealing with one of the subjects nearest her heart, and that she published a novel of the same kind, added nothing to her fame. She was wholly an orator with an instinctive knowledge of the way to play on the emotions of her listeners. Her faults were the faults of an intense nature too early obliged to grapple with hard problems; her virtues were those of a strong, independent, unselfish nature. It has been said that she rose to fame on the crest of three waves: the negro wave, the war wave, and the woman wave. If that is so, then was her success as a public speaker something of which to be proud, for to have spoken on such subjects surely betokens a great nature. Anna Dickinson has been called the "Joan of Arc" of her day and country. If she had not the delicate spiritual vision of the Maid of France, she had her superb courage in reaching up toward an ideal. What she was and what she accomplished as an American girl, who was an orator at eighteen, gives an incentive and a new enthusiasm to young Americans of the twentieth century, for what girls have done girls can do, and we believe, with that greatest of poets, that "the best is yet to be."

Made in the USA
San Bernardino, CA
25 July 2020

TEN LANDSCAPE

ROCKPORT

TEN LANDSCAPES

STEPHEN STIMSON ASSOCIATES

EDITED BY JAMES GRAYSON TRULOVE

ROCKPORT PUBLISHERS

First published in the United States of America by:

Rockport Publishers, Inc.
33 Commercial Street
Gloucester, Massachusetts 01930-5089
Telephone: (978) 282-9590
Facsimile: (978) 283-2742
www.rockpub.com

Cover photo: Charles Mayer

ISBN: 1-56496-858-8

10 9 8 7 6 5 4 3 2 1

Printed in China.

Charles Mayer is a Boston-based photographer who collaborates with architects, landscape architects, and installation artists to document designed space and to explore the many facets of our built environment. His simple, direct compositions capture the sense of place within a space. His work can be found in numerous national and international publications. Please visit the Web site at cmayerphoto.com.

Jane Amidon is the principal of Amidon Design & Communications, a site design/venue design and communications firm. She lectures and teaches in the U.S. and in Europe and has authored several books on contemporary landscape architecture. With a focus on the intersection of natural and urban systems, Amidon Design & Communications participates in projects ranging from residential to civic and from temporary installations to permanent works.

James Grayson Trulove is a book publisher and editor in the fields of landscape architecture, art, graphic design, and architecture. He has published, written, and edited over 40 books, including, most recently, *The New American Swimming Pool, Hot Dirt Cool Straw, Ten Landscapes: Topher Delaney, Ten Landscapes: Michael Balston,* and *New Design: Amsterdam.* Trulove is a recipient of the Loeb Fellowship from Harvard University's Graduate School of Design. He resides in Washington, D.C., and New York, N.Y.

CONTENTS

FOREWORD

By Michael Van Valkenburgh

Few things have been more welcomed than the invitation to write a foreword for this book on Steve Stimson's work. Over the years, I have had the pleasure of visiting some of Steve's gardens on Martha's Vineyard. A couple of years back, a landscape contractor I was working with on the Vineyard asked me to look at a stone wall in a garden that he thought I should see. The garden was a splendid mix of contemporary forms and also more timeless concerns — the new stone walls looked old and some pavement looked very modern and these were juxtaposed; the garden's rich planting palette was thoughtful and obviously was intended to (and would) bring much joy and magic to the people who would inhabit the garden. Only well into my visit to this garden did I realize it was designed by Steve. Since I know Steve and several of his associates extremely well, it was a great test to not know the garden was theirs before I decided that I liked it. And I did.

The integrity, the joy, and the beauty that are so much a part of Steve's work reflect the man I know as much as they do anything else. The beauty of the gardens produced by Steve and his staff extends in part from Steve's own tremendous qualities as a person: he is magnanimous, gentle, affable, winning, inquisitive, impish in a good way, and perhaps most of all, he has a total lack of cynicism about landscape design. We live in a time when intelligence of the heart is trusted far less than it should be. Steve has this intelligence in spades, and it shows in his work. It has been a great pleasure to watch Steve's work grow and mature, and it will be even more fun to see what is next. This important first book of his work records these pivotal early years.

Michael Van Valkenburgh—26 September 2001

Michael Van Valkenburgh is a landscape architect with offices in New York and Boston and has taught at the Harvard Graduate School of Design since 1982.

Introduction: Making a Place for Buildings and People to Dwell

By Jane Amidon

The goal is to create that memorable outdoor space…. And the challenge: to amplify while bringing the design to its simplest form.

The process of creating built landscapes is complex. It involves respecting a site's past while honing a vision for its future. One must have an in-depth understanding, or at least working knowledge, of how living systems function and how cultural models evolve. It is the intersection of the two – nature and culture – that proves to be fertile ground for the design practice of Stephen Stimson Associates (SSA).

Nationally operative but regionally responsive, Stephen Stimson Associates seeks to discover, define and develop the unique qualities of each site. Inspiration is taken equally from environmental factors such as geology, vegetation, climate and orientation and vernacular influences such as construction techniques and local materials. Introduced elements and fragments of past land use are tightly woven. Observation and interpretation lead to bold, architectural strokes that catch the eye, yet the work possesses a quiet dignity that should endure over time. A contemporary concept of space and place is deftly explored, yet respect for regional traditions is apparent. SSA wields a visible design language that grows from the particulars of each site, client and program, but there is a consistency across the firm's body of work that has to do with attitude. Crisp lines define edges and transitions. Intersections matter. Corners matter. The manner in which materials are used and the orchestration of movement through the site are inseparable.

When visiting a landscape created by SSA, the keen eye begins to discern site and sight legends that provide clues to use and meaning — just as a farmer's shaping of the land is pragmatic but results in a certain measured beauty. Graceful arcs and well-proportioned quadrilaterals serve as connective tissue between indoor spaces and the greater outdoors. Subtle shifts in the ground plane (expressed by stone steps, grass ramps and minimal stone curbing) signal receding or strengthening relationships to the heart of the site. One's movement and perception are purposefully directed to fuel awareness of the affinity between architecture, designed landscape and natural context. Innovative, custom-crafted details turn up unexpectedly, enlivening the rational design structure. SSA understands the landscape as a vitally dynamic medium, both culturally and ecologically, and seeks to establish lasting spatial orders into which particulars of time and place are incorporated.

Foundation

The focus of Stephen Stimson Associates' practice is broad, ranging from large-scale private gardens to a growing roster of institutional, corporate and civic works. Stephen Stimson, founder and principal, trained as an undergraduate in the Environmental Design program at the University of Massachusetts and subsequently worked at the Manhattan firm of Blumberg & Butter PC, an architecture and site planning practice that exposed him to a variety of projects in the urban context. Stimson received a Masters Degree from Harvard's Graduate School of Design in 1987 and upon graduation formed the firm Bunker Stimson Solien Inc. with Harvard classmates. The trio worked through a number of private and public commissions in the Boston and Cape Cod region, providing a strong foundation for the establishment of Stephen Stimson Associates in 1992.

In this time, Stimson built a personal design philosophy inspired by three figures seminal in his education: Michael

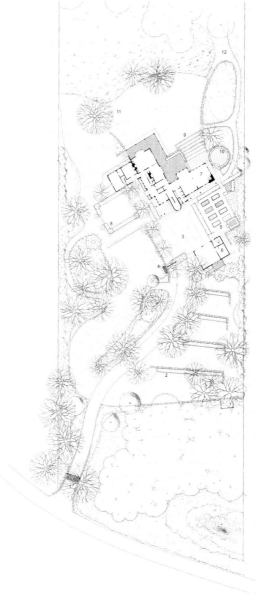

BELOW: *Woods Hole Residence, site plan.*

LEGEND
1 Entry Court
2 Terrace
3 Parking Court
4 Water Basin
5 Vegetable Garden
6 Garage
7 House
8 Rose Garden
9 Grass Treads
10 Screen House
11 Lawn
12 Beach Path

0   32 ft

Van Valkenburgh (for whom he worked for three years during graduate school), Peter Walker and Dan Kiley. Importantly, Stimson's upbringing in a rural setting underlies his appreciation of these masters of modern space. Raised on a tenth-generation dairy farm in central Massachusetts, he learned early on the evocative power of land contoured by agricultural practices. Exposure to the visual nuances of the agrarian realm engendered a respect for efficient site relationships and an awareness of the effects of continual change. The spatial mosaic of fields and windrows, the patterning of crops, and the cycling of seasons imprinted Stimson's perception of place-making. Clearly a native spirit runs throughout his work, an instinctual approach to design that has its roots in New England but these days is a direct reaction to the location of the individual project. Stimson seeks out historic elements and remnants of past land use, giving his work a sense of new woven with old. One sees evidence of Shaker influence in the studied minimalism and purposeful lines of SSA's forms; Stimson speaks of the graceful utility, proportioned balance and authenticity of materials found in Shaker architecture and landscapes as an ongoing inspiration.

Fellow principals at SSA include Edward C. Marshall and Richard Johnson. With a master's degree in landscape architecture from the Harvard Graduate School of Design and an undergraduate degree in environmental design, Marshall spent a decade as a Corporate Landscape Architect for IBM. He consequently brings significant institutional and corporate client experience to bear in SSA projects. Also a graduate of Harvard's program, Richard Johnson holds additional graduate degrees, including a master's and a PhD in Horticultural Sciences. Stints at Morgan Wheelock Incorporated, Michael Van Valkenburgh Associates and as a professor of horticulture have given Johnson a multi-faceted approach backed by extensive plant knowledge.

Amplification

As a mid-sized studio, Stephen Stimson Associates strives to put forth a consistent language of design that resonates with clients and colleagues. Although diverse in scale, program, and location, the body of work is unified by the clarity of dialog between architecture and landscape. Close collaboration with architects and other specialists is a key component of SSA's design approach. Inside SSA, the act of drawing and rendering is considered essential. From initial gestural sketches through meticulously produced plans and perspectives, drawing pushes evolution of design intent. Principal and founder Stephen Stimson — who learned to draw sketching cows in his family's dairy barn — brings a true

BELOW: *Zeeside.*
BOTTOM: *Isabella Stewart Gardner Museum garden court, cross section.*

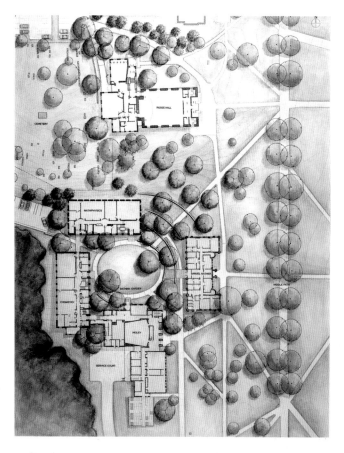

passion for artistic expression and notable drawing skills to SSA's graphic presentation and communication techniques.

An increasing number of SSA projects are for corporate, civic, and institutional clients. The Dr. Seuss National Memorial in Springfield, Massachusetts, (designed in 1998 and currently under construction) signals the firm's transition from primarily private gardens to larger-scale works. Recent projects include a masterplan for the Woods Hole Oceanographic Institution, the International Fund for Animal Welfare Headquarters masterplan, the Shapiro Student Center at Brandeis University, the Kenyon College Science and Music Quadrangle, the Isabella Stewart Gardner Museum Garden, the University of Connecticut Business

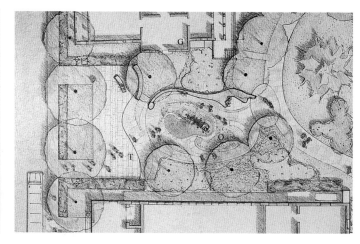

School, and the Harvard University Science Center Courtyard renovation.

The design strategy for this scale of work is remarkably similar to that of smaller projects. Earth is carved and wrapped to link buildings and people to the site. Grading schemes generate from the existing landforms; they are strong, generally planar statements, not abstract impositions. Ingredients of the surrounding context are selectively drawn in to fuse the site framework to its surrounds, visually and ecologically. The undiluted boundaries between "cultivated" and "wild" are etched with monolithic elements such as retaining walls, walkways and water works. Specific sequential experiences (arrival, circulation, moving from interior to exterior, prospects) are announced by functional stone, wood, and metal features and are reinforced by plantings. Planted forms (lines of shade trees, orchard grids, clipped or naturalized hedge lines) are used to define or filter spatial volumes, to describe site geometries, and to distinguish circulation and

sight corridors. Water features and built elements are site-referential and have an air of focused simplicity. Individual components are considered in section, not merely as a surface or veneer. Protrusions, overlapping and layering of materials are purposeful clues to site hierarchies. A care for distinctive detailing and concisely defined parts of the whole is writ large.

Order and Eloquence

Inciting perception is perhaps an appropriate summation of the intent of these collected works of Stephen Stimson Associates. The projects presented in this book reveal a self-imposed mandate: to make the designed landscape visible. Central in this effort is a heightening of the interplay between the manmade and the natural, a revelation of the inherent tension not of opposites but of two entities so entwined that they are often rendered imperceptible. With an eye to detail that communicates without reliance on ornamental flourishes, SSA creates and then pares to the essentials. Their technologically-savvy design is founded upon an intuitive understanding of vernacular sensibilities. Their work is site-specific but stems from age-old ideals of graceful utility. Be it garden, streetscape or campus, the works presented here invite you to observe a quiet confidence in the fundamental principles of order and eloquence.

BOLDWATER FARM

Edgartown, Massachusetts, 1993
Mark Hutker & Associates, architects

ABOVE: *At Boldwater Farm a pure arc drawn by a stone wall holds the inhabited landscape apart from the forest.*

OPPOSITE PAGE: *The contrast between smoothly mowed lawn and native vegetation is heightened by the presence of a simple boundary. The wall's width invites one to walk on its top, creating an element that is both visual and interactive.*

Set on a low outwash moraine, Boldwater Farm occupies thirty acres next to Great Salt Pond outside of Edgartown on Martha's Vineyard. The masterplan includes a number of introduced boundaries, both visual and physical, which call out designed elements while integrating them into the historic and ecologic fabric of the land. An awareness of distinctly different types — and the unity of thesis and antithesis — is heightened by these partitions that clarify edges, perimeters and formal relationships. The site is entered on the north through an orchard of Donald Wyman crabapple trees, a vestibule of sorts that is enclosed by a stone wall. Gated on all four sides and bisected from north to south by the entry drive, the orchard is an arrival yard reminiscent of the Vineyard's traditional stray livestock pounds. The drylaid stone work is also locally inspired, recalling both the delicate "lace" walls that network over the island and the heaped stone walls built by New England farmers as they cleared their fields for crops. The orchard's geometric grid orients visitors and will, as the trees mature, develop into a spatial volume through which one enters and exits the site.

In the future a barn, paddocks, guest house and caretaker's cottage will be built just west of the orchard. A manmade pond (with one side architecturally defined by a stone edge, the other sides softened by reeds and grasses) anchors this area and will link to the planned livestock facilities via a long water trough. As the entry drive runs southward, it passes through fields newly cleared for pasturing and hay. It then enters a thick forest of oak, beech and maple before opening into the circular parking court at the heart of the site.

The main residence is broken into three low-slung masses angled to embrace a central lawn and water view on the south side. Balancing the residence's canted configuration, an arc of stone encircles the entire domestic realm. A long-standing collaboration between architect and landscape architect resulted here at Boldwater in a notable degree of integrity in the connection between house and land. For example, subtle level changes in the residence are responded to in the landscape. The south porch and the lawn are at the same elevation as the finished interior floor, creating a planar flow of space that reaches outward toward the view horizontally-framed between the circling wall and the gnarled tree canopy.

The curving stone wall, compelling in its simplicity and earnest geometry, is a datum from which one reads diverse elements as parts of a coherent composition. The arc bounds the inner, cultivated landscape and sets up a crisp contrast with the antithesis of man's order: the seemingly untouched native vegetation that crowds the other side of the wall. Outside, sandy soils and strong, salty winds have reduced the trees to a collection of stunted scrub oaks rising out of densely textured undergrowth. Importantly, the wall is interrupted twice, once by the parking court and again by a sunken viewing garden just off the master wing. The top-of-wall elevation remains constant, revealing the land's sloping contours as the wall is just three inches high at the pool area to the north and stands twenty-four inches high at its terminus to the southeast.

RIGHT: *A view of the entry orchard before the crabapple installation. The enclosure is derived in part from stray livestock pounds found around the island. The design of the stone wall is inspired by the area's historic "lace" walls.*

OPPOSITE PAGE: *The Boldwater Farm master plan illustrates the rhythm of enclosed, open, and forested areas that characterize passage through the site. The detail plan, above, shows the monolithic sweep of wall that bounds and connects the outdoor living areas.*

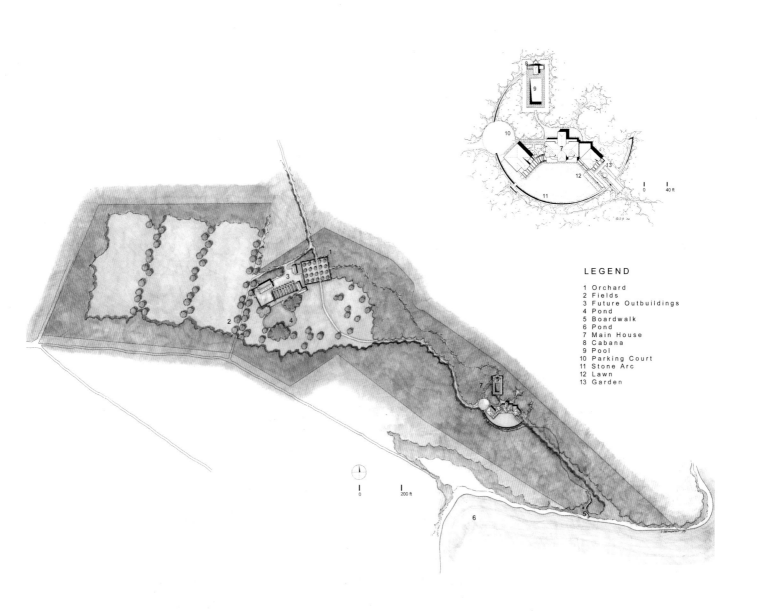

LEGEND

1 Orchard
2 Fields
3 Future Outbuildings
4 Pond
5 Boardwalk
6 Pond
7 Main House
8 Cabana
9 Pool
10 Parking Court
11 Stone Arc
12 Lawn
13 Garden

ABOVE: *The parking court's granite paving is patterned to extend the movement of the curving entry drive.*

RIGHT: *Boardwalks stretch between the residence — which is set back from the water's edge, protected by scrub oaks — and the shoreline of Great Salt Pond.*

OPPOSITE PAGE: *The Circle Garden lies between the master suite and the forest. Clean geometry forces perspective and draws the eye to the distant view. Linear beds of heather and grasses are steel edged to maintain graphic clarity. Paving materials relate to the colors and textures of the planted and native vegetation. The circular pool contains Koi fish, a favorite of the client.*

ABOVE LEFT: *Looking east through the entry orchard.*

LEFT: *A concept sketch of the orchard, looking west.*

OPPOSITE PAGE: *As the entry drive emerges from deep shade at the property's perimeter, the walled orchard is the first hint of cultivation within the native landscape. Granite piers call out the crafted gates.*

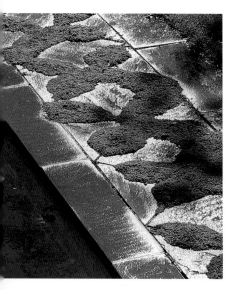

ABOVE: *Thyme embroiders the pool terrace.*

RIGHT: *Initially native trees formed a light curtain between the main house and the swimming pool. Over time the forest has re-established itself and now encloses the pool area in a thick cloak of foliage. The custom-designed fence recalls the silhouette of branching patterns.*

TOP LEFT: *A water trough will one day link the barn to the pond. The retaining wall and weir provide a tectonic edge on one side of the pond.*
LEFT: *Cattails and reeds grow along the water line. Much of the pond planting has been carried out by the client who has an interest in aquatic gardens.*
FOLLOWING PAGES: *Working from a primarily flat site, minimal changes in grade are carefully integrated to respect the planar nature of the landscape. Together the lawn, wall, and limbed oaks create a horizontal force that flows outward towards the water's edge.*

THOMAS PRINCE SCHOOL

Princeton, Massachusetts, 1996

ABOVE: *Children play beneath the semisphere vine trellis.*
OPPOSITE PAGE: *The redbud grove creates a canopy over crushed stone at the north end of the courtyard.*

Rallying around the vision of an innovative outdoor teaching space that could be much more than the typical schoolyard, parents, teachers, students, the building committee and the local garden club enlisted SSA to create a courtyard at the Thomas Prince School. Just 50 feet by 130 feet, the courtyard provides visual interest for people within the adjacent corridors and classrooms and is also an outside room for gatherings and instructional groups. Layered over the simple design structure is a choice of materials that relates directly to local archetypes of cultural practice and natural process.

Serving kindergarten through eighth grade students in a rural New England community, the school is a focal point of symbolic as well as institutional value. Just as members of the community reach into the school for educational fodder, so too does this central courtyard use the surrounding countryside as a resource to inform its physical expression. Its elements are pragmatic translations of indigenous ingredients. In this site design, a forest edge, a riparian corridor, a successional field, a remnant stone wall and huts of the local native American population become pieces of a school landscape that serve the everyday needs of students and teachers. Abstracted beyond immediate recognition and placed in an insular context, the core elements allow flexible interpretation of their source and meaning, yet are intuitively understood as components of a purposeful narrative.

A redbud bosque set in crushed stone anchors the south-facing end of the courtyard. The grove's leafy canopy in the summertime, autumn foliage and bare winter branches are reminiscent of the deciduous forests that border the region's farm fields. A string of individual fieldstones marks the transition from the gravel ground plane beneath the bosque to the neighboring stretch of grass. This lithic line is an abstraction of the old stone walls that network the area's hillsides, while the contemporary eye reads the boulders as an inviting place to sit.

A concrete walkway edged by colorful annuals, perennials and bulbs curves out from the redbud bosque with a stream-like meander and stretches the length of the rectangular lawn. Varying in width, the walkway is both a functional element of circulation and a visual link between the two ends of the enclosed space. Loosely arranged evergreens embrace the vine structure on the south end of the courtyard, their growth mimicking the evolution of a successional field. These junipers also act as vertical elements that define an energized field of space to balance the redbud grove. The remaining open lawn is maintained for instructional activities, group gatherings and events.

Recipient of a Merit Award for design excellence from the Boston Society of Landscape Architects in 1996 and a Merit Award from the American Society of Landscape Architects in 1999, the teaching courtyard is the product of volunteer efforts and community involvement. It is an exhibit of sorts, a living, inhabitable interpretation of contextual influences intended to educate and to amuse.

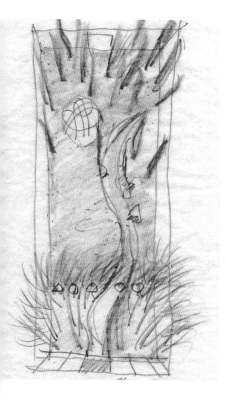

ABOVE: *An early concept sketch for the courtyard.*
NEAR RIGHT: *Looking upward through the top of the vine structure.*
FAR RIGHT: *After several growing seasons wisteria vines shroud the wire frame.*

BELOW: *Site plan.*

RIGHT: *An aerial view of the courtyard.*

LEGEND

1 Redbud Grove
2 Granite Boulders
3 Lawn
4 Concrete Path
5 Perennial Beds
6 Juniper Grove
7 Vine Structure

0   20 ft

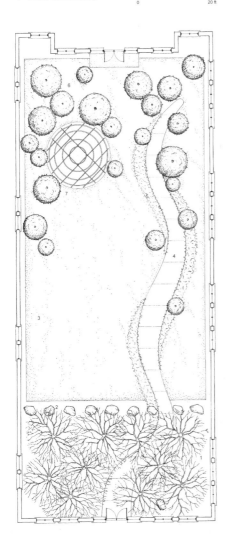

ABOVE RIGHT: *The Building Committee sought an imaginative solution that would go beyond the typical school yard.*

RIGHT: *A diagram of the seasonal changes in the courtyard, with spring at left and winter at right.*

OPPOSITE PAGE: *The redbud grove is a shady veil through which one views and enters the courtyard.*

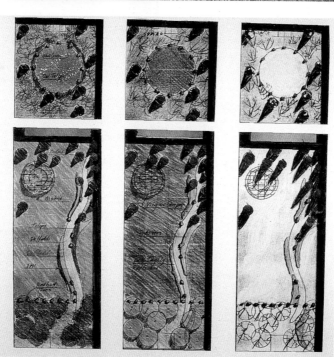

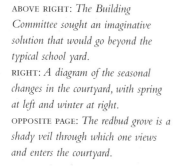

CASCADE POOL

Central Massachusetts, 1999
Hart Associates, architects

Surrounded by an upland mixture of oak, maple, beech, hemlock and pine, Cascade Pool House is perched at the edge of a bluff sixty feet above a river. The entry drive approaches from the north and curves through native woodland alongside a crab apple orchard, the peaceful scene belying an interlocking drama of topography, hydrology and geology that awaits on the south side of the residence. Couched in the language of local agricultural traditions and architectural styles, the arrival sequence is a demure foil for the visual and material intensity at the heart of the site.

Emerging from the shaded forest into the open arrival court, visitors are met by a wide granite fieldstone wall that defines one side of the arrival area. This wall is a key compositional line that creates a subtle spatial volume and stitches the sloping grid of the orchard to the orientation of the house. The wall's detailing, from its unusual dimensions to the fact that it stands free from neighboring wall segments rather than returning as a continuous element, foreshadows the extensive stone infrastructure on the south side of the residence. A bed of laurel, rhododendron, vinca and European ginger accents the main entrance and softens the edge of the parking court where it meets the house foundation.

As one moves around to the south side of the residence, everything changes as the structurally complex interplay of water and topography becomes apparent. The landscape's

ABOVE: *A walkway below the cascade offers an intimate experience of falling water and sparkling mist. The right side of the walk is a reservoir that catches and recycles the water.*
OPPOSITE PAGE: *The pool's shape works with the existing forest frame and hillside contours to emphasize a sense of prospect. Sky and water reflect each other.*

orthogonal frames give way to a series of massive, arcing retaining walls. Each stone arc is a terrace that relates to adjacent rooms of the house — a kitchen garden, a dog run, a living/dining patio, a swimming pool off the exercise room. Together, the loosely concentric slices form a multi-level platform that holds the house into the hillside, and corresponds to rounded contours that descend to the river. The convexity of the terraces emphasizes that this is a place of prospect.

Set into the lowest of the three terraces, the pool interrupts the sweeping stone arc to release a waterfall. The pool challenges conventional form and is shaped to relate the house outward to the view (framed in part by the adjacent white pine). Meticulously crafted, the weir edge consists of an inner gunite wall and an outer concrete wall with a fieldstone veneer and a battered granite cap. The waterfall is perfectly placid as it flows over the cap. It then varies from a streaming sheet at high volume to a sparkling curtain at low volume that catches on the stone underneath. At any level, the sound of falling water permeates. Uplights magnify the liquid flow at night. From above, the pool — itself sometimes appearing as a sliver of atmosphere hovering in the treetops — reflects passing clouds and echoes distant wet meadows across the Concord River.

In some instances the degree of high tech manipulation at the Cascade Pool House is evident, such as the ability of the zero-edge pool overflow to be adjusted to cascade at three different volumes. In other cases, state-of-the-art engineering is cloaked in low tech craft, such as the simple bronze gate that appears to catch innocently in the stone threshold but whose operation is monitored by a concealed security system. Throughout, a consistent logic of materials reveals certain attitudes. For example, bluestone is intended to have a sense of geologic layering to it. Never used simply as a veneer, the four to six-inch thick pieces always appear in section, a quarried aesthetic that speaks of solidity and terrestrial structure. Overall, crisp delineations and the dynamic slicing of the terrace walls achieve a memorable transition from interior space to the exterior experience of the greater landscape.

ABOVE: *The stair from the upper terrace is oriented to intersect the pool edge and to move outward toward the greater landscape.*

RIGHT TOP: *A perspective sketch of the arrival court as the drive emerges from the shaded forest.*

RIGHT BOTTOM: *View through maple trees over the court wall and out to the young orchard.*

BELOW: *Site plan.*

LEGEND

1 Orchard
2 Court
3 House
4 Living Terrace
5 Pool Terrace
6 River

ABOVE: *At the top of the cascade water glides over a granite cap. On the right end of the weir a snapping turtle sculpture guides current away from the wall.*

RIGHT: *Amelanchier foliage filters sight lines down to the pool. In the foreground, a ring of perennials outlines the edge of the upper living terrace.*

ABOVE LEFT: *The stone wall that defines one edge of the arrival court is composed of freestanding segments that slide past each other.*

LEFT: *Inside the arcing stone retaining wall granite steps negotiate small level changes.*

OPPOSITE PAGE: *Planted on a staggered grid, the orchard will mature into a strong spatial structure set against the native forest.*

FOLLOWING PAGES: *Individual terraces spill concentrically outward from the house. On the lowest level, the solidity of the encircling wall changes momentarily to shimmering liquid as the pool breaks through the stone arc.*

MEADOW HOUSE

Dover, Massachusetts, 1993
William Rawn Associates, architects

ABOVE: *Traditional architecture and vernacular landscape fuse with the site and its New England context.*
OPPOSITE PAGE: *Red maples line the entry drive, evoking memories of the region's historic tree-lined roadways.*

Spare but deliberate, the designed landscape frame of Meadow House is a contemporary adaptation of the traditional New England farmstead. Locally familiar materials and a native plant palette connect the site to its regional setting. In response to the topography (five acres of gently rolling fields) and the architectural language (Greek revival), the farmhouse is set on a grass plinth bordered to the south by a stand of mature pines. The plinth is retained by a beautifully aged field stone wall that emerges from grade at the threshold of the arrival court, spans the east face of the residence, and returns westward. The elevated expanse of lawn contrasts with the rough meadow grass beyond and calls out man's order against the encompassing natural context.

Architectural lines extend off of the house into the immediate landscape, establishing a subtly structured spatial progression that compliments the classic proportioning of the residence. A brick walkway travels east to west along the south side of the house, linking the front porch to the rear terrace as well as the kitchen and living room stoops. The walkway's linearity is reiterated by a perennial and herb border. Although clearly associated with the adjacent architecture (the front porch and the back terrace) the walkway breaks through the lines of these elements, extending into the lawn. This small but important detail relieves a potentially static relationship and calls attention to the walkway as an individual component. This clue to intrinsic hierarchies is also found at the granite steps and bluestone pavers on the south side of the house — each pushes into the neighboring material by inches, emphasizing contrasts of color and texture while simultaneously making a connection.

A lilac hedge underplanted with vinca and fern runs northward from the residence to define one side of the parking court. Cars pivot around a single linden tree to access the garage. A pair of granite posts and an inlaid band of granite mark the threshold between entry drive and the inner parking court with material and formal simplicity that is inspired by the regional aesthetic.

Moving outward from the house, major elements originate within the amplified architectural framework but then gently cant to meet the surrounding landscape. A row of red maples lines the entry drive and in plan reads as a pinwheeling spoke linking the residence to the town road. On the north side, a magnificent viburnum hedge stretches another spoke into the surrounding fields, reaching towards a group of towering pines and embracing the greater view. In the south meadow, a young orchard provides a hint of agrarian-inspired geometry. The choice of plant materials forges a powerful connection to the historical and regional context: from the seasonal show of the crab apple orchard, the viburnum and the lilac hedges to the brilliant red foliage of the maples, Meadow House is firmly grounded in age-old cycles that define the local environment.

This project received a Merit Award from the Boston Society of Landscape Architects in 1995.

ABOVE: *An early sketch illustrates the ordered relationship of house, garage, entry drive and landscape elements.*
OPPOSITE PAGE: *Site plan.*

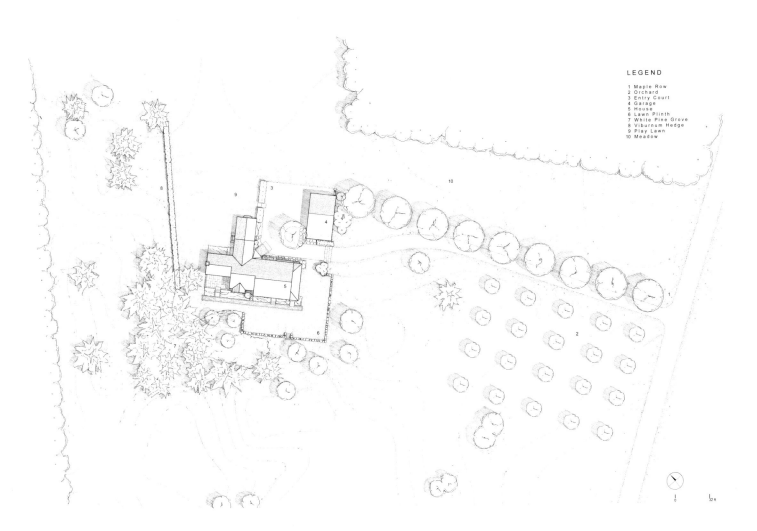

LEGEND

1 Maple Row
2 Orchard
3 Entry Court
4 Garage
5 House
6 Lawn Plinth
7 White Pine Grove
8 Viburnum Hedge
9 Play Lawn
10 Meadow

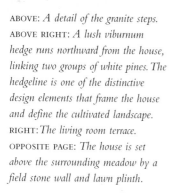

ABOVE: *A detail of the granite steps.*
ABOVE RIGHT: *A lush viburnum hedge runs northward from the house, linking two groups of white pines. The hedgeline is one of the distinctive design elements that frame the house and define the cultivated landscape.*
RIGHT: *The living room terrace.*
OPPOSITE PAGE: *The house is set above the surrounding meadow by a field stone wall and lawn plinth.*

RIGHT: *Steps that descend from the lawn to the meadow are integrated quietly into the plinth rather than extended past the line of the wall.*
OPPOSITE PAGE TOP: *Built and planted elements respond to existing trees and to the scale of the open fields.*
OPPOSITE PAGE BOTTOM: *A detail of the granite steps.*

ABOVE LEFT: *The maple line estab-lishes a regular interval of trunks that measure passage along the entry drive.*
LEFT: *Looking back through the vibur-num line to the house.*
OPPOSITE PAGE: *Red maples in their autumn splendor.*

HAWK RISE

Nantucket, Massachusetts, 2001
Lyman S.A. Perry Architects, Inc., architects

Not invisible, but more sensed than seen, the interplay of glacial history and ocean expanse at Hawk Rise creates an impression of immensity within which resides an array of more detailed experiences. A shrub barren upland bracketed by beech stands, sassafras colonies and tupelo wetlands, the site's vegetation gives clues to soil conditions, hydrology and degree of exposure to the elements. Throughout the thirty-acre property a minimized palette of plant materials and simplified, pure forms reveal a designed landscape whose character is simultaneously rich and stark, vast and intimate, current and timeless.

Long hedgerows and stone walls organize the property into a collection of open pockets that hold the main house, guest house, garage, pool, pool house, tennis court and five future family residences. During construction, seventy-five native scrub oaks were transplanted to surround new elements with site-specific plantings. Several of the most gnarled oaks, stunted by salt air and strong winds, were pruned and replanted in the arrival area to highlight their natural distortions and mottled bark. The entry drive, designed to accentuate topography, enters from the south and traverses rolling dips and knolls and skirts contours before arriving at the main house, guest house and garage. Stone clad and hunkered into the earth (one steps down three feet to enter the house), these structures appear to catch and distill the undulating land into a singular plane that then descends toward the ocean from the north side. Architecture and landscape are knit together by a continuous band of stone that runs

ABOVE: *Throughout the designed landscape the use of stone is deliberately bold and minimal, bringing forth a dynamic dialog between macro and micro scales.*
OPPOSITE PAGE: *A layered landscape captures imagination and brings depth to the perception of site.*

ABOVE: *A long view down one of the arm-like walls that bracket the central lawn.*
OPPOSITE PAGE, LEFT: *Site plan.*
OPPOSITE PAGE, RIGHT: *Mowed paths meander through the wildflower meadow.*

the length of the south façade. Appearing alternately above ground as a freestanding wall, then slicing through earth to retain the grade around a sunken garden, then piercing the house itself to become an interior wall and chimney, this artful component represents significant collaboration between architect and landscape architect.

A second important result of the shared design process is the placement of the residence. Instead of locating the sizeable structure at the water's edge, a decision was made to pull the building back into the site, gaining elevation, valuable foreground and optimized sight lines. The journey through the site is enriched, as one first travels the shrub moorland by car, arrives at the house, and then moves through layers of terrace, lawn, wildflower meadow, scrub oaks and bluff by foot. Visible as a destination but not interrupting the visual connection between the main house and the ocean, a swimming pool, pool house and pergola sit down by the water's edge. In essence, the program has been attenuated to stretch the length of the site.

Emerging from grade, massive stone arms reach down the east and west sides of the wide north terrace and lawn. Part boundary, part visual aid to guide perceptual progress through the landscape, the stone walls align with existing scrub oaks and long views to the harbor. Rather than compete with the magnificent setting, the elevated north lawn and below it the wildflower meadow heighten awareness of the prospect. The resulting scale and simplicity of the space are striking. Native and planted vegetation push on the outside of the inner cultivated area, seasonal color and texture contrasting with the purity of the smooth grass surface. There is a crisp resonance to the ramped, architecturally banked expanse of lawn that speaks to the monumentality of the ocean without challenging it. It is a reminder that glaciers, the ocean and man all possess the ability — although working at notably different rates — to radically transform topography.

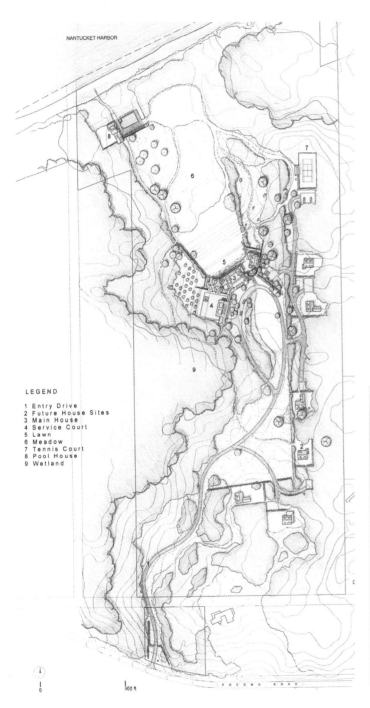

NANTUCKET HARBOR

LEGEND

1 Entry Drive
2 Future House Sites
3 Main House
4 Service Court
5 Lawn
6 Meadow
7 Tennis Court
8 Pool House
9 Wetland

THIS PAGE: *Detailed moments of purity and of contrast between the native and the designed landscape.*
OPPOSITE PAGE: *An unusual degree of collaboration between architect and landscape architect resulted in a symbiotic use of stone. Granite and bluestone move effortlessly between interior and exterior spaces.*

ABOVE LEFT: *A "water hedge" sprays up from the island. The pool is divided to provide a play area and lap lanes.*

LEFT: *The pool terrace is a final built edge atop the bluff before the terrain gives way to the ocean shoreline.*

OPPOSITE PAGE: *Pergola columns frame serene twilight at the pool.*

FOLLOWING PAGES: *Massive, stepped stone walls reach outward from the house, shaping the view and imbedding the inhabited landscape into the existing contours.*

SOUTH SHORE LANDSCAPE

Coastal Massachusetts, 1994
Dewing & Schmid, architects

ABOVE: *Rigorously sculpted slopes and a sense of engineered precision bring to mind land works of the classic French chateaux.*

OPPOSITE PAGE: *At the southern residence, a birch grove acts as a portal both into the parking court and, shown here, approaching the sitting terrace.*

Carved into the mixed forest along Boston's South Shore, this fourteen-acre residential site presents a number of highly orchestrated features that recall the grand gardens of 18th- and 19th-century Europe. In the first phase of the masterplan, a new residence with a parking court, garage, pool, pergola, cabana, lawn and gardens were constructed at the south end of the property. Subsequently, a significant redesign of the arrival court at the existing main house and additional design elements were completed.

Marked by bedrock outcroppings and descending at its center to a shallow ravine bisected by a small brook with a proposed circular pond, the oceanfront site is a play of topographical relationships. Architecturally cut slopes and extensive stone retaining walls set up a progression of lawn terraces that move from tightly controlled, ornately paved and planted surfaces adjacent to the houses out to expanses of mowed turf. The entry drive, called out by a double row of columnar maples, rises and falls with the contours as it passes alongside the multitiered great lawn.

Classically proportioned with symmetrical geometries, the arrival courts are truly outdoor rooms that extend elaborate interior detailing into the landscape. But the use of stone and the arrangement of plant palettes tends to be simplified and bold, leading to an overall impression of ordered unity instead of excessive decoration. At the original residence, a

ABOVE: *Bronze railings designed with the sculptor Sebastien Richer are inspired by a nearby beech tree.*
BELOW RIGHT: *An allee of columnar maple define the lower entry drive.*
OPPOSITE PAGE: *Site plan.*

patterned granite surface surrounds a central circular fountain. Each corner of the court holds a parterre of annuals edged by boxwood. Stone scuppers spill water over the south side into a trough bordered by a rose garden on the narrow lawn tiers below. Together the waterworks and the linear gardens reiterate the gesture of the walls as they trace the fall line of the slope. To the east, a birch grove introduces an informality that becomes a transition to the woodland beyond. At both residences grouped birch trees play a variety of roles, from portal and frame to poché and curtain.

At the second residence, geometry and control again provide a strong framework. The spatial ordering of the arrival court, dining terrace, pool area and circular play lawn, well-defined by plantings and walls, is closely related to the floor plan of the house. Birch groves, lilac, hydrangea, and yew hedges form architectural enclosures that separate the constructed landscape from the forest. On the north side, the prospect opens to look over the length of the property. In overall concept and in detail, the design of this South Shore property is a careful balance between historical influences and creative response to site conditions.

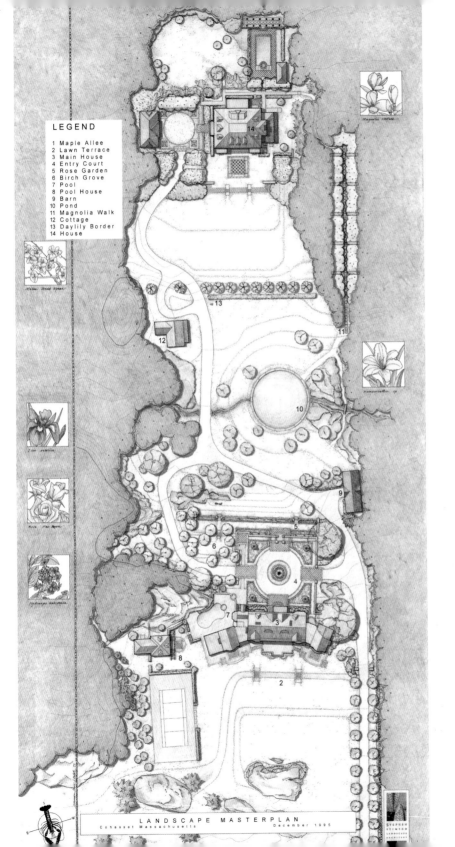

LEGEND

1 Maple Allee
2 Lawn Terrace
3 Main House
4 Entry Court
5 Rose Garden
6 Birch Grove
7 Pool
8 Pool House
9 Barn
10 Pond
11 Magnolia Walk
12 Cottage
13 Daylily Border
14 House

LANDSCAPE MASTERPLAN
Cohasset Massachusetts   December 1995

ABOVE: *A detail of the granite steps.*
RIGHT: *A system of retaining walls lead from the parking court at the main house down to the rose garden. Capstones are cut wide to strengthen the visual effect of the walls as a continuous element.*

OPPOSITE PAGE: *The view southward from the main house. In its simplified form and straightforward geometry the central fountain draws attention to the kinetic aspects of water rather than to ornament. The bluestone and granite cobble court slopes to a circular bronze drain.*

CLOCKWISE FROM TOP LEFT: *Cut bluestone scuppers; a detail of the parking court ground plane; terrace walls; an arc of granite cobbles.*
OPPOSITE PAGE: *At the south residence the pool enjoys rich surrounds: a wisteria arbor, cabana and spa are set into a bluestone terrace outlined by yew, licac and hydrangea hedges. To the left the circular play lawn carves into the forest.*

ABOVE, LEFT AND OPPOSITE PAGE:
*Groves of river birch create a spatial
volume that contrasts with adjacent
open areas. The trunks are a loose filter
between parking court, entry drive and
play lawn. Casting dappled light onto
crushed stone, the birch fit into a black
and white color scheme that underlies
the site detailing.*

STONE MEADOW

Chilmark, Massachusetts, 1993
MacNelly Cohen, architects

ABOVE: *White oak, granite and bronze hang in balanced harmony.*
OPPOSITE PAGE: *The wide plinth wall is a view line and an elevated path.*

In the Shaker tradition a particular grace is found in solutions of refined utility, in simple orders and purposeful lines that are proportionally balanced. These same qualities are evident at Stone Meadow, where crafted details define a sense of place and aware clients respect an artful approach to the design of landscape. Ambient elements of the six-acre site's setting are pulled into a loose composition of spatial sequences that becomes increasingly legible as one moves through the property from the entrance at the east to the western edge.

Succinct samplings of materials (native vegetation, local stone) and of environmental factors (the vast ocean view, the wild meadow, the undulating topography) are incorporated to create site structure. At the same time, the introduction of distinct design features - a plinth of mowed lawn, shifting levels in the ground plane, a vocabulary of paving materials, beautifully crafted gates - provide reference points against which to gauge the experience of context.

Designed in collaboration with several craftsmen, the entry gate provides the first clue to the attention to detail displayed throughout Stone Meadow. Forces of gravity and balance determined the gate's construction detailing, resulting in an arrival feature of spare elegance. Passing through the gate, fields of native grasses and wildflowers bracket the entry drive as it winds westward. The roadway gently rises to reveal a sweeping ocean prospect, one of the many subtle manipulations of grade that influence site and sight perception. A pair of sentry stones set back from the drive on the highest point of land is aligned with distant views of Squibnocket.

Descending towards the main house, the entry drive is slightly elevated as it passes over a wet meadow and through a tupelo grove, one of several planted forms that give the site an internal framework and coherent geometry while linking to the pre-existing native plant palette. The arrival sequence terminates against a beach plum orchard in a crushed stone court. A massive, three-piece granite slab stoop steps up to the front door. Similar, smaller slabs mark all entrances and site thresholds, each a fragment of the system of materials that characterizes Stone Meadow.

While the north side of the house is lodged into the land and vegetation, the south façade is exposed, rising off of a broad grass plinth. The platform extends outwards into the meadow and presents an unambiguous baseline that parallels the distant horizon. A simple plane retained by a low granite stone wall, the smooth expanse is a silent but evocative foreground that directs the eye upward and outward. The width of the retaining wall invites people to walk along its top while making a concise visual distinction between the work of man and of nature. A small grove of honeylocust set at one corner of the house frames views; individual red cedars in the outer meadow are focal points that define the middle ground between the residential core and the ocean horizon. Steps and paths cut into the high meadow grass link the pedestrian experience of the elevated, open platform to the greater landscape.

A line of black locust pulled from the neighboring woodland slides as a curtain between the main house and the adjacent guest house. The grade elevates twenty-four inches above the guest area to hold a stone-edged swimming pool. Screened on its west side by a sculpted privet hedge, the pool appears secluded and serene, free from typical fencing. Moving westward, a series of free- standing remnant stone walls, planted red cedars and black locust form inter-connected spatial volumes into which a par-three golf range is fit - an adept fusion of old and new. At Stone Meadow, minimal, purposeful moves and a sense of graceful functionality interpret the critical role played by specifics of place and the passage of time.

LEGEND

1 Gate
2 Causeway
3 Court
4 Main House
5 Lawn Plinth
6 Meadow
7 Pool
8 Guest House
9 Play House
10 Garage

PLANTED FORMS

 Tupelo Grove
Lawn Terrace
Beach Plum Orchard
Black Locust Hedgerow
Privet Hedge
Red Cedar Hedgerow

ABOVE: *A secret stair descends from the pool lawn through the privet hedge.*

RIGHT: *Perovskia and fragrant plants line the base of the pool wall.*

OPPOSITE PAGE: *Raised above the adjacent landscape, the pool is given a sense of removal and privacy by clipped privet and lilac hedges. Stone and lawn provide a simple frame for the pool.*

ABOVE: *A detail of bronze bands inlaid into the granite platform.*

RIGHT: *The landscape unfolds in layers leading outward to the ocean. A focal point / play stage is sited as a strong termination of the front wall. A grass ramp slips between segements of wall to connect upper and lower lawn levels.*

OPPOSITE PAGE: *Narrow stone bands are part steps, part wall that cut the slope neatly. The bands tie into the plinth wall and are a subtle device that is more distinct than simply sloping the grade.*

RIGHT: *Three honeylocust trees establish a foreground that increases perception of the distant landscape.*

ABOVE LEFT: *The plinth wall breaks and opens to allow steps down to the meadow pathways.*

LEFT: *The northwest corner of the plinth is marked by a shallow carved water basin integrated into the top of wall. A mowed line marks the transition from cultivated lawn to wildflower meadow.*

CAPE COD RESIDENCE

Coastal Massachusetts, 2001
Dewing & Schmid, architects

A landscape of ascent and prospect, this property occupies a high point on Cape Cod's southern shoreline, below which the land falls away to a shallow network of tidal marshes. The main house, guest house, garage, pool and pool house are integrated into the steep hillside via level changes that minimize the scale of the structures by setting them into the contours. Together the architect and landscape architect worked to synchronize changes in the interior floor levels with the terraced terrain.

The entry drive provides the first clue to the site's nature as it winds upward through several switchbacks. The drive is lined with banks of beach plum, rosa rugosa, choke cherry and bayberry, hearty species that will mature into a thicket rich with seasonal color. As one ascends, three stepped stone retaining walls appear on the south side of the drive, parsing the hillside's flow to form a winding grass ramp. The roadway swings around a knob of planted black pine and arrives at a granite-paved plateau between the main house and garage. Given the steep climb, one expects a broad view, but this is not revealed until one passes through or around the house.

On the south side of the residence, fieldstone walls retain a multi-tiered terrace that leads down to the pool. Jutting outward, the pool is a shining visual connection to (and a sharp dividing line between) the domestic landscape and the ocean. Its lipless edge pulls the eye outward to vast bodies of water and the distant horizon. A narrow runnel receives overflow from the freestanding spa, zig zags across the bluestone terrace and spills into the pool. The channel's glistening, angular meander is inspired by the linear mosquito ditches cut into the estuary marshes as well as by fingers of water and remnant inlets that reach into the body of the Cape and nearby islands. This landscape anchors a private residence into dramatic coastal terrain with a precise strategy of cutting, carving and holding.

RIGHT: *Changes in ground level are used to integrate the house into the vertiginous topography. Fieldstone retaining walls and hedge lines hold and visually define each platform.*
BELOW: *Elevation looking west. The house is pressed into the hillside rather than perched on top.of the rise. Inside, floor levels step upward from east to west to traverse the slope.*
OPPOSITE PAGE:*Site plan*
FOLLOWING PAGES: *Fieldstone walls guide movement as one descends from the house across the south terraces to the pool level.*

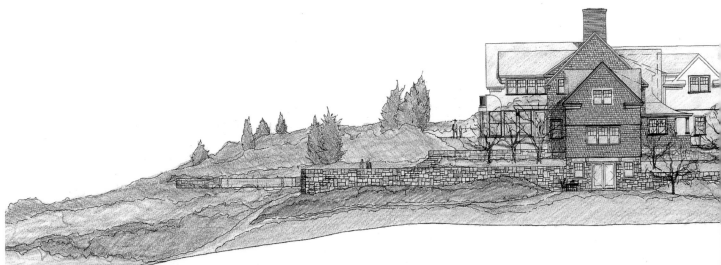

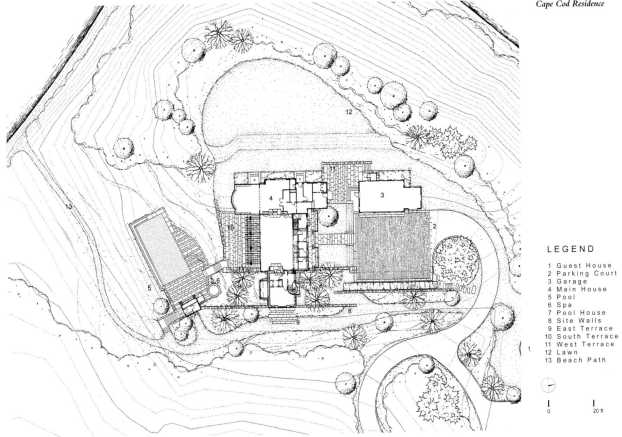

LEGEND

1 Guest House
2 Parking Court
3 Garage
4 Main House
5 Pool
6 Spa
7 Pool House
8 Site Walls
9 East Terrace
10 South Terrace
11 West Terrace
12 Lawn
13 Beach Path

0   20 ft

LEFT: *Minimal forms and muted tones of paving, water and sky fuse the manmade with the natural environment.*

OPPOSITE PAGE, LEFT: *Layered view from spa.*

OPPOSITE PAGE, RIGHT: *A runnel cut into the bluestone surface carries flow from spa to pool, echoing water channels in the distance and providing a place for children to play. The stone slab bridge leads to steps from the upper terrace.*

WOODLAND HOME

Sherborn, Massachusetts, 1998
Deborah Epstein, architect

Flowing contours embrace and emanate from Woodland Home, situating architect Deborah Epstein's addition and renovations within a self-contained topographical context. A sloped clearing surrounded by mature upland forest, the site is anchored at its center by the house and garden. Colors and textures of landscape materials (such as lilac bluestone paving and copper accents) respond to idiosyncrasies of the architecture. At the same time, objectified grade transitions and quietly defined exterior volumes provide a spatial superstructure to which the house's placement and expression (such as the sweeping entry stair, windows on the north face and the pool arcade) appear to relate. As evidence of fruitful collaboration between landscape architect and architect, the site plan and the renovated residence speak with individual voices yet the two easily harmonize.

On the south side of the house, a small bluestone terrace sits between the guest bedroom and game room. Bracketed by a pair of existing blue Atlas cedar and punctuated by a small basin and water jet visible from the main living areas of the house, the terrace draws the eye with its purplish hue and inset copper bands. Stone steps, cranked to meet the fall line of the adjacent lawn on the perpendicular, gesturally balance the pool and cause one to shift orientation when moving from inside to outside. The south lawn is a sunken oval set several feet below the terrace, its outer edge thickened with native flowering shrubs and trees. To the east, the grade rises steadily through a planted woodland garden of redbud, dogwood and viburnum.

On the north side a significant amount of earth was excavated to create the amphitheater that now cradles the house. Stepped fingers span the concave lawn and reach into the forest. The narrow granite ribs originate at regular intervals that coordinate with the fenestration rhythm of the facade, but the arcs' radii increase as they move up the slope. The expanding arcs encourage movement outward from the interior core of the site. River birches scattered across the inner bowl are intended to read as a unified canopy rather than as unique objects. Groupings of viburnum occupy the upper levels of the north lawn.

Throughout the Woodland Home site, small but studied changes in grade create dynamic relationships. Quirky, smart detailing draws the eye to features that customarily go unnoticed. The designed landscape rests within the all-encompassing woodland without becoming integrated, a secret clearing that is not of the forest but that would not exist without the power of the forest.

ABOVE: *A pair of blue atlas cedars frame the view over the intimate south terrace to the bowled lawn.*
RIGHT: *Copper bands punctuate the purplish bluestone paving entry walk.*
OPPOSITE PAGE, LEFT: *Site plan.*
OPPOSITE PAGE, RIGHT: *Steps set into the grade are angled to shift orientation from interior spaces to the contoured edge of the south lawn.*

LEGEND
1 Parking Court
2 Entry Terrace
3 South Lawn
4 South Terrace
5 House
6 Granite Arcs
7 Birch Grove

ABOVE: *A detail of the chiseled granite curbs.*

RIGHT: *The white of the stone bands and birch bark brighten the wooded enclave.*

OPPOSITE PAGE: *Granite arcs are pulled off of the building and reach across the lawn into the forest.*

Cove House

Coastal Massachusetts, 2001
Thompson and Rose, architects

Straightforward, refined elements and an emphasis on materiality qualify this young residential landscape as a future hallmark of SSA's design approach. Intersections, adjacencies, and edges are carefully considered and consistently treated in a manner that brings clarity and coherence to the site. From the outset, one has the sense that the site design conducts movement and perception, leading sequentially from the well-defined arrival court eventually to the open expanse at the ocean's edge. There is a visual energy manifest in the juxtaposition of terse, eloquent walls and purposeful plantings. Stone and wood surfaces are crafted to call out functional areas: broad slabs of lavender bluestone in the entry walk; crisp wood decking around the pool (secured with internal fasteners that avoid the need for nails and leave the surface unmarked); radial wood decking banded by stone on the west terrace. Hedge lines and tree groupings fortify spatial volumes, screen boundaries, frame views and pose as sculptural accents.

The most notable feature of this compact site are the low, primarily freestanding stone walls that arc around the oval play lawn elevated above the waterfront. The first wall stretches across the west face of the residence, edging the deck as a vertical element and, as a horizontal device, guiding movement to either end of its curved length. Resisting the temptation to step directly down from the living area to the lawn, this wall is a final layer through or around which one must pass to gain the site's promise.

ABOVE: *Looking north, the arced wall activates an energy between architecture and landscape. As with many SSA projects, the walls straddle an ambiguous line between being a horizontal datum against which one reads terrain, sky and water and being a vertical instrument that controls movement through the site, a barrier or threshold.*
OPPOSITE PAGE: *The oval lawn, embraced by stone walls, serves as a play and event lawn elevated above the cove. Manipulation of the lawn grade is subtle but critical to the perception of site and context.*

The second wall originates flush with the decking on the south corner of the house, then swings toward the pier. Its wide bluestone cap, a continuation of the detailing on the adjacent deck, invites one to stroll out along the arced length. The top-of-wall width tapers as the wall moves away from the house and as its height increases — a subtle trick that strengthens the effects of forced perspective. Syntheses of walkway, boundary, and artful object, the walls instigate a fluid gesture that grounds the house and embraces the convex contours emanating toward the shoreline. This residential landscape makes a careful distinction between the manmade and nature's work. In doing so, it ignites a vibrant tension not of opposites but of two entities skillfully counterbalanced in the service of graceful utility.

ABOVE: *The use of wood extends from within the residence out to the decking and renovated pier.*

RIGHT: *The wide walls guide movement to the sides of the deck but also invite one to experience them as a walkway or a seat.*

OPPOSITE PAGE: *Site plan.*

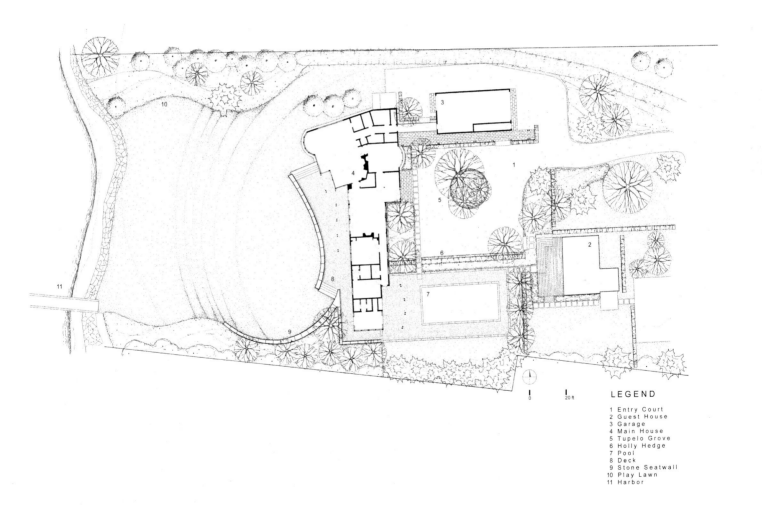

LEGEND

1 Entry Court
2 Guest House
3 Garage
4 Main House
5 Tupelo Grove
6 Holly Hedge
7 Pool
8 Deck
9 Stone Seatwall
10 Play Lawn
11 Harbor

ABOVE: *The arc walls are constructed of split flat rough bluestone with a lilac bluestone cap. Integrated detailing defines the entire design, from the manner in which the wood deck meets stone to the bullnosed wall cap.*

OPPOSITE PAGE: *There is a purposeful shifting of planes from interior to exterior spaces. Grade changes tend to occur at gates, walls and transitions. Clear geometries strengthen the link between architecture and site and foster a visual energy that pulls one through the landscape.*

ABOVE RIGHT: *In the entry court native forest gives way to a legible destination defined by hedge lines, trees, pergola and paving.*

RIGHT: *Looking from the pool back toward the entry court, vertical planes or layered elements pull the eye with varying colors and textures.*

OPPOSITE PAGE: *Stones read equally as a cadenced edge and a walkway. Planted boundaries frame views and give privacy. A delicate custom wood and bronze gate leads from entry court to pool terrace.*

FOLLOWING PAGE: *The swimming pool borders are planted with blue and lilac perennials.*

Stephen Stimson Associates would like to acknowledge the indispensable contributions of the following people:

Julie Bargmann
Anita Berrizbeitia
Derek Bowser
Tom Bunker
Dede Clark
Mary Ellen Donald
Susannah Drake
Danielle Dupuis
Rebecca Galat
Ronald Henderson
Kris Horiuchi
Benjamin Houghton
Richard Johnson
Ah-Yeon Kim
Warren Knight
Sing-Ning Kuo
Byoung Hoon Lee
Michael Ludington
Jennifer Malila
Edward Marshall
Kevin McKeon
Kimberly Mercurio
Tracey Miller
Manuel Morales
Jill Neubauer
Hillary Noyes
Michelle Oliva
Nancy Parmentier
Joni Palmer
Chris Reed
Kristen Reimann
James Royce
Jeff Ryther
Derek Simpson
Dan Solien
Jeeun Song
David Smith
Lisa Swansey
Bethany White
Trisha Woods

PROJECT CREDITS

Boldwater Farm
Project Manager: Stephen Stimson, Bunker Stimson Solien, Inc.
Architect: Mark Hutker Associates
General Contractor: Andrew Flake
Pool Contractor: Luzietti Pool and Spa, Inc.
Landscape Contractor: Landscope, Clay Merrill
Masonry Contractor: Francisco Tavares, Gary Stead

Thomas Prince School
Project Manager: Stephen Stimson, SSA
Landscape Contractors: Colonial Landscaping, AJF Environmental Services, Bigelow Nurseries,.R. Mason Landscape
Principal: Dr. Louis Giantris
Garden Club: Jane Weisman
Building Committee: Tom Sullivan

Cascade Pool
Project Manager: Richard Johnson, SSA
Architect: Hart Associates
General Contractor: Thoughtforms Corp., Aquaknot Pools, Inc.
Landscape Contractors: R.P. Marzilli & Company, Inc., Hayden Hillsgrove
Structural Engineer: LeMessurier Consultants, Inc.
Artist: Rosalind Waters

Meadow House
Project Manager: Stephen Stimson, Bunker Stimson Solien, Inc.
Architect: William Rawn Associates
General Contractor: Malcolm Construction
Landscape Contractor: Green Earth

Hawk Rise
Project Manager: Richard Johnson, SSA
Architect: Lyman S.A. Perry Architects, Inc.
General Contractor: Thirty Acre Wood, LLC
Landscape Contractor: Francisco Tavares, Inc.
Pool Contractor: Luzietti Pool and Spa, Inc.
Tree Mover: Instant Shade, Inc.
Metalsmith: Sebastien Richer, Richer Metal

South Shore Landscape
Project Manager: Richard Johnson, SSA
Architect: Dewing & Schmid Architects
Pool Contractor: Aquaknot Pools
Landscape Contractor: R.P. Marzilli & Company, Inc.
Masonry Contractor: Schumacher Landscape, Castelluci, Inc.
General Contractor: Thoughtforms Corporation

Stone Meadow
Project Managers: Kristen Reimann, Hillary Noyes, SSA
Architect: MacNelly Cohen Architects, Inc.
Masonry Contractor: Francisco Tavares, Inc.
Landscape Contractor: Landscope
Metalsmith: Sebastien Richer
Metal Fencing: Concannon Fence Co.
Artist: Ethan Fierro

Cape Cod Residence
Project Manager: James Royce, SSA
Architect: Dewing and Schmid, Inc.
Civil Engineer: Ryder and Wilcox, Inc.
General Contractor: Fellman Brothers, Inc.
Landscape Contractor: R.P. Marzilli and Company, Inc.
Earthwork: AMA Excavating
Pool Contractor: Custom Quality Pools, Inc.

Woodland Home
Project Manager: Lisa Swansey, SSA
Architect: Deborah Epstein Architect
General Contractor: Kistler & Knapp Builders, Inc.
Landscape Contractor: R.P. Marzilli & Company, Inc.

Cove House
Project Manager: Kim Mercurio, SSA
Architect: Thompson & Rose Architect, Inc
General Contractor: Gentile Remodeling
Landscape Contractor: R.P. Marzilli and Company, Inc.
Pool Contractor: Custom Quality Pools, Inc.
Metalsmith: Cape Cod Fabrications, Inc.

PHOTO CREDITS

All photographs by Charles Mayer, except as noted.
Stimson Portrait: Jill Neubauer
Thomas Prince: Edward Marshall
Thomas Prince Color Plan: Edward Marshall (p.30)
Kenyon College model photo: Edward Marshall
Boldwater Aerial: Aerphoto/S. Turner
Boldwater: Edward Marshall (p.22)
Boldwater-Pool: Steve Rosenthal

DRAWING CREDITS

Woods Hole plan: Lisa Swansey, Ah-Yeon Kim
Woods Hole Oceanographic Institution sketch: Stephen Stimson
Isabella Stewart Gardner Museum: Manuel Morales, Stephen Stimson, Ron Henderson
Dr. Seuss national Memorial Plan: Ron Henderson, James Royce, Kim Mercurio
Kenyon College plan: Jennifer Malila
Kenyon College models: Jeeun Song, Kim Mercurio, Edward Marshall
IFAW perspective: Ah-Yeon Kim, Stephen Stimson

Meadow House plan: Rebecca Galat, Stephen Stimson, Kris Horiuchi
Thomas Prince School plan: Stephen Stimson, Kristen Reimann
Thomas Prince School plan: Stephen Stimson, Rebecca Galat
Cascade Pool plan: Derek Bowser, Kevin McKeon, Jeeun Song, Richard Johnson, Ah-Yeon Kim
Cascade Pool perspective: Stephen Stimson
Cascade Pool section: Derek Bowser, Jeeun Song, Stephen Stimson
South Shore plan: Hillary Noyes, Rebecca Galat, Stephen Stimson
Boldwater plans: Tom Bunker, Jeff Ryther, Stephen Stimson
Stone Meadow plan: Kristen Reimann, Stephen Stimson
Stone Meadow diagram: Edward Marshall, Ah-Yeon Kim, Lisa Swansey
Hawk Rise plan: Jennifer Malila, Richard Johnson, Nancy Parmentier, Stephen Stimson
Cape Cod Residence plan: James Royce, Ah-Yeon Kim, Jennifer Malila
Cape Cod Residence section: Jennifer Malila
Woodland Home plan: Lisa Swansey, Stephen Stimson
Zinner plan: Kim Mercurio, Ah-Yeon Kim

FIRM PROFILE

Stephen Stimson Associates produces original landscapes of insight, responsiveness, and resonance.

Insight is derived from careful consideration of a client's program, budget and long-term goals.

Responsiveness is our calibrated strategy for issues of environmental, cultural and aesthetic context.

Resonance results as our landscapes mature into vital spaces of experience, learning, and celebration.

Stephen Stimson Associates (SSA) has received numerous awards for institutional, corporate, urban, and residential landscape design, including an Award for Design Excellence from the Boston Society of Architects (2000) and a number of Merit Awards for Design from the American Society of Landscapes Architects. Our work is respected for its capacity to build dialogue between buildings and landscape, between man's work and nature's systems. We are dedicated to providing clients with the highest quality of design services.

At Stephen Stimson Associates three principals with 55 cumulative years of experience lead a diverse staff of professional landscape architects, planners and horticultural experts. Our principals are active in both the design field and in academics, giving the firm a vibrant intellectual framework from which to approach each project as a unique set of circumstances. SSA has significant project management experience, enabling us to guide clients through complex design and construction processes. Our scope of capabilities is wide and is frequently augmented by close collaboration with architects, engineers, ecologists, and specialized fields such as soils, irrigation, lighting, acoustics, exhibit and graphic design.

We strive to find solutions that fit adeptly with site conditions and client needs. We are sensitive to environmental concerns and work to minimize unnecessary site impacts. We promote landscapes that reveal information about use, culture, history, weather, geology, hydrology, and wildlife. In the work of SSA, crafted moments are embedded into larger spatial sequences to speak over time and across generations.

The work of SSA appears in these and other publications: New American Gardens, New American Pools, Pocket Gardens, Landscape Architecture Magazine (1999, 1998, 1991), Town & Country Magazine (2001), Metropolitan Home (1997), The Boston Globe Magazine.

Principals

Stephen Stimson is a registered landscape architect with significant design and project leadership experience. Before founding SSA in 1992, Steve worked at Michael Van Valkenburgh Associates and, subsequently, a founding partner and principal of Bunker Stimson Solien Inc. Steve received an undergraduate degree from the University of Massachusetts, a Masters Degree in Landscape Architecture from Harvard's Graduate School of Design (1986) and was awarded a Penny White Traveling Fellowship. Steve has served as a Visiting Lecturer in design and drawing studios at Harvard and at Roger Williams University.

Edward C. Marshall is a registered landscape architect with over two decades of experience in corporate, institutional, and civic work. Holding a Masters Degree in Landscape Architecture from Harvard's Graduate School of Design (1986) and a Bachelor of Science in Environmental Design (University of Massachusetts, 1978), Edward served as Corporate Landscape Architect for IBM for ten years and as Landscape Architect at Morgan Wheelock Associates for seven years before joining SSA. Edward has published articles in Think Magazine, Dallas Times Herald, and Landscape Architect and Specifier News.

Richard T. Johnson is a registered landscape architect with a PhD. in Horticultural Science (University of Minnesota, 1983) and a Masters Degree in Landscape Architecture (Harvard Graduate School of Design, 1989). Prior to joining SSA in 1995, Richard acted as Project Landscape Architect at Morgan Wheelock Associates, Paul C.K. Lu and Associates, and Michael Van Valkenburgh Associates. As an Assistant Professor at Virginia Polytechnic Institute and State University, Richard taught courses in plant materials, ecology, and history of landscape architecture. Richard has exhibited work at the National Building Museum and at the Harvard Graduate School of Design. He was the recipient of the Frederick Sheldon Traveling Fellowship (Harvard, 1989), and has received awards from the American Society of Landscape Architects.

Afterword

The list of colleagues, clients, and mentors to whom I am indebted is long, and at the very top is my architect wife, Jill Neubauer. Her insight, support and critical design advice have been invaluable to this book and to the growth of my practice. My daughters, Annie and Lizzie, help me see with a fresh perspective every day.

I hold great appreciation for the dedication, professionalism and friendship of fellow principals, Edward Marshall and Richard Johnson. I deeply value the creative collaboration that our firm has enjoyed with a number of gifted architects, sculptors, craftspeople and contractors. I have learned much from them and from their enthusiasm for the process of building landscapes to endure. Over the years our staff has included numerous talented individuals who have produced a tremendous body of work. Many thanks to those in the office who spent hours and days with me, Chuck Mayer and Jane Amidon in the production of this publication. Without the patience and skills of Chuck Mayer, we would not have won daunting battles against site elements to obtain outstanding photography. Of course the greatest debt of gratitude is owed to our clients, whose encouragement and vision have led the way to fruitful design explorations. Together creative impulse and drawings are brought to reality.

Anne Lister *of* Shibden Hall

Introduction

This book serves as an introduction to Anne Lister (1791–1840) who lived at and eventually owned and managed Shibden Hall and Estate near Halifax, West Yorkshire. Her home of Shibden Hall has survived over 500 years and is open to the public to visit. It is managed by Calderdale Museums Service, part of Calderdale Council. In addition to her home, some of her possessions and a vast archive relating to the Hall and Estate have survived. Anne Lister was a diarist, and recorded her life in great detail from 1806 to 1840 and the volumes of over five million words survive, along with hundreds of letters, account books and miscellaneous papers, all revealing a fascinating woman and life in the early 19th century.

Although never famous in her own time, Anne Lister's legacy has revealed her to be a remarkable scholar, traveller, business woman and property owner. Her diaries also reveal she was a lesbian and defied the norms of the time, not only in her relationships with other women, but also in how she dressed and conducted herself, resulting in her nickname, Gentleman Jack.

Known locally as a land owner, business woman and member of the Halifax Literary and Philosophical Society, it was not until Anne's diaries were published by Helena Whitbread in 1988 and her intimate relationships with other women were revealed that she grew in notoriety. This interest has increased steadily since then with a number of publications, ever increasing media coverage and the BBC television series, *Gentleman Jack,* based on Anne Lister written by Sally Wainwright.

In light of this increased interest it became apparent that there is no definitive account of Anne's life and what can be seen today relating to her. Focus has tended to be on the diaries themselves, which are a rich source of information, whilst her home and possessions and the rest of the archives, including volumes of travel notes and hundreds of letters, all contribute to discovering and getting to know this remarkable woman.

Whilst some sections of the diaries have been explored in more depth in other publications, we focus on her legacy and how her story has been discovered and shared over the last century to today.

Portrait of Anne Lister attributed to Joshua Horner (also on the front cover) and her signature, taken from one of her music books.

As Collections Manager for Calderdale Museums I am honoured to introduce Anne Lister, an enigmatic and high achieving woman who is becoming known throughout the world, far beyond her home of Halifax, West Yorkshire.

Angela Clare, 2019.

Shibden Hall and Estate

Painting of Shibden Hall by John Horner (1784-1867).

Shibden Hall was first recorded in 1420 as home to the Otes family. The Hall and Estate stand about two miles from Halifax and are hidden from the town by a steep hill. It was subsequently lived in by the wealthy Saviles at the start of the 16th century, and then by the entrepreneurial Waterhouses, who extended and improved the property.

In 1612 Shibden had to be sold by Edward Waterhouse, to stave off impending bankruptcy and was bought by members of the Hemmingway family who were cousins of the Listers. The tenant in 1614 was Samuel Lister, a clothier, who by the marriage of his sons to their Lister cousins, brought Shibden into Lister family ownership in 1619.

The Listers were professional people, clothiers, apothecaries, headmasters, Virginian pioneers and soldiers. The Estate itself, about 400 acres, survived on rents, agriculture and mineral extraction, particularly coal.

Otes, Savile and Waterhouse crests despicted in the windows at Shibden Hall.

All these portraits are on display at Shibden Hall. The three to the left were restored by local artist John Horner (1784-1867) and reframed by Anne Lister in 1833, ordered from Millbourne & Sons, London. John Horner suggested the paintings were by Thomas Hudson (1701–1779). However, on the reverse of Reverend John Lister's someone has pencilled 'Richard Lynes' and on Samuel's portrait is pencilled 'F. Heufell'.

Reverend John Lister (1703-1759).　　James Lister (1705-1763).　　Samuel Lister (1706-1766).

Reverend John Lister (1703-1759) inherited Shibden in 1729. He did not marry and died in a hunting accident in 1759, leaving Shibden to his brothers James, Samuel and Jeremy.

Jeremy had three sons, James (1748-1826), Joseph (1750-1817) and Jeremy (1752-1836) and two daughters, Martha (1763-1809) and Anne (1765-1836).

children, two girls and four boys. Anne was the second eldest child.

Anne Lister had moved into Shibden Hall with her Aunt Anne and Uncle James in 1815. All four of her brothers had died by the time her Uncle died in 1826, and he left the Hall and Estate to Anne, along with her father Jeremy and Aunt Anne. Her younger sister Marian

also later lived at Shibden. Anne took over management of the Estate and in 1836 when both her Father and Aunt died, she inherited fully.

The eldest son James Lister inherited Shibden and lived there with his sister Anne. His brother Joseph lived at Northgate House, part of the Shibden Estate in the centre of Halifax and Jeremy, the youngest, was commissioned into 10th Regiment of Foot (Lincolnshire Regiment) in 1769. He later became a recruiting officer after an injury.

Captain Jeremy Lister married Rebecca Battle (d.1817) in 1788 and the couple had six

Uncle James (1748-1826), posthumous, by Joshua Horner (1811-1881).

Aunt Anne (1765-1836) by Thomas Binns, commissioned in 1833.

Marian Lister c1855 (1797-1882).

Shibden's Residents

William Otes (1420)

William Otes and Margaret Waterhouse

Joan Otes and Robert Savile

William Otes

Hands of the court from 1491-1504

William had previously left the hall to his daughter Joan but after his wife's death he remarried and had another son Gilbert (1428-1508) and tried to change his will to favour him. The Savile family contested this. Eventually the hall passed to Joan. Gilbert received an income from the property during his lifetime.

John Waterhouse (1523-1583) and Joan Bosville

Robert Waterhouse (1498-1578) and Sybil Savile (?-1524)

Robert Waterhouse (1544-1598) and Joan Waterton

Robert was a barrister at the Inner Temple: a successful lawyer in York. He inherited the house in 1584 and made extensive improvements to the hall. In 1584 he was elected MP for Aldborough in North Yorkshire and moved to London. In 1580 he married Joan Waterton and they had ten children, the first son died in infancy and their second son Edward inherited the hall.

Edward Waterhouse (1581-16??) and Abigail Parker

Jane Crowther, for nephew John Hemmingway

James was an apothecary and made and sold medicines at his shop near Hall End, Halifax. He inherited the hall from his great-grandfather Samuel Lister. The case was challenged but James obtained possession in 1709. He married Mary Issot in 1699. They had 13 children. James emigrated to America in the 1730s with two of his sons but returned later. The estate passed to his eldest surviving son John.

Samuel Lister (1570 -1632) and Susan Drake

Thomas Lister (1599-1677) and Sibell Hemmingway (16??-1633)

Wealthy local lady bought the hall for her nephew John Hemmingway.

Samuel Lister (1673-1702) and Dorothy Priestley (16??-1709)

Samuel Lister (1623-1694) and Hester Oates

Dorothy Priestley (16??-1709)

James Lister (1673-1729) and Mary Issot

Reverend John Lister (1703-1759)

On John's death the estate passed to his brother Jeremy. He had emigrated with his brother Thomas to Virginia but returned to England in 1736. In 1744 he married Anne Hall and they had eight children.

Jeremy Lister (1713-1788) and Anne Hall

James Lister (1748-1826) and sister Anne Lister (1765-1836)

Jeremy Lister (1752-1836) Anne Lister (1791-1840) and Marian Lister (1797-1882)

Ann Walker (1803-1854)

Ann was Anne Lister's lifelong companion who had lived at Shibden with her. She was forcibly removed from the house in 1843 after Anne's death.

Various families from 1843-1855

John was a local antiquarian and was a founder member of the Halifax Labour Union and the Independent Labour Party. He never married but lived with his sister Anne at the hall. He became bankrupt in 1923 and was forced to sell the estate.

John Lister(1847-1933) and sister Anne Lister (1852-1929)

Dr John Lister (1802-1867) and Louisa Grant (1815-1892)

Shibden was donated to the **Halifax Corporation** who opened the park in 1926 and the hall in 1933.

'Yet the thought of exile from poor Shibden always makes me melancholy - come what may, I have been happier here than anywhere else. [...] I am attached to my own people- they are accustomed to my oddities, are kind, are civilized to me.' - Sunday 16th December 1832.

Anne Lister (1791–1840)

It was no surprise that Anne wanted to have the freedom of ownership of property and in turn, that she was very capable of managing it. Anne was very intelligent and was fortunate to have received an education when young, which she continued to pursue her entire life.

Anne was born in Halifax on the 3rd April 1791. She was the second child of Jeremy and Elizabeth Lister. Their first child John was born in 1789 and died the same year. Anne was brought up in Skelfler House, Market Weighton and made frequent visits to her Aunt Anne and Uncle James at Shibden Hall. Samuel, who Anne was closest to, died in a boating accident whilst in the Army in 1813. The other two brothers

Jeremy (1801-1802) and John (1795-1810) had both died, leaving just Anne and her sister Marian to inherit.

Anne was sent to school in Ripon and also educated at home with tutors. In 1805, at fourteen-years-old Anne went to Manor House School in York. She attended lectures in Paris and continued to self-educate throughout her life. In 1831 Anne was the first woman elected to the committee of the Halifax Literary and Philosophical Society.

In 1815 Anne moved in permanently with her Aunt Anne and Uncle James at Shibden Hall. Her mother Rebecca died not long after in 1817.

It was whilst she was at Manor House School that Anne began to write her first diary in 1806, which starts with the words 'Eliza left us.' Eliza Raine was Anne's first girlfriend.

Throughout her diaries Anne documents that she was only interested in women. She had 'marriage' ceremonies with Mariana Lawton and later Ann Walker, who would eventually move in with her at Shibden Hall.

It was also clear that Anne was different from society's expectations of a woman at the time. Anne not only did not wish to marry, but she also did not want to conform to what was expected of her and chose to cast her own mould. She decided to only wear

Three portraits reputedly of Anne Lister. The oil painting on the right was done posthumously and attributed to Joshua Horner (1811-1881).

black, spent a great deal of time studying, managed her own estates and sought business opportunities, travelled widely and even climbed mountains.

In 1809 Anne met Isabella Norcliffe of Langton Hall, near Malton and they had a relationship, but Anne did not seem content with Isabella. Anne met Mariana Belcombe in York in 1810, who seems to have been the love of her life. Mariana married Charles Lawton in 1816, possibly in the hopes he would not live overly long, but Anne and Mariana were only ever able to have an affair and the two women never got to live together as Anne hoped.

Anne had several relationships over the years but was often heartbroken, constantly searching for someone to live with her at Shibden.

She met Ann Walker (1803-1854) in 1832. They had met previously but now became well acquainted. By 1834 Ann had moved in to join Anne and they set up a joint household at Shibden Hall.

Ann Walker had inherited Crow Nest Estate when her brother John (1804-1830) died on his honeymoon in Naples. His widow was pregnant but the child was stillborn. Ann shared her inheritance with her sister Elizabeth. When she finally settled on Ann Walker, Anne Lister gained not only the companion she wanted but also access to considerable wealth.

In 1836 Anne's Aunt and Father both died leaving Anne to fully inherit Shibden Hall and Estate. Her sister Marian returned to live in Market Weighton in 1836.

Anne had first travelled to Paris in 1819 for three weeks with her Aunt and over the coming years made journeys to Switzerland, Italy, Belgium, Netherlands and the Pyrenees, and spent two years living in France. Her travels were cut short when her Aunt became ill and then after the deaths of her Aunt and Father she focussed on managing Shibden Hall and making great changes to the Hall and Estate. By the time Anne had the time and resources to travel again in 1839, she was 48 years old. She had now gained more income to pay for her adventures and also a companion, in the form of neighbouring heiress Ann Walker.

Anne had never been able to settle for long, and her plans to travel further afield lured her away from Shibden Hall. Taking Ann Walker with her, they set off to reach Georgia in June 1839 on a two-year expedition. Anne Lister would not return to see Shibden again. She died in Koutais in Georgia on 22nd September 1840. She seems to have died of fever, but the exact cause is unknown. Her diary finishes on 11th August 1840 through lack of page space, so she may have written more elsewhere.

Anne's passport to Russia, 1839. Image courtesy of West Yorkshire Archive Service (SH:7/ML/1077).

Anne's Diaries and Archives

The reason we know so much about Anne's life as a landowner, business woman, intrepid traveller, mountaineer and lesbian stems from her legacy of diaries, letters and archives.

Anne Lister first started to write a diary in 1806 which became a daily ritual, recording every detail of her life. By her death in 1840 she had completed 26 volumes, 7,722 pages of around five million words.

This unique set of diaries along with letters and other archives relating to the Hall and Estate not only reveal the details of Anne's life and her own thoughts and feelings, but provide information for almost every aspect of early 19th century life in England. They are a vital source of information on women's and lesbian history and social, political and economic history. They also give insights into technology, theology, linguistic and medical history of the time. Anne's detailed diaries reveal her personal journey with an emotionally honest account of lesbian life, recorded alongside local and national events and overseas travel experiences.

In 2011 the diaries were included in UNESCO's Memory of the World Register because of their importance.

The diaries were written into small notebooks and written up later as part of a daily ritual for Anne. She meticulously recorded the daily

'I owe a great deal to this Journal. By unburdening my mind on paper I feel, as it were, in some degree to help get rid of it; it seems made over to a friend that hears it patiently, keeps it faithfully, and by never forgetting anything is always ready to compare the past and present and thus to cheer and edify the future.'
Friday 22nd June 1821

weather, temperature and clock references to all of her activities, such as what she was reading, how long it took to walk to places and letters sent and received. She also added indexes to the backs of the volumes for reference.

Her earliest diaries were in smaller volumes and loose pages but from 1816 she set about recording her life in good quality bound volumes of unlined paper with page numbers at the top and dates in the margins. The hard bound volumes cover 24 years of her life in great detail.

For her more personal thoughts, including her relationships with women and financial information, Anne had devised a code which she called her 'crypt hand' using a range of symbols, numbers and Greek letters.

Anne's diaries, travel notes and Shibden Hall's archives are all looked after by West Yorkshire Archives, housed within Halifax Central Library.

Anne Lister's travel case.
The red insert folds down to create a writing surface.

> "I propose fr. Ys. Day to keep an exact journal of my actions and studies, both to assist my memory & to accustom me to set a Due value on my time." Introductn. to Mr. Gibbon's Journal —
>
> A. Lister

Written on the inside page of Anne's 1817 diary.

In 2018 the diaries and travel notes of Anne Lister were conserved and digitized by Calderdale Museums in conjunction with West Yorkshire Archives, and Townsweb Archiving service. The project to digitize, conserve and work towards transcribing the diaries has been funded through Sally Wainwright.

Whilst work has been done transcribing certain sections of the diaries by Helena Whitbread, Jill Liddington and Anne Choma, amongst others, the job of fully transcribing, editing and making the diaries searchable is a long process. A large amount of the diaries are in Anne's code (with no spacing or punctuation), which also slows the process.

The conservation and digitization in 2018 were the first stages in trying to make the diaries as accessible as possible and hopefully enable easier transcription.

Digitizing the diaries also aims to help preserve them for the future, as researchers are able to access high resolution scans which can be enlarged for easier reading, through West Yorkshire Archive Service.

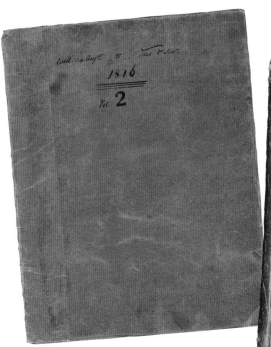

Anne's diaries from 1816, 1832 and 1840.

1806

Monday August 11th Eliza left us
Had a Letter from her on Wednesday
morning by Mr Ratcliffe the 13th Inst
Wrote to her on Thursday 14th by Mr Lund
Wrote to her again on Sunday 17th put into
the Post office at Leeds on the Monday following
that Evening the 18th had a parcel from
her Music Letter & Lavender ——————
had a Letter Wednesday August 20th ——
Answered on the 21st
Sunday 24th wrote to ER put into the Post on monday
Wednesday 27th had a Letter from her in answer to two
Friday 28th rec'd a parcel from ER by Mr Lund
Sunday 30th Wrote to ER in answer to her 2 letters ER
by Mr Lund ~ Sunday 7 of September wrote
Tuesday 9th had a Letter from her
Wednesday 10th had a Letter from ER —
Friday 12th had a Letter from ER
Thursday 11th wrote to ER in answer to hers of the 10th
Sunday Sept 14th Wrote to ER by my Uncle &
Aunt I Listen going to Hull on the same
day a short Note to Miss Hargrave enclosed
with 3 P Handkerchiefs 1 Slip in a parcel
with my Letter to ER in answer to one
from her on Saturday 13th by Mr Vastlet
enclosing me a Cornelian Broach ————
Monday August 25th 1806 Rode with Mr
Mitchell to Bakeup the first time I ever
was out of Yorkshire
Tuesday Sept 16th had a Letter from ER in answer to
mine by my Uncle J Lyon, By the Post they being at Hull
Wednesday rode with Mr Mitchell to fixby through Elland
Rastrick and Brighouse on that day was the Pretoria
at Elland Wednesday Sep 17th 1806

A selection of pages from Anne's diaries including the first known page from 1806 on the left.

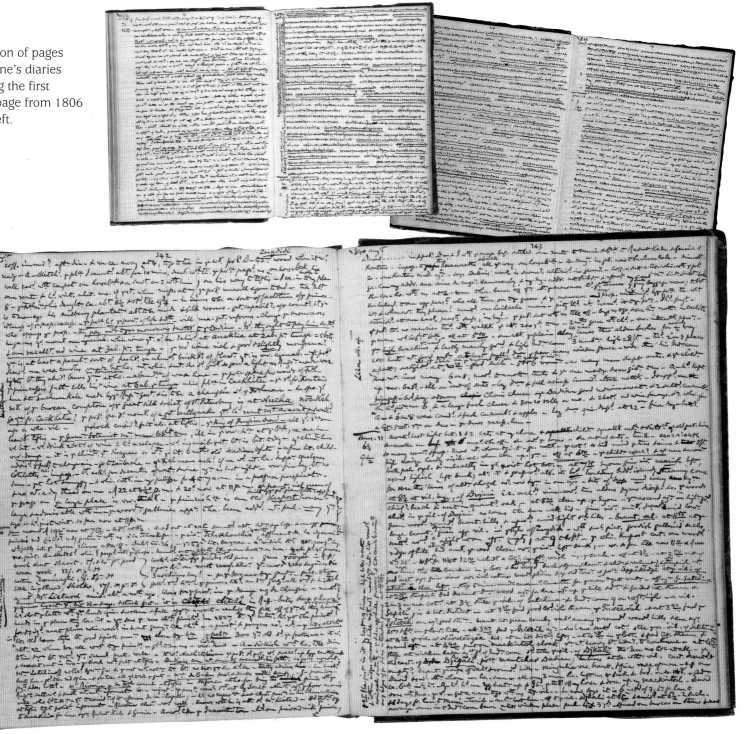

Anne's Travel Notes

Anne also left behind 14 volumes of travel notes and maps of France and Norway. She must have decided to write these accounts in addition to her diaries, possibly for potential publication.

The notebooks from her travels in 1829 and 1830 have many pages crossed through, suggesting these were written up again elsewhere with a view to sharing them.

Above right, Anne's volumes of travel notes. Below, map of the Pyrenees.

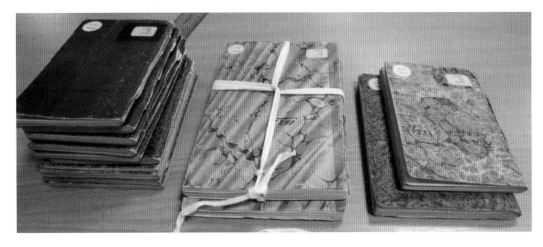

These volumes are mainly from her overseas trips, but Anne also travelled a great deal within the United Kingdom to the Lake District, Scotland and North Wales, including a trip on the newly opened railway from Manchester to Liverpool in 1831.

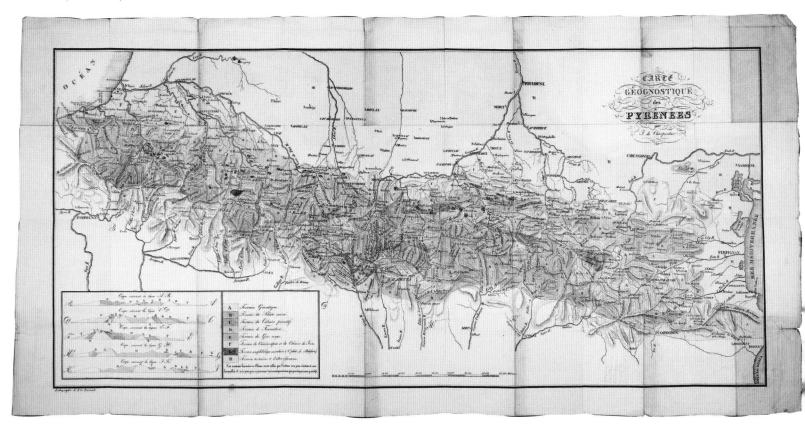

> *'On the snow without quitting it 'til 9.08, then rested on a little, grassy knoll 'til 9.20. Took off crampons at 10.10 then rested on top of second crête at 11.15. I lay down a little. Sun – put my cloak on and did not feel the air cold. Thick – clear all the morning except about sunrise and for about an hour. Now at 11.40 clouds gathering round.'*

Tuesday 7th August 1838

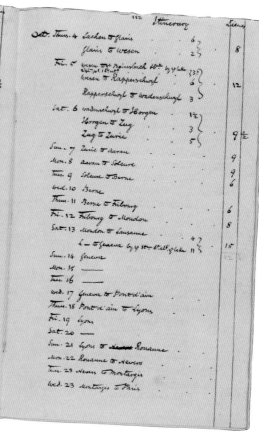

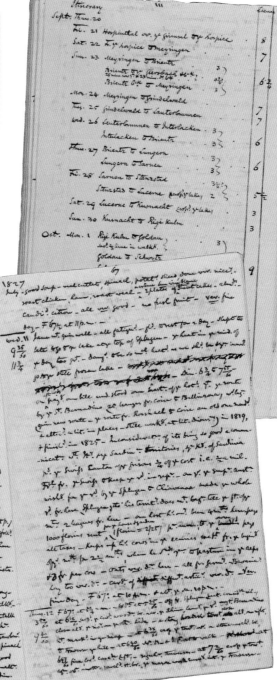

The first two volumes are from 1827 when Anne travelled to Switzerland and Italy.

The second two volumes are from 1829 when she travelled to Belgium and the Netherlands.

Pages of Anne's travel notes from 1827.

Anne's Travel Notes

There are four softbound green notebooks and a hardbound notebook from 1829 and 1830 in which many of the pages are crossed through, all from Anne's travels to France and the Pyrenees.

A volume with 59 pages dated August 4th to the 25th 1831 is from when Anne travelled to Holland with Mariana Lawton.

Another volume with 30 pages dated September 12th to October 10th 1831 has several pages removed from the back of the book. This is from when Anne travelled to visit friends in Hampshire and visited the Isle of Wight and Sussex.

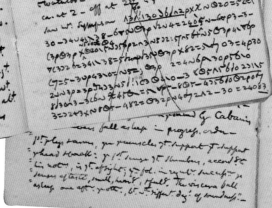

Pages of Anne's travel notes.

Three volumes are from Anne's last journey to Russia in 1839. The first volume is dated July 20th to August 20th 1839. The second volume is dated August 20th to September 14th 1839 and the third volume dates from September 14th to October 6th 1839.

They travelled via Dunkerque, Belgium, Germany, Copenhagen, through Norway, Sweden, Finland and Russia into Astrakhan (now Georgia) where Anne died in Koutais on 22nd September 1840. There are no travel notes surviving after October 1839,

leaving a large gap in her story. Her final diary entry on 11th August 1840 was due to lack of writing space, suggesting again, that other diaries and notebooks may have existed.

Anne's Letters

In addition to her diaries there are 1,200 letters between Anne Lister, family, friends and business contacts, including her Aunt Anne, Eliza Raine, Mariana Lawton, Maria Barlow, Lady Stuart de Rothsay, Lady Gordon, Sibella MacLean, Ann Walker and members of the Norcliffe family, written between 1800 and 1840.

Anne refers to her letters in the diaries and it is clear what we have is a small fraction of what would have been written and received. Many letters of a confidential nature may well have been destroyed either by Anne herself or perhaps by Ann Walker, or later lost or disposed of.

Librarian Muriel Green studied the letters when they were moved into the local archives from Shibden Hall in 1938 and wrote her thesis on some of them. She later published in 1992 the book *Miss Lister of Shibden Hall: Selected Letters (1800–1840)*.

There are also notebooks comprising of about 500 draft business letters to people including Robert Parker, her Halifax solicitor, David Booth her last steward, John Harper her architect and Grays her solicitors. In addition there are 32 volumes of account and day books covering household, estate and travelling expenses, eleven volumes of school books and notebooks, eleven volumes of extracts of books read by Anne, lecture notes and miscellaneous notes.

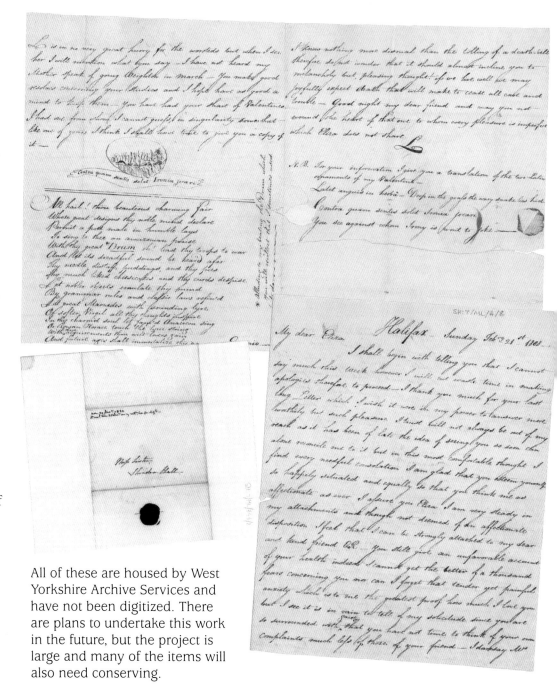

All of these are housed by West Yorkshire Archive Services and have not been digitized. There are plans to undertake this work in the future, but the project is large and many of the items will also need conserving.

Above, letter from Anne to Eliza Raine 21st February 1808 (SH:7/ML/A/8) and envelope of a letter to Anne from Ann Walker in 1832 (SH:7/ML/644). Images courtesy of West Yorkshire Archive Service. Opposite, a page of Anne's diary from 1826 in her crypt-hand.

This painting of Shibden Dale was commissioned by Anne Lister from John Horner (1784-1867) in 1833 as a gift for her sister Marian. It hangs on the staircase at Shibden Hall.

Anne's Impact on Shibden Hall

The Shibden Estate produced income from agriculture, coal mining, stone quarrying and brick making. The Listers also had some income from canal shares, Turnpike Road Trusts and pew rents. It was the stable income of rents from the farms and cottages on the Estate that gave Anne a firm base from which she could branch out into riskier investments.

Once Anne had management of the Hall and Estate she commissioned John Harper (1809 -1842) an architect from York. She initially asked him for plans for Northgate House, another Lister property in the centre of Halifax, which she wanted to convert into a hotel and casino. She was impressed with his work and turned her attention to Shibden Hall. Anne wanted a far more grand and imposing property.

'Mr. Harper had brought plans of Shibden Hall... with just a perfect drawing of the South front.'

27th October 1835

'... only afraid of making the house too large-looking and important.'

16th April 1836

John Harper's plans for the south front of Shibden Hall. Image courtesy of West Yorkshire Archive Service (SH:2/M/2/7).

John Harper's plans for Shibden Hall. Images courtesy of West Yorkshire Archive Service (SH:2/M/2/5-9).

The initial plans by Harper were rather elaborate and costly but they settled on an addition of a new three-story gothic tower with a library and modern water closets on the west side and an east wing with new kitchen, servant's quarters and dressing rooms.

Anne certainly left her impact on the Hall and Estate making many changes to improve the look and size of the Hall and increase the grandeur of the Estate.

Anne's Impact on Shibden Hall

Painting of Shibden Hall's Housebody by Henry Sykes in 1877 on display at Shibden Hall.

Internally rooms were adapted with panelling installed and new fireplaces, and major changes were made to increase the size of the main hall, known as the Housebody.

Anne added a grand staircase off the main hall, raised the ceiling, installed a new fireplace, (copied from one in a nearby house she admired), added panelling and carved figures, as well as her initials and the Lister motto 'Just and true of purpose' in Latin into the carvings, all of which can be seen today.

Photograph of staircase in the housebody and close-up of the carved Lister Lion.

To keep servants out of sight Anne commissioned the digging of cellars beneath the hall to link the buttery, kitchen and new tower.

By 1839 the initial alterations were complete, but Anne died whilst travelling in 1840 so never got to see her Gothic tower ready to house a library. Indentations can be seen on the tower's exterior where there would have eventually been more additions to the building work in the future, if Anne had returned. Shibden Hall would have ended up as a castle like building, alluding to Anne's love of Norman and Early Medieval architecture.

Architect John Harper died in 1842 in Italy from malaria aged just 33, so no more of Anne's plans were completed. Subsequent residents also made changes to Shibden Hall but all of Anne's improvements can still be seen today.

Plan of the tower by Harper. Image courtesy of West Yorkshire Archive Service (SH:2/M/2/9) and photograph of the tower showing recesses for future building additions.

Anne Lister's Parklands

Outside the Hall Anne ordered the rendering to be stripped off and the half-timbered look restored.

It was not only the Hall itself that Anne set about changing. In order to improve the look of Shibden Estate, Anne decided to turn 85 acres surrounding the Hall into a landscaped park. She also raised the terrace of the lawn to create a level standing and added the wall and gardener's tunnel. When it was renovated more recently it seems there may have been plans for a tunnel leading to the house.

All of the parklands work was designed by Mr. Gray. Anne added fish ponds and high rockwork to create a cascade between them, a walled garden and a garden cottage.

Garden turret with door leading from the gardener's tunnel.

The wilderness garden, with its cascade and pools leads to the tunnel under Shibden Hall Road and on through to Cunnery Wood, the site of a kitchen garden and two ponds to provide water for the domestic supply. The stones used weighed between five and seven tonnes and were lifted into place using a pulley system. Anne recorded having nightmares about one of the stones falling down. The terraces were also part of this grand series of designs for a picturesque landscape.

An early photograph of the wilderness garden and cascade with young John and Charles Lister, c1860.

In February 1836 work began on the Meer, a lake at the bottom of valley, using Red Beck, named after the polluting red oxides from the coal mines. It is 163 yards wide by 40 yards, to give the impression of a river running through the valley and was completed in 1838.

Black and white photograph of the Meer in the 1930s and a view of Shiben Hall from the pond.

Anne Lister's Parklands

Anne also commissioned the gatehouse and Lister's Lane carriage drive. John Harper was the architect again and the gatehouse is a copy of the one at Kirkham Priory, North Yorkshire. The driveway between the gatehouse and Hall was finished and first used on 27th June 1837 when Anne visited Halifax to hear the proclamation of Queen Victoria. She celebrated the completion of the gatehouse shortly after by buying the masons drinks at Stump Cross Inn.

Below, the gatehouse and opposite, the stone lion, carved for Anne in 1837.

'... but the air of my own native hills has done me good and spite of fate, the shades of Shibden have still some charm for me.'
- Thursday 10th May 1832.

Shibden Hall after Anne

When Anne died on the 22nd September 1840 whilst travelling, her partner Ann Walker was left to return to England accompanying Anne's body.

Ann Walker was not quite as enthusiastic a traveller as Anne Lister was and Anne's diaries reveal tensions between her and Ann during their trip together. Ann Walker was also prone to bouts of melancholia and it is hard to imagine how difficult the journey home, without Anne leading the way, and in the company of a dead body, would have been for her.

Anne had said of Ann Walker in her diary that 'she had everything to be wished for but the power of enjoying it,' 19th December 1832.

A report of Anne Lister's death was in the *Halifax Guardian* on 31st October 1840 and on 1st May 1841, nearly eight months later, the newspaper reports that her remains 'arrived at Shibden Hall on Saturday night, and were interred in the parish church, on Thursday morning.'

The Listers had a section of the church where it would be expected for Anne to be buried. It is said that because of the size of the coffin she had been placed in she would not fit, so was buried in a different section of the church. When this area was later excavated to make room for alterations a broken tombstone was recovered. There are no details of any remains being moved or why the stone is broken and incomplete, but from what remains of the stone it is clear this is Anne Lister's.

Old paintings of exterior and interior of Halifax Minster in Calderdale Museums collections.

Pieces of a tombstone at Halifax Parish Church, now Halifax Minster. Anne's body was returned and buried there on 29th April 1841.

The red frieze in the Red Room.

had to take the door off its hinges. Ann was taken to York Asylum and her brother-in-law moved into Shibden Hall. Ann never returned to Shibden and she died at Cliffe Hill in 1854.

Whilst Ann Walker was still alive several different families lived at Shibden and one of them sold off Anne's library at auction. Luckily the archives were safely stored away. On Ann Walker's death the property reverted to Lister family ownership and the estate was inherited by Dr John Lister (1802-1867). John Lister moved in with his wife Louisa Anne Grant (1815-1892) and their two sons, John (1847-1933) and Charles (1848-1889) and daughter Anne (1852-1929) in 1855.

Under the terms of Anne's will, her partner Ann Walker inherited Shibden Hall. There are little records of this time but it is known that Ann Walker was removed from Shibden Hall in 1843.

There is an account that she had locked herself in the Red Room (known from the red frieze on the wood around the top of the walls), and to get to her they

Anne's funeral hatchment.

Funeral hatchments were a custom of the period and were hung outside homes of the deceased after their death. There are three funeral hatchments which have been saved and now reside at Shibden Hall. One of them is purportedly Anne's and is on permanent display at the Hall.

Photographs of Dr John Lister, c1855 and Louisa and Charles and John, their two sons.

Shibden Hall as a Museum

In the 1850s a Paisley Shawl garden was designed for the terrace by Joshua Major, a leading landscape designer of the time.

Dr John Lister also had a home in Swansea and the family moved between the two places. John made further improvements to the coal mines and farm at Shibden and added a greenhouse, ornamental pond and flower gardens. He also purchased a peacock to roam the grounds.

Their eldest son John inherited Shibden in 1867 when he was twenty-years-old. John had attained an MA from Brasenose College, Oxford and soon acquired a new library to rival Anne's. His mother Louisa lived at Shibden with him and his younger sister Anne. John published articles about the family's history and extracts from

Anne's diaries. He set up Shibden Industrial School in 1877 with the Roman Catholic Church to teach young people a trade to help them gain employment. At one time there were 200 students listed here.

SOCIAL AND POLITICAL LIFE IN HALIFAX FIFTY YEARS AGO.

SOME EXTRACTS FROM THE DIARY OF A HALIFAX LADY.

By the courtesy of J. Lister, Esq., M.A., Shibden Hall, we are enabled to place before our readers some interesting extracts from the diary of the late Miss Lister, of Shibden Hall. It should be stated that these entries were made for private perusal, and were never intended for publication; but they are of special interest at the present time, as they throw great light on some features of the social life in the town, in the year when Her Majesty ascended to the throne, and they refer to matters for which a person might search in vain in the files of an old newspaper. The first extract refers to that ever debate

TOUR IN RUSSIA IN 1840.

EXTRACTS FROM THE DIARY OF A HALIFAX LADY.—No. CXX.

TIFLIS, THE ANCIENT CAPITAL OF GEORGIA.

Monday, April 20th, 1840.—"At the Garden at 12.40. The door opened, and what a panorama! Gazed in mute admiration at the town, the river, the range of snow-clad mountains. How fine! how new and asiatic to us! We had looked down from the Arx, the citadel, the acropolis of the ancient capital of Georgia—a noble rock, which hosts of half the peoples of the world had passed and gazed on. The Kur still bathes its foot as when Cyrus himself was here."

A FAMOUS IMAGE.

Tuesday, April 30th.—"All off to the Monastery of St. David. Went into the houses of the religieuses—Armenian-like divans. Pilgrims often sleep there. Two of these devout ladies were asleep after their fatigues. An image there famous for giving children to those who lack and pray for them. If one makes a stone stick against the wall of the church, whatever one wishes is to come true."

AROINT THEE, WITCH!

Saturday, May 2nd.—"Hajie Yoosoof, and Mr. Stadler came, and went with us to the Gymnase—a large and handsome building. The Master of the School shewed us his translation into Russian of Romeo and Juliet, and his Baudry-Paris edition of Shakspeare. He is a well-informed, gentlemanly man. Turned to Macbeth, the beginning—'aroint thee,' witch. The glossary explained it: Avaunt—begone; and I mentioned the conjecture of a learned Scotsman (Dr. Hunter, ages ago, to my Aunt Anne) that 'aroint thee' should, probably, be a rowan tree, which i.e., the rowan tree, or mountain ash, was a spell against witchcraft;

Anne Lister (1852-1929) aged 8.

John Lister (1847-1933).

John and his sister Anne were the last two residents of Shibden Hall. Unfortunately, John spent all his money on charitable works and maintaining Shibden and became bankrupt.

Shibden estate was bought from John Lister by his friend Arthur Selby McCrea in 1923. He donated the parkland to the Halifax Corporation for the people of Halifax and allowed John and Anne to live at the Hall for the remainder of their lives. On the opening of the park on 15th October 1926, new paths, walks and planting had been created, transforming the lower parts of the estate to formal parkland.

Anne died in 1929 and on John Lister's death in 1933, Shibden Hall also came into the ownership of the Halifax Corporation, today Calderdale Council.

The Hall was opened as a museum with much of the original furniture left on display on the 4th June 1934 and continues to welcome visitors today. The 17th century aisled barn was also preserved and is home to the unique early 18th century Lister chaise. In 2001 the fabric of the Grade 2 Listed barn was restored.

In 1953 a Folk Museum was opened as an addition to the Hall and barn by Dr. Frank Atkinson (1924-2014), who later set up Beamish. The Folk Museum displayed traditional trades and crafts, many of which are now rarely used such as an apothecary shop, coopering, wheelwright and blacksmiths' workshops, a brewhouse, the Crispin Inn, a tack room, a saddler's shop and a farm worker's cottage. In the 1960's the Museums Service also collected a wide range of carriages and carts to be displayed in the aisled barn.

In 2003 Calderdale Council was able to restore the fabric of the Hall, also a Grade 2 listed building with the help of over £358,000 from the Heritage Lottery Fund.

Shibden Hall remains open to the public today. The Calderdale Museums website has up to date opening times, information and details of events.

The Prince of Wales planting a tree to commemorate the opening of Shibden Parkland to the public in 1926.

Anne Lister's Legacy

Interest in Anne Lister has steadily grown over the years since Helena Whitbread's first publication revealing Anne's sexuality in 1988. Focus has been on her sexuality and her exploits as a business woman, traveller, scholar and mountaineer.

Shibden Hall has on display collections that relate directly to Anne. One key item is Anne's travel writing case. Although Anne's library was auctioned off many years ago, a few books remain with her signature and also two music books.

The Hall and grounds can reveal a great deal about Anne and her time living there managing the Hall and Estate. Lots of the furniture at Shibden was there during Anne's time, as well as the Lister chaise, which is on display in the barn.

Anne's diaries had their own journey of discovery. John Lister, the last resident of Shibden Hall, was the founding president of the Halifax Antiquarian Society and published information on his family and his home, including articles about Anne. John read the diaries but at first was unable to read the coded sections, written in Anne's crypt hand.

John published edited sections of the diaries in the *Halifax Guardian* newspaper between 1887 and 1892. It was John and his friend Arthur Burrell in the 1890s who first cracked Anne's secret code in which she had written the more personal and intimate parts of her diaries. Arthur Burrell reported that 'The part written in cipher- turned out after examination to be entirely unpublishable. Mr Lister was distressed but he refused to take my advice, which was that he should burn all 26 volumes.' Fortunately John chose not to.

The Shibden Hall archives were vast and it took librarians two years just to catalogue John Lister's library. The diaries were just one small part of this.

In 1937 Arthur Burrell provided the key to Anne's 'crypt' for use. Muriel Green who first examined the diaries after John, commented in her publication in 1992 that 'with very few exceptions the passages in 'crypt' alphabet are of no historical interest whatsoever'.

She added 'and it can be taken for granted that the longer the passage the less it is worth the tedium of decoding.'

She also suggested a very small part of the journal were in code, but it is now estimated about a sixth of the journals are in code.

The Porch Chamber at Shibden, a small room next to Anne's bedroom where she may have written her diaries. There are shelves within the panelling in this room so it is likely the diaries were stored in here.

'What a comfort my journal is. How I can write in crypt all as it really is and throw it off my mind and console myself. Thank God for it.'
July 1833

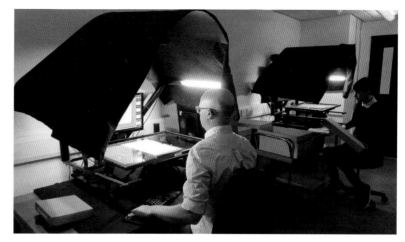

Photographs of the scanning of Anne's diaries in 2018.

In the 1950s the diaries were read by Dr. Phyllis Ramsden and Vivien Ingham. They published articles in 1969 and 1970 focussing on Anne's travels but never published a biography. Dr Ramsden commented that 'there are long accounts in crypt writing of her sentimental exchanges with her deemed friends, excruciatingly tedious to the modern mind.'

In 1970 the diaries and archives were taken into the local archives department for safe keeping and cataloguing. In 1984 a *Guardian* article about the diaries reached a wider audience and gained some interest from scholars in Anne Lister.

Once in the archives, local researcher Helena Whitbread was offered some of the pages to read. This eventually led to her 1988 publication *I Know My Own Heart*. Muriel Green's book on Anne's letters followed in 1992 along with a second publication by Helena, *No Priest But Love* in 1992.

In 1994 Jill Liddington published *Presenting the Past: Anne Lister of Halifax 1791-1840,* then *Female Fortune* in 1998 and *Nature's Domain* in 2003.

With growing interest in Anne Lister and the diaries, Calderdale Council's Museums Services produced an *Anne Lister Research Directory* in 1997.

Most of the diaries were scanned onto microfilm in 1979 and in 2003 the University of Huddersfield digitized the microfilm into images and put them online as part of their 'History to Herstory' project. www.historytoherstory.ac.uk

In 2015, Calderdale Museums Service created an interactive display of Anne Lister's diaries showing pages of the diaries, transcribed extracts, information about Anne the traveller, socialite, landowner, scholar and businesswoman, with assistance from Helena Whitbread. The unit was created as part of an Arts Council England funded project, part of which

was to refurbish some of the non-historically set rooms at Shibden and include more information for visitors, including Anne Lister's life and impact on Shibden.

In 2018 the Museum Service led on the conservation and digitization of the original diaries and travel notes to preserve them for the future and make them more accessible. The next stage will be to look at the letters and other related archives to Anne's life to eventually create a full digital catalogue.

Shibden Hall hosts regular Anne Lister based tours to show visitors the changes Anne made to the Hall and Estate and the legacy she has left. The Museums Service also hosts Anne Lister conferences and event days, where a range of speakers share their research and interest in Anne.

The Calderdale Museums website has up-to-date opening times, information and details of future events.

The Lister Chaise on display in the Aisled Barn. Possibly the one recorded in Samuel Lister's inventory of 1766.

Anne Lister in the Media

Anne has featured in a number of TV and radio dramas and documentaries over the years.

Mary Cooper wrote a radio play based on Anne Lister called *Such Sweet Possession* for BBC Radio 4 in 2002, featuring Deborah McAndrew as Anne Lister. In 2009 Anne Lister was the subject of a *Woman's Hour* programme for BBC Radio 4.

In 2010, BBC2 showed a feature length drama based on Anne Lister, written by Jane English called *The Secret Diaries of Miss Anne Lister* featuring Maxine Peake as Anne. The same year the BBC created a documentary about Anne Lister hosted by Sue Perkins.

Shibden Hall featured in Historic England's Pride of Place project in 2016.

Screen shots from the promotional film *Visit Shibden*.

Screen shots from *The Anne Lister Story*, featuring Helena Whitbread.

Also that year, the Museums Service commissioned a documentary about Anne Lister featuring Helena Whitbread. The twenty-five minute film is shown at Shibden Hall. The same year, a new promotional film about Shibden Hall was commissioned and again featured Anne Lister's story. Short versions of both films can be viewed on the Museum Service's website.

Anne Lister's story was featured in Channel 4's *Britain's Great Gay Buildings* in 2017. Mary Portas visited Shibden Hall to find out more about Anne Lister. The programme was hosted by Stephen Fry.

Suranne Jones as Anne Lister. Copyright Lookout Point 2019.

Anne Lister is the focus of the TV drama *Gentleman Jack* written by Sally Wainwright, exploring Anne's life and those who lived in the Hall and Estate. Suranne Jones plays the role of Anne Lister and Shibden Hall is a key filming location. Other cast include Gemma Whelan as her sister Marian Lister, Timothy West as her father Jeremy and Gemma Jones as Aunt Anne. Sophie Rundle plays Ann Walker and Stephanie Cole is her Aunt.

Find out more

Online resources

Calderdale Museums have information about Anne on their website including a full list of articles and publications. Also links to information from the BBC on the *Gentleman Jack* TV series, the University of Huddersfield's archive site and West Yorkshire Archive Service, who house the diaries and Shibden Hall's archive collection.

Contacts

If you have a specific enquiry about Shibden Hall or Anne Lister please contact **collections@calderdale.gov.uk**

If you would like more information on any of the archives please contact **calderdale@wyjas.org.uk**

Key publications include:

Helena Whitbread, (1988). *I Know My Own Heart: The Diaries of Anne Lister 1791- 1840*. Virago, 1988, and New York University Press, 1990.

Helena Whitbread, (1992). *No Priest But Love: The Journals of Anne Lister from 1824 - 1826*. Smith Settle.

Muriel Green, (1992). *Miss Lister of Shibden Hall: Selected Letters (1800 -1840)*. The Book Guild.

Jill Liddington, (1994). *Presenting the Past: Anne Lister of Halifax 1791 – 1840*. Pennine Pens.

Jill Liddington, (1998). *Female Fortune: Land, Gender and Authority*. Rivers Oram.

Jill Liddington, (2003). *Nature's Domain: Anne Lister and the Landscape of Desire*. Pennine Pens.

Helena Whitbread, (2010). *The Secret Diaries of Miss Anne Lister*. (An updated version of *I Know My Own Heart*).

Anne Choma, (2019). *Gentleman Jack*. BBC Books.

The Kitchen at Shibden Hall.

The Dining Room at Shibden Hall.